THY
KINGDOM
COME

THY KINGDOM COME

DELIVER US FROM EVIL
BOOK I

International Bestselling Author
MONICA JAMES

THY KINGDOM COME

This book is a work of fiction. Names, characters, places and incidents
are the product of the author's imagination, or are used fictitiously.
Any resemblance to actual events, locales, or persons living or dead, is
coincidental. Any trademarks, service marks, product names or named
features are assumed to be the property of their respective owners and are
used only for reference.

Copyright © 2021 by Monica James

Cover Design: Perfect Pear Creative Covers
Photographer: Michelle Lancaster
Cover Model: Lochie Carey
Editing: Editing 4 Indies
Formatting: E.M. Tippetts Book Designs

Follow me on:
authormonicajames.com

OTHER BOOKS BY
MONICA JAMES

DEDICATION

For Dacca. Every word written was done so with you by my side. I miss you.

AUTHOR'S NOTE

PROLOGUE

"**O**h my God…they found me."

Punky peers up from his coloring book, unsure why his ma looks so troubled, so anxious because that is unlike her. Cara Kelly is usually composed and refined, but she's been forced to live this way. A woman of her standing has no other choice.

Punky is Cara's world. She has done everything to protect her son, but now, she fears she's made a dire mistake, and her only child will pay for her crimes.

She didn't think they'd find her here. She thought they were safe.

"Punky!" she exclaims, clutching onto his small arm and forcing him to stand as she bends to look him in the eye. "Listen to yer mummy. Come now, ya have to hide."

"Why, Ma? What's tha matter?" Punky asks, heart in his throat as he hates seeing his mother upset. But when a loud bang sounds, his questions remain unanswered.

Cara peers around the bedroom, frantically looking for a place to hide her son, but she's running out of time, so the wardrobe will have to do.

Cara guides Punky over to the white wardrobe, desperately opening the door. "Ya need to be quiet. Quieter than a mouse. Okay, my wee son? Promise me."

Punky stubbornly shakes his head, tugging his small arm from her grip. "No. I wanna stay with ya. A'll protect ya."

He reaches for a toy knife on the white carpet, arming himself as he stands in front of her.

When frantic footsteps pound down the hallway, Cara's blue eyes, eyes just like her son's, fill with tears. She knows there is no running this time.

Punky is stubborn, and he always has been. She hopes he will hold onto this attribute long into his life. But she won't be alive to see him grow into the strong, powerful man she knows he's destined to become.

With the Kelly name, Punky's future is already mapped out for him. He may only be five years old, but his fate was decided the day he was born. He has no other choice, which is why Cara pushes him into the wardrobe—her sacrifice will not be in vain.

"Ma!" Punky shouts, trying to fight her.

She reaches for the face paints hidden on the top shelf. "Here," she says, looking over her shoulder at the locked bedroom door. She's running out of time. "I want ya to be someone else. I want ya to pretend yer anywhere but here. Whatever ya see, whatever ya hear, I want ya to know it's not real because yer not really here."

Punky's eyes widen, as his dad, Connor Kelly, had spanked Punky silly for painting his face, saying no son of his would be wearing makeup like some "queer." Punky hates his father. He doesn't understand how his mother loves a monster like him.

When deafening pounding ricochets against the door, a tear trickles down Cara's cheek. She failed her son. All she wanted to do was save him from this life, but she condemned them both.

Punky reaches forward where his mother is crouched and wipes the tear away with his small thumb. "Don't cry. I'll hide. I promise. A'll not make a sound."

Cara holds back her sobs, nodding quickly. "Good boy. Mummy loves ya. So much. Never forget it."

She kisses Punky's forehead, inhaling his scent, memorizing the only good thing that came out of marrying Connor Kelly.

She gives Punky his face paints and coaxes him to hide in the corner of the wardrobe. She presses her finger over her lips, gesturing he's to stay quiet, no matter what. He nods, and she takes one last look at her son.

Closing the wardrobe door, she presses her back against it

and wipes away her tears as she locks it. No way will she cower. She will stand tall.

The bedroom door is kicked open, and Cara is confronted by three masked men. They're wearing all black. Nothing distinguishes them, but Cara knows who they are, which is why she'll never see a sunrise ever again.

They're big and strong, but she walks into the middle of the room and faces them without fear. "Get out!" she sneers, folding her arms. "How dare ye come into my home? Do ya know who I am?"

The three predators enter the room, their eyes animated due to what is about to transpire.

"We know who ye're, ya whore," says one of the men in a thick Irish accent. "That's why we're here."

Punky creeps forward on his hands and knees. He knows he promised his ma he would stay put, but he wants to know what's going on. The slatted wardrobe doors allow him to see three men standing in front of his ma. Their balaclavas hide their faces. Their long sleeves and trousers cover their body.

When one of them reaches out and slaps his ma's cheek, Punky cups his mouth to mute his screams. He promised his ma he would be quiet, quieter than a mouse.

"How 'bout a dance, Cara?" one of the men say, walking over to the radio to turn up the song. "C'mere to me."

He grabs Cara, forcing her to dance with him, but she fights him, her small fists pummeling against his broad chest. The two other men laugh, relishing in Cara's fight, because they know there is only one outcome for her.

She chose her fate when she decided to take on the Kelly name. In this war, you're either a Kelly or you're a Doyle, and sadly for Cara, she chose the wrong side. And now, her death will be a warning for all future Kellys.

Cara continues to fight; she won't surrender with ease. Her dancing partner doesn't appreciate her insolence, so to subdue her, he punches her in the face. Blood pours from Cara's broken nose, staining the white carpet red.

The bloodshed rouses the bloodlust.

"My turn," one of the men says, dragging a screaming Cara into his arms.

Punky knows he made a promise, but he can't watch his ma being treated this way. He lunges for the handle, but it doesn't budge because the door is locked.

"Ma!" he screams, banging on the door until his fists begin to ache. But his cries are muted by Frank Sinatra playing loudly over the radio. "Mummy, open the door!"

The men take it in turns, passing Cara between them, her limp body nothing but a ragdoll as her spirit begins to wither and die.

Punky can't see straight as his vision is blurred with tears, and when Elvis Presley's "It's Now or Never" comes on the radio, Punky does what his ma asked—he becomes someone else. He pretends to be anywhere but here.

With trembling hands, he reaches for the white face paint and unscrews the lid. His mother's pained shrieks have him dipping his fingers into the paint and circling his cheeks and forehead to coat his skin white.

When one of the men produces a hunting knife, intent on silencing Cara's screams for good, Punky then swaps the white paint for the black. As his mother's mouth gets slit from ear to ear, Punky repeats the same action with his black face paint, which is shaped as a crayon.

He runs the tip from the apple of his cheek to his mouth, where he draws lines across his lips, wishing to silence his screams, then repeats the action on the other side of his cheek. He now wears a grin as big as his ma's. With precise strokes, he draws slashes downward along the line he just drew, emphasizing his grin as something sinister, something grotesque.

When one of the men bites down on Cara's nose and her ear, Punky draws a messy black dot on his own nose, and with the black dye he squirts into his hand, he uses his fingers to flick paint onto his ear and down his neck so it resembles the blood splatter his ma wears.

Cara drops onto her stomach when the men let her go, but they're not done, not yet. They lift her dress and tear off her knickers.

"Whatever ya see, whatever ya hear, I want ya to know it's not real because yer not really here."

Cara's words play over and over in Punky's head as he

watches the men take turns mounting his ma, riding her like Punky saw the stray neighborhood dog do to his Border Collie before his dad shot it dead.

As the men holler, biting and fondling a near unconscious Cara, Punky paints black around his eyes, not wanting to bear witness to his ma being defiled over and over again. Once they're done taking it in turns, the area around Punky's eyes is coated in thick black paint.

But he can still see.

One of the men lifts her limp head by her snarled hair and bangs her head onto the carpet. A jagged gash forms on the left side of her forehead, so Punky draws a small line to replicate his ma's wounds.

The men laugh, cheering and high-fiving one another, proud of their efforts. Punky hopes it's over.

But it's not.

One of the men, the man who danced with her first, stands over Cara's broken body and seems to examine the mess he's made.

"I never wanted this for ya, Cara. But ya didn't listen."

Punky doesn't know what that means. But he knows his mother did something bad.

The man bends down and lifts Cara's head back by her hair, exposing her neck. Cara moans, her face barely recognizable. Her bloodshot eyes focus on the wardrobe door where she knows Punky is watching. She reaches out with a quivering

MONICA JAMES

arm, wanting to touch him, to tell him it'll be all right.

She wishes he never saw what he did.

The bright light catches the sharp silver of the blade which slits Cara's throat. Blood pours from the wound as Cara wheezes for breath.

Punky's eyes widen, but he reminds himself it's not real. He's not really here. He focuses on Cara's favorite rose brooch. His ma loves flowers. She loves nature. But she'll never be able to feel the sunshine on her skin ever again.

He snares the bottle of black paint and squirts it down his neck where he runs his fingers through it, smearing it across his throat. Everything his ma feels, he feels too.

The man lets Cara go, where she flops onto her face, bleeding out.

He wipes the bloody blade on the back of her dress before coming to a stand. Punky peers up and up as the man is tall. When one of the men begins to hunt through Cara's jewelry box, Punky sees a crucifix tattooed on his left wrist.

He draws one on his too.

The man who slit Cara's throat focuses his attention on the wardrobe. Punky holds his breath. With no hurry, he walks over and inhales deeply, placing his hands on the door.

Punky reaches for the toy knife, armed and ready. Slathered in war paint, his face is a reflection of the injuries inflicted on his ma, and he's ready to go to war.

The man, however, doesn't want to hurt Punky. He simply

unlocks the door.

"We're away to the car," he orders the other two men pilfering like common thieves.

They take one last look at the mess they made, snickering about the Kelly geebag. They're out the door, but the man, the tall man turns over his shoulder, once again looking at the wardrobe door. He places his bloody pointer over his smirking lips, gesturing Punky isn't to make a sound.

He's gone a moment later.

Punky waits for silence, and although he promised his ma he'd stay hidden, he slowly opens the door. The song on the radio switches from Elvis to a song Punky's mum sings to him to keep the nightmares away. But when he crawls toward his ma, he realizes his nightmares have just begun.

The song is "Stand by Me" by Ben E. King, and Punky begins to hum the chorus as he gets closer to his ma. There is so much blood, but Cara said it's not real. She's going to wake at any moment. She has to.

"Ma," Punky says, reaching out with black and white painted hands, nudging her shoulder softly. "Wake up. I did whatcha asked. It's time to wake up now."

But Cara doesn't wake. She never will.

"Mummy!" Punky's pleas are a little louder, more desperate because he doesn't like this game. "Please wake up. I wanna go home."

Punky looks down at his hands, covered in his ma's blood.

He turns them over and over, not understanding what he's seeing.

"Are ye sleepin'? Ye knackered, Ma? It's Baltic in here. I'll keep ya warm."

Punky pulls the blanket off the bed and curls up beside his dead ma, tucking it around them. He's suddenly so tired. He wraps her arm around him, snuggling close to the only person in the world who showed him any love.

Before he succumbs to sleep, Punky reaches out and dips three fingers into a coagulated pool of blood just inches away. He then runs those fingers down the middle of his forehead, leaving three bloodied slashes in their wake. His face is a grotesque picture of everything he saw—a black, white, and red imagery, reflecting the death of his childhood.

Three men changed his life forever, and as long as it takes, no matter what Punky has to do, he's going to find those men and paint their faces too...before he rips them from their mutilated corpses.

A kaleidoscope of black and white lays before Punky, but he'll soon realize...nothing in life ever is.

ONE

PUNKY

"How hammered are ya?" asks Orla Ryan as she drags my wasted arse up the stairs of her parents' home. Strangers look on, gossiping behind their hands.

I moan in response, sinking further into her as she tightens her hold around my waist.

Orla has had a crush on me since I cut off one of her pigtails in primary school. I never understood why. I still don't. I don't understand why most girls have a crush on me.

My mates tell me it's because I'm dark and mysterious or something naff like that. With a hooped piercing in my nose and one in my lip, I don't really look the part of Prince Charming, but it doesn't seem to matter. I thought my tattoos would steer them away, but again, it only enticed them all the more. This has worked in my favor for many reasons—just like right now—and I hate it.

My long fringe flips forward as my chin drops to my chest. My dirty blond hair is cut short on the sides and long on top, and I wear it this way just to see my father ragin'. Just thinking about that fucker has me clenching my jaw.

He's the reason I'm here. He's the reason for all this.

Focusing on Orla and where she's taking me, I shake my floppy head. "Yer parents' room," I mumble, semi-coherent.

"Yer so bad, Puck Kelly," she whispers excitedly and changes course, obeying my command.

She opens the door and flicks on the light, still clinging to me, and leads me toward the bed. We both collapse onto it, a trail of giggles spilling free from her. I'm on my back, and Orla doesn't waste a second as she straddles me, lowering her mouth to mine.

She kisses me softly, cupping my cheek and coaxing me to reciprocate, but that's not why I'm here.

I don't like intimacy. Honestly, I hate it. I don't like being touched. The only person whose touch I crave is dead, and when she died, I died with her. To the outside world, I look relatively "normal," but it's a whole different story on the inside.

On the inside, all I think about is revenge and blood...my mum's blood staining the white carpet a bright red.

Cupping the back of Orla's neck, I give her what she wants,

returning her kisses with a brutal passion and pushing aside the need to hurt her. This is the only way I know how to be. I wish I could be gentle and enjoy the things most twenty-one-year-olds do, but I can't.

The only thing coursing through me is vengeance, and, being a Kelly, I must deal with that in the most deplorable of ways. Just like right now.

Orla runs her fingers over my T-shirt, circling the barbell in my nipple before stopping at the button on my ripped black jeans. When she flicks it open, I reach down and stop her.

"Ya don't wanna?" she breathlessly pants against my lips. Her hot breath reminds of me of the warm blood that coated my knuckles last week when I paid a visit to one of my dad's customers who was late with their payment.

"I do," I confirm, threading my fingers through her hair. "But could I trouble ye for some water?"

Orla's disappointment is clear, but she's a good Protestant girl and nods. "Aye, no bother."

She gingerly slides off me and arranges her dress, not wanting to alert the partygoers downstairs what we were just doing.

"I won't be long."

Nodding, I throw an arm over my eyes as if snuffing out the bright light. In reality, I'm blocking out all the atrocities I've done.

The closing of the door announces her departure, which is

my cue to follow, but just not in the way Orla thinks.

I spring to my feet, my drunken state miraculously gone because I'm not plastered. I never was. Locking the door, I get to work for the real reason I'm here.

The corner of my mouth lifts when I open the bedside dresser and see Mrs. Ryan's pink dildo. I wonder if Nolen Ryan is privy to the fact that his Holy Joe of a wife has a battery-operated friend feet away. Unable to help myself, I swipe it and slide it in my back pocket.

Closing her drawer, I round the bed, and when I open Nolen's dresser, I curse under my breath.

The bastard was right.

Reaching into my backpack—which I slipped under the bed earlier—for my phone, I snap a picture of the evidence before taking it and the *Catholic* rosary beads from the drawer. I slip everything into my backpack. My job here is done.

The party is in full swing downstairs, and I know it's only a matter of time before Orla comes back. I walk toward the window, unlock it, and look at the two-story drop.

"Ach, finally," says my best friend, Cian Davies, peering up at me as he flicks his feg into the bushes.

I've known Cian since I was born. Our fathers have been best friends since their teens, and it was expected we were to follow in their footsteps. His father is an eejit, but thankfully, his son just so happens to be the coolest person I know.

We're often mistaken for brothers because many have said

he's my double. It's helped with our alibis in the past.

"Stop faffin' around. Rory is keepin' dick for us down the street. Get a move on before the peelers come."

This is so like Cian—always worrying about the what-ifs, the complete opposite to who I am.

Clucking my tongue, I calmly say, "Houl yer whisht, y'll jinx us. I've a present for ye."

Before he can ask what it is, I reach into my back pocket and toss Mrs. Ryan's dildo down to him. On instinct, he catches it, and it takes him a few seconds to realize what it is. When he does, he shrieks and flings it into the bushes.

Laughing, I climb over the windowsill and peer downward.

"Punky, yer not gonna jump, are ya?"

Of course, he'd assume I'd scale down the drainpipe, as that's what any normal person would do, but I never claimed to be normal. What's that? While most people are inside, hiding from the thunderstorms, I'm outside, playing in the rain.

Before Cian can protest, I use my legs and launch out the window, relishing in the adrenaline rush as my boots hit the soft grass. I wish it was higher. It's only in the face of danger that I feel alive.

"Ya jammy bastard!"

"Luck has nothin' to with it, Cian," I say with a grin as we commence a discreet walk across the Ryans' front garden.

It's in the wrong, corrupt, and violent where I thrive.

Keeping my head down as I'm supposed to be wasted and

passed out upstairs, we avoid bumping into anyone and head down the street to where our friend, Rory Walsh, is keeping a lookout. When he sees us, he flashes the lights on his car.

After we all quickly get into his BMW, he puts the car into drive and speeds off down the street. Like thieves in the night, we've gotten away unscathed. It shouldn't be this simple, but it is.

Even if anyone suspected us, they wouldn't dare wage a war against the Kellys, the Davieses, or the Walshes as our families rule all of Northern Ireland. Belfast is our base, but paramilitary groups who run their own "areas" are still under our control. There are a few paramilitary groups in the past who have fought against each other, but they soon learned that we don't tolerate rebellion.

It's been this way for generations, and we're expected to take over from our fathers when the time comes.

I never chose this life. It was my birthright, according to my dad, but all I see is the curse that it is. It's because of the Kelly name that my mum was slain by the Doyles—our Catholic cunt counterpart in Dublin.

They don't come into Belfast, and we don't go into Dublin. If a Doyle dares to flounder these century-old laws, they will pay with their life. Some have tried, but all have failed. And I'm just waiting, anticipating the day one smug arsehole tries his luck.

When he does, I'll be there waiting, because the Doyles will pay for what they did to my ma.

My dad may have been able to move on with his life—remarrying and having twins, like his first wife wasn't murdered because she bore *his* name—but I cannot. She paid for being a Kelly. Her death was supposed to incite a war, but my father simply laid down his arms like the coward he is.

I don't even know why she died. My dad refuses to tell me why, and that makes her murder all the worse. He's happy to forget she existed while I exist only to avenge her death.

I stayed nestled with her corpse for three days before my father came. At five years old, I didn't understand the concept of death.

My face was painted, reflecting her injuries and tallying how many men caused her the heinous injuries she sustained. This was my way to shoulder her pain when I couldn't help her because I was locked in a wardrobe, thanks to my ma saving me until the very end. It was also to ensure I never forgot who was responsible for killing her; not that I ever could.

I remember bits and pieces, like a moving picture flickering in and out of focus, but I'll never forget the man who turned toward the wardrobe and gestured for me to stay quiet. He knew I was there, so the question is, why did I not face the same punishment as my ma?

My dad has a single photo of me from that night. He keeps it locked away in his desk drawer, but when I was ten, I found it. It was a reminder that the nightmares were real. That *she* really existed. But he never answered my questions, and after a while, I realized if I wanted answers, I'd have to find them for myself.

The three bloody lines fingered down the middle of my forehead were in honor of the three men who took away the only person who ever loved me. This is their future, imprinted on my skin because they're already dead—they just don't know it yet.

Rubbing over the crucifix tattooed on my left wrist, I remember one of the men who brutalized my ma had the same brand. I had it tattooed so that every time I look down at it, it provokes this burning desire to kill every last Doyle who walks this god forsaken earth.

I hated my father growing up, but now, that hatred has grown into something else.

He did nothing to avenge my ma, and I need to know why. His brother, my uncle, Sean, is the only person who seems to give a shit about her. I often wish he was my father instead of Connor Kelly. He was the one who told me the Catholics had broken into the bungalow Ma bought without my father knowing and killed her to start a war over territory.

The Kellys deal drugs, stolen guns, dabble in money laundering, and everything in between. If you were expecting us to be moral citizens, I hate to disappoint. We're anything but.

The Doyles are the same. They keep to their area in Dublin, and we to ours in Belfast, but it seems they wanted that to change when they took the life of my mum. Utter blasphemy, as Uncle Sean speculates that the Catholics not only wanted to steal our territory but they wanted to sell to the Protestants on the down low as well.

They would be seen as traitors in the eyes of other devout Catholics, but they wouldn't tell them. The Doyles wanted it all. They wanted our turf, our business, and our people. Killing my mum was them challenging my dad, but she was innocent. This war was never hers, yet she paid the ultimate price.

What I don't understand is why my mum bought that bungalow without my father's knowledge. Where was my dad for three days? And how did the Doyles find us?

I have more questions than answers, which is the only reason I do my father's dirty work. One day, he's going to slip up, and I will uncover what happened on that cold November night. It's the only reason I'm still here.

It's the only reason he's still alive.

"Did ya find it?" Rory asks, looking at me in the rearview mirror.

Nodding, I hunt through my backpack for the Catholic Bible and rosary beads. "Nolen Ryan is so fucked."

Rory whistles when he sees the evidence my father ordered me to find and bring back to him.

Nolen is a trusted confidant of my dad's, but my dad suspected he was double-crossing him when someone reported seeing him at Sunday Mass—a *Catholic* Mass near Dublin. It goes without saying, this cannot go unpunished, and Nolen will be made an example of.

Orla will soon be left with only one parent because Dad won't let Nolen live. If you side with the Catholics, no matter your surname, it may as well be Doyle because you'll be treated the same way.

"Shall we get a wee pint before we head home?"

I smirk because there's no such thing as a wee pint when Rory is involved. "That sounds a bitta craic, but I can't. If I don't get home, my aul' fella will be ragin'."

Both boys nod, knowing better than to keep Connor Kelly waiting.

Rory's phone dings, and when Cian dives for it and starts laughing, I know who it is.

"Darcy Duffy yer girlfriend now?" Cian asks, playfully moving the phone out of Rory's reach as he tries to steal it back and drive his car.

"Ack, stop acting the maggot. We're just friends."

But Cian is not convinced. "Do ya think I came up the Lagan in a bubble? I don't blame ya. She's a ride. I don't know what she's doing with you, though."

Darcy Duffy is the eldest daughter of Patrick Duffy—a self-made millionaire operating the biggest construction company in Northern Ireland.

If this were an American sitcom, Darcy would be the popular cheerleader every jock wanted to date. I've known her since we were kids, and although my da wanted us to be friends—for his own selfish reasons, of course—we've hardly spoken ten words to one another, though it's not on the account of her not trying.

It's me.

I'm not interested in meaningless conversation. Actually, I'm not interested in conversing at all. I have one goal in life, and that doesn't involve a fairy tale ending.

"I don't care whatcha think. She's sound. Don'tcha think, Punky?"

With a shrug, I peer out the window. "Aye, sure, why nat?"

My response is hardly convincing, and Cian laughs. "Ack, dry yer eyes, Rory, before I boke."

It's with the boys that I can try this humanity suit on for size. Sometimes, I can convince myself that I'm just like them, but I'm not. None of this stuff interests me. What most laugh at, I don't. I don't take pleasure in girls, getting wasted, or having fun, because I'm dead inside.

I may smile and look like I belong, but the truth is, I much prefer to be alone.

Another text message comes through, and Cian reads it aloud. "I wanna get hammered. Come over."

Rory shakes his head, giving up on the idea of ever getting his phone back.

"That sounds like good craic. Cian and I will be over soon," Cian types out, laughing as he's just gatecrashed the romantic pull.

With that as my cue, I unsnap my seat belt. "Pull over here. I'll walk the rest of the way."

"Away on!" Rory says, peering through his windscreen at the darkness in front of him. "Ye sure?"

"Aye," I reply, putting the Bible into my backpack and the rosary beads into my pocket. Besides, my house is in the opposite direction of Darcy's. This allows my mates more time with Darcy and her friends.

Rory knows not to argue and pulls over. We're in the middle of nowhere, but it's in the dark where I thrive. I've seen the bogeyman. He doesn't scare me anymore.

Opening the door, I bid my friends farewell. "Thanks a million. I'll chat to ye later."

Cian turns over his shoulder and smirks. "Be careful of the culchies."

"Ack, they need to be careful of him," Rory retorts playfully.

With a smile, I close the car door and watch my friends drive off into the night, faffin' about like normal twenty-one-year-olds should. I start to dander home.

The full moon provides some light, but the darkness doesn't scare me. It's the daylight that does. But it wasn't always this way. When Ma was alive, I used to love digging with her in her garden. She loved roses.

Peering down at the rose tattooed on the back of my hand, I sigh. Her memory fades every single day, and I'm afraid it won't be long until she's gone forever. Reaching into my pocket,

I finger over her rose brooch which I've carried with me since her death.

It was the only thing my dad let me keep of hers. Everything else, he threw away. It seemed he wanted to erase any memory of her. I wanted to believe it had something to do with my stepma, my ma's once best friend.

But I soon learned this was all my dad.

A dim light up ahead catches me off guard because I'm literally in the middle of nowhere. It looks like the screen on someone's phone. I have my knife and brass knuckles within reach, but when I get closer, I see that I won't be needing them.

The first thing I notice is her hair—it's almost silver under the moonlight and tied in two loose ponytails. The black headband contrasts the platinum color. As I get closer, I see that she's wearing a short navy skirt and matching top.

When she hears me, she spins around, using a small torch to see who's there.

"Hello?" she yelps in a posh accent.

"What's the craic?"

She cocks her head to the side, obviously confused. She's definitely not from around here.

"What's goin' on?" I say, the universal language for why the fuck is she out here, all alone in the middle of the night and the middle of nowhere.

"Oh," she says, brushing back a stray piece of hair behind her ear. "My bike broke."

She flashes the torch on the pink bike which lays on its side.

"I was riding home from a party, hence the costume," she explains, as if needing to clarify why she's riding a bike in thigh-high stockings and boots.

Not that I care because she looks a ride.

Taking a closer look at her outfit, I smirk, but am suddenly alarmed I responded this way because it's not forced. "Babydoll?"

She seems surprised I know she's dressed as a character from one of my favorite comics. "Yes!" she says happily. "I'm glad someone has a clue around here."

Compliments make me uncomfortable, so I clear my throat. "I'll take a look at yer bike."

"Thanks."

I crouch down to see what the damage is. Instantly, I see the bike chain has come loose. "Wee buns. Y'll be on yer way in no time."

She cautiously walks over, watching as I go to work fixing the chain. "What are you doing out here?" she asks, pointing her torch my way to provide more light.

"Just out for a dander."

"A what?"

Smirking, again surprising myself, I clarify, "A walk. Where ya from?"

"Oh," she says, giggling. "I'm from London. I just moved here with my aunt."

No wonder she has a posh accent.

"Are you from around here? My name is Poppy Yates. I'm a Pisces. I prefer thunderstorms over sunshine. And my favorite color is blue."

I know she's trying to be funny, trying to break the ice, but I don't reply. Instead, I focus on fixing her bike so she and her vanilla-smelling self can ride the hell away from here.

"How about you?"

"How 'bout me, what?" I counter quickly, before silently cursing myself. She's just trying to be friendly.

"That's your lead-in to tell me all about yourself. It's called making conversation," she replies lightly.

"Right, well I'm not interested in makin' conversation. All done," I reveal, not answering her question or giving her my name.

Coming to a stand, I almost bump into her because she's standing so close. She's short, maybe five-three. I'm six-three, so I guess most people are relatively short compared to me.

"Th-thanks," she falters, taking a step back.

I move the kickstand so the bike is ready for her, but she quickly reaches out and grips my wrist.

On instinct, I recoil forcibly. "Any more of this and there'll be less of it."

"Oh, I'm sorry," she quickly apologizes, her cheeks taking a reddener. Even though she's probably lost in translation, my firm tone has hinted what I mean. "I just wanted to thank you for helping me."

"No bother. See ya." I need to leave, but am stopped in my tracks.

"Are you always this rude? Or is it just me?" she says bluntly, placing her hands on her hips.

I am shook by her confidence and can't seem to stop grinning when she's near. She's annoyed, and it gives me great satisfaction seeing her pissed off.

"Don't flatter yerself, Babydoll," I frankly reply. I don't care what her name is. She's Babydoll to me.

When a lopsided smirk falls across her full lips, I want to reach out and touch them; I want to know what a genuine smile feels like. I haven't smiled for so long, I'm almost envious of her lips.

But I'm also curious to how they'd feel; how they'd taste.

"Oh, so you're always a rude sod then. Good to know." Her smile soon turns to a scowl as she hops onto her bike.

I laugh deeply in response. The surprises just keep on coming.

A part of me wants to stop her as I actually don't want her to go. She interests me, and I don't know why. Aye, she's parful, but that's not it. There is something…more.

She rides past me, head held high, and doesn't see the pothole. The wheel of her bike gets caught, and she shrieks, falling off or, more accurately, falling onto me. I break her fall, and we both tumble onto the gravel road.

I'm lying on my back with her pressed to my chest and her

face inches away.

Her breathing is uneven as she clearly had a fright. Mine, however, are measured and calm. She is soft against me, and her warmth doesn't suffocate me like others have.

I take a moment to admire her beauty. Her eyes are green, her lashes long. Her pink, glossy lips are full. I can see the arch of freckles across her cheeks and nose.

What *is* this feeling inside me?

She licks her lips, and I have the urge to follow her tongue.

She whimpers, moving in my arms. It's then that I realize I'm touching her without wanting to claw out of my skin. I suddenly don't like it. I don't like this vulnerability she infuses in me. We both shift at the same time, appearing to realize this moment is a little too intimate for mere strangers. I know better than to be distracted by a pretty face.

She gracefully gets off, ensuring she's not flashing any arse in her short skirt as she picks up her bike, quickly mounting it. "Thanks a-again," she calls out, riding away as if the devil is at her heels.

Looking down at myself, I realize he is.

Coming to a stand, I wipe the gravel from my clothes, confused as to what the fuck just happened. Sure, I've had girls show interest in me. I'm not being cocky; it's what happens when you bear the Kelly name, but this was different.

Why?

Because I wanted her too.

I don't like this sinking in the pit of my stomach. Is this what…feelings are? I don't know. How can I? I watched the only person full of feelings be slaughtered in front of my eyes. The only person to teach me what emotions are is my dad, and he'd rather teach me how to shoot or kneecap someone than deal with something he said I'd never need.

"Emotions make ya weak. They get ya killed."

My phone rings, thankfully interrupting these thoughts which will eat at me until I drown them in a bottle of Buckie.

It's my uncle Sean. "Bout ye?"

"Sound. On the way home."

"Yer da is waitin' for ya."

Shite.

He wasn't supposed to be back for another hour or so.

"I'm about halfa way."

"Yer coddin'," he says, and I can imagine him shaking his head. "Where ya at? A'll come get ye."

I hang up and text my uncle the GPS coordinate from my maps. He's here within twenty minutes.

Uncle Sean is quiet, which means things will be anything but at home. When we pull up the graveled drive, I sigh, seeing this once castle as nothing but a prison. This house has been in my family for generations.

Its beauty is undeniable, but I don't live in the main building. I can't.

Every inch of the interior has been replaced with my

stepma's things. That's the first thing she did when she moved in. She redecorated, saying the place needed a facelift. But I know what she really meant was that she wanted to remove any trace of my ma.

I live in the stable yard building behind the main house. It has everything I need, and it's far away enough that I don't have to see my dad unless I need to. I make sure that's not a lot of the time.

We exit the car and before we enter the house, Uncle Sean gently grabs my arm. "Don't provoke him tonight, cub."

"Course not," I quip with a slanted smirk.

"Catch yerself on!" he rebukes, not appreciating my cheek tonight. "He's in a mood."

"That's nothin' new."

"Punky," he warns with a stiff upper lip.

He's the reason everyone calls me Punky. My name is Puck Connor Kelly, but when I was younger, much to the distaste of my father, I couldn't pronounce my own name. I would try to say my whole name, as I knew it would please my dad if I could, but it just sounded like Punky. So, my uncle called me Punky, not wanting to ridicule me like my dad, and it just stuck.

"Ack, sure ya know yerself," I reply, putting his worries at ease.

With a sigh, he lets me go, and we enter the lion's den. Many have marveled at the large reception hall and domed ceilings, but the only good thing about this place is my twin half-siblings. They're one of the only reasons I stay here as I know if I move out, I'll never be allowed to see them again.

I've left home many times, intent on never returning. I stayed with Rory or Cian while I tried to figure out what to do, but the problem with that was my dad always knew where I was. If I wanted to break free from the Kelly name, I had to leave Northern Ireland and change my name.

But I soon learned there's no running from being a Kelly, especially being the eldest son of the most powerful man in Northern Ireland. I had to start new.

With no family, and the only friends I had being linked to my dad, that was impossible. I wasn't afraid of having nothing and building a new life from scratch, but rather, I knew if I decided to emancipate myself, I would never avenge my ma.

I would be dead to my dad, and if anyone was caught trying to help me, so would they.

So this is why I stay. Being a Kelly allows me to dig because no matter how long it takes, I will find out what happened to my ma.

When the twins see me, they come running forward, demanding hugs.

Bending down to pick them up, I scold them playfully, kissing their warm cheeks. "What about ye? Why ya still awake?"

Hannah, the eldest twin by two minutes, squeezes me tight. "Ya promised to read us a story," she replies, her blue eyes so pure, so innocent to the atrocities of this world.

Ethan, the younger twin, yawns. "Ya gonna paint yer face again?"

It seems my siblings also have a flair for art. When they discovered my paints, they begged me to paint their faces and my own. I told them those paints were for painting on a canvas, a hobby of mine which helps silence the voices for a while.

But when they begged, I went out and bought some. It was bittersweet as I couldn't help but think of my ma. She was the one who encouraged my creative side. She was an amazing painter; it's something I inherited from her. And the weird thing was, the moment the first stroke of paint coated my face, I felt at home.

It should frighten me, considering I should only associate horrible memories with such an act, but it doesn't. I feel more comfortable in someone else's shadow when I paint my face to reflect the demons within me, unleashing the pain with every stroke.

"You little rascals!" says the playful voice of their nanny, Amber.

Amber is an American nanny in her early twenties. She's been here for over a year and treats the wains better than my dad and stepma. It's been good craic having her here. She's educated me in all things American, and I find myself slipping into her accent often because it's nice to pretend I'm someone other than me.

I know she's interested in me, but I don't see her that way. I don't see anyone that way—until tonight, that is.

My mind circles back to Babydoll. How can someone I met for mere minutes have this kind of impact on me? I need and want it to stop.

And it does the moment Connor Kelly enters the room.

His sharp blue eyes narrow when he sees Amber and the children. "I'm so sorry, Mr. Kelly. They wanted to wait up for Punk—" She licks her lips, quickly backtracking. "For Puck."

My dad is highly opposed to my nickname, which is why I continue to use it.

"Ack, I want to fly to tha moon, but we can't be havin' everythin' we want. Go to bed. Now."

"But, Da!" Hannah and Ethan whine at the same time, but soon stop when our father gives them the "don't fuck with me" look.

"Good night. I'll see ya in the mornin.'" Giving them both a quick kiss on their foreheads, I lower them to the carpet, giving Amber a reassuring look. I don't want them to be anywhere near him right now. I'll deal with his sour bake.

She quickly ushers them from the room, not looking back.

Da looks at me, not hiding his disgust that his firstborn isn't what he wanted him to be. He wants me to be some "jock" as Amber would say, dressing like him in pressed trousers and polos and with short, conservative hair. But most days, I don't wear anything unless it's black and has a hole in it.

He curls his lip when he looks at the grayscale tattoo sleeve down my arm. I designed the artwork. It's a collaboration of nature combined with horror. But it's my ma's name tattooed along my knuckles which disgusts him the most.

"Come."

That's all it takes for Connor. One demand and we're to jump to command.

Uncle Sean nudges me, however, in a silent warning not to test Dad.

We walk through the castle, and I see my stepma, Fiona has added a new painting—a family portrait, bar me. It should hurt, but it doesn't.

Once we enter my dad's office, we all take a seat.

"How'd you get on?"

Nodding, I lean back in my leather chair. "Grand. Yer right. Nolen Ryan is a dick." I pass him my phone, showing him the photo evidence I found in his top drawer.

He slams his fist onto the desk. "That lying fuck! He must be made an example of. No man of mine is a fucking Catholic. No man."

And this is the only thing my father and I agree on.

It's in my blood to hate Catholics. How could I possibly not after what they did to my ma? But it's more than that. To understand my stance, we have to go back in time.

Certain parts of Northern Ireland are Protestant, whereas others are Catholic. Some of these areas are divided by a wall—the Peace Line. As wains, Cian, Rory, and I knew it was dangerous to venture into the neighborhoods of the Catholics.

We couldn't play thick as the enormous paintings on various buildings clearly show what area you were in. But that just tempted us all the more. As kids, we would sneak in just to get a glimpse of the unknown. And that's what almost got Cian killed.

One night, we wandered too far, and some Catholic didn't appreciate three wee hoods in his garden. He shot Cian in the back, no warning shot. Thankfully, Cian lived, but the same can't be said for the Catholic.

Back then, the majority of the peelers in Northern Ireland were Protestant; therefore, they didn't take too lightly to a Catholic harming their "own." Although they said there was no prejudice, we knew different, which is why the IRA served as a special "police force" for the Catholics.

But don't assume Catholics have been hard done by. They keep to their own as well.

We've been shunned, spat on, and cursed at for being Protestant by many Catholics throughout our lives. Cian, Rory, and I were minding our business when a Catholic gang beat us up for no reason. We were eight. This is why my dad taught me how to fight.

My dad is proud of his heritage. His ancestors are from England and Scotland, and have always been Protestant. But many people in Northern Ireland are descendants of the original population and are Catholic.

So, we're faced with a split populace belonging to different religious backgrounds. Hence, the hatred between the two religions.

Long story short—I was taught all Catholics are the enemy. And after what they did to my ma, to Cian, and the experiences I've had with them since I was a wain, I believe it to be true.

"I need ya to take care of it," my dad states, surprising me.

"Connor," Uncle Sean warns. "He's just a cub."

"Wind yer neck in," Dad argues. "We need to keep a low profile with the peelers sniffin' around."

With the new chief constable just appointed, Da has to test the waters to see which side of the law he sits. In the past, Da has been able to bribe many peelers to turn the other way, but now, he isn't sure if the chief constable is a friend or foe.

"Think you can handle it?" Dad asks, watching me closely.

"Aye, I'll get it sorted."

I've been doing my father's dirty work since I was eleven. If someone didn't pay for their order, whether that be drugs, guns, or protection, I went around and made sure they paid. We aren't a charity.

But I've never killed anyone. Sure, I've roughed them up good and lamped them within an inch of their lives—hence why my dad wanted to name me Puck—but it seems Da wants me to take the next step, the step every Kelly is expected to eventually take.

I could justify what I did by reasoning they were the bad guys, not me, but in reality, I am the worst of them all.

I try not to think about how my actions will impact Orla. Her father made a choice, and it was the wrong one. Now, he must suffer the consequences.

"Good lad. There's something else I want ya to do for me."

I arch a brow, indicating I'm listening.

"I want ya to be nice to Darcy Duffy."

"I *am* nice to her," I counter, wishing he'd give up on this idea.

"Grand, 'cause we've been invited to the Duffys' tomorrow for tea."

"I wish you'd let this go, aul' lad," I say as no matter how many teas we attend, Darcy and I will never be a thing.

But it seems Da won't take no for an answer this time. "Is yer head cut? Who d'ya think yer speakin' to, ya ungrateful fucker?"

Uncle Sean grips my arm, a silent warning not to rebel. But not this time.

"Ungrateful?" I challenge, my gaze never wavering from his. "That's a wee bit contradictory, seein' as ye had no issue moving on from Ma before she was even buried in the ground!"

Da grips the desk, his cheeks turning a bright red. "Ya want a clip on the lug? Is that it?"

Uncle Sean pinches the bridge of his nose, inhaling deeply. He's always been the peacekeeper, but it seems to be getting harder for him each day because I'm not a wee cub anymore. It's only a matter of time before my father and I end up in a fight with only one man left standing.

Da senses I'm in no mood to deal with his shite, and if he wants me to continue doing his dirty work, then he has to show me some respect.

He inhales, as if leveling himself. "Show me what ya nicked from the Ryans."

I've won this war—for now.

Opening my backpack, I slide the Bible across the desk toward my da. His nostrils flare when he sees the Catholic abomination in his house. I hoke through my pocket for the rosary beads but come up empty. I quickly check my other pocket, revealing the same outcome—they're gone, as is my ma's brooch.

Coming to a stand, I pat myself down, not understanding where they could be. I know I put the rosary in my pocket. So where are they?

As I retrace my steps, a realization slams into me, and I curse myself for being such an eejit. I know the rosary and my mum's brooch were in my pocket. I know they didn't fall out. So that means, I also know the reason they're not here is because Babydoll stole them from right under my nose.

She staged the entire incident of accidentally falling off her bike so she could steal from me. I can't even…

Dad senses something is wrong and comes to a stand. "Ya

spoofin', ye wee want? Or you just plain stupid?"

"I lost them," I reply, aware of what's coming. "But I'll get them back."

"Wha? You had one job. One fucking job! Yer fucking thick."

Before I can fight him off, Da rounds his desk and punches me in the face.

I stagger back, shook. No matter how many times he hits me, it always feels like the first time. But I accept his blows because better I suffer than he takes his temper out on the twins.

"Aye, for fuck's sake!" Uncle Sean exclaims, standing quickly and getting out of harm's way. He knows better than to intervene, but he tries, nonetheless. "That's enough, Connor. Y'll kill him."

I cup my bleeding nose. It's not broken—yet.

"I fucked up, so I did. I'm sorry," I exclaim, ragin' at myself for allowing this to happen.

But Dad doesn't want to hear apologies. He views apologies as weaknesses, and no son of his is meant to be weak.

He punches me again, connecting with my jaw, but still, I don't surrender. I stand tall, accepting this beating because I deserve it. I couldn't care less about the rosary beads, but my ma's brooch? How could I have been so careless?

I let my guard down for a pretty face. Never again.

Dad hits me in the stomach, knocking the wind from my lungs. I drop to my knees, and when he knees under my chin, I collapse onto my back.

"Is that the best ya got, aul' lad?" I provoke, a pained wheeze leaving me as he stomps on my knee.

"Ya fucking smart-arse!" He doesn't stop his assault. He kicks my ribs, my stomach, screaming that I'm worthless and should have died with my ma.

I accept his slurs and punches because he's right, but instead of Mum dying, it should have been me. But her death will not be in vain. Every Doyle is going to pay for what they did. My dad isn't with me, so all I've got is me, which is no different to how I've lived my entire life.

I've waited long enough. The Doyles incited a war—it's time the Kellys finally answered back.

But first, there's a wee doll I need to find.

TWO

PUNKY

Groaning, I open my right eye because my left one is almost closed over, thanks to the beating I got last night.

"Bout ye? Ya look like shite."

Turning my cheek, I see Cian sitting in the armchair, skimming through a copy of *Macbeth*.

"Ach, happy days," I reply, flinching as I shift to lean against the headboard. I'm breathless from the simple action.

"He lamped ya good this time, didn't he?"

It's not uncommon for Cian to find me black and blue, thanks to my dad's fists. It's a sight he's seen many times over the years. But this time is different because I'm going to fight back; just not in the way everyone thinks.

"I need yer help," I say, which has Cian placing the book on the armrest. "I want to go to Dublin."

Cian blinks once, appearing to need a moment to process what I just said. "Dublin?" he asks, in case he's had a lapse in hearing.

I nod firmly.

He shoots up from the chair and begins pacing the room. "A don't believe ya! Stop actin' the eejit. Ya wanna get killed?"

"Stop bein' so dramatic," I counter, pulling back the blankets. Cian flinches when he sees my bruised ribs. "I just want to have a wee look, that's all."

"A wee look at what?" Cian exclaims, hands out wide, but he knows. He knew it would eventually come to this.

"I can't let those fuckers walk around without any repercussions for what they did to my mum. Every day they live is just an insult to her memory!

"The aul' lad is nothin' but a coward. The only reason I'm still here is 'cause I hoped to learn somethin' about Ma's death. But I'm done waitin'. I know I can't do this on my own. I have to be smart."

"Ya can't just go danderin' into Dublin, Punky. Would ya quit actin' reckless?"

Placing my feet onto the carpet, I take a moment to pace myself. "Sure, this is it, but I'll be careful. Besides, youse big lads are gonna keep dick for me, aye?"

Cian pales and abruptly stops in his tracks. "This is a bad

idea. But we're with ya. Besides, a wee look can't hurt?"

"Aye, sure why nat?"

My flippant response does nothing to ease Cian's worries, but I mean it. I'll proceed with caution. I just want to take a look around. That's all.

But that look will eventually lead to bloodshed, one way or another.

"Is that why ya got a hidin'? Ya told him yer goin' to Dublin?"

"Ack, no," I hiss, my eyes darting to the door to ensure no one is listening in. "No one can know about this but us. Once I have a plan, we go. All right?"

"Sound." Cian nods, running a hand through his dark brown hair. "So why did he belt ya?"

Clearing my throat, I stand casually. The room spins, but I stay upright—for now. "'Cause I lost the rosary beads."

"Shut your bake! How?"

I'm utterly scundered when I confess, "A wee doll stole it… when I helped her last night."

Cian's mouth twists into an amused grin as me helping strangers, or anyone for that matter, is a quare rare thing. "Helped her with what?"

"Helped fix her bike," I explain, but he thinks it's code for sex.

"Yeo!" he hollers, but there is nothing to be excited about. "She a ride then?"

"Cian, what she is, is in trouble. I need to find her. She took my mum's brooch too."

His smirk soon dies as he understands my urgency to seek her out. "Sure, this is it. I'll help ya find her. Whatcha gonna do when ya do?"

And that's a question I don't have an answer to.

If this were anyone else, they would pay and pay painfully slow, but with Babydoll, the thought of hurting her doesn't get me off like it would with most. I'm fair ragin', but after last night's strange response to her, I don't want to punish her with pain.

So what do I want to punish her with?

Thoughts of her tied to my bed and squirming while I make her beg come to mind. Sex for me is something carnal. It always has been. There's never any commitment; no chance at falling in love, because I don't want love.

I just want the pain to go away for a small fraction of time.

Running a hand through my snarled hair, I decide to take a quick shower and work out my plan of attack. Cian plays a video game while he waits for me as I limp toward the bathroom.

The simple act of showering hurts, and I wonder what excuse Dad will use at tonight's tea for me looking like someone's punching bag. This is another reason for me to pursue something I should have years ago. I am done being his lackey.

I'm not stupid, I know I can't go into Dublin, guns blazing. I need a plan, and a smart one at that. Even though I've never met Brody Doyle, the kingpin of Dublin and the arsehole who ordered the hit on my ma, I've heard stories which make Da look like Father Christmas compared to him.

Uncle Sean said there wasn't any proof, but he was certain it came from the top as nothing happens unless it goes through Brody first. I begged him to tell me more, but he said it was better to let sleeping dogs lie. But I don't understand how.

How can they allow my ma's death to go unpunished?

When your dad is feared in all of Northern Ireland, it's hard to get any dirt on him, as everyone is too afraid to talk bad about him in case it comes back to bite them in the arse. So getting any information from his confidants was impossible.

I don't know my mum's family. I don't even know if they exist. Growing up, all I knew was the Kelly family as my dad said that was all that mattered. I've grown up only knowing half of my identity. It's time that changed.

I don't care what Ma did, but I imagine she betrayed my dad in one way or another for him to forget she existed and not avenge her death. I'm going to get to the bottom of the Kelly family secrets and ensure those who were involved pay.

Looking down at the crucifix tattoo on my wrist, I decide to start with this first piece in the large, intricate puzzle. I need to get into my da's office to look at the photo he took for any clues.

It's a long shot, but when you've got nothing, it's a start.

Drying off, I put on ripped jeans and a black T-shirt. I loop the silver chain around my neck before running my fingers through my wet hair. I avoid the mirror and enter my bedroom. Hannah and Ethan have taken over the PlayStation from Cian, but when they see me, they stop their game, their eyes wide.

"Hey! How are ya?" Hannah says, chewing on her bottom lip when she notices my injured face.

"Stickin' out, wee rascal," I reply, playing off my injuries. Hannah and I have a special relationship. I love them both the same, but there is something about Hannah.

I hate them seeing me this way because even though they're only six, they understand that something bad happened.

Dad hasn't raised a hand to them, and if he ever did, I would make sure it was the last thing he did. I look at Ethan, silently promising to never let Da use him the way he's used me.

Amber pokes her head into my doorway and sighs in relief when she sees the twins. "Oh, thank God. You two are going to give me a heart attack one of these days."

Cian instantly sits taller when he sees Amber. "Good mornin'," he says with a smile.

Cian doesn't lack female attention as, according to his mum, he's a handsome devil, but he grows bored easily, a product of growing up and having it all.

We're both looking for something...more, in every aspect of our lives. Something more that'll help drive the demons away, and I found more last night, so much more. I crack my knuckles, just thinking of Babydoll.

Amber gasps when she notices my face. "Punky, what did he—"

But I cut her off, not wanting the twins to overhear. "The aul' lad gone then?"

Amber wipes away a tear, before nodding.

Her kindness still shocks me sometimes. I don't understand why she cares. And this is why I believe I'm dead inside. I don't feel what others do. I can't remember the last time I cried or cared. I wake, shower, run errands for my da—repeat.

I function on autopilot, waiting for some big revelation to appear. But it never does.

However, the thought of killing every Doyle alive shifts this emptiness I feel. It's the first time in forever I've felt like I'm on the right path. I know that path will be laced with danger, carnage, and blood, but it's here where I belong.

I look at Cian, hinting the plan starts now.

He gets up reluctantly, clearly wanting to spend more time with Amber, but that can wait. Da has some business meetings this morning; I know because I checked his weekly planner. He'll be back soon, so we don't have much time.

"Do you want me to bring them back inside?" Amber asks, looking at the twins who are thoroughly engrossed in their video game.

"They're all right to stay here."

Amber nods and commences making my bed, knowing

how pedantic I am. I would usually do it myself, but at the moment, it hurts to breathe.

Nodding my thanks, I kiss the twin's foreheads before Cian and I make our way to the main house. My lungs are screaming at me to stop, but I persevere.

"How'd ya get on last night with Darcy?" I ask, hoping he shares that Rory and Darcy are now seeing one another. This will get Dad off my back.

"Ack, Rory fancies her something shockin', but she's not interested. She asked about ya."

Gripping my side, I inhale sharply to measure my choppy breaths. "Fuck."

"What's goin' on?" he asks, sensing my distress.

"We're callin' on the Duffys' for tea tonight. I think my dad is trying to set somethin' up with Darcy and me."

Cian's eyes widen. "Shite. Rory is really hung up on her."

"I know. It doesn't matter what Dad wants. He's away in the head if he thinks this is happenin'. I don't want her. I don't want anyone."

"Except for the wee doll from last night, aye?"

He grunts when I elbow him in the ribs.

"I don't want her. She…interested me, aye, but she fuckin' stole from me."

"And?" he poses. "Ya steal from everyone."

"Remind me why yer still my friend?" I quip.

Cian knows not to press. I don't do feelings or emotions. I

never have. He'd love nothing more than to talk about girls over a pint, but I've never been interested in that.

But the conversation turns serious when Cian asks, "What happens if yer dad won't take no for an answer?"

I don't reply, and instead, focus on getting into Dad's office.

We enter through the back door where Fiona's personal chefs are busy preparing her breakfast. I have no idea what she does. She doesn't cook, clean, or look after the twins. I stay out of her way, and mostly, she does the same with me.

She married my dad a few months after my ma was murdered. She often says she never planned to fall in love with her dead best friend's husband, but we all know what a load of shite that is. The church allowed their union because my dad wasn't divorced—he was a widower.

Just thinking about how fucked up my childhood was, I curl my lip and continue walking through the castle, ensuring we keep out of anyone's way. Cian stands close behind me, always having my back.

When we get to my dad's office, I look down the long hallway. When the coast is clear, I slip off my silver chain with a key dangling off the end. The key unlocks this office door.

"Yeo," Cian whispers with a smirk.

Slipping the key into the lock, I turn it, and when it clicks over, I open the door. We enter Dad's office, then close the door softly behind us.

I head straight for my dad's desk and drop to a crouch to

open the bottom drawer. Taking care to keep everything the way Da left it, I flick through the files until I come to the folder I want. Opening it, I reach for the timeworn photograph that still has the ability to shock me after all this time.

Cian peers over my shoulder, gasping when he sees it. "That's you?"

"Aye," I reply, looking into the sad eyes of five-year-old me.

Even though I don't remember this photograph being taken, I do remember the pools of blood on the white carpet. I trace my finger over one in the background—it was where my ma took her last breath.

"Who did that to yer face?"

"I did," I reply, remembering drawing each line with precision to reflect the injuries inflicted on my ma. "This is what they did to her, Cian. They took a knife and slit her mouth, ear to ear, to silence her screams.

"And after they were done rapin' her broken body, they slit her throat," I reveal, running two fingers over the black paint over my throat.

"Fuckin' hell, mate. I'm sorry," Cian says, his disgust clear.

I've never told him or Rory the details of what happened that night. I didn't see the point. But now, they both need to know it all to understand why I'm about to start a war.

"She told me to pretend I was someone else, that I wasn't really there. But all I could paint was what they did to her. It was my way to help carry her pain because I was locked in the wardrobe, watchin' them kill my ma."

"Is that why ya don't like confined spaces?"

Not much scares me anymore, but being locked up with no escape route is my worst nightmare. I'm awful claustrophobic, but no one knows it. This is a weakness my enemies would exploit.

"Aye."

Cian is quiet, digesting what I just shared. This is why I don't tell anyone about my past. I don't want sympathy or anyone to look at me with pity in their eyes.

"I remember bits and pieces, but I'll always remember her sacrifice. And this photograph just reinforces what I have to do.

"I think even as a wain, I knew that drawin' what I saw, a reflection of what they did to her, would help me avenge her death. I remember blood. Her screams. Her body coolin' as I lay beside her for three days.

"But these three lines"—I slide my finger over the three red slashes on my forehead—"they represent the three arseholes who took her life. I drew them to ensure I never forgot.

"One of them, the one who slit her throat, knew I was there."

"Away on!" he wheezes, shook.

"He unlocked the door, but left me there unharmed...why? This has always confused me because I don't understand. If he knew I was there, why didn't he kill me too?"

"That fucker. I'm sorry, I didn't know."

Returning my focus to the photograph I've looked at

countless times, I examine every inch of it for anything I may have missed. But nothing looks different.

Frustrated, I close my eyes, trying to transport myself back in time.

"I never wanted this for ya, Cara. But ya didn't listen."

Screams and then a gurgle of blood.

What didn't she listen to?

And that voice…do I know it?

Groaning, I slam my fist against the carpet, angry I can't recall more. I've tried for many years, hoping to remember something I may have missed, a small detail that would help identify who these men are.

But I'm always faced with a black mass that won't shift. Holes in my memory? Or my brain's way of self-preservation? I don't know.

"Fuck!" I curse, angered that this has failed.

Opening my eyes, I replace the photograph and put everything back where I found it, so as not to alert my dad that I've been snooping. As I go to close the drawer, something falls behind it, preventing it from closing all the way.

Angling my head to the side to see if I can uncover why it's jammed, I notice a piece of paper stuck behind the drawer. This is new.

Without delay, I pull the drawer out completely and reach for the folded piece of paper. When I unfold it, all I see is an address. It's in Dublin.

My heart doesn't usually race, nor does my breathing accelerate, even when I've beaten someone within an inch of their lives. I usually operate on a monotone, but that changes when I see this piece of information because it may be the key to where I need to start.

Reaching into my pocket, I use my phone to take a picture of the address. Cian does the same. Always have a backup. Not sure where this piece of paper was stacked in this drawer, I place it between two folders and hope for the best.

"Let's go," Cian anxiously says, knowing if my dad catches us in here, it'll be hell for us both.

Ensuring everything is where we found it, I slowly open the door and take a juke down the hallway. When it's clear, I step out, and Cian follows. I lock the door, and we dander, not wanting to alert anyone to our snooping.

We turn the corner and bump into Uncle Sean. "What 'bout ye?"

"Beezer," I reply, but my injuries contradict my aloof reply.

Uncle Sean grips my chin, turning my face to look at the damage. "Why do ya provoke him, cub?"

Uncle Sean's touch is the only one I can stomach—only just. "The aul' lad is such a dick. I can't believe yer his kin."

Uncle Sean sighs, letting me go. "Aye, sometimes I wonder that myself. Since yer ma—" But he soon pauses, stopping himself from sharing the Kelly secrets.

I don't bother asking him to continue because I know he won't, which is why as soon as this naff tea is done tonight, I'm going to Dublin.

"Yer so much like him. Yer both so bleedin' stubborn."

"Please don't insult me, Uncle Sean," I sternly say. "I'm nothin' like that bastard."

Uncle Sean knows better than to argue. "That's the truth, so it is. Have fun tonight," he quips, knowing how opposed to the idea I am. "Make sure yer not runnin' late."

He gives us one final look before we part ways, and I'm onto the next state of affairs for the day.

When we're out of earshot, Cian exhales in relief. But the fun is only just beginning, and he knows it.

"Ya didn't tell me the wee ride's name."

A mix of emotions come over me when I think about her. Even though I am rippin' that she stole from me, a small, insane part is actually impressed she was able to nick from me in the first place. I haven't been caught unaware in a long time.

But regardless of that, she's going to pay for taking something that isn't hers.

Only when we're in my car do I reply, "Babydoll," before turning up the radio.

"Oh, fuck," Cian groans, shaking his head as he fastens his seat belt, knowing this is about to get bumpy.

As I'm knotting my black tie in the bathroom mirror, I scoff, hating everything about tonight. My face looks a mess, and no matter that I'm sporting a pressed white shirt and tie, it doesn't deter from the black and blue mess my face is.

My tie is loosely knotted, and two buttons are left undone on my shirt. My dad is not going to be happy that I replaced my black trousers with ripped black jeans and black combat boots, but he's lucky I'm going at all.

My mood is foul because Cian and I didn't find anything on Babydoll. We went back to where I last saw her but came up empty. In the daylight, it was even more isolated than it looked at night. There wasn't a house for miles, which has me wondering, just what was she doing out there?

I haven't given up, however.

I *will* find her. I just need to figure out how.

My hair is a tousled mess with the longer blond strands flicked to the left to cover the bruises around my eye.

Once I'm ready, I grab everything I need and jump into my Jeep. I'm not riding with Da as I don't plan on staying long. The moment this tea is over with, I plan on making an excuse to leave. It'll take about an hour and a half to get to Dublin, so I have no time to waste.

The drive to the Duffys' is quite peaceful. Filled with lush greenery and old homes, I appreciate how "fortunate" I am to bear the Kelly name at times. I've never had to worry about money, and my house, which was once a castle, is the envy of many.

I begin to wonder what Dublin will be like. The unknown excites me. I know I have to be careful, as even our lingo differs, so it won't be hard to spot the odd man out. I need to blend in.

When the Duffys' mansion comes into view, I put all thoughts on hold because I need to get through this fucking tea first. Parking my Jeep, I send Cian and Rory a quick text, telling them to be ready for my call. I can only hope tonight is over with soon.

I don't even have a chance to ring the doorbell before the door opens, and I'm greeted by a butler. "Can I take your—" He peers at my clothes and just smiles uncomfortably instead.

Entering the grand foyer and whistling an annoying tune, he gestures that my dad and Mr. Duffy are in the living room. I can hear my da laughing, which is a rare occurrence, but I know it's all for show. He's a lickarse as he clearly wants something from Patrick Duffy.

At a guess, I'd say he wants in on his business.

Patrick's construction company is very valuable to my da, and not just financially. To have access to abandoned buildings and neighborhoods where Dad can run his operations would benefit him immensely, especially now that he's unsure if Chief

Constable Moore will turn a blind eye to the Kellys illegal dealings.

My dad's most effective means of drug transportation has been concealing cannabis in loads of vegetables on lorries. The drivers are aware of what they're doing. Nolen Ryan is one of those drivers, which is why Dad wants him dealt with.

If he can't be trusted with his religious beliefs, how can he be trusted with transporting over 600 kilos of cannabis?

Uncle Sean and Dad take care of the logistics while I deal with anyone who dares to defy them. There are a few, but the Kelly name is notorious in Northern Ireland. So most know better than to challenge a Kelly.

I enter the living room, and the moment Patrick sees me, his eyes widen. "What happened?"

Dad speaks for me before I can. "Karate. The wee lad forgot to dodge," he playfully says. This is believable because I am a black belt, and it could be assumed someone got in a lucky shot. But because of my reputation, Patrick will probably guess I got into a fight, but he'd never anticipate with who.

"Ack, yer poor critter."

Dad looks at me, hinting I'm to play along with his wee fairy tale, so I merely nod.

"Darcy and my wife are still getting ready. Can I get you a drink?"

I shake my head. "Naw, I'm all right."

My dad is sulking for whatever reason, but that reason can

wait because something strange happens. I don't know how to explain it, other than that bubble of excitement that wells in yer stomach before a fight—that's what I feel.

When I turn around and see the reason, I don't know whether to be happy or rippin' because this bold doll has been on my mind since the moment we met. And she shouldn't be because Babydoll is a fucking thief.

Her fear is clear when she sees me, and the tray of drinks she holds falters in her hands. But she soon recovers, not wanting to make a scene. Patrick and Dad seem unaware of what's happening.

"Ack, hurry, love," Patrick orders, annoyed she's taking so long.

Babydoll nods, avoiding eye contact with me as she offers her tray to Patrick and Dad. My dad looks at Babydoll, obviously liking what he sees.

On instinct, I curl my hands into fists by my side, wanting to punch the aul' lad for looking at her that way. She's in yet another costume, but I eat her up all the same.

Her black dress with a white collar is about a size too big, but regardless, she's parful looking. Her white apron angers me because she's too good to be serving ballbags like Patrick Duffy. Is this why she stole from me? Does she need the money?

The fact she appears to be the Duffys' new housekeeper confirms that she does.

"Who's this, then?" asks Dad, taking a glass of champagne

from the silver tray Babydoll holds.

"This is Poppy," Patrick reveals with a smile; a smile I want to slap from his bake. "She just moved here from London. She came highly recommended by the Clerys."

"Is that right, love?" Da asks with a grin.

Babydoll nods nervously.

Under the bright lights, her blonde hair glows, but her dark eyebrows reveal her natural hair color is light brown. It's my job to notice these things. Knowing the enemy is what a smart predator does because that's what Babydoll is.

I keep calm, not wanting to alert anyone to the fact that I'm about to corner Babydoll and demand she give me back what she stole.

"Hi," Darcy says as she enters the room, oblivious to what's going on as she politely gives my dad a kiss on the cheek.

Babydoll quickly makes a beeline for the exit, but I think not. She's not getting away, not again. Discreetly reaching out, I snare her wrist, stopping her. The glasses on the tray rattle. She licks her lips, her chest rising and falling rapidly.

"Y've got somethin' of mine…I want it back." My low tone is firm. I take great pleasure in seeing her pretty pink lips part as she gulps in a mouthful of air. "I care not about the rosary beads. But the brooch, I want it back, and I want it back *now*."

Her eyes dart to Darcy making gracious conversation with the aul' fellas. "I don't know what you're t-talking about," she frantically whispers, insulting me further.

When she tries to remove herself from my grip, I tighten my hold and pull her toward me. "Will ya do me a kindness? Don't fuck with me, Babydoll," I warn, eyeing her closely. "Ya won't like the consequences if ya do."

"Let me go," she hisses angrily, fruitlessly trying to break free.

Why isn't she afraid of me like everyone else? It's time that changes.

With a cocky grin, I bend low, completely ignoring her personal space. "Ye may be able to fool others with yer shy act," I hum, slowly running my thumb along her bottom lip and leveling her with a scowl. "But I see ya for what you are. Yer a thief, and ya stole from the wrong lad. Well, good luck with that 'cause I'm huntin' ya, wee doll."

And only then do I let her go.

She's shaking, but I'm unsure if it's from fear or rage, and that just excites me all the more.

We stare at one another, and the static between us is so toxic I can barely breathe. But I stand tall, not letting on what being in her presence does to me.

She's out the door fairly lively, as she's not thick—she knows I meant what I said.

Darcy turns toward me, where I smile, pretending my heart isn't beating faster than it has ever beaten before. It's the most confusing of emotions because in one heartbeat, I want to hurt Babydoll, but in the next, all I want to do is press her body against mine and steal her warmth like I did last night.

Fair play to her because she's the first person to ever provoke this in me.

"Bout ye, Puck," Darcy says, kissing my cheek and reminding me where I am.

"Dead-on," I reply, subtly moving away from her, unlike with Babydoll, who I couldn't get close enough to. I'm up to high doh from our encounter.

"I thought ye'd come last night with the boys," she says, lowering her voice so her da doesn't hear.

"I was busy," I vaguely reply, noticing our fathers happily overlooking our exchange. Is Patrick all for this, too?

"No bother." She smiles, and I suddenly feel unsettled. "Do ya think then when yer not busy…we could go out to the pictures or maybe a swall?"

"Why d'ya say that for?" I ask quickly, confused.

"Why not?" she counters with a grin.

"'Cause a lovely wee bird like yerself doesn't want to go out with someone like me. I'm sure ya have lots of other fellas, like Rory, who would be happy to take ya."

Darcy stands on her toes to whisper into my ear, "I don't want another fella. I want you."

I pull away, stunned. "Are ye havin' a laugh?"

She brushes a strand of brown hair behind her ear. "No, I'm not. I like ya, Puck Kelly."

Right, this has turned to shite in a matter of seconds.

Before I can tell her that'll *never* happen, Patrick and my da come over, smiling happily. But they don't know their arses from their elbows if they think this is happening. However, as Darcy shifts closer to me, not at all deterred by my obvious rejection, I realize this is a lot worse than I thought.

THREE

PUNKY

"She said that?" Rory asks, his mouth slack.

"Aye, sorry, big lad. I don't know if her dad has got to her, but the whole night, she made it awful obvious she was interested in me. I don't know why," I add because the feeling was definitely not reciprocated.

We're in a rental as we would never drive our own cars into Dublin, but I suddenly wish I was because Rory is sulking. I wanted to be honest and let him know what happened tonight. However, now I wish I'd kept my bake shut.

"I can't get my head around it. I mean, we kissed a couple of nights ago."

I shrug because I don't have an answer. I'm just as confused as he is.

"Darcy is a melt," Cian says, trying to lighten the mood. "At least ya know now."

But Rory doesn't see it in that way. He's been mad about Darcy for as long as I can remember, so I can imagine knowing this has him rippin'.

"Ack, what does yer dad want with the Duffys anyway?"

"Fuck if I know. But at a guess, Patrick's portfolio is probably a good place to start."

"Yer dad is a real wanker," Rory angrily says.

I don't argue because I agree.

Tea at the Duffys' was painful and long, and Darcy trying to discreetly play footsie with me under the table made it worse. I don't know what's caused this forward response from her, but I don't like it.

Nothing she says or does will change my mind and having Babydoll feet away just confirmed it. It just proved I'll never want Darcy the way I do Babydoll.

I don't understand these feelings I have for her. I hardly know her. But I can't deny that whenever she's near, I seek her out. I'm drawn to her.

She ignored me the entire time I was at the Duffys', but her breathless whimpers when she leant over to refill my glass or collect an empty dish revealed she also feels whatever *this* is. There is still one small problem, and that is, Babydoll is a thief. Therefore, I can't trust her nor should I trust whatever this feeling is.

"So ya left without yer mum's brooch?" asks Cian, interrupting my thoughts.

"Aye. What could I do? I couldn't exactly frisk her between the main course and afters. Now that I know where she is, I can act, but not tonight. I have other important things to deal with."

The car falls quiet.

We're about twenty minutes from arriving at the border, twenty minutes where everything is about to change. We went over everything we know about the Doyles or, more specifically, Brody Doyle. This information is either hearsay or things we've earwigged on.

Our parents would rather the Doyles didn't exist; therefore, talk about them has been sacrilegious our entire lives, but I can't live that way any longer. I need answers. I need those who hurt my ma to pay. And tonight is the first step toward achieving that.

"So, we know that Brody has three kids. Two boys and one girl."

Cian nods, opening his notepad and reading over his scribble. "Aye. The lads are older. The wee girl is the wain of the family.

"The eldest is Liam. He's dead spit of his da. Hugh is second eldest. He is a wee rip. Likes to punch first, ask questions later. He's the one we have to look out for. Liam is discreet. Hugh is not."

"And the daughter?" I ask, needing to arm myself with as

much information as I can.

"I couldn't get much information on her, which makes her dangerous. She could be anyone."

He's right. We need to be alert.

The research into the address reveals it's a pub. When we searched it online, it didn't say who the owners were. We're guessing it belongs to the Doyles, but honestly, we could be walking into anything.

Rory taps his fingers against the steering wheel, clearly caught up in other thoughts—such as Darcy. I wish I could empathize with him, but all I see is a huffy bastard. She doesn't like him, so I'm not sure why he's stressing over something out of his control.

But that's just me. I'm not wired like everyone else.

"I still can't believe Babydoll is the Duffys' new maid. What a small world, do ya not think?" Cian probes, desperately trying to get a response from me.

"I don't think anythin," I retort, loosening my tie.

Both Cian and Rory smirk, not convinced, but I don't care what they think because the moment we cross the border, all I care about is revenge.

We're all quiet, marveling at this foreign land that's been forbidden our whole lives, but now that we're here, it's made what we're about to do real. I thought I would come into Dublin with Dad, avenging my ma, but it's just up to me.

Rory keeps to the speed limit, which is now in kilometers,

not wanting to draw any attention to us being here.

I don't know what I expected Dublin to look like. Being from the north, I never took much interest in the south, but it certainly doesn't look like the hellhole I thought it to be. I suppose I am biased, as I have no problem with the city itself; it's the inhabitants who make this place hell on earth.

The map says we're five minutes away.

"Right, boys," I say, rolling down the sleeves of my shirt as I don't want my tattoos to be on show. "Nice and quick, yeah?"

"So, we have a wee drink and a juke?" Rory asks, an excited energy radiating from him.

This is why we're best friends—all three of us thrive in the darkness, the corrupt, and this right now is probably the most danger we've been involved in. Our parents thought we'd forget this vendetta, that Cian and Rory would talk me out of acting in haste if this time ever came.

But they don't know what true friendship is because these lads have had my back since I can remember. They don't have to be here, as this is my retribution, not theirs, but they wouldn't let me do this alone.

"Aye. We won't be long in there. We're just three lads out for a wee drink. That's all."

They nod.

Rory parks the car a few blocks away, inhaling deeply as he puts on a hat backward to conceal his tousled brown hair. Cian smirks, slipping into his coat to hide the tattoo sleeve on his right arm. I hunt through my backpack and slip on my black-rimmed glasses, then take out my nose and lip piercing.

I don't know what the Doyles know about us, so to blend in, we have to look like everyone else. Piercings and tattoos can be used to identify us, and we can't have that. Tugging at the sleeve of my shirt to cover my crucifix tattoo, I know firsthand how disastrous it can be if that information falls into the wrong hands.

We exit the car and slip our masks into place. To onlookers, we're just three mates out for a good night.

Dublin has a cosmopolitan atmosphere, while Belfast is small and has a country town feeling to it. I can imagine many come to Dublin and get lost as you can be anyone in such a large city. I instantly miss home. But the closer we get to the pub, the more excited I become—excited by the possibility of spilling Doyle blood. When we're feet away, I look overhead at the glowing green sign.

The Craic's 90

A classic Irish phrase which means a good time.

The building is painted red with small Irish flags draped along the balcony's ledge. It's in a good, busy location, and is modern, but has an aul' feel to it. It's jammed full of patrons, which is a blessing as well as a curse.

We can blend in, but as far as earwigging, we won't be able

to hear a thing above the rowdy drunks.

With nothing but confidence, we enter, taking everything in.

It's everything you'd expect to see inside a traditional Irish pub. The walls are dark brown with green and white accents. Wooden barstools surround the kegs acting as tables, and some tasteful light fixtures help brighten the room.

But the noisy drinkers aren't here for the décor. They're here to get plastered.

We walk inside, heading straight for the bar. I take a moment to listen and watch, like a smart predator does. Instantly, I'm drawn to a pretty blonde behind the bar. She's pouring pints with skill, hinting this isn't her first night behind the bar.

Cian notices me looking. Standing at six-four, he can clearly see where my attention is. Rory soon catches up to speed. We wait in line, soaking up the atmosphere for an entirely different reason to everyone else here.

"C'mere till I tell ya," shouts a hammered eejit two patrons in front of us to his friends. "I'm gonna ask Erin to have a drink with me."

His mates laugh, slapping him on the back as if they don't believe him. "Yer a real bungalow. A pretty thing like Erin Doyle wouldn't touch ya."

Rory makes eye contact with me as he heard what I did.

Looking around the room, I see a pretty girl sitting with a group of friends.

Tapping the man in front of me, I try my best to smile when he turns over his broad shoulder to look at me. He doesn't hide his disgust that someone like me would dare speak to him.

"Excuse me, but I overheard that girl over there tell her friends ya were bleedin' massive."

The man follows where I'm pointing, and his attitude soon changes.

"Janey Mack," he says, smirking. "Excuse me, lads."

This ballbag *would* believe a table of pretty birds are interested in him because he's a cocky cunt. He doesn't need any further encouragement and heads off into their direction.

Cian shakes his head, just as disgusted as I am. "Oh, yer excused, cockhead. Ack, these fuckers sound like buck eejits," he says under his breath.

And he's right.

Their slang and accents are different. I studied some basic lingo and hope it'll get us through without being detected for who we are. But the reason I sent that knob away is because now I can subtly earwig on the conversation in front of us.

"I don't care whatcha think. I'm askin' her," the eejit with red hair persists.

His friends all laugh, apparently not having much faith in his pickup attempts.

"Yer full of wind and piss. Besides, a girl like Erin is too good for a gom like you."

"And her two brothers are scary as all shite. They rule

Dublin. Stay away. I'm not savin' yer pig-ignorant arse. Again."

"Run yer lamps over her," the infatuated eejit says to his friends.

Cian, Rory, and I follow his line of sight and when we see he's drooling over the blonde bartender, we all make the same assumption.

This is Erin Doyle—the only daughter of Brody Doyle.

Cian grips my bicep to stop me from advancing. It was an involuntary movement. My body is prepared to fight as this pub has a Doyle working behind the bar. I doubt it's because she needs the money. This pub is owned by the Doyles and is definitely a front for something.

And I intend to find out what that something is.

The three men wait until Erin can serve them, and when she makes eye contact with the eejit, she rolls them.

"What'll it be then?" she shouts to be heard over the music.

"If yer not on the menu, I'll have three pints of the black stuff."

Cian snorts while I try not to boke at the lame pickup line. No wonder his mates were having a laugh at him.

Erin doesn't crack a smile when she pours the three drinks and places them on the bar. "Anything else?"

I don't hear the eejit's reply because my attention is diverted to the big lad who just walked behind the bar. Erin doesn't seem bothered that he's helping himself to the top shelf whiskey. He's tall and has light brown hair.

His hard face reveals he doesn't take shite from anyone. He has a sense of control, entitlement, which means he has to be a Doyle. And the way girls are falling over themselves to get a juke at him confirms this.

I'm guessing this is Liam—the eldest Doyle sibling.

They say he's dead spit of his dad, so I take a close look at him, memorizing the face of a monster. He grabs some glasses and walks over to a table in the corner of the room. I see three older men, laughing rowdily without a care in the world.

I gesture with my head that Cian and Rory are to go check it out while I deal with Erin.

The eejit doesn't take no for an answer, and as Erin waits for him to finish whatever nonsense he's carrying on with, her gaze lands on me. I expect her to look away, but she doesn't. She makes it very clear that she's checking me out and likes what she sees.

My skin crawls, but my mask is firmly in place as I grin, then raise my eyes to the heavens as if bored by the cockhead in front of me. Erin smiles, brushing a piece of blonde hair behind her ears.

The eejit finally gets the hint, and he and his friends leave, which gives me room to step forward. "Three pints of Guinness, thanks," I say in an American accent that would make Amber proud.

Erin nods and commences pouring my drinks.

She is very pretty, but I don't let her good looks have me

away with the fairies. No matter what she is, first and last, she will always be a Doyle, and her gold crucifix necklace is just confirmation of this. She is the enemy, a dangerous enemy with a pretty face.

"Yer American then?"

"Yes," I reply coolly. "I'm here on vacation with friends."

"Ah, some craic. How ya liking it here?"

"It's awesome. Although, it's fucking cold."

She laughs while I mentally catalogue everything I can about her. "Have you worked here for long?"

"Aye, my whole life. My family owns this pub," she clarifies when I don't respond. "It's expected of me to be here, regardless of if I want to be or not."

She doesn't seem happy of that fact.

"I know that feeling all too well," I reply, pushing my glasses up the bridge of my nose.

"I imagine you would," she says, making a point to look at my bruised face. "I'm Erin, by the way."

"Mike," I reply with a smile.

"Well, Mike, that'll be ten euros."

I pay her, ensuring our fingers touch when I pass her the money. "Keep the change, Erin. It was nice meeting you."

I grab my drinks, hoping my aloof act works—it does.

"I have a break in half an hour. I hope yer still here."

Smiling, I don't bother saying anything as I walk away with drinks in hand. Rory and Cian are doing a good job at blending in, and when they see me, they can read the buzzin' expression on my bake. Setting the glasses down onto the table, I casually turn my back toward Liam, not wanting to raise any red flags.

"How'd it go then?" Rory asks from behind the rim of his glass.

"Grand. It's her," I affirm as her comment about her family owning this pub means we're on Doyle turf.

"Yer sure?" Cian asks softly, keeping his eyes peeled to the table behind me.

"Aye, she told me her family owns this pub. She's got to be Brody's daughter."

"She could be a relative," Rory reasons, and he's right. She could be. But I feel it in the pit of my stomach that she and the cunt behind me are Brody's kids.

"What else did she say?"

"Nothin'. Just that she's havin' a break soon and hopes I'm here when she does."

Rory jokingly pretends to boke while Cian shakes his head. "Ach, yer breakin' hearts even in Dublin."

"Fuck off," I playfully reply, throwing back my drink.

The men behind me are talking softly, which just confirms they're talking business, and when one of them stands, excusing himself to use the jacks, this is my cue to find out what they're discussing.

I finish my drink, then follow him.

The jacks are empty, apart from the man taking a piss at the urinals. I keep my eyes up front and use the urinal two away from him. It's as awkward as it sounds, making conversation when taking a piss, but thankfully, the shithead doesn't seem to mind.

"Look at the bleeding state o' you, lad."

Turning to look at him, I smile. "I ran into a door," I reply with cheek.

He laughs loudly. "Ack, you Americans are bitta craic. My name's Aidan."

"Mike," I reply, thankful when I hear Aidan do up his fly. He walks over to the sink to wash his hands. When I'm done, I join him.

"Ye can fight then?"

"You should see the other guy." I whistle, lathering my hands with soap.

Aidan laughs, turning off the taps. And when he does, a crucifix tattooed on his left wrist catches my eye.

Time stands still.

I blink once, needing a moment to process what I'm seeing in case my eyes are playing tricks on me. But it's there, bringing back a downpour of emotions.

Ma's screams, her wheezing for breath, all of it comes crashing to the surface, threatening to drag me under and silence the memories for good.

But I need to hold it together because Aidan has something I want, something I've been looking for since I was five years old.

Answers…and his fucking head.

"Yes, I can fight, why?" I ask, needing to keep this conversation going. "You need someone to fight for you?"

Aidan dries his hands on the paper towel, appearing to weigh over my question. "Yer offering?"

Aidan is guarded, and so he should be. I would be suspicious if he welcomed me into his circle with open arms. But I will do anything to gain his trust because it'll make what I plan to do to him wild craic. I am not going to merely kill him—I'm going to paint Dublin with his blood.

The door opens and the person who enters has me clenching my fist, but I need to calm down, as I can't stir any suspicion.

"I thought ya fell in."

Aidan laughs. "Ye know what happens when ya break the seal. Was just talkin' to this nice fella. Liam, this is Mike from America."

I have no idea why my nationality makes a difference, and right now, I don't care because I was right—this fucker is Liam Doyle.

Liam eyes me closely. I wonder what he sees.

Once I finish drying my hands, I offer one to Liam. He looks down at it and eventually shakes it. When we connect, sheer fury overwhelms me, and it takes every ounce of control I have not to kill them both where they stand.

"How's the form?" He asks how I am, but I play thick,

seeing as I'm supposed to be American.

"How's the what?"

A grin spreads across Liam's bake. This was a test. And I passed.

"What happened to yer face?" he asks, looking at me closely.

"Oh. Someone had a smart mouth. I didn't like it." I don't elaborate.

Aidan looks at Liam, clearly attempting to read what's going on behind those cold blue eyes.

"Have a drink with us?" Liam phrased it as a question, but I know I don't have a choice.

"Sure. Sounds good."

Aidan chuckles, slapping me on the back like we're old friends. If only he knew how I wish to break every bone in his body. We exit the jacks while Liam remains behind to take a piss. When Rory and Cian see me walk out with Aidan, their eyes widen, but they remain calm when they don't sense any threat.

"These yer friends?" Aidan asks, as he clearly noticed us standing by them. He offers his hand, which both boys shake.

"Yeah, these are my boys," I reply, ensuring they hear me speak with my American accent to alert them to think fast as they cannot be Irish.

"Nice to meet you," Rory says with a French accent. I mentally thank Estelle, Rory's first girlfriend and exchange student from Paris, as he's adopted the accent perfectly. "I'm

Paul."

Cian smiles. "G'day mate, mi name's Kanga. Bloody ripper to meet ya." Looks like his obsession with *Crocodile Dundee* has paid off.

These lads are smart, playing along perfectly. Their accents are flawless.

Liam appears a moment later, grinning when he sees he has company. Just what is he playing at? "Grand to meet ya, lads, mi name's Liam Doyle."

Just hearing his name aloud is so surreal. I have been hunting him and his clan for so long, so to be here, it almost feels like a dream. But this is no dream. This is real life, and I'm really going to end the Doyle bloodline, even if it takes the rest of my life to do so.

Cian and Rory continue with their roleplaying, introducing themselves.

"What do ya get when an Irishman, an Australian, a Frenchman, and an American walk into a bar?" Liam says playfully, attempting to set a lighthearted mood.

But we know better. However, we all play along, laughing and fueling his already large ego.

The other men introduce themselves, but they're of no interest to me as I assume they're acquaintances. I have a wee hunch this may be a casual business meeting as such. It makes sense for it to occur on Doyle turf.

Liam wants this to appear informal, but if they dare step

out of line, they'll be punished as Liam has home ground advantage.

Cian and Rory make light conversation with the other two men, but Liam and Aidan make clear their interest is with me. "How long ya in Dublin for?"

"A couple of weeks," I reply, sipping my Guinness.

Every time Aidan talks, laughs, or breathes, I want to slam his head onto the table and make him bleed. I'm inches away from ma's killer, and I can't do a thing about it. Not yet, anyway. I need to remind myself of this because the urge to inflict pain on him is almost unbearable.

"So, yer a bit of a rebel then?" Liam says, lowering his voice.

I just smile in response.

"Did ya want to make some extra money while yer here?" And the real reason Liam has shown interest in me has been revealed.

"Doing what?" I ask, not wanting to appear too eager.

"Chance yer arm and trust me, bucko." Liam throws back a shot of whiskey, waiting for me to reply.

"Okay, I'm in."

Cian and Rory have heard the exchange, and by their stiff upper lips, they're seconds away from telling me to wise up, but this is happening. I don't know what I'm needed for, but I'm going to find out. I can't let this opportunity go.

Liam hollers, slapping my back happily. "Good lad. We do have a wee initiation process."

"What is it?" I keep my cool as I knew there was a catch.

Liam pours a shot of whiskey and slides the glass my way. "Yer a good fighter?"

Nodding, I accept the whiskey and knock it back.

"Gas. Let's see how good ya are then."

Aidan gulps down his whiskey, making a face as he stands, hinting this is happening now.

"Thanks for coming, lads. I'll be in touch." Liam dismisses the two men as their business is done for now. They don't argue and shake hands before leaving us alone.

Liam grabs the bottle of whiskey and heads for the front door.

"The fuck ya playin' at?" Cian whispers into my ear as we push our way through the crowd.

"Houl yer whisht," I reply softly, not wanting to set off alarm bells. "That fucker, Aidan, has a tattoo on his wrist."

Cian's eyes widen. He understands the importance of that comment.

"Wise up!" Rory frantically utters, always the level thinker of us three. "I thought ya said nice and quick? This is not either of those things. With yer temper, Punky, this will end badly."

And he's right.

I just never thought I'd find myself in a situation such as this. I didn't know what I expected to find coming here, but I need to know why the Doyles' pub address was locked away in my da's drawer.

Just as I'm about to exit the pub, Erin grabs my arm. I refrain from recoiling, but only just.

"Where ya going with my brother?" she asks, eyes darting to the doorway where Liam has stopped to talk to some bird.

"Oh, Liam is your brother?" I ask, playing dumb.

"Aye, and he's someone ya don't want to be messin' with. Please, just go home."

"I'll be fine. Thanks for the heads-up," I reply, surprised that she seems genuine.

"Jaysus," she mutters under her breath, reminding me why I'm here. "Mind yerself."

Nodding, I don't faff about and leave Erin behind as the boys and I follow Aidan and Liam around the corner. They walk casually, hinting nothing is wrong. We're just a bunch of mates, out for a casual dander.

But whatever faces me, I know won't be good.

When we turn down an alley, things become real. A big lad is waiting for us. Cian and Rory come to a sudden stop while I merely take a close look at him, wanting to know who he is.

"This is my brother, Hugh," Liam reveals. The luck of the Irish seems to be true for me tonight because I've just met the three Doyle siblings.

I can see why Hugh has the reputation that he has. He's built like a brick shithouse. The scar across his left cheek adds to his hard appearance. His eyes are dark. His head shaved.

"What's up?" I casually say while Hugh snickers when he

hears I'm "American."

"Some neck on ya bringing this bleedin' clown to me."

This cunt has opted to use slang with the belief that I won't understand him. But I understand him, all right.

Liam ignores Hugh and turns to me with a predatory smile. "Think ya can take him?"

I take a moment, pretending to size him up. I don't want to appear too arrogant, but with confidence, I take off my glasses and unthread my tie, giving them to Cian for safekeeping. He looks at me, scared.

"That's the way!" Liam exclaims, clapping wildly.

Hugh grins, before taking off his T-shirt. The dim lighting in the entryway allows me to see the many scars across his chest. This fucker is a hard nut.

"So, what're the rules?" I ask, keeping my focus on Hugh who bounces on the spot, cracking his neck from side to side.

"Don't die," Liam replies with a laugh, before Hugh advances and throws the first punch.

Instantly, I dodge his attack and belt him in the ribs. A pained hiss leaves him, but he's soon to recover and launches an onslaught of punches. He connects with my chin, then my cheek. My head snaps back, the warm metallic taste of blood fueling the devil within me.

This is my dream come true—spilling Doyle blood.

We circle one another as Hugh suddenly realizes I can fight. His cocky attitude soon fades, and he focuses on winning something he thought was already won. He dives on top of me, but I kick him in the guts, sending him tumbling backward. My sensei would be proud.

I don't hesitate and pin him to the ground as I connect with his face repeatedly. The sound, the feel, it's all too much, and a savage rush of adrenaline courses through my body, fueling the fire in my stomach. My knuckles and my face are coated in blood, and I want more.

The back of Hugh's head slams into the hard ground, and I know with a few more digs, he'll go down for good. He desperately tries to fight me off, and when he grips my shirt in his fists, he soon gets the chance.

I don't know why, but I take a juke at his wrist and what I see has me losing focus—a crucifix is tattooed on his left wrist.

How and why is this possible?

The moment of distraction allows Hugh to buck me off and switch positions so I'm the one now pinned to the ground. He belts me ruthlessly as he doesn't like being made an eejit of. Hugh doesn't like to lose.

Cian is swearing in French, which confirms this looks as bad as it feels.

"Had enough?" Hugh mocks, breaking my nose.

With blood gushing from my neb, I laugh manically. "Is that the best you got, motherfucker?"

Hugh roars, pinning one shoulder down to the ground as he continues to belt me.

It would be easier if I gave up as my head isn't cut, and I know Hugh will kill me if I don't submit. But suddenly, images of my mum, images of her being pressed into the carpet as some cunt rides her, slam into me, and I wheeze in air, desperate to breathe; just how she was.

I remember the way she extended her arm, her last desperate attempt to assure me everything would be all right.

I can't let her down—not again.

I turn my cheek, seeing the tattoo on Hugh's wrist as a clear fuck you, so with a new lease on life, I rear up and bite over it— hard. He presses the heel of his palm to my forehead, attempting to pry me off him, but I only bite down harder, tasting Doyle blood. It's heaven on my tongue.

"Ye fucking cunt, get off me!" Hugh screams, the hand he used to lamp me, now frantically trying to free his wrist from my jaws.

I wrap my fingers around his wrist, holding him captive as I gnaw through skin and muscle. The bloodlust leaves me hungry for so much more. Only when I have a hunk of his flesh in my mouth do I release him, bringing up my knee to catch him with a nice ringsend uppercut.

His wheezes leave me lured, and I shove him off, coming to a quick stand. I spit out the lump of flesh in my bake. It lands at Liam's Nikes with a wet plop.

Blood runs down my chin, and I slowly wipe it away with the back of my hand, never breaking eye contact with Liam. My chest is rising and falling quickly, my lungs desperately trying to catch up—I've never felt more alive.

Did I pass his wee test?

Hugh rolls around on the ground like a wee wain, and I curl my lip in disgust. His cries are music to my depraved soul. It takes all of my willpower not to kill this fucker, but not now. Things have only just begun.

Liam toes over the hunk of flesh before bursting into loud laughter. "Yer off yer nut!" he bellows, rushing over to me and slapping me on the back cheerfully.

"I just kicked the shit out of your brother, and you're congratulating me?" I ask, bowed in half and clutching my side as I attempt to breathe.

"Aye, ya did what not many have done before. This is a cause for celebration."

He offers me his hand, and as he does so, the cuff of his shirt rides up, allowing me to see that he, too, has the mark which suddenly doesn't seem so rare.

A crucifix tattoo.

What? How is this possible?

It's like one sprouted on Liam, seeing as I ripped into Hugh's with my teeth.

My theory that Aidan took my ma's life is now not so certain. It seems the Doyle men bear this mark, which means… any Doyle could be one of the three men I'm hunting. But first things first, I need to uncover the significance of this tattoo.

I thought it paid homage to their Catholic faith, but now, I believe it's something else, and I will do anything to find out what that is.

Aidan bends down to pick up Hugh, but he slaps his hands away, not wanting any help. He's feeling wick I beat him. He comes to a shaky stand on his own, looking shook. He clearly didn't think I could fight.

In response, I press two fingers over my bake and blow him a smug kiss.

With a growl, he advances forward, but Aidan grips his forearm, stopping him. I wonder who Aidan is to the Doyles.

Liam digs into his pocket and asks for my number as he produces his mobile phone. I give him the number to my prepaid phone that can't be traced back to me.

"All right, bucko, I'll be in touch."

And just like that…I'm one step closer to avenging my ma.

Cian and Rory don't help as I turn and limp my way down the entry. They allow me to gloat in victory.

A part of me believes this is too good to be true—that just by kicking Hugh Doyle's arse, I was able to fleece the Doyles and earn their trust. But when no one comes after me, it's evident this spur-of-the-moment plan worked far better than I thought it ever could.

I take the corner and almost bump into Erin, who is having a feg. "Feck me, ya surprised me, Mike from America."

Did she witness me belting her brother? If so, she doesn't

look awful upset he got his arse kicked.

"Well, thanks, I think."

She laughs, turning a few heads with the sound. Erin Doyle, just like her brothers, has a magnetism surrounding her. But I'll never be fooled by what she represents.

"I'll be seeing ya then," she casually says, but we both know there is nothing casual about this. A pact with the devil has just been signed. But the Doyles are unaware that devil is me.

"Later."

My laidback farewell has her smiling.

With nothing further left to say, I continue my hobble toward the car with Cian and Rory following close by. When we're out of earshot, Cian clucks his tongue.

"What the fuck is goin' on with that? Y've just started a war, Puck Kelly."

With a smile on my bake, I tip my face toward the heavens and inhale. A shooting star ignites the night sky, a sign of things to come.

"Keep her lit, lads, ats us nai."

FOUR

Babydoll

I *shouldn't be here.*

Stopping in my tracks, I place a trembling hand over my chest and take three deep breaths, hoping it'll help calm me down.

It doesn't.

I'm going to be in so much trouble, especially after what I went through to get it, but it's wrong. God knows, I need it, but it doesn't belong to me.

Taking one last breath, I continue my walk toward the house or, rather, castle.

The Kellys' home is utterly enchanting. It's something you'd expect to see in a Disney film, but no Prince Charming exists behind these doors.

Puck Kelly, or Punky as I overheard Darcy call him, is anything but a gentleman. He is rude, arrogant, and a fucking arsehole. Yes, he has every right to be mad at me as I did steal from him, but he was a jerk even before that happened.

So why am I here?

I owe him nothing, yet after last night, I can't stop thinking about how underneath his anger, I sensed pain. The brooch means something to him, and I can't hold onto it knowing that. This doesn't make sense, but neither does my entire life, so carpe diem.

The rocks beneath my brown ankle boots crunch as I make my way toward the front door. I could leave the brooch in the mailbox, but if someone stole it, then all of this would have been for nothing. So I suck it up, straighten out my black dress, and ring the doorbell.

Children's playful shrills sound in the distance.

I shouldn't be here.

Turning quickly, ready to flee, I close my eyes and curse under my breath when the door opens. "Hi. Can I help you?"

An American?

Finding my courage, I turn back around and smile at the gorgeous woman standing in the Kellys' doorway. "Er, hello. I'm sorry to bother you, but is…Punky home?"

The woman folds her arms across her chest, clearly sizing me up. I wonder what she sees.

"He's not here," she replies, and I get the feeling she doesn't like me much. Is she Punky's girlfriend?

A wave of…jealousy sweeps over me, though it's completely irrational. I hate Puck Kelly, I remind myself. I'm only here to return what's his. It doesn't matter who he's screwing.

So why do I have the sudden urge to pull out every strand of this stranger's lush brown hair?

When she doesn't offer to tell me where he is, or when he'll be back, I get the hint. "Okay then, sorry to bother you."

Suddenly, two curious faces peer around the doorjamb before creeping past the woman so they can get a better look at me.

"Hiya!" the girl says, smiling broadly. "What's yer name? I'm Hannah."

"Yer pretty," the boy quickly follows. "I'm Ethan."

I can't help but smile because these two are absolutely adorable. "Hi, Hannah, I'm Poppy. It's nice to meet you. And thank you, Ethan, I think you're pretty too," I say to both of them.

"Boys can't be pretty," Ethan replies, scrunching up his cherub face.

Bending low, I wink. "And why not? They can be whatever they want to be."

"You talk funny."

Laughing, I give my attention to Hannah. "That's because I'm from London."

Her eyes widen before she whispers not so quietly, "Amber,

she knows Paddington Bear!"

The stranger has a name. Amber. And Amber is pissed off I'm still here.

"Well, Poppy, if you'll excuse me, I have to give these rug rats some breakfast. Sorry I couldn't help you with Punky."

"You know our brother? I love him soooooo much," Hannah says, jumping on the spot. "He's sleepin'?"

Looking up at Amber, I slowly come to stand at full height.

She's just been caught out in a lie, but instead of apologizing, she simply stares, challenging me to call her out on it. She's definitely into him. The green-eyed monster returns.

"He doesn't live in here. He lives out back."

"Ethan, that's enough!" Amber scolds, gently ruffling his hair. "Come on, your eggs are going to get cold."

"Bye!" the kids cheerfully holler, pushing past Amber and skipping down the hallway.

"Bye," I reply, knowing what I'm going to do. "It was nice meeting y'all."

Amber makes it clear she's not closing the door until I get off her front lawn, so I smile and wave goodbye. I hear the door slam shut seconds later.

This should be an omen, that I should continue walking down this driveway and not go in search of Punky, who lives out back. But my feet disagree because when I think Amber has stopped manning the fort, I turn around and make a mad dash in the opposite direction of where I should be going.

I half expect the hounds to be unleashed, biting at my heels, or better still, Amber to come charging out, shotgun in hand. But none of that happens.

I keep running, and when I see a stable yard building in the distance, I realize what "out back" means. Punky lives out here as he clearly has no interest residing in the main residence. I have an inkling that's because he doesn't get along with his dad.

Last night, they barely said three words to one another, and when Connor did speak, I noticed the way Punky would either shift uncomfortably or clench his fist around whatever was in reach. I don't see a Mrs. Kelly, which has me assuming she's passed, and this brooch once belonged to her.

Tears well in my eyes, but I quickly wipe them away.

Once I'm close to the stable yard building, I come to a stop and catch my breath. I haven't given much thought to what I'm going to say because I didn't think I'd have the balls to actually come here. But I am here, and nerves suddenly overtake me.

I don't know what it is about Punky, but he makes me nervous. But underneath those nerves, I can't deny that there is an exhilaration I haven't felt before. When he touches me—like last night when he ran his thumb along my lip—the noise, the chaos, it all fades into the background, and I feel…alive.

It doesn't make sense. It shouldn't. I barely know him, but I can't deny Punky intrigues me.

He doesn't realize how attractive he is, which, in itself, is a complete turn-on. He's arrogant, yes, but that arrogance isn't in the way he looks, but rather, the way he composes himself and the control he wields in everyday activities.

He's tall, and his body is lean, muscular, like a fighter's physique. I use this term because his face was bruised, but he was still standing, which has me believing he knows how to throw a punch. His eyes are the bluest in color, and he styles his tousled dirty blond hair in a way that accents his bad-boy look.

His piercings, tattoos, and bad attitude should all be a warning to keep away, but they just interest me all the more.

I stop overthinking and walk to the glass front door. I'm about to knock, but I notice the door is slightly ajar. I should not—absolutely should not—enter, but I softly push open the door before my brain has a say. I freeze because I'm suddenly hit with a delectable rich, sexy, and sensual fragrance—Punky.

Being in his private domain feels utterly sinful, and I like it. I want more.

Tiptoeing through his home, I take a look around, immersed in history with a modern-day feel. The exterior is brick, matching the main house, but the interior has been outfitted with modern white walls. There is wooden furniture and modern appliances, but what catches my eye are the beautifully sketched artworks adorning the walls.

One in particular fascinates me; it's just a white canvas with charcoal lines, but the way in which those lines are sketched, I find myself lost in the silence while also deafened by the noise. I wonder who the artist is.

The furnishings and appliances are what you'd expect to find in most homes, but considering Punky shares these grounds with a castle, it's modest in comparison, and I like it. He doesn't show off his wealth. Everything in here has a place.

The mystery of Puck Kelly just continues to grow.

There is a beautiful chandelier hanging in the middle of the room, and I peer up at it, mesmerized by the sunlight streaming in from the windows and catching the low-hanging jewels. They send mini rainbows across the carpet, giving off the illusion that everything isn't fucked up beyond repair.

Digging into my handbag, I run a finger over the rose brooch, not missing the similarities of it and the one tattooed on the back of Punky's right hand. I can't read what is written across his knuckles, and I have a feeling this was done with intent.

His tattoos are for him and not for the world to see. And I like that.

I'm about to leave the brooch on the kitchen counter as this was a bad idea and I'm clearly insane for even being here, but suddenly, it's too late. The world is about to eat me whole.

The hair at the back of my neck stands on end, and the room is filled with a spine-tingling spark, threatening to electrocute me where I stand. Just as I'm about to spin around, a pair of muscular arms wrap around my waist and draw me into a warm, hard, heaven and hell.

"See anythin' ya like, Babydoll?" His voice is hoarse,

honeyed, and goddamn, goose bumps prickle every inch of my skin, especially when I hear him use the nickname he's pegged for me.

But I'll be damned if he knows that.

"No, not particularly," I reply with bite as I struggle to free myself. "Let me go."

"Ack, I think not. What ye doin' in my home?"

"I got lost," I quip, ignoring the heat of his bare chest pressed against my back. "But I'll be on my way."

Punky laughs in response, hinting I'm not going anywhere.

He towers over me, and God knows, I should be frightened being held prisoner in his arms, but I'm not afraid. I'm aroused.

He tightens his hold around me, making it near impossible to breathe. Turning over my shoulder, I get a glimpse of a silver barbell in his nipple and script writing, which looks Latin, inked across his chest. Both have me biting the inside of my cheek to stop my whimper of approval.

"Yer not going anywhere until ya answer my question."

His deep, honeyed Northern Irish accent does things to me that heat my cheeks, but I can't be distracted. I've established that I'm incredibly attracted to Punky, but that shouldn't deter me from the fact he is a downright arsehole who I want to slap half the time.

I know he won't let me go until I tell him the truth, so I open my palm and show him the brooch. "Here, sorry I took it. Who does it belong to, anyway?"

I don't want to make a fuss, so I play nonchalant. His grip on me slackens when he sees the offering.

"Ya wee thief," he says, clucking his tongue but not answering my question.

"Sticks and stones, now let me go." I struggle once more, and this time, he loosens his hold so I can break free.

Spinning around, I'm ready to slap his cheek for having the gall to touch me, but stop dead in my tracks when I see his face. If possible, he has even more bruising, but these cuts are fresh. What happened after he left the Duffys' last night?

"What happened to your face?" I ask, curiosity getting the better of me.

"That's none of yer concern," he replies, gesturing with his hand that he wants the brooch back.

I give it to him, wishing he'd tell me what happened.

His hard, angry exterior is replaced with what I can only describe as genuine relief and a flash of happiness. It's gone a second later.

"Why'd ya take it then?" he asks as if remembering I'm still here.

"You're welcome," I smartly reply, ignoring his naked, defined chest and abs inches away.

His hair is mussed, his long fringe flicked to the high heavens. I must have woken him even though I was quiet. He clearly sleeps with one eye open as nothing slips past him.

"I'll not tell ya again," he warns, not in the mood to play

games.

"Why'd you think I took it?" I declare, hating how weak my admission makes me sound. "I'm the Duffys' fucking servant, for Christ's sake. Do the maths and spare me the fucking lecture."

He seems caught off guard by my response, as I can imagine most wouldn't dare speak to a Kelly this way. But I'm not most.

"How'd ya know where I live?"

"It's not exactly a secret," I reply, rolling my eyes. "I know how to use Google."

Punky's lips lift into an amused grin. "If that's true, ya know all about the Kelly name then?"

I swallow subtly, my bravado soon fading. I know all about the Kellys. Some pieces of information I wish I didn't know. But I play coy.

"Not really. I don't care, to be honest with you. I came here because I wanted to do the right thing, and now that I have, I'm leaving and plan on never returning. Good day."

I turn in vain because we both know I'm not going anywhere.

Punky seizes my wrist, drawing me into his chest. I put my arms up, a defensive move to protect my chest from being pressed to his. But sadly, all that it does is allow my hands to touch his warm, hardened flesh.

A sigh escapes me in betrayal, and I curse it, and this illogical response I have to him. I need it to stop. But when his heartbeat thumps beneath my fingers, I know stopping is nigh on impossible.

His scent is comparable to a warm summer's day, but on the flipside, I can smell an approaching thunderstorm beneath the surface. He has one hand wrapped around my wrist, but with the other, he cautiously brushes a strand of hair from my cheek.

The simple action has the ability to leave me breathless.

We're inches apart, and the world soon fades into the background so it's merely us. It's quiet here.

I take a moment to examine him unguarded because I need to know why I'm so drawn to him. The silver hoop in his bottom lip emphasizes its fullness, and the one in his nose draws attention to how elegantly straight it is—or was before he was beaten to a bloody pulp. It's slightly upturned, which just adds to the air of arrogance he owns with each breath he takes.

His jawline is chiseled, a sprinkle of dark scruff hinting he hasn't yet shaved. His body is muscular, but lean. Every muscle is defined, taut, and when my gaze drops to his rock-hard V-muscle and dusting of hair leading from his belly button into the sweats which sit low on his tapered waist, I need to remember to swallow.

He is bloody beautiful.

"Why aren't ya afraid?" he queries, watching me with those astute eyes.

"Afraid of w-what?" I question, my heart beating madly, threatening to break free as I peer up at him from under my lashes.

He licks his bottom lip, his tongue brushing over the ball in the hoop. "Of me."

His question isn't cocky. He seems genuinely curious as to why I'm not recoiling from his touch. If only he knew the truth.

"Because there are nastier things in this world than you, Punky," I reply, saying more than I should.

He cocks his head to the side, appearing to weigh my confession. "I doubt that," he counters heavily, still watching me as if trying to work me out.

This is a dangerous game; one I have to lose.

"Where were ya comin' from the other night? I went back to find ya, but there wasn't a gaff for miles."

And this is my cue to leave.

"Good talk, but I've got to go. I gave back what's yours, so let's never do this again." Sarcasm is my security blanket. It's how I cope with awkward situations—like right now.

I yank out of his hold, making a beeline for the front door, but Punky quickly sidesteps to block my exit. "What's the rush, love?" he says with a lopsided grin. "I was just gettin' to know ya."

"Yeah, well, I have no interest in knowing you. So please let me leave." I attempt to push past him, but he doesn't budge.

"Ack, now yer just hurtin' my feelings. Yer the one who broke into my gaff."

"I did no such thing," I argue, offended. "You really should lock your door."

Punky appears taken aback by my revelation.

"Your brother and sister told me you lived out here. So don't worry, I'm not stalking you. I'm sure you have enough of those—stalkers, I mean." It's on the tip of my tongue to ask who Amber is, but I don't. I'm already in too deep.

Punky bursts into husky laughter, surprising me. "I don't know about that. I don't have time for such nonsense."

"But you surely have enough time to be a bloody arsehole!" I spit before I can stop myself.

I expect Punky to be tired of my insolence by now and throw me out, but he does nothing of the sort.

"Aye, that I am, but at least ya know. I don't know what to be expectin' with ye. Ya steal from me, with no explanation, and then ya come into my home, like everythin' is going to be sound. What do ya want from me?"

And this is the reason I shouldn't have come.

Punky is smart, and he will eventually figure out why I'm here. That's a given. What remains unknown is what he will do when he does.

"Nothing," I reply, and I mean it.

"I don't believe ya," he rebukes calmly. "I think yer here for a reason. I just haven't figured out what that reason is."

The reddening of my cheeks betrays my horror because if he continues to dig, I wonder what he'll find.

"Well, good luck with that. Goodbye, Puck Kelly." I push

past him, and this time, he lets me leave. With my back turned, hand poised on the door handle, Punky makes it clear, however, that I can't run forever.

"But I will, Babydoll. I promise ya that."

His cautioning isn't meant to scare, but rather, warn me of what's ahead.

Needing to get out of here before I crumple, I quickly open the door and walk briskly down the driveway with Punky's warning sounding loudly in my ears.

I am so fucked.

FIVE

PUNKY

The moon is full, setting an ominous mood for what's ahead.

I was right. My dad is now best friends with Patrick Duffy because he wants access to his real estate, or more accurately, he wants to use abandoned buildings around town as his personal dumping grounds. I know this because I'm standing in an aul' building which will soon be torn down to make way for trendy waterfront apartments.

But for now, it'll serve as the place Nolen Ryan takes his last breath.

With the River Lagan at my disposal, getting rid of Nolen's body won't be a problem. My dad said he'll have reinforcements waiting for me, which means, once I'm done, they'll take care of the body.

Nolen made the wrong choice, and now, it's time he paid his dues.

He'll be here any minute in the belief we're picking up a shipment of 200 kilograms of cocaine. The van he drives has been modified to conceal the drugs. Large metal drawers hidden underneath a false floor is how we transport our goods.

My dad has thought of everything, which is why he's been able to get away with the shite that he does. Mr. Walsh and Mr. Davies are his business partners, but my dad is the kingpin. Mr. Walsh takes care of the money side of things, making smart business moves so the authorities are not alerted to the money laundering our families are involved in. While Mr. Davies takes care of the business side, as dealing drugs in a modern world isn't what it used to be.

A three-tier hierarchy is what the drug business involves these days.

The lower tier consists of highly disadvantaged youths spreading fear on behalf of the Kellys. Cian and Rory oversee the dealings, ensuring no one steps out of line. They also run the "hotlines" where people can order drugs.

The second tier involves people who engage in high-risk, low-reward activities. They are the muscle. They can also be the dealers. They inflict beatings and serious intimidation on behalf of the top tier players—my dad, Mr. Davies, and Mr. Walsh.

The second tier is where I belong, but as I bear the Kelly

name, I oversee who does what. Nolen works for me, which is why I have to deal with him accordingly.

Cian, Rory, and I do all the legwork while our fathers deal with where the shipments come from and who buys them. We have a large network of drug dealers and drivers, all of whom are discreet and trusted, except for Nolen.

The top tier is, of course, where my dad sits.

The lower tier is most important to our business, which is why my dad and Mr. Davies choose with care. Most of the time, Mr. Davies recruits the lads who owe money for drugs they can't pay for. He offers them an opportunity to pay off their debt by doing petty crimes. But that soon leads them down the rabbit hole.

My father prides himself on the fact he and his two friends have recruited boys and young men to carry out violence and intimidation to collect drug debts from users. He thinks they're rather brilliant for governing an operation such as this.

I understand no one is holding a gun to these lads' heads, or even to the users who are desperate to shoot up and get high, but the exploitation of the weak makes me sick.

I'm not putting myself on a pedestal, as I, too, engage in violence and intimidation on behalf of Connor Kelly, but I don't target kids who made a stupid choice—I deal with the big fish. Like big-shot men who think they can steal from the Kellys and undercut us.

Drugs will be dealt, that's the reality of the world, but I'd rather it be us than some other cockhead whose moral compass is so banjaxed, they'd sell to anyone and everyone. Cian and Rory's "hotline" catalogues every buyer, and if they're going too hard, Cian won't sell to them.

They can get their product elsewhere.

Our dads aren't aware of this little clause in the contract, which is why Rory, the technology king, has many online accounts set up so that we always have a stream of business coming through every avenue. If a disgruntled buyer decided to tell his mates that we refused service, then the odds are, they wouldn't go through that vein again.

But having multiple accounts means more people will tell their friends that channel A, B, C dealt them some grade A product, and word will spread. Most of the time, the knobs don't even know they're dealing with the same people.

And the user we refuse to deal with—only looking out for their well-being—they can either wait, or they can seek out shite product elsewhere. We've come to learn that they wait, because not only is our product good, it's also cost effective.

In this case, this most definitely is two wrongs don't make a right, but Rory swears this method has saved lives. For instance, a cub—just fifteen years old—was hooked on heroin. He wanted Rory to deal him more gear only a few hours after his last hit.

Rory refused, knowing the cub would likely OD, and instead sold him some cannabis to tide him over until his next fix. He's still alive, and as fucked as that is, Rory knows monitoring the distribution, especially to kids, is the lesser of two evils.

Our lives are fucked up, but this is all we know.

Cracking my neck from side to side, I need to focus on what I'm about to do. I don't want to think about taking Nolen's life. I plan on delivering justice swiftly.

Most would let him off with a warning, but that doesn't exist in our world. If you're not with us, you're against us, and that means the difference between life and death. Nolen could be a traitor, an inside man for the Doyles.

We can't take any risks.

He knew the consequences working for the Kellys. No one is to blame for his choices but him alone.

On instinct, I reach for the brooch in my pocket, thankful, but still confused why Babydoll gave it back. But to be honest, I'm confused—period—when it comes to her.

She said my door was open, but I know I locked it which means someone was in my room. The thought leaves me ragin' because I want to know who it was. I checked if anything was stolen, but nothing was. Amber promised she nor the kids were in my room. She looked pissed off when she asked me who Babydoll was.

I told her she's no one, but she didn't seem convinced. When I asked her what Babydoll had said, she replied that she didn't remember, which is a lie. Amber seems suspicious about Babydoll too, and I plan on finding out why.

I changed the locks on the door, but if whoever wants to get in is determined, no lock will stop them.

Without a doubt, Babydoll is hiding something. I know firsthand what it's like to live a lie. Rory is currently doing every search possible on her, and I hope he finds something which will shed some light on who she is.

I still don't know why she stole from me as she answered a question with a question. She insinuated she took it because, as being a servant for the Duffys would imply, she isn't as fortunate as I am. So if that's the case, then why didn't she sell it? Just by looking at it, she'd know it was worth a lot of money.

Nothing about her makes any sense and I know she is trouble, but that just has me wanting her all the more.

I have no problems touching her. I find myself reaching out for her without thought. That's something that's never happened before. She's toxic, I can feel it in my bones, but the mystery of who she is and why I'm drawn to her outweigh good sense.

I will get to the bottom of this, one way or another, and then the question is, what will I do?

But all of that can wait when the door opens and Nolen Ryan's silhouette is outlined by the moon.

"Punky?" he questions, clearly shook I'm here and not my da.

"What's the craic, Nolen?"

He pauses in the doorway, but enters as he knows he can willingly do so—or I'll force him to. The gun in the small of my back will aid me if need be.

The single light bulb hanging from the banjaxed ceiling provides some light, but I don't need it to know that Nolen is scared. He knows what I can do. He's seen it. But he never thought I'd do those unspeakable things to him.

"Everythin' all right then?" he nervously asks, taking a juke at our mingin' surroundings.

Curling my lip, I shrug casually. "I don't know. Is it?"

The room is filled with an uncomfortable tension, and as much as I don't want to hurt Nolen, he can't leave here alive.

With a sigh, I reach into my backpack and produce the damning piece of evidence—his Catholic Bible.

The moment he sees what I'm holding, he drops to his knees and interlaces his hands. "Please, naw. It's not what ya think."

"No?" I counter, flicking through the pages in disgust. "So, this isn't yer Bible?"

When he lowers his chin, whimpering, I lose patience and slam the book against his cheek. His head snaps to the left.

"I'll not tell ya again."

"Please, let me go. Y'll never see me again," he begs, lifting his chin and the full moon catches the tears in his eyes.

"Aye, that's where yer right. I won't see ya 'cause y'll be dead."

"Oh, shite," he cries, shaking his head frantically. "Punky, I've a family."

If this is supposed to move me, Nolen needs to try another tactic because all he's doing is boring me with his excuses.

"So did I," I reveal, the Bible clenched in my hand. "Until your kind decided to kill her. I can't let ya live, Nolen. Ya know that. Yer a traitor. Yer a fucking *Catholic*. How do I know yer not involved with the Doyles?"

"I would never!" he gasps, pleading I believe him.

"How can I believe ya? Ya see the position y've put me in? I let ya go, how do I know yer not gonna run to Brody Doyle and tell him Connor Kelly's eldest son is a pussy."

"I'm not messed up with Brody Doyle!" he exclaims, the white of his eyes almost glowing under the light. "I swear down. I fucked up, so I did. I'm sorry. But my wife, she's Catholic. What was I supposed to do? I've not told anyone because I knew what would happen.

"Please don't kill me. I know yer friends with Orla. Think of her."

"*You* should have thought of her," I spit, not appreciating him guilt tripping me. "What did ye think was gonna happen?"

"This hatred, Puck, this isn't you. It's because of yer da that ye think like this. Yer a good lad. Ya can't hate someone because of their religion. This isn't the Middle Ages anymore."

Tipping my face to the ceiling, I inhale, needing a minute. "In the name of *their* God, they slaughtered my ma. So I can hate whoever I want. Do I hate Catholics? Aye, and the reason is, all Doyles are Catholics. To me, the Doyle name is what I have most issues with. Their religion is secondary."

It's been forced onto me that I was to hate Catholics. They

were the enemy. And after my hostile experiences with every Catholic I've met, how could I not? But Nolen is right.

A small part of me agrees with him. To hate someone because of their beliefs is ridiculous. Would I go out and harm an innocent person because of what God they kneel before? No. But that doesn't mean I want to be their chum either. Or have anything to do with them. As long as they stay away from me, we're sound.

The problem with Nolen is that he can't be trusted, religion aside. He lied because he knew if he told us the truth, there was no way he would work for the Kellys. He should have found a job doing something else because now, he's going to find out what happens to liars firsthand.

"I understand that, but we've got nothin' to do with the Doyles. Please, lad, let me go. Yer a good—" Before he can finish, I whack his cheek with the Bible once again.

He moans, blood trickling from the corner of his mouth.

"Why'd ya have to lie?" I question, tossing the Bible at Nolen. "Pick it up. I want ya to read me yer favorite passage."

"Wh-what?" he stutters, eyes wide.

"Read to me," I repeat, grabbing an aul' wooden chair and sitting on it backward.

Nolen cops on that I'm serious and opens the Bible, unable to turn the pages because his hands are trembling so badly. He licks his finger and slowly peruses through the passages until he stops. He raises his eyes and meets mine.

"For You have armed me with strength for the battle; You have subdued under me those who rose up against me. You have also given me the necks of my enemies, so that I destroyed those who hate me."

With a slanted smirk, I clap slowly. "Ye wee fucker. Ya think yer funny then?"

By reading this passage, he's pretty much telling me to go fuck myself.

"Yer gonna kill me, anyway. I may as well go down fightin'," he replies, closing the Bible and extending it out to me. "Will ya give this to my wife?"

I respect Nolen for accepting his fate, instead of groveling like a wee pussy. But that doesn't change what I'm about to do.

Coming to a stand, I look down at the man whose life I'm about to end. I think about how my actions will impact the lives of his family and friends. I think about Orla and how when I see her next, I'll know something that she never will.

I'll know that I killed her father.

"Make the right choice, Puck. Yer ma—"

The moment Nolen attempts to use my ma as collateral, something inside me snaps. He didn't know her. He has no right to speak her name. With a roundhouse kick, I connect with Nolen's temple. He collapses onto the hard ground.

"Don't you dare speak her name!" I exclaim, lifting Nolen up by the lapels of his shirt.

I headbutt him, but don't let go. His head snaps back with

an awful crack, and his body goes limp. He doesn't put up a fight as I toss his arse into the chair. He flops forward, his chin drooping to his chest. He's pathetic.

"Fight me!" I demand, yanking his head back by his snarled hair.

"Naw," he breathlessly replies, looking up at me, refusing to cower. "Ya wanna kill me, go on then. I'm not givin' ya an excuse to justify yer actions."

His refusal angers me and I punch him in the face, breaking his nose.

Blood splatters onto the ground, but it doesn't give me the satisfaction it should. I punch him in the ribs, a pained *oof* escaping him, yet he still doesn't fight back.

I've had no issues with violence in the past, so why is this time different? It's then I realize it's because the others, they deserved it. Nolen is a traitor and a liar, aye, but does that warrant his death?

As he helplessly slumps in the chair, bloody and struggling to breathe, I know the answer is no.

With a roar, I fist my hair and begin to pace. I need to get out of my head and remember what Nolen is. Not all Catholics are in cahoots with the Doyles, but Nolen is involved in illegal dealings, which means he isn't a Catholic minding his business.

If I let him live and he is with the Doyles, it'll be on me. I'll be seen as the pussy who choked.

"I know ye don't wanna hear it," he pants, shifting as he

clutches his side. "But yer a good lad. No matter what yer da says. I see yer ma in ya."

Coming to a sudden stop, I turn my cheek slowly. "What did ya say?"

Nolen doesn't wipe away the blood I spilled. He lets me see what I've done and what I plan to do. "I knew yer ma," he reveals, leaving me awful shocked. "Cara was so parful. Ya were the love of her life. She'd do anythin' to protect ya."

"Yer aul' arse," I snarl, barely holding back the urge to cut out his tongue for spewing forth such lies.

But Nolen doesn't waver. "Believe whatcha want, but it's true."

"And why haven't ya mentioned this until now?" I ask, watching for any signs of deceit. Nolen did lie to us for years about his religion. What's stopping him from lying right now to save his arse?

But what he does next catches me by surprise.

He laughs loudly.

"You away in the head?" My question just has him laughing harder.

Blood mixes with tears as he confesses, "For years, I've kept this secret, but no more. Yer not an eejit, lad, even though yer da treats ya like one."

"What secret?" I ask between clenched teeth.

When Nolen just continues to laugh, appearing to have lost the plot, I angrily spring forward and slap his cheek. "Yer a fierce cunt, so ya are. I'm about to slit yer throat and yer laughin'. What's the matter with ya?"

His laughter is soon replaced with nothing but tears. "Get a move on then!" he shouts, but we're not done until he explains himself.

"Answer my question!" I demand, yanking him forward so we're pressed nose to nose.

"I tell ye and then what?" Nolen has realized that he just may have an advantage that could save his life.

Shoving him back into the chair, I stand tall. "That depends on what ya tell me," I warn because he isn't in control. I am.

"I'll tell ye what it is, but yer to promise to let me go."

"Will I, yea?" I state, because that's something I can't do. But a small bothersome voice reasons that this is a compromise I'm willing to make.

If he has information which could prove to be useful to me, then I have to agree. I could just kill him afterward, but I don't work that way. If I give him my word, then I plan on sticking to it. And I would have saved Orla the heartache of not knowing what happened to her da.

A voice I've not heard in so long tackles me from out of nowhere. *"I'm so proud of ya, my wee son."*

Ma?

It can't be. It must be wishful thinking, or my mind playing tricks because if my ma were to speak to me, those aren't the words she'd say. I've hurt more people than I've loved, which is nothing to be proud of. But I can't help it. This is who I am. I don't know how else to be.

"All right then," I utter, watching as a wave of relief washes over Nolen. "I give ya my word. But if yer lyin' to me, I promise ya…ya won't like the consequences."

Nolen nods eagerly, understanding the seriousness of my words.

"Thank ye, Puck," he wheezes, adjusting his position to get comfortable. "I'm sorry I lied to ya. But I had to protect my family."

"Enough," I snap, not interested in having a deep and meaningful conversation. "Start talkin'."

Nolen takes three deep breaths, wiping away the blood from his broken nose. "Yer whole life, he's been lyin' to ya."

"Who has?" I fold my arms across my chest, watching Nolen closely. "And lyin' about what?"

I don't know why, but my stomach suddenly sinks. I have this overwhelming feeling that whatever Nolen is about to reveal is going to change everything forever.

He sits tall, meeting my eyes, and I see it. He knows what happened to my ma. "Yer da—"

But his confession will never be heard because in its place is a thunderous bang.

I reach for my gun in the small of my back and spin around frantically, locked and loaded on whoever just shot Nolen dead. Who I see in the dim lighting leaves me shook.

"Uncle Sean?" I exclaim, shocked but also ragin'. He just shot the answers I've been searching for, for sixteen years, right between the eyes.

With a flop, Nolen's neck droops backward, and I hear a drip…drip…drip of blood onto the cold ground.

"Why d'ya do that?" I bellow, furious at him. "Do ya realize what y've done?"

"Aye, cub, I'm savin' yer life," he counters, lowering his gun.

I, however, can't do the same. My gun is aimed at him as I attempt to process what's just happened.

"He was no threat!" I shout, shaking my head. "He had information I needed."

"And ya believe him?" Uncle Sean reprimands, walking into the room. "I taught ya better than this. A desperate man will say anythin' to live. Ye know this!"

"How'd ya know?" I yell, waving my gun in emphasis.

Uncle Sean isn't scared that he currently has a firearm pointed at him. He continues walking toward me.

"Because Nolen Ryan is a liar. That's the reason he's here. That's the reason you were supposed to kill him. But ye were gonna let him go." His disappointment in the decision I made is evident.

"It's not like that," I reply, but when looking at the situation in black and white, that's exactly what it is.

"Naw? Ya weren't gonna let him go then?"

Silence.

Uncle Sean stands in front of me and grips my wrist, placing the muzzle against his chest. "Ya wanna kill me? Yer own flesh and blood? Go on then."

My grip on the gun falters and my arm grows slack. "Course not."

Uncle Sean sighs and lets me go, and I replace the gun at the small of my back. "Ach, I knew ya weren't ready for this. Yer dad is so fucking stubborn! That's why I'm here, just in case."

I shouldn't be angry with Uncle Sean because he's right. A desperate man will say anything to save his own arse. But I can't forget the look in Nolen's eyes. He was telling the truth.

"Yer not ready."

"Don't tell me what I am." I'm affronted he thinks so little of me. "I had it under control."

"From where I was standin', it certainly didn't look that way. He'd tell ya what ya wanted to hear and ye'd let him go, only for him to see yer clemency as a weakness. The Kellys can't be weak, cub. If this got out…ya know what it would mean for us?"

Nodding firmly, I accept him reprimanding me because as always, he only has my best interests at heart.

"Good, lad. I'm sorry yer angry with me, but I'd rather ya be mad at me than dead, which is what would happen if yer da found out ya let a traitor go free."

"He said he knew Ma," I confess, her voice long gone from the violence which took her life.

Uncle Sean's face turns nostalgic. "Everyone knew her, Punky," he shares, which is news to me. "She was an angel."

"Then why does no one talk about her? It's like she never existed. But she did, Uncle Sean. She was my ma, yer sister-in-law. I'm sick of the lies and the secrecy. I want to know what happened to her."

"Ack, lad, let it go," he says, shaking his head.

"Naw. I will not," I stubbornly argue. "How can ya ask that of me? Ya know what happened to her. Ya know Dad is a fucking pussy and won't confront the Doyles once and for all."

"Y'll just have to get over it, Punky. There's no other way."

"But I'm not like him. I can't forget her. I won't. The Doyles can't get away with this."

Uncle Sean's nostalgia fades and is replaced with annoyance. "And what's that supposed to mean?"

This is the first time I've spoken those words aloud to him. I've made it clear that I'm disgusted with my dad's inaction, but I've never hinted I'm about to change that.

"Answer me, lad."

"I hate this secrecy," I reveal angrily. "I don't even know who my ma's family are. Why not?"

"'Cause they're not worth knowin'," he bitterly spits, but I've heard it all before. "That's the truth, so it is."

"How about ya let me decide that. I'm not a wee chile anymore."

"I don't care how aul' y'are, y'll always be my cub."

I appreciate his concern, but he can't protect me forever.

"I'll never forgive myself for what happened with ya. I should have done more," he says with regret, running his hands through his dark brown hair.

"What more could ya have done? You didn't know where we were."

"Naw, I didn't, and I'll never forgive Cara for that. She was so stubborn. And that got her killed. She had no business being in Movil—"

He pauses, but it's too late because I heard him—loud and clear. I never knew where the bungalow was…until now.

Moville.

That's what Uncle Sean was going to say before he realized he shared more than he should. I can either continue to pump him for information, or I can pretend it never happened.

I decide on the latter…for now.

"That didn't get her killed; the Doyles did that," I correct because I won't stand by and allow her to be blamed for something that wasn't her fault.

"Aye, those fuckers," he spits with contempt, appearing thankful I didn't probe.

"Why didn't Dad fight for her?" I question for the hundredth time.

Uncle Sean's cheeks billow as he weighs over his response like he always does. "Some things are better left alone, Punky. Please trust me. I'm doin' this for yer own good."

There's no point arguing. I face this answer every single time.

"My own good leaves my head melted."

"And what do ya plan on doin' to change that?" Uncle Sean asks, his blue eyes narrowing.

"Nothin'," I reply, not because I'm scared, but because I know Uncle Sean will stop me from pursuing this. I need to approach this carefully, not just with the Doyles, but with the Kellys, as well.

But he knows me better than I know myself at times. "If yer thinkin' of doing somethin' stupid, please don't. I love ya like my own son. Ya know that?"

I don't know why Uncle Sean never married. He's not short of admirers. When I asked him why not, he said it was because he hadn't found the right woman.

"Ach, yer such a big softie these days, aul' lad," I tease, wanting to change the subject because Uncle Sean is the only person who, if he dug deep enough, could unravel my plan. And I can't have that happening.

No matter what he tells me, and no matter how many times he warns me to let it go, I will not. It only enforces what I need to do.

"Ach, yer a smart-arse. Away now, I'll take care of this."

I'm suddenly reminded there is a cooling corpse behind me.

Taking one last look at Nolen, I push aside the guilt at

seeing his lifeless body slumped in a chair because I could have helped him. I'll never know what he was going to share with me, but that's the least of my worries when I think of Orla.

He'll never share anything with her ever again.

Swallowing down my regret, I slap Uncle Sean on the back and make my way out the door. I don't know what's going to happen to Nolen, but I do know his body will never be found.

When I'm far enough away from Uncle Sean, I dig into my back pocket for my phone and call Rory.

"What's the craic with Babydoll?" I ask when he answers.

"Ack, nothin' excitin'. I'll keep lookin' and askin' around."

"Grand, I need ya to look into somethin' else for me."

"What is it then?"

Ensuring no one is within earshot, I reply, "Real estate. My ma's bungalow is in Moville."

Rory's silence hints that he's shook. This is one question which has baffled me for years, but now that I have the answer, it almost doesn't feel real. I never knew her bungalow was located in the Republic.

I just assumed it was here in the North. But this changes everything.

"Are ye all right?" he asks with concern.

"Aye, I'm fine. But I'd be even better if you can find me an address." When the silence continues, I add, "Out with it, Rory."

Rory isn't one to sugarcoat anything, so his silence leaves me awful restless.

"Yer not gonna like it, but ya know who'd have all the answers?"

Digging into my pocket for my car keys, I reply, "Who's that then?"

"Patrick Duffy."

I freeze from unlocking my car, needing a minute. "Yer right, but how do I manage that? I can't exactly ask him to show me what I need."

When Rory sighs, I clue in that he wasn't suggesting I ask Patrick.

"Oh, fuck," I mutter under my breath. "I'm sorry, Rory, I know ya like Darcy, but I gotta—"

He doesn't let me finish. "It would fit ya better if ya did this with Darcy. I understand that."

Just because he understands, doesn't mean he likes the idea, but this shows what a true mate he is.

"I promise no funny business. As soon as I get what I need, I'll go. I'll put in a good word for ya," I add, wanting to do something for him.

But we both know it doesn't matter how many words are said, Darcy isn't interested in him.

"I'll call ya if I find anythin' on Babydoll."

"Thanks. I really appreciate everythin' youse are doing for me."

"We're family. Ya don't have to thank me."

I don't know where I would be without these lads. They

are more of a family to me than my own flesh and blood. We understand one another and what it means to be who we are. I would die for these boys and I know the feeling is mutual.

"I'll talk to ya later." Hanging up, I take a moment to process what I need to do.

Every part of my body is rebelling at the thought, but Rory is right. Patrick Duffy is my way in and I'm prepared to do what I must to get what I want; which is why I scroll through my contacts and stop on the letter D.

As I dial Darcy's number, I peer into the starless sky—there's no hope of ever making a wish and it coming true.

Luckily, however, I don't believe in fairy tales.

SIX

Babydoll

"Get up!"

My groggy brain takes a moment to come to, but when it does, I wish I could slip into a coma and never wake.

"I said, get up!"

Wiping the sleep from my eyes, I quickly pull back the scratchy blanket on my single bed and get into position—on my knees. This is what's expected of me, and if I don't obey, I get punished. And so does everyone I love.

Which is the only reason I submit. It's the reason I do the despicable things that I do.

"Where is it?"

"Where's what?"

It's too late by the time I realize what I've said. I pay for my error with a slap to my cheek. My head snaps to the left with a sharp crack.

"What did ya say?"

"Where's wh-what...m-master?" I repeat, my eyes downcast.

"Aye, that's better," he says happily. My humiliation gives him great pleasure. "The brooch."

Keeping my nerves under control, I lick my dry lips. "I don't know. I haven't seen it. The last time—"

"Shut yer bake," he interrupts, not appreciating my lies. "Yer full of shite. Where is thon brooch?"

I prepared myself for this situation as I knew it was coming. By giving the brooch back to Punky, I knew what it would mean for me. But I'll deal with the repercussions because I did the right thing—for once.

"I don't know."

The silence is heavy. I brace for what comes next.

"Ya need reminding of yer place?" I don't know why he phrased it as a question because there are no choices. That privilege was stripped from me when I agreed to sell my soul to the devil.

My silence usually pleases him, but not today.

He slaps my other cheek, hollering when I grunt under the force. Yet I still don't snitch. This earns me a punch to my stomach. Groaning, I fold in half, attempting to catch my breath.

"I'll ask ye again, where is it?"

Gasping for air, I measure my breathing until eventually, I come back into an upright position. This just enrages him further. He wants me to surrender, but I can't. He wants me to break, but it's going to take a lot more than him beating me black and blue to break my spirit.

I will withstand everything he delivers because it brings me one step closer to why I'm here. There is only one person who matters; they're the reason for all of this.

"I-I don't know."

"Fine, have it yer way then."

I hear the familiar sound which no longer scares me—his belt unfastening and slipping through the beltloops.

"Take it off," he orders, and I don't resist. What would be the point? It just delays the inevitable.

Slipping the thin nightgown over my head, I cover my modesty as best I can, but it doesn't matter. He's seen it all. He's humiliated me in every possible way that there is.

"Look at the bleedin' state of ya. Yer disgusting."

The belt cracks across my back, a fresh lash added to the ones he delivered three days ago. Flinching, I bite down on my tongue so hard, I taste blood. But I don't cry out for help because who would help me? I'm alone.

Again, he whips me, this time across my arse. The pain is excruciating, but still, I don't scream. I know if I just submit the torture will stop, but if I do that, he wins. Therefore, I will endure every punch, slap, bite, and whip he inflicts because each one proves that I'm stronger than him.

I'll never admit defeat.

He whips me again and again, screaming that I'm to surrender.

In response, I don't make a sound. I don't move.

The belt drops to the hard floor and I close my eyes as I know what comes next. He kicks me in the ribs, before stomping on my calf. But he never punches me in the face because he doesn't want anyone to see what a monster he truly is.

My injuries are easily covered because he's a coward; a coward who will pay for everything he's done.

With one final blow to my ribs, he exhales, tipping his face to the ceiling, elated by the violence he's caused. But it's not enough. It's never enough. He comes to stand in front of me, roughly gripping my chin and arching my neck back so I can look up at him.

I don't cry.

I don't scream.

I simply exist for the day he'll suffer at *my* hands.

He rubs his thumb over my bottom lip, a feral look reflected in his cold blue eyes. "There's more than one way to make ye talk."

He forces his thumb into my mouth, slipping it in and out, a clear innuendo for what he wants. His erection presses against the front of his trousers. My stomach roils in disgust.

He removes his thumb, which he replaces with two fingers. He forces them down my throat and when I gag, he hums in approval. He awkwardly tugs down his trousers, freeing his revolting cock and forcing me to gag for another reason.

As he strokes over his swollen shaft, he continues to work his fingers in and out of my mouth, grunting as the tempo gets faster and faster.

It takes all my willpower not to bite down, not to gnaw off this motherfucker's fingers and reveal why I'm really here. But not yet. It's not time. I refuse to let all of this be for nothing. I'm their only hope.

This is only a shell; one he can break time and time again. But he'll never take my will to survive. And survive, I will.

So, I watch uninterested as the corded veins in his neck pop, him grunting and jerking himself off with that poor excuse of a cock. We never break eye contact as he wants me to yield.

In response, I smirk around his fingers, a clear fuck you.

He roars, angered, forcing my mouth open as he yanks down on my bottom jaw. My mouth is hinged ajar, his fingers down my throat. I gag violently, which is what he wanted. With three quick pumps, he removes his fingers and comes inside my mouth, grunting fervently.

Just as I'm about to spit, he cups my chin, pressing my mouth shut. He then pinches my nose, knowing sooner or later, I'll need to breathe.

My cheeks grow hot as my lungs demand air, and just when I'm about to fight him, he lets my nose go. On instinct, I open my mouth, gasping for air as he releases me. This results in most of his seed spilling down my throat, while some dribbles out of the corner of my mouth.

Spitting hysterically, I attempt to rid his foul taste from my mouth, but it's too late. He's a part of me now.

"One day, it won't be my fingers down yer throat." He wipes away the trickle from my chin, smirking victoriously as he pulls up his trousers.

I don't cower. I am expressionless as he waits for me to do something, anything. But it'll be a cold day in hell when I show defeat.

Angered, he spits in my face before turning and slamming the door shut behind him.

Only when I hear his irritated footsteps grow softer and softer, do I crumple. Wiping the spittle from my cheek, I reach for my nightgown with trembling fingers. Once dressed, I come to a shaky stand and stagger into the bathroom where I lift the toilet seat and crouch. This time, I force my own fingers down my throat.

Gagging a few times, I persevere until I throw up nothing but bile, but that's okay because I know I'm expelling the vile bastard from my system. When I've got nothing left to bring up, I cradle the porcelain bowl, slamming my fist against the side of it as tears of anger stream down my face.

No matter what it takes, no matter how long, I'm going to kill every last…Doyle and burn their motherfucking kingdom to the ground.

"The black? Or the green?"

Flinching, as it hurts to breathe, I look over my shoulder to see Darcy holding up two dresses. She wiggles each coat hanger, hinting she's waiting for me to reply.

Honestly, both look like they're missing about eight inches off the hemline, but good luck to her if she wants to catch pneumonia.

"The green," I say, trying my best to sound interested.

Darcy looks at the green dress, pursing her lips. "The black it is."

She turns on her heel and leaves me to scrubbing her toilet while she gets ready for wherever the hell she's going.

Turning back around, I curse under my breath, reminding myself why I'm here. It's the only reason I haven't told these narcissistic arseholes to sod off. I can't believe how unbelievably obscene and cruel these people are.

To the outside world, they are respected, admired for their hard work and determination, but I've seen who they really are behind closed doors. Once their masks are removed, I see the ugliness which truly lurks beneath the surface.

All but one.

Punky.

I don't know what it is about him, but he's unlike the others. Something about him makes him stand out from the rest. Yes, he is a Kelly, therefore, he is the enemy, but not by choice. He was born into this; as was I.

What's in a name? That which we call a rose by any other name would smell as sweet.

Shakespeare said it best, but Punky and I are no Romeo and Juliet. We aren't star-crossed lovers. We never can be. I know that. So why can't I stop thinking about him?

These are dangerous waters I tread because so much relies on getting what I want, but to hurt someone like Punky to achieve this doesn't seem right. He's as much a victim as I am.

With a sigh, I continue scrubbing Darcy's toilet as I have a day filled with chores ahead of me. Once I'm done cleaning the bathroom, I enter her bedroom and try my best not to cry out in pain with each step I take.

She looks incredibly dolled up, so I'm guessing she's going on a date. I wonder who the unlucky fella is.

Darcy is pretty if you like that perfect kind of look, which is what every guy likes, bar Punky it seems. He didn't hide his distaste of her at dinner. She could have cartwheeled in the nude in front of him, and it wouldn't have mattered.

That probing stare of his penetrated my very core as I tried my best to remain unmoved by his presence. But he makes me nervous, and he knows it. Simple tasks such as breathing are a chore with him close by. I've never felt this before.

I'm twenty years old, and although I've had a couple of casual boyfriends, none of them were able to elicit these feelings in me. Being near Punky excites me, and I think he feels the same way about me.

I can see it.

I can feel it.

And that's what worries me the most.

I need him to be strong because my resolve is slipping. If he doesn't deny me, then I sure as hell can't deny him. I'm playing with fire…especially if he finds out who I really am.

"I have a guest arriving soon. Please don't interrupt us." She pauses from applying her red lipstick, and her mirror image smirks at me. "If ye know what I mean."

"Of course, Miss Duffy," I reply, nodding quickly. That won't be a problem. I don't want to be anywhere near her PDA.

"Grand." She goes back to finishing her makeup, puckering once she's done. "I've been trying for years to get his attention, and it's finally worked. When he called me, I was so surprised. But I knew he'd give in sooner or later. I always get what I want," she adds, turning around to face me.

I don't know if this is supposed to be a two-way conversation, so I keep quiet, focusing on making Queen Darcy's bed. She asked I change her sheets to the pink silk set. No guessing why that is.

"But I suppose someone like you wouldn't know anything about that."

Biting the inside of my cheek, I don't take the bait.

"Did you always want to be a—" She pauses, appearing to search for the right word. "A maid."

Maid is a polite way of saying fucking servant because what twenty-year-old woman can't make her own bed? Darcy can do it, but why would she when she has me to do it for her? This is how the rich work. They use and abuse those "beneath" them because that's what we're here for—to serve them.

She doesn't give me a chance to reply because she doesn't want me to. This isn't two friends gossiping about boys. It's two distinct classes co-existing because they have to. Darcy isn't sharing this as a friend; she's bragging about everything I'll never have.

Thankfully, the doorbell rings.

Darcy takes two deep breaths, before squealing and primping her appearance one last time. "How do I look?"

"Lovely," I reply half-heartedly, rolling my eyes as I turn my back to tuck in her sheet.

She seems satisfied with my response and is out the door, primed on greeting the poor chap downstairs.

I quickly finish making her bed as I don't want to be anywhere near here if she's planning on giving her guest the grand tour of her bedroom.

Once everything is in order, I go about cleaning the rest of the house. Mr. and Mrs. Duffy are away for the weekend, which is why I jumped at the chance to do some extra chores around the house when Mrs. Duffy asked.

Without them here, I can put my plan of attack into motion.

Faint voices drift up the stairs, and when I hear the side door open, I sigh in relief. Darcy has taken her guest into the gardens, which gives me an opportunity to snoop around. Using the feather duster as a decoy, I pretend to be dusting the invisible cobwebs as I pass by Mr. Duffy's office door.

Peering from left to right and seeing the coast is clear, I try the door handle. No surprise, it's locked. But that's not a dead end—it's merely a speedhump.

Removing my hairpin, I carefully insert it into the lock and wiggle it. To the left. To the right. Up and down. I continue working it because I know with experience, eventually, you'll find the sweet spot…like right now.

The lock clicks, permitting me entry. I don't waste a minute and quickly enter, softly closing the door behind me.

Patrick Duffy's office is meticulous, not that I expected anything less, so I have to ensure I leave everything as I found it. Opening the filing cabinet, I reach for my phone and flick through the alphabetically organized files.

There is no such thing as too much information, so I take an abundant number of photos of files which I think will be of use. I stop when I reach the letter N. I don't want to push my luck as

I assume Darcy will want to show her guest her bedroom soon.

Quietly closing the filing cabinet, I take a look around, backtracking to a painting which hangs over the fireplace. Tilting my neck to the side, I examine the way the watercolor painting of a horse is sitting a couple of inches away from the wall.

To the untrained eye, it would go undetected, but not to me. It's my "job" to notice these things. It's what helped me survive all these years. Lifting the corner with my pointer, I see the reason it's not flush with the wall is because there is a safe mounted behind the painting.

Taking a quick photo of the safe, I ensure the painting is hanging the way I found it and decide to look for the code another time because I can hear Darcy's laughter from downstairs.

Doing a quick sweep and ensuring everything is in order, I softly open the door and peek my head out into the long hallway. It's clear.

Locking the door, I continue my ruse of dusting, a rush of adrenaline thrumming through me at not being caught. If only the Duffys knew the real reason I'm here. But they will. Soon enough.

Once I'm done dusting, I collect the supplies I need to clean the main bedroom. I'll take a quick look around as I haven't been able to do so with Mrs. Duffy around. I'm feeling good about this because it's only a matter of time until I can leave this hellhole for good and go home.

I miss them. So much.

My mind is so lost to a place I yearn to return, that I'm not aware of my surroundings until it's too late. I turn the corner and bump into a delectable smelling wall. However, that doesn't make a lick of sense because I'm in the hallway.

I peer up and up and see the wall is actually the muscled chest of the last person I expected to see here.

"Punky?" I can't hide my surprise because what in the ever-living hell is he doing here?

However, it doesn't take me long to catch up to speed when I see he's wearing a pressed white shirt and black ripped jeans. His long fringe is flicked to the left, styled this way to accent his bad-boy look.

He looks incredible.

But no matter how incredible he looks, him being here leaves the most bitter taste in my mouth because *he* is Darcy's guest. I'm going to be sick.

"Babydoll?" he says, his surprise clear. "I didn't think ya were workin' today."

Needing to get my head back in the game, a game where Punky does not exist, I pull back my shoulders and ensure my mask is firmly in place. "Well, I am. If you'll excuse me."

I attempt to push past him, but he doesn't let me move an inch.

Gripping my wrist, he looks at me closely. He examines my

face, down my chest, and then ends with my feet. I'm covered, so there is no way he can see the atrocities which remain hidden beneath my uniform. But I nervously lick my lips, nonetheless.

"What happened to yer face?" he asks, his eyes narrowing.

Shit.

I slathered on the makeup, and no one has noticed thus far. But Punky isn't no one. I should know that by now.

"That's none of your concern." I use his own response as ammo back at him because when I asked the same question, he had no intention of sharing. And neither do I.

Yanking out of his hold, I shove past him, but again, he stops me, and this time, he ensures I'm not going anywhere as he pushes me and pins me to the wall. He places his hands either side of my head, caging me in. I shove against his chest.

He doesn't speak, but in this case, actions speak a lot louder than words. He examines every inch of me, those blue eyes looking for any clues.

"I'm sure your *date* will be looking for you," I sarcastically bite, still unbelieving he is here of his own accord.

But he ignores the jab.

He keeps one hand fixed to the wall, but with the other, he gently runs his thumb over my chin. I flinch as I'm not used to such a tender touch. It surprises me. As do the trail of goose bumps which coat my skin.

No matter how hard I try to stay calm, my labored breathing gives me away. Being this close to Punky is a drug, and like a junkie, I want more…more…more.

A look I can't quite place overcomes him, and I'm too late to stop him when he pulls down the sleeve of my loose-fitting dress, exposing the purply blue bruise on my shoulder, courtesy of my beating three days ago.

"Who did this to you?" he orders, his voice frighteningly low.

Frantically, I attempt to pull up the sleeve of my dress, but he won't permit me to cover my shame. "I fell down the stairs," I whisper angrily, not wanting Darcy or anyone else to hear our exchange.

"Bullshit!" he growls, not caring who hears it seems. "Tell me."

I fight him, desperate he doesn't continue disrobing me as I'm afraid of what he'll see. But the harder I fight, the more evident it becomes I've got something to hide. Punky yanks down both sleeves and spins me around so my bare back faces him.

A horrified breath escapes him when he sees the ghastly mess. The fresh welts from this morning's beating are swirled among the bruising I've withstood since coming to this god forsaken country.

I drop my chin to my chest, wishing I could just disappear.

"The fuck? Ya got…whipped?" His surprise is clear because being whipped without the kink is just punishment, a brutal form of torture.

I hold back my tears, and his question remains unanswered. I can't tell him what happened, no matter how badly I want to.

"Go back to your perfect date and forget this ha-happened," I assert, but the quiver to my voice betrays my bravado.

I'm clutching onto the front of my dress, the material bunched in my tight fists as I wait for Punky to let me go. He's seen the ugliness as these scars come with baggage, and what sort of man wants to deal with that.

But what he does next has a single tear trickling down my cheek.

At first, I think my fragile mind has conjured up such an occurrence to deal with the humiliation, the pain, but when I feel the unmistakable glide of flesh upon flesh, I know that this is really happening—Punky is stroking over my wounds. He isn't repulsed by my humiliation.

"I can't forget," he confesses, his fingers gently tracing over the welts on my back. "I don't want to. And I don't want perfect...I want real."

I allow myself this moment of silence because I know it won't last. It can't.

"I'm sorry this has happened to ya. I know what it's like," he shares with regret. "My aul' lad, he knocked me out. And then the next night, I got into a fight. That's what happened to my face. And the brooch...it, it belonged to my mum."

His confession is laced with so much pain, I feel it all the way to my core. I now know why I gravitated toward him. We both share something life changing which has shaped us into the damaged people we are today.

I don't need him to explain what happened to her. I can guess. Him speaking about his mother in the past tense says it all, and that breaks my heart because it hits close to home.

"So thanks for giving it back."

"It's okay," I reply softly. "I shouldn't have taken it in the first place."

"Who did this to ya, Baby?"

I like this nickname for me too.

"It doesn't matter."

"Course, it matters. No one has the right to lay a hand on ya. I'll break every bone in their fucking body for doin' so." He strokes over the large welt across my back; his touch filled with nothing but compassion.

I can't take his kindness. I don't deserve it.

Gently shrugging away, he gets the hint and lets me get dressed with my back turned. I wish I could slip away and forget this encounter ever occurred, but he shared something personal with me, and I don't want to throw that back in his face by not at least acknowledging it.

With courage filling my lungs, I turn around and slowly lift my chin to face Punky. I see nothing but sincerity reflected in those clear blue eyes. "Thank you, but I can look after myself. I better get back to work. And you better get back to Darcy."

I wish I did a better job at concealing my jealousy because

being jealous means I care, and I can't care about Puck Kelly.

"I'm not here 'cause I want to be," he reveals, shaking his head and thumbing over my bottom lip slowly.

"Then why are you?" His touch sets me alight.

"She has somethin' I need," he reveals, finally releasing me from this spell he's cast.

"And what's that?" I ask, suddenly very curious and elated at the same time.

He tongues his cheek, as if weighing over what he should tell me. "I need access to her father's files. Or, more specifically, I need all the housin' information he has in Moville."

I know that place because I took photos of that file a few minutes ago. But if I tell Punky that, he'll know I broke into Patrick's office to obtain that information and then the questions will start. Questions I cannot answer.

But I think about his admission and how I doubt he needs real estate information because he's interested in investing. So what does he need it for?

"Punky! Did ya get lost?" Darcy calls out, her footsteps pounding up the stairs.

"Ah, just fuck off, will ya?" he mutters under his breath, running a hand through his hair.

His honest response has me going against my gut and whispering quickly, "What's your number?"

His eyes widen, but when he reads the urgency to my question, he recites it speedily.

Memorizing it, I grab my things and hurriedly walk down the hallway, diving into the safety of the main bedroom, avoiding an awkward encounter with Darcy.

Leaning up against the wall, I measure my breaths and dig into my pocket for my phone. Scrolling through my pictures, I sigh, pausing over the documents Punky needs. I do this, and there's no turning back. Thinking about the reason I'm here, I enter Punky's number and send him the photos with tears in my eyes.

Regret and shame overwhelm me because Punky will believe I sent these to help him. But the truth is…I did it to help myself. Puck Kelly is the reason I'm here. He's the reason for all of this. He just doesn't know it.

Yet.

SEVEN

PUNKY

We're all quiet because, thanks to Babydoll, things are about to change. We don't know how, but I can feel it. We all can.

I'm driving, while Cian is riding shotgun and Rory is in the back. Rory was relieved when I told him I didn't need Darcy after all as Babydoll had the information I was looking for.

Darcy was going to eat the head off me when I told her I had to go. I didn't give her an excuse, just that I had to leg it.

The moment I stepped outside, I got into my car, drove home and punched the shite outta my punching bag for an hour. All I could see was Babydoll's bruises and welts. The bruising indicates she's been hit before. And the welts were fresh.

I wish this was a one off, but I know better, which is why

I'm not going to stop until I find out who did this to her.

It doesn't make sense, but the attraction I feel for Babydoll just continues to grow. She is strong; she's a fighter. Her battle scars prove this. I have no doubt she took each lash without surrender, challenging the fucker to do his best.

She has every right to tell me to go fuck myself, but she hasn't. She gave back my ma's brooch, and now she's given me information which led me down this dark, gravel road. I owe her.

"How's it goin'?" Cian asks, sensing my thoughts are elsewhere.

"Sound," I reply, half arsed.

I didn't go into details about what happened with Babydoll. All the boys know is that someone hurt her, and that someone is going to be in the hospital for an awful long time once I find them.

"It's about half a mile ahead," Rory says, as he's the using GPS on his phone.

There isn't a house in sight, just acres upon acres of green, farmlands, and lots of cows. There are no street lights, so when I park my car and turn off the blinders, we know we've got to adjust to the dark. Locking the car, we commence our walk down the deserted road.

"What's the craic then?" Cian asks, his voice echoing out here in the middle of nowhere.

"I walk up to the front door and knock."

He laughs, but when he realizes I'm serious, he shakes his head. "Fair play to ya, mate. Yer bollocks are bigger than mine."

Both Rory and Cian think I'm not the full shilling, but I didn't come this far to faff about. When Babydoll sent me every listing in Moville, it wasn't hard to find which one once belonged to my ma because there was only one owner before the current residents—Cara Foster.

It couldn't be a coincidence. Cara Foster had to be my mum.

I don't know how I feel about this. Finding out so much, so fast, has been information overload. I need to process it, but time is something I don't have. If my da gets wind of what I'm up to, he'll do everything in his power to stop me.

But I won't allow that and this time, I *will* fight back.

Creeping through the night has me wondering about that fateful night which changed my life forever. Are these the same footsteps my ma's murderers took? Why wasn't she in Northern Ireland? What was here for her to choose this location?

It's in the middle of nowhere with a population coming in at under two thousand.

This quiet, simple life is so different to Belfast. So different to being a Kelly. Is that why she came here? To run away?

When the bungalow comes into view, I delve deep into my psyche, hoping to unearth repressed memories which may resurface being here. But all I'm faced with is a black mass which won't shift.

Cian slaps me on the back encouragingly, while Rory vows,

"We've got yer back, mate, so we have."

I want to thank them, but I'm so lost to this surreal feeling that I merely nod in acknowledgment.

The closer we get, the more unsettled I become, but I squash down the uncertainty and only focus on the answers I will get. The full moon provides the light for me to see the bungalow is painted white with a gray roof. Smoke plumes from the chimney, hinting someone is home.

The property itself is huge, but it's gone to waste as no crops or animals are in sight. When we reach the long drive, I stop and close my eyes. Was she happy here?

"Yer all right then?" Cian asks.

Nodding, I open my eyes and focus on the bungalow in the distance. There are gardens with shrubs, trees, and hedges. Was it this way when I was last here?

"It's so quiet out here. No one would have heard her scream," I utter, surprisingly calm. "Youse stay here. I'll call out if I need ya."

Rory and Cian nod, understanding this is something I need to do on my own.

With no time to waste, I commence my walk toward the bungalow with no expectations; this avoids disappointment. On the listing, it has a D. Morrison as the current owner. They've lived here for fifteen years, which tells me they bought this place not long after my mum died.

A sensor light switches on when I get within a few feet of

the front door. No turning back now. There is no doorbell, so I knock on the wooden door.

There is light from a TV flickering through the sheer front curtain and I'm about to take a peek inside, but when the front door opens and an aul' doll greets me in a blue dressing gown, I smile.

"How ya doin'? Sorry to disturb ye, but I was wonderin' if I could trouble ya with some questions?"

She narrows her blue eyes.

She has every right to be suspicious. A strange lad *is* on her doorstep at nine p.m.

"What questions?" she asks with a thick Irish accent, ensuring she holds onto the door in case she needs to shut it quickly.

Rubbing the back of my neck, I decide to lead with my gut because it's now or never. "'Bout the woman who lived here before youse. Her name was Cara Fost—"

Suddenly, the door is yanked open, and the muzzle of a shotgun is inches from my forehead. "Away with ya," says the aul' lad who is wielding the shotgun.

Slowly raising my hands, wishing to show them I want no trouble, I say, "I mean no harm. I just wondered if you knew her—"

"Ah'll knack yer bollocks in. Chase yerself!" he warns, his grip firm on the shotgun.

"Boys a dear," the aul' doll gasps, clutching at the cross

around her neck.

"Really sorry, but I can't do that. Not until ya answer my question." I won't surrender. Not when I've come this far. "Do ya know what happened here?"

"Wise up, cub! Did ya not hear me? Away on! Ya got naw business being 'ere."

The aul' lad gestures with the gun that I'm to go, but when the aul' doll's eyes fill with tears, it confirms it *is* my business. I'm not going anywhere.

I direct my question at her. "The woman, Cara, she was—" But the aul' lad doesn't let me finish.

"Don'tcha listen to him, Imogen," he warns, his gaze never wavering from me. "Are ye deaf? Call the peelers, I will."

If I wanted to, I could drive that shotgun into his chest, setting him off balance and force my way in. But I don't want that. This bungalow has seen enough violence.

Imogen reaches for a tissue out of her pocket and wipes her nose. "Who are ya, wee lad?" she asks, ignoring the man, who I'm assuming is her husband. "Why ya askin' after Cara?"

"Y'knew her?"

A sniffle escapes Imogen, which is a strange response for someone she didn't know.

"You did know her," I press, reaching forward to gently grip her wrist. "Please, just tell me how."

But the aul' lad has had enough.

Without warning, he flips the shotgun and delivers a

buttstroke to the center of my forehead. I stagger back two steps and clutch at my bleeding head, stunned at the bollocks on this aul' lad.

"Keegan! If yer mother were still alive, that would kill her," Imogen scolds, but Keegan, aka the aul' lad who just kicked my arse, ignores her and comes chasing after me with the shotgun.

"Is that you? Or ye away in the head?"

My vision is blurred, but I manage to dodge the gun-wielding lunatic as he tries to hit me again.

"I don't want any trouble," I pant, raising one hand in surrender while the other cradles my brow.

"Yer head's full of wee sweetie mice. Trouble's been had."

"I'm not leavin' until ya tell me how ya knew Cara," I persevere. The only way I'm leaving here without any answers is if he kills me.

"Stop saying her name!" he screams, advancing once again. "Give ma head peace."

I recoil, impressed with this aul' lad's stamina and how stubborn he is. But I'm not leaving until he gives me answers.

Cian and Rory come running up the drive, guns drawn as they heard the commotion. When they see the blood gushing from my forehead and that I'm being held at gunpoint, they instantly spring into attack.

Imogen shrieks.

"Naw!" I bellow when they make a move for Keegan. "Don't touch him."

Cian and Rory freeze, looking at me like I've gone mad, and I may just have. But I don't want to hurt either of these people. They're not the enemy. They're only protecting their home and one another.

"Yer bleedin'," Cian says, as if needing to remind me the reason for my injuries is holding us hostage with his shotgun.

"Slap it up ye!" Keegan spits, pointing the shotgun at Rory and Cian. "Call the peelers, Imogen."

This is my last chance.

Submitting is not in my nature, and it appears it's not in Keegan's either, which is why I slowly drop to my knees, admitting defeat.

He won.

"Cara was—" I lick my lips, tasting nothing but the sharp metallic sting of my blood. Visions assault me, or rather, memories leave me winded because I'm suddenly inside this bungalow, locked away in that wardrobe as I watch my ma being killed.

I clearly see my five-year-old self, painting my face; each stroke denoting what those three fuckers are doing to her as she screams for them to stop.

I can feel her skin cooling as I lay nestled in her arms.

I smell the stink of decay.

Memories my brain had suppressed are reborn, refueling this desperate need to avenge my ma and stop at nothing until I do.

"Cara, she was my ma," I state, unsure if I said it aloud.

But when the shotgun drops to the ground with a hollowed thud, I know that I did.

"Houl on, what did ye say?"

Shaking my head, I return to the now and observe Keegan turning a terrible shade of white.

"Cara was my mum," I repeat, still on my knees. "My name is—"

But I never get to reveal who I am, and that's because they already know.

"Puck?" Imogen gasps, placing her weathered hand over her mouth.

"How'd ya know my name?" I ask, looking from her to Keegan.

"Boys a dear," she utters, shaking her head, eyes wide like she's seen a ghost.

Keegan blinks once, as he too appears like he's gone into shock. "Get up from there, lad."

I do as he says, hoping one of them will explain what the fuck is going on.

"Says I to her, don't marry that good for nothin' sleekit. But she didn't listen. And look what happened," he says, talking to himself.

I have no idea what's going on.

"Married who?" I ask, wiping the blood from my eyes and hoping to clear away the confusion as well.

"Yer dad," Imogen replies softly, coming out of the doorway and walking toward me. "Cara is our daughter, Puck. Yer our grandson."

The gash on my forehead suddenly pales in comparison to the one on my heart because there must be some mistake. I came here for answers, not to find long-lost relatives. But before me stands just that.

"I don't believe it." Imogen gasps, staring at me. "Ya look just like her."

When she attempts to touch me, I recoil violently as I need a minute. Or two.

These strangers are my *grandparents*? Do they look like my mum? I don't know. I can't really remember what she looks like. I don't remember them. I know where I got my temper from, however.

I have so many questions. I don't know where to start.

"Yer so big," Imogen says in awe, unable to take her eyes off me.

"Aye, yer a big mawn. How old are ye?" Keegan asks, which has me arching a brow.

"Twenty-one," I reply, needing to address the obvious. "Did ya know I was alive all this time?"

Imogen draws the lapels of her dressing gown across her chest. "Aye, but yer da—"

"We tried, lad," Keegan interrupts, sensing the sudden shift in the air.

All I hear are excuses.

"You should have tried harder. How can ya live in there?" I ask, peering at the bungalow with disgust.

"This isn't our home. It's our son's. Yer uncle's."

An uncle? I have another uncle.

"He's on holidays with his family. We're mindin' his dogs."

I don't know how to process this. I have this entire other family, and they've moved on, moved on without me. They've made a life without me when all I ever wanted was to make a life with them.

"Come inside," Imogen begs when she notices me processing what they've just shared.

Clenching my jaw, I can't hide my rage as I spit, "Are ye jokin' me? I don't wanna set foot in there. Do ya know what I saw? What this house represents? This place should be burned to the ground. It's soaked in my mum's blood."

Imogen muffles her cries, while Keegan lowers his eyes, ashamed. "Cara was awful stubborn," he says, shaking his head with regret. "We told her if she married that hallion, we'd never speak to her again. She didn't listen."

"And that excuses ya for abandonin' her?" I ask, barely reining in my temper. "She came here to escape my da? Am I right?"

"Aye."

"She had no one," I state, nothing but anger filling my words. "Her family disowned her because she chose the wrong man to marry. And she died here—alone. Ya may as well have killed her."

"Don'tcha say that," Imogen cries, wiping her tears away with trembling fingers.

"Why not? It's the truth. She didn't come to ya because she obviously didn't think she was welcome. How old was she when she got married?"

"Sixteen," Keegan replies with regret.

"And my dad?"

"Twenty-eight."

"For fuck's sake, she was only a chile. How could ya allow her to marry him?"

Keegan doesn't appreciate me pointing fingers, but what the fuck? Why didn't they stop her? She'd need the consent from a parent or guardian to be married at such a young age, but I suppose the church was happy to bend the rules for a Kelly.

"Ya don't know yer ma. She—"

"That's right," I interject, curling my lip. "I don't 'cause she was murdered in front of me."

Imogen crosses herself with fresh tears in her eyes. "Yer dad has told ya nothin' 'bout this?"

"Naw, but he should have done. I know nothin' about her. The only memories I have are of her covered in blood!"

"Oh, Puck, I'm sorry. We tried to see ya. But yer dad wouldn't allow it. He's a Kelly."

"And so was yer daughter," I counter, like that excuse is

supposed to make everything all right.

"We're not perfect," Keegan says, running a hand over his thinning, gray hair. "And we should have done more. But there was no stoppin' her."

"Why did she buy this place?"

"'Cause she was leavin' yer da," Imogen reveals, confirming the blanks I've tried to fill in for years. "And she was takin' ya with her. You were her life, Puck. But leavin' Connor Kelly wasn't an easy thing. She knew he'd kill her, so she planned carefully."

"But not careful enough," Keegan adds with anger.

"The day before she...she was killed, she called me. She told me she knew somethin' that would ruin the Kellys if it ever got out. I believe she thought this was her way out. But she never told me what it was."

The hair at the back of my neck stands on end. "What're ya saying then?"

Keegan levels me with nothing but sincerity as he rattles my world forever. "Whatcha think, lad? Yer da is responsible for yer ma's death. She wanted to leave him and had a secret that could ruin him. What do ya think he'd do?"

I've heard him loud and clear, yet I can't accept what he just said.

This isn't possible. Aye, my dad never avenged my ma, but he didn't kill her.

Or did he?

The past sixteen years overwhelm me, and I hiss in a winded breath. The unanswered questions which plagued me night after night…Have I had the answers all along? Has my ma's murderer been under my nose this entire time?

I think I'm going to be sick.

I don't want to believe them, but this makes more sense than my da laying down arms and not avenging his wife's death. He never took vengeance because he was the one who killed her. This story of the Doyles being responsible was merely fabricated to placate the rumors. And to pacify me.

Better I believe our rivals are responsible—who I've been raised to hate—than my own father.

I wanted answers. And I got them.

"Who's D. Morrison?" I ask about the "owner."

"It's a friend of ours," Keegan replies. "We didn't want yer dad knowin' we bought the place."

Imogen sniffles, before turning around and going inside.

"And why did ya? No offense, *Grandpa*, but that's awful fucked up."

He nods, his fight no longer thriving. "This was the last place yer ma was. It's the only thing we have left of her."

He realizes what he just said, but it's too little, too late.

"My uncle Sean was right. Yer not worth knowin'," I state emotionlessly. "You shoulda been there for her when she was alive. Now, yer holdin' onto memories instead of her."

Imogen comes hobbling back out, something in her hand.

"We just got ya back. Please don't go."

With a wrathful smirk, I affirm, "Y've never had me in the first place. Ya could have, but ya turned yer back on me, like ya did my mum. I'm a Kelly. I'll never be a Foster. And for once in my fucking life, I'm proud of that."

She nods, accepting my insult because how can she refute the truth?

With nothing further to say, I go to turn, but she offers me the photograph she has in her hand. "Y'll always be a Foster, Puck. Yer ma's blood runs through ya whether ya like it or not."

Accepting the photo, I don't look at it. Instead, I shove it into my pocket and leave. I don't bother with goodbyes because I didn't even say hello. Cian and Rory's footsteps alert me that they're following, but I can't talk to them right now.

I can't do anything but think about what Keegan said.

"Whatcha think, lad? Yer da is responsible for yer ma's death. She wanted to leave him and had a secret that could ruin him. What do ya think he'd do?"

Those words haunt me, and I break into a sprint, wishing to escape the pain they bring. But the faster I run, the deeper they cut, and I know only one thing will center my world once again. The gravel kicks up under my feet as I run toward my car, and when I'm within reach, I unleash my anger the only way I know how; the only way I was taught by the monster who murdered my ma.

I bate my fist into the car bonnet over and over again, but

it does nothing to subdue the demons. It only feeds them. And they're hungry.

"Ah, stop it, y'll break yer hand," Cian says, attempting to calm me down. But that ship has sailed.

Only when I'm hitting or destroying something do I feel better. However, there is only one person who will be able to stop me ragin'. I need to go home. I need to look my da in the eye and ask him if he killed my ma.

And if he says yes…then I'll do unto him what he did to my ma.

"Whatcha gonna do, Punky?" Rory asks, keeping far back, knowing better than to touch me.

"What I have to," I reply, lamping the bonnet one last time.

"Ya believe them?" he asks, but that's the thing—I don't know who to believe.

With a roar, I kick the tire and finally contest defeat.

Breathless, I dig into my pocket to retrieve the photograph, and although it's dark, the moonlight allows me to see the image is that of a woman and a wee boy. That wee boy is me.

With bloodied fingers, I bring the photograph closer so I can look at the woman sitting in front of an easel with a set of paints close by. Her blonde hair matches mine in color and so do her eyes. I trace over her kind face, unbelieving this is my ma.

The images of her in my head match this woman perfectly. I didn't even know I knew her…until now.

I remember her tender voice, singing to me as she rocked me to sleep. I remember her sweet smell; she always smelled of roses. I remember how she shoved me into that wardrobe, protecting me with her life.

I remember…

And I'll never forget.

Digging into my pocket, I give the keys to Rory. "Well there ya are now."

He nods, realizing this is far from over.

I want nothing more than to kick open my dad's bedroom door and beat the truth outta him. But I can't.

When that happens, and it'll happen soon, the twins can't be here. Neither can Fiona. It just needs to be me and my dad because this is between us.

On the drive home, I thought about calling Uncle Sean and confronting him with what I've uncovered. But honestly, I am fucking knackered. I need a clear head when I tackle this because I know I have one chance, and one chance only.

The boys left some hours ago, and although they offered to stay, I told them to go home. I can't be around anyone right now. I can't even be around myself.

I've showered, but I haven't left the bathroom. I've stared

at my reflection for hours, hoping to see the resemblances between my ma and me. Her photo is taped to the mirror, and as I stare at her, memories begin to materialize.

I remember bouncing on her lap as she sat in front of her easel, painting colorful images which made no sense to me, but they did to her. Regardless of how unhappy she was, her paintings helped her escape, just as mine do for me.

Gripping the sink, I arch my back, measuring my breathing as I attempt to calm these images racing inside my head.

"Ya need to be quiet. Quieter than a mouse. Okay, my wee son? Promise me."

The harder I try, the more predominant they become.

"How 'bout a dance, Cara?" one of the men says, walking over to the radio to turn up the song. "C'mere to me."

Elvis suddenly replaces the deep voice of Ma's attacker.

Kiss me, my darling...

That song...it's the song that was playing on the radio.

I scream, slamming my fist into the side of the sink, squeezing my eyes shut. This joyful song is the perfect oxymoron for what horrors the smooth voice of the King was concealing.

It's now or never, indeed.

Jolting up, I race through my bedroom and turn on my laptop. I search for the song which is on a loop inside my head and press play. The moment it sounds, I stagger backward, clutching my chest.

I want to claw out of my skin.

I see my ma's bloody face as she reaches for me, her twisted body as the knife cuts through her flesh with ease. I see it all. The memories I tried so hard to remember come flooding back, and I do the only thing I can.

My room appears ransacked as I hunt for them, and when I find them, they tremble in my hand.

With Elvis on repeat, I collectedly walk into the bathroom and sweep everything off the vanity. Staring at my reflection, I laugh maniacally, certain I've lost what small shred of sanity I've clung to.

Reaching for the container, I unscrew the lid, humming in happiness because I've come home. Picking up the brush, I dip the bristles into the makeup—appropriately named clown white—and commence spreading the paint across my face.

Before long, my face is slathered in white paint. The starkness concealing the red and purple bruises allows me to be someone else. But this is just a blank canvas, just like my mum needed to create the paintings which transported her away from this cruel thing they call life.

I swap the white paint for the black, and with a thinner brush, I draw a steady line from the apple of my cheek to my mouth. I repeat the same action on the other side. Once I'm done, I paint across the black line, so I have downward slashes along my cheeks. I then stroke vertically across my lips— silencing my screams. My grin is sinister.

But it's not enough.

Coating the brush bristles in black, I color in my nose, paying homage to the white makeup I just applied.

My eyes are next.

With precision, I paint around them, accenting the darkness with strokes branching out from the blackness. They come out like tentacles, and when I join one with a single stroke to my nose, I smile, happy with the brutality.

I shade in the strokes, adding depth, adding carnage to the grotesque man beneath this mask. My skull face represents the demons inside of me.

It's perfect.

The white container drops into the sink, going round and round, the imagery similar to what's going on inside my head.

Reaching for the tube of black body paint, I unscrew the lid and squirt it over my neck and chest, where I run my fingers through it, coating my skin black. With the leftover paint, I flick it over my ear and down my face, envisioning it red as it resembles blood—the blood my mum spilled.

I leave black handprints on the white sink as I grasp it and lean closer into the mirror, studying my creation. *This* is who has remained hidden all these years. Hidden away in a wardrobe, waiting for the memories to revive him.

Now is that time.

However, there is one last thing I need to do. A mask is never complete without any wounds.

Unscrewing the container, I peer into the red paint, the

slickness singing to the depravity which lives inside me—it always has. I smear three fingers in red and stare into the mirror as I slowly sweep downward across the middle of my forehead.

These signify the three lives who ruined mine. But after tonight, I wonder, how many more I need to add?

My hair is still wet from my shower, so I run my fingers through it, styling it so it's tousled. The tattoo on my knuckles catches the light, and my ma's name almost shines.

"I'll avenge ya. I promise ya that," I avow to my mirror image. "I don't care what y've done. If *he* was the one who took yer life…then I'll take his."

My entire life has been based on a lie.

This is the first time I've painted my face this way since that night. I remembered because of the photograph, but tonight, I painted it from memory, and that only ignites my need for revenge.

My face is the canvas, and this painting is one I wear with pride. Each stroke is in honor of my ma, and I will bear this mask to punish those who hurt her.

Suddenly, the hair at the back of my neck stands on end, and without a sound, I reach for the gun in the top drawer of the vanity. Elvis muffles my footsteps as I creep through the bathroom, peering around the doorjamb into the living room, gun poised and ready to use, but who I see has the depravity reflected on my face burning my soul.

Why is she here?

She stands in front of the charcoal sketching hanging over the fireplace, her head cocked to the side as if attempting to decode what each stroke means. Good luck to her. This is a look inside my mind. It doesn't make sense—up is down, down is up. Nothing is what it seems…just like me.

Her blonde hair is loose, and I have the urge to wrap it around my fist as she drops to her knees before me. These thoughts need to stop, but I lost control the moment I met her. She intrigues me because without a doubt, she's not who she says she is.

I sure as shite don't trust her, but that doesn't stop me from wanting her. And so, I do the one thing I've not done before—I give in.

With a measured pace, I walk into the living room, and the closer I get to her, the hotter the fire burns. She is pure sin wrapped in a big red bow. When I'm feet away, she spins quickly, her trance broken, but when she sees me, she gasps, taking a step back.

I wonder what she sees.

I come to a stop, thrilled by the way her heated gaze openly examines me. I'm in nothing but ripped black jeans. But I imagine my face is what she's most intrigued and…terrified by. A breath escapes her as she walks forward, closer and closer until she halts.

We stand face-to-face, inches apart, not saying a word.

Wearing this mask allows me to study her without

reluctance because I feel like someone other than me. There has always been an attraction between us, but something feels different. This feels like we're at a crossroads, and the direction we choose to take will change the course of everything.

Babydoll bites her bottom lip, appearing to weigh over her next move, and when she reaches out with hesitation, I realize why that is. With two fingers, she cautiously caresses down my cheek, examining the design beneath her touch.

She doesn't know the story of why I would choose to paint my face this way. This war paint is as much a part of me as my neutral face, and I suppose in some ways, I wear two faces.

"What does this mean?" she whispers, her eyes chasing her touch.

"This is my true face," I reply, standing perfectly still when she runs her fingers along the line across my cheek and traces the slashes over my mouth. "Everythin' else is just a pretty distraction."

She strokes over my lip piercing, taking a moment to digest what I've just shared. "Why does this face look so...sad?"

Sad?

To most, this makeup would appear frightening, monstrous, but of course, Babydoll isn't like most.

"Why're ya here?" I question, peering down at her, the closeness between us suddenly not close enough.

Her fingers are leading to my forehead, but my hand snaps out, capturing her wrist. "What do these three lines mean?"

She sees the significance for what it is and doesn't disregard it as merely a theatrical flair. She seems to understand that each stroke serves a purpose, that nothing was done by accident. How can she read me so well?

"Their lives are mine," I ambiguously answer, eyes locked with hers. "I know who they are…it's only a matter of time."

"And what happens when you take them?"

Her question catches me off guard because I haven't thought that far ahead. Up until tonight, I didn't even know that one of those lives could be my da's.

"What happened to you, Punky?"

Hissing, I pull her toward me, so we're pressed chest to chest. She doesn't cower. She dares me to do my best.

"If I tell ya that, I'm gonna have to kill ya."

She licks her bottom lip nervously, but what she replies brings me to my knees. "You can try."

I know this is a bad idea, but that's never stopped me before. In reality, I have no self-control when it comes to Babydoll, and finally, I give in to what I've wanted to do since we first met and slam my lips against hers.

A gasp escapes her, but that soon turns into a moan when she stands on her toes and kisses me back with fire. She pulls at my hair, whimpering when I bite her bottom lip. She flicks her tongue across my piercing, then tugs it gently between her teeth.

The sharp sting has every part of me hardening, and kissing

is suddenly not enough.

With our lips still attached, I walk her backward until her knees hit the couch. She tumbles onto it with a yelp, but I don't follow. I stand before her, breathless and so incredibly turned on. She scoots backward on her elbows, her eyes never leaving mine.

When her back hits the armrest, she inhales slowly, her cheeks turning a deep red as I openly explore every inch of her. Her mouth is slathered in black and white paint, making her all the more delectable.

Her blue summer dress dips low at the collar. Her chest is rising and falling with uneven breaths, and I like that I'm the one who provoked this response from her.

"I'm n-not sure if I should trust you," she confesses, and I hum in delight.

"Good," I reply, watching the way she slips off her shoes, eagerly awaiting my response. "Don't."

Just as she's about to rise, I climb onto the couch and sit back on my heels because this is happening and it's happening now. We're on opposite sides of the sofa, giving her a false sense of security because when she tries to get up again, I grip her ankles and drag her toward me.

A yelp leaves her, and she grips the cushions, needing something to anchor her for what's about to come. Placing my hands on either side of her hips, I hold her prisoner, keeping my weight off her as I press my lips over her racing pulse.

She arches her neck, permitting me to take and take I do. With no hurry, I run my nose over her skin, lost in her vanilla scent. She smells good enough to eat…which is exactly what I plan on doing.

I slither down her body, her curves molding to mine, and come to a stop at the junction of her thighs. She shuffles back and leans against the armrest, knowing what I want as she opens her legs timidly. She slowly pulls up the hem of her dress, exposing her black lace underwear.

They're see-through, allowing me to admire what that flimsy piece of material conceals. Her pussy is bare, and I run my tongue over the ball in my lip piercing, obsessed with what I see. I don't ask, I take, as I run my hand up her thigh and circle the outside of her underwear.

I'm surprised to feel the material is wet.

I wish I could be gentle and give her what she deserves, but I can't. I don't know how.

She repositions herself, bending one leg while she spreads the other wide, granting me full access to her beautiful cunt. Her breaths are hot and heavy as I shift her underwear to one side, baring herself to my deviancy. Her pretty flesh seems to turn scarlet all over.

With two fingers, I stroke up and down the outside of her pussy, excited by the way her body responds to my touch. She whimpers, gripping the couch cushions.

Her skin grows slicker, and never breaking eye contact, I

offer her two fingers from my other hand, where she does as I coax and draws them into her mouth to suck on them. Barely holding back my growl of approval, I continue stroking her while she suckles my fingers, circling her tongue around them.

Her cheeks hollow as she sucks me deep, which has my dick stirring in approval.

Once my fingers are well lubricated, I remove them from her mouth. They slide free with a pop. The noise, coupled with the feeling, just increases the need to eat her whole. She leans back against the armrest, her throat quivering as she swallows deeply, awaiting my next move.

She's on fire in my hand, but when I sink my finger that was inside her mouth seconds ago into her pussy, she detonates.

"Oh my God," she moans, throwing her head back.

I work my finger in and out, in and out, watching closely as Babydoll comes undone. With my thumb, I circle over her clit, in awe at the way her body responds to my touch. I'm used to my hands causing pain, not pleasure, so I can't get enough of her breathless cries and small shudders that rock her body.

She reaches down, placing her hand over mine, begging I speed up the tempo. Seeing her beg is a new drug to me, so instead of increasing the rhythm, I sink in another finger.

Her back bows as she squeezes her eyes shut, her body trembling, demanding more.

With sluggish strokes, I penetrate her deep. Her warmth sucks me in, and I never want to leave. She's so slick, I slide in and out with ease. To feel how turned on she is pleases me in ways I never thought possible.

"Please," she begs hoarsely, raising her hips, hoping to deepen the angle.

"Please what, Babydoll?" I question, her pleas only adding to the tension building inside me.

"More," she shamelessly demands. "I want more."

Her underwear is in the way, which frustrates her. She shoves them aside, opening herself further up to me, but I chuckle smugly as that's the reason I left them on—to have her on the cusp of exploding before I give in.

As I work her into a wild mess, I play with her clit, unable to get over the sight of her coming undone because of me. I enjoy going down on women. I prefer it to sex, to be honest. Being able to dominate someone to the point of them losing complete control is what I like.

Sex is the hard part. The intimacy makes me uncomfortable because someone always wants more, and I don't have any more to give. Being with them, vulnerable that way, isn't something I enjoy. But now, all I want is to be lost in Babydoll as I know my demons will play well with hers.

I just want to let go.

With a guttural groan, I give her what we both want, and with a sharp tug, tear off her underwear. Her pussy glistens under the light, the slickness awakening an even deeper hunger within. Without thought, I lie down on my stomach, position one of her legs over my shoulder, and take her cunt into my mouth.

Babydoll cries out, clutching the top of my arms for support as I devour her without apology. She tastes how she smells—like vanilla—and I want more.

Rubbing her flesh against my face, I slather myself with her honey, taking her into my mouth as I sink my tongue in deep. Up and down, in and out, I fuck her with my tongue and mouth, licking, sucking, leaving no part of her untouched.

She bucks against my face, using the heel of her foot to coax me in deeper. She is the one holding me prisoner, and usually, I wouldn't like it. I would feel suffocated, claustrophobic, but not with her. She tenderly runs her fingers through my hair, moaning and shuddering with each flick of my tongue.

Her pussy is scalding, burning me alive, but I want more, so I add a finger to the mix, showing no mercy as I eat her out. Gripping her thigh, I extend it out further as I want her all over me. I want her aching, her legs resembling jelly, so she'll think of me tomorrow with each step she takes.

My finger and tongue are in a race with one another, sprinting toward the finish line as I punish Babydoll with torturous strokes. Her back bows off the couch, and she uses my hair as reins, pinning me to her pussy. She is confident and knows what she wants—and that is the kind of lover I want.

I want someone to take from me, demand I serve her like a queen. I want an equal, in every way there is. I want someone to challenge me, infuriate me until I'm ready to explode, because that eruption will result in something utterly sinful…just like this.

"Ahh, Punky!"

Gripping her waist, I keep her restrained as I work her into a frenzy. She writhes and moans. "Please, oh God…it hurts… but it hurts…so damn good."

It pleases me that Babydoll doesn't mind a little pain because I can give her that. Everything else is foreign to me. But being with her this way feels almost innate as though we've done this a thousand times before.

We click, in every way, which has never happened before.

She is slathered all over me, and I wonder what my face looks like because her pussy is covered in slashes of black and white. My dick is so hard, I'm afraid I'll come in my pants like a horny wee lad.

Babydoll pumps her hips against my face, fucking me as I'm fucking her, and when I suck her clit, she comes loud and hard. I keep her pinned, holding her pussy prisoner as I milk every last tremor from her body.

Her curses are moaned, and holy fuck, if it's not the hottest sound I've heard, then I don't know what is. The last shudder leaves her, and her body grows lax. With one last kiss over her perfect pussy, I sit up and wipe my mouth because I'm a messy eater, but I thoroughly enjoyed that meal.

Sprawled across the couch, Babydoll attempts to catch her

breath. I like seeing her here, in my home, sated because of me.

I'm about to stand because my erection threatens to have me walking with a permanent limp, but the moment I do, Babydoll slides over and straddles me. She loops her arms around my neck, still breathless and spent. Her cheeks are scarlet, and a satisfied look paints her face.

Instantly, I stiffen as I don't like this intimacy. She's too close. I turn my cheek, but she stops me, coaxing me to look at her as she places a finger under my chin.

"You just ate me out like I was your last meal, and now you can't bear to touch me?"

"It's not that," I reply, not wishing to offend her.

"Then what?"

"I, I don't like this sort of…touchin'."

She arches a brow, confused.

"I don't like being this close to someone," I confess, feeling emotionally inapt. "I feel…caged in. I feel like I can't breathe."

She purses her lips, weighing over what I've just shared, but she doesn't get off. She isn't repulsed or mad. "What happened to you?"

"Ya don't want to know," I counter, gripping the cushion beneath me.

"Yes, I do," she gently argues. "That's why I asked."

She looks at me, waiting for me to divulge all the sins of my past, but she'll be waiting a long time. My walls are instantly re-erected, and I click over into defense mode.

"Just 'cause I ate yer pussy, doesn't mean we're gonna cuddle and share our deepest, darkest secrets. Ya got what ya came here for. Now away with ya."

She blinks once, clearly offended, and she has every right to be.

But this isn't personal. This is who I am. I'm fucked up in the head. I know that. There is no fixing me, and I don't want to be fixed.

When she realizes I'm serious, she angrily stands, frantically putting on her shoes. She won't look at me, and it hurts, but I brought this onto myself.

"You're a real arsehole, you know that?"

Leaning back against the couch, I smirk. "Aye, I think we've established that, but ya can't seem to stay away, can ye? Any time ya want that grand pussy ate—"

I don't get to finish my sentence because she springs forward and slaps my cheek—hard. "You shut your filthy mouth," she sneers, eyes narrowed and making no apology for her actions.

Good, she hates me. Hopefully, this is enough to keep her away because I don't have the strength to do so.

Rubbing my cheek, I merely grin smugly. She reads this for what it is.

She spins to leave, but stops and levels me with nothing but pure hatred as she reveals, "I came here to check on you. I wanted to make sure everything was all right after I sent you that information. I was worried," she says, scoffing. "What a bloody idiot I am."

I remain impassive, not wanting her to see how her words have affected me. This was her final ploy to get through to me, but she failed, by no fault of hers. When she realizes this conversation is done, she turns on her heel, slamming the door behind her.

Once she's gone, I lean my head back against the cushions and place an arm over my eyes, wishing to block out the pain I've caused. It's going to take a lot more than that, however.

I just did Babydoll a favor…she just doesn't know it.

EIGHT

Babydoll

He wants to see me. I don't know why. Has something happened? I gulp at the thought.

Walking through the luxurious home, I pay no attention to the riches because this wealth is merely a reminder of everything I need but will never have unless I do something so deplorable, I'll question my morals forever.

I'm already halfway there, however.

I'm sore, thanks to Punky giving me the best orgasm of my life before throwing me out like some common whore. I clench my fists just thinking about that son of a bitch. How dare he.

This shouldn't be personal, but it suddenly feels like it is. I'm in way over my head.

Puck Kelly has gotten under my skin. I should have been

more careful, but I never expected to feel...this connection to him. But after last night, that connection has been severed because I will not be treated like a whore.

However, when I knock on *his* office door, I know that this choice isn't mine anymore. I'm here to serve a purpose. He permits me admission, and I enter, head bowed; just as he commanded I do.

I don't take a seat. I know better. Someone like me isn't fit to sit before someone like him. I smell his trademark pine cologne underneath the cigar smoke. It makes me want to gag. I wait for him to address me, but he draws it out. It's all just a powerplay, but I can never forget who's in charge.

"Bout ye?" he asks as if I'm here because I want to be.

"Fine," I reply, keeping my answer short.

"Did ya find anythin' out?"

Measuring my breathing, I nod. "Yes, he asked about a house in Moville. I gave him what I found at Mr. Duffy's."

"Aye, good, love. What else?"

"His face was painted." My body still tingles at the memory of finding him that way. He looked so frighteningly hot.

Silence.

"He had three red lines down the middle of his forehead. They signify the lives he's going to take."

"And he knows who they are?"

"Yes. He didn't tell me who."

He claps loudly, clearly happy with the update. "And his

father was the one who beat him up?"

Nodding, I swallow down my disgust at the thought.

"Well done. What else?"

I know what he wants me to tell him—that I seduced Punky into telling me all his secrets—but he doesn't know Punky. And he doesn't know me.

"I've got photos of all the files you wanted," I reveal, which is not the information he wanted, but it'll do—for now.

"Nice one. I want ya to keep at it, though. I need ya to break him."

Tears well, because I don't want that. I never wanted any of this. But that's why I'm here. Puck thinks he's a monster, but monsters come in all different shapes and sizes. His mask last night was a reflection of who he thinks he is.

What happens if he saw mine?

"He's not easily broken," I counter softly. "It's going to take a lot more than—"

When I hear the leather of his chair creak, indicating he's risen, I seal my lips, terrified. I shouldn't have contradicted him. But I can't stand this.

The plush carpet announces his arrival, and when he lifts my chin with his finger, my mask, the one I've tried so hard to master, slips into place. He examines my face, but I can't read what's going on behind those steel gray eyes. His mask is rock-solid.

"Try harder," he calmly says—but make no mistake, this is

a warning. "Ya know what happens if ya don't?"

Biting the inside of my cheek to stop the tears of anger, I nod firmly.

This motherfucker loves to assert his power as if anyone could ever forget. "Yer here for one reason only. And what's that?"

I stand tall, hating myself more than I already do as I stonily reply, "To…seduce Puck Kelly and make him fall in love with me."

And there it is…the ugly truth. The reason I've helped Punky. The reason I can't leave him be.

At first, he was merely a means to an end, but the moment we met, I realized he was something more. But regardless of my feelings, if Punky ever knew who I really was and why I was sent to him, he'd have no qualms killing me for my betrayal.

He nods happily, brushing over my trembling bottom lip. "And?"

"And to uncover everything I can about the Kellys."

"And what does that make ya?"

A tear trickles down my cheek. "It makes me a liar."

"Aye, and no one could ever love a liar," he says, wiping away my tear. "Ya think yer meeting was by chance? None of this is by chance. Ye all played right into my hands.

"I knew dressin' the way ya did would spark his interest. As would doing something which would have him lookin' for ya.

Stealing from him was perfect. I gave ye orders, and ya ran with them. None of this makes sense. But it will."

I hate him, and he knows it.

"Yer nothing but a liar. And a good one at that. The apple doesn't fall far from the tree. Never forget that. I own ya."

I'll never forget because no one can hate me more than I do myself.

He walks toward his desk and picks up the phone. He dials and offers it to me. *This* is the reason I'm doing this. This is the reason I've sold my soul to the devil.

I quickly accept, and when I hear that voice, I know what I have to do. Puck Kelly will hate me, but I'll deal with the repercussions because nothing else matters...but this.

"Hello?" the voice says, heavy with burden.

I don't speak. It's been so long since I've heard that voice. I just want to absorb this rare moment in time because I'm happy. It soothes me, even this far away from home.

"Hi," I finally reply, squeezing the phone tight, wishing it was them instead.

He's watching me, so I can't say what I want. I'm a prisoner—in every sense of the word.

"Oh, baby, I've missed you! Are you all right?"

He looks at me with a cocky grin, daring me to tell them otherwise.

"I'm fine. How are you, more importantly?"

"I'm okay. Just worried about you. Is it over?"

And that's the million-pound question.

"Camilla?" the voice presses, reminding me this isn't over…

Things have only just begun.

NINE

PUNKY

I'm angry.

This isn't an uncommon occurrence for me, but this anger is different. I'm angry with myself. As I hit the punching bag hanging off a rafter in the unused barn, all I can think about is Babydoll and how fucking stupid I am.

I hurt her feelings, and usually, I couldn't give a fuck, but with her, I do.

She confessed to being worried about me, after I insinuated she came to see me because she wanted to get off.

Groaning, I slam my fists into the bag, wishing I could punch away this guilt in my chest. But it only seems to get worse. With heavy metal blaring in my earbuds, I don't hear anything until it's too late. The punching bag swings, revealing my dad standing on the other side of it.

He is the last person I want to see, especially after everything I uncovered two nights ago. He's here because he wants something as we don't do small talk. But I don't take my earbuds out, nor do I stop punching the bag. Instead, I envision it's his face I'm punching as I belt the red bag.

Sadly, I can't ignore him forever.

"Ya smart-arse." I only catch the end of his sentence as he spins me around and snatches the earbuds out from my ears.

Controlling my temper, I glare at him, demanding that if he has something to say, then to do so now.

"I need ya to talk to one of the men. His delivery was short a couple of kilos."

When he says talk, he means beat him within an inch of his life.

Nodding, I attempt to replace my earbuds, but he slaps my hand away. "Don'tcha fucking touch me, aul' lad," I warn, shaking my head.

He merely laughs in response. "Ack, look at ya. Yer growin' hair on yer bollocks, then?"

"Fuck off," I spit, not interested in conversing with this knobhead.

His laughter soon dies, and I know things are about to turn dire. "Yer a wee want. A'll give ya a dig in the bake for that gob on ya."

Usually, I wouldn't bother. But not today.

"Ach, ya can try."

"What did you say to me?"

"You heard me," I reply, folding my arms across my broad chest. "I know whatcha did."

"Cool yer jets, lad. What're ye yappin' 'bout?"

I didn't want it to go down this way, but it's now or never...

"I had a wild craic conversation the other night with some people."

"Aye? Who was it then?"

"My grandparents," I reply with no hesitation, deadpanning him.

I take great pleasure in seeing him pale. He soon composes himself, however. "Ack, what did those culchies have to say for themselves?"

"A lot, actually." I clench my taped fists; certain this conversation will end in bloodshed.

"They told me ya killed Mum," I reveal, as there is no sugarcoating this. "That she was leavin' ya. Takin' me with her. She knew a secret which could ruin the Kellys. What do ya think about that?"

I wait for him to react. To confirm the truth. But he just stands before me, expressionless.

"Are ya deef, or what?" I exclaim, angered he's standing here, not saying a word.

He shrugs, digging his hands into his pockets. "Dry yer eyes, will ya? Yer pathetic. Always been a mammy's boy. Things don't change."

"That's it?" I question, disgusted he would respond this way. I shouldn't expect more from him, but this is the first time I've mentioned my grandparents. "That's all y've got to say for yerself?"

"What do ya want me to say, lad? That yer ma was a saint?"

"Ach, shut yer mouth!" I warn, my temper about ready to explode.

"I will not," he counters. "Yer so desperate for the truth, here it is. Yer ma was not the angel ya think she was. She was out fuckin' every man in town while I was the one who changed yer nappies. Made sure ya were fed!"

I shake my head, refusing to believe him.

"Aye, yer grandparents were right…she *was* leavin' me 'cause I kicked her out. Our marriage was over because the secret…the one she thought she could ruin me with, is that she was fucking Brody Doyle!"

"*What*?" I stagger back, unable to process what he just said. There's no way, no way she was sleeping with a Doyle. "I don't believe ya."

"Believe whatcha want," he spits, unmoved. "I never told ya any of this 'cause I didn't wanna hurt ya, lad. But yer so fucking stubborn. So this is the truth, the truth ya asked for. Once ya know this, cub, ya can't take it back."

"Know what?" I question, because this is the answer I've been searching for my entire life.

Dad runs a hand through his hair, and for the first time in his life, he looks exhausted. "Yer ma was killed because she was fucking Brody Doyle and wanted more. He didn't. She became a nuisance, and once he had his fun, he disposed of her. It's that simple. There was no drug war. No war over turf. Yer uncle and I made that up to spare yer feelin's."

"Yer a fucking liar!" I scream, tears of anger stinging my eyes.

"I may be a bastard, but a liar, I am not. That's why I did nothin'. She got what she deserved for fucking my enemy. I never fought for her because she gave me nothin' to fight for. She made her choice, Puck."

"Ye'd say anythin' to save yer arse! She's not here to defend herself."

"Ya don't believe me? Ask yer uncle," he says, knowing how that'll hurt me. "The reason I've been so tough on ya is 'cause… when I look at ya, all I see is yer ma, and her betrayal."

My brain cannot accept his words. They're lies. All lies. "I'm still yer son! Both yours and Mum's!" I bellow, arms out wide, but when he lowers his eyes, I realize I've misread this entire story and what her betrayal really means.

"Naw, Puck, that's the thing… I don't know that ya are."

For the first time in my life, Connor Kelly has shocked me beyond words, and the reason for that is because I believe him.

It makes sense why he's been so cruel to me. Sometimes, he looks at me like I'm nothing but a stranger, the enemy, and I understand why that is.

"Who's my father then?" I ask in vain because I know, I know but I need him to shatter my world beyond repair.

He sighs, appearing beaten as he shakes his head. "I don't know."

"Ack, bullshit! Don't stop now."

When he refuses to answer me, I advance and shove him in the chest. He staggers back, as this is the first time I've laid my hands on him.

"Don't start somethin' ya can't finish," he cautions, giving me one chance and one chance only to retreat.

But that ship has sailed.

"Let's finish this then, aul' lad, once and for all. Tell me who I am."

It's a standoff, and only one man will be left standing.

"Are ya away in the head, lad? I told ya…I don't know!"

Looks like he needs some encouragement.

Without hesitation, I strike out and connect with my da's jaw. His head snaps back with a satisfying crack. This is the first time I've hit him, and I'm instantly addicted to the taste.

"Let's try again," I smartly say, grinning as he wipes away the blood trickling from his mouth with the back of his hand.

"Ya wee fucker."

Regardless of the bombshell he just dropped, he doesn't let me off and comes charging toward me. I get into position, ready to fight until the death. He swings, but I dodge and connect with his ribs. It doesn't stop him, however.

We circle one another, fists raised, ready to tear the other apart—just how I knew it would always end.

"Yer ma was fucking a Catholic!" He spits on the ground, expressing his repulsion at the fact. "Ya could be anyone's son for all I know."

His words just fuel this out of control anger, and I strike out, belting him in the stomach. He bends in half, but I don't show any mercy because he's never done so to me. I kick him in the face, setting him off balance as he tumbles onto his back.

I dive on top of him, pinning one shoulder to the ground as I punch him in the face over and over again. His warm blood coats my knuckles, blood which may not run through my veins. With an indignant howl, I grip his cheeks and slam his head onto the hard ground.

He laughs in response, bloody and beaten. "Ye may not be my son, but ye fight like a Kelly."

"Ya fucker!" I scream, and just as I raise my fist, prepared to knock him out for good, strong hands scoop under my arms and drag me off him.

I fight wildly, but my uncle Sean hushes me, pinning me to his chest. "Catch yerself on! Enough!"

But not this time. He can't calm this over.

I shove him away, and he staggers back, shook, as it's the first time I've been forceful with him.

"What's going on here?" he asks, looking between me and

my da.

But he doesn't get to play peacemaker. He is as much to blame as my da.

"How could you lie to me? I expected it from him, but not from you," I say, shaking my head, ragin' but also, hurt.

Uncle Sean sighs, interlacing his hands atop his head.

"So it's true then? My ma was…fucking Brody Doyle?"

This is it; the truth I sought so hard for.

"Aye, lad. I'm sorry ya found out. I wished for ya to never know the truth," he says regretfully.

"Ya lied to me!" I shout, unable to accept this because the only person who showed me an ounce of decency was in on this ruse.

"Only 'cause I wanted to protect ya from the truth."

"And what is the truth, Uncle?" I question, peering down at my hands coated in Kelly blood. "Am I a Kelly? Or am I a… Doyle?"

There it is—the truth which has been staring me in the face.

My da or, rather, Connor comes into a sitting position, flinching as he clutches his ribs.

Uncle Sean looks at Connor, who nods. Connor knows I'll only believe Uncle Sean to tell me the truth.

"Lad, we don't know, but we think so. We think Brody Doyle is yer father. When yer ma fell pregnant, yer da and she were separated. The time don't match up for Connor to be yer da. We never thought much of it, but when yer ma's deceit became clear, we joined the dots."

I shake my head, shook.

"We never avenged yer ma 'cause she was goin' to sell yer da out. The secret she kept was that she would ruin the Kellys by revealin' to everyone that she was havin' an affair with yer da's archnemesis.

"Can ya imagine how that'd look? We'd be the laughin' stock of Northern Ireland. Connor Kelly can't control his wife; how was he to manage a multimillion-pound illegal business? How were his men supposed to look at him with respect?

"How were the enemies supposed to be afraid? This would ruin us. Ya know that. But it was leverage yer ma had. She thought she had the upper hand. She was cocky and careless and demanded things in a world she didn't understand.

"Yer da tolerated yer ma's rebellion because he loved her. But Brody didn't; this is why he had yer ma killed. She was becomin' a liability to him, as at the end of the day, she was always a Protestant and he a Catholic. I'm sorry, Punky, but it's the truth."

I need a minute to digest this because it feels like a bad dream.

I wonder if my ma only slept with Brody to get back at my da. Did Brody do the same thing? I can only imagine what an accomplishment it would be to sleep with yer sworn enemy's wife. And what about me? Does he know that I could be his son?

It's too much. I can't breathe.

"How do I know you didn't do her in?" I ask Connor, who is still slumped on the ground. "Ya had grounds to."

"Ack, yer right. But I only found this out by the note she left when she kidnapped ya. The note which cruelly stated you were not my wee chile. The note which implied you were a Doyle.

"Brody bought that bungalow for her, so he knew where she was. I didn't even know it existed. That's why it took me three days to find ya, Puck. Yer ma and I always had problems, but I didn't know any of this until she left for Moville. The Doyles knew where she was. They always did."

I want to fight him, but the tattoo on my wrist burns me with the truth. The tattoo, the same one I saw when I was five years old, the one I saw the other night on the Doyles' wrists, proves to me he's telling the truth.

I always knew the Doyles were responsible for her death. However, I never really knew why—until now.

My entire life has been a lie.

"Why didn't ya give me away?" I ask Connor, not wanting his sympathy. I just need to know why.

He shifts, flinching as he tries to stand. "'Cause I reared ya like my own."

"Yer a Kelly, no matter what," Uncle Sean says with love, offering a hand to his brother.

I suddenly feel sick to my stomach. I don't even know who I am anymore. The man I've hated my entire life, the man I believed was responsible for all of this is actually the hero in this story?

It can't be.

I need space. I need time to think.

Leaving behind the family who I now look at in a different light, I leave the barn, and the moment I walk outside, I tip my face to the skies and scream. I scream so loud, I'm certain my hollowed cries can be heard in Dublin.

Angry doesn't describe what I'm feeling right now because this extends past that. I've never felt this sort of fury before. Once I'm done cursing the world, I walk toward my house, intent on only one thing.

When inside, I call both Rory and Cian. They don't speak as they sense something huge just went down from the tone of my voice.

"I understand if youse say no, but I'm going to Dublin. Tonight. I can't wait for Liam to call. I need to go to him."

"And then what?" Rory asks.

"Then I'm goin' to find out once and for all what that tattoo means. And when I do, then I'm goin' for Brody Doyle."

I can hear Cian choke on his beer. "What?" he wheezes.

Brody Doyle was always in my sights, but now, he's my number one target.

"What happened?"

"What happened is that I found out Connor Kelly isn't my father."

Both boys sound shook, but they haven't heard anything yet.

"And that Brody Doyle may be."

I wonder what they'll say.

"I'll see ya in twenty minutes," Cian says.

"Aye, I'll be there in fifteen."

Ending the call, I realize no matter what surname I bear, they'll always be my friends.

We're quiet, but I compare it to the calm before the storm.

The streets of Dublin are busy, with many laughing and having a pint with friends. But I'm here for another reason, and that's to speed up the inevitable.

I can't wait for Liam to maybe call me. I need to show initiative, which is the reason we casually walk into *The Craic's 90*. To onlookers, we're just three friends out for a drink. But when I see Erin Doyle behind the bar, the truth to why I'm here surfaces.

If I believe Connor and Uncle Sean, then Erin is my half-sister, which makes her very valuable to me but not because I'm interested in a family reunion. Naw. She's my stepping-stone.

We stand in line, waiting for our turn to be served. The place is packed, which allows us to blend in. Erin showed interest in me when I was here last, but I can't work that angle anymore. No matter how desperate I am, I won't cross that line.

Until I find out for certain just who she is, just who *I* am, I need to treat what Connor and Uncle Sean said as the truth, which leaves me with only one option—Cian.

Rory is too hung up on Darcy to make this convincing, so that leaves Cian. I know girls back home consider him a ride, so I just need Erin to think the same. He looks grand in jeans and a shirt, which allows Erin to see he works out.

When we're next in line, Erin does a double take when she sees me. Her smile reveals she's happy that I'm here.

"Ack, this is a bad idea," Cian whispers into my ear. "She's thick as champ over ya."

"Keep 'er lit. This'll work," I reply, waving at Erin.

"Mike from America," she says when we walk up to the bar.

"Erin from Dublin," I reply playfully. "I didn't get a chance to introduce my friends. This is Kanga and Paul."

She politely nods, but makes it clear she's not interested in either of them. "What can I get ya then?"

It's almost impossible to believe she could be my sister. We look nothing alike, but that doesn't mean we're not related. My stomach churns at the thought.

"Blonde with a black skirt," Cian says in his staged Australian accent.

Erin smirks as she commences pouring our pints of stout. "Yer Irish is deadly. Massive."

Cian leans forward, laying on the charm. "I'm full of surprises, love."

Rory rolls his eyes while I chuckle. He's slipped into the role of Casanova easily.

"Is your brother, Liam, in?" I ask casually, but Erin seems to think nothing is by chance when her brother is involved.

"Whatcha want with him?"

I don't get a chance to reply because the devil himself speaks for me. "Mike, it's been donkey's years," Liam says with cheek.

Reining in the need to headbutt him, I turn to my right and offer him my hand. "You don't call, you don't write. I thought we shared a moment when I kicked your brother's ass."

Liam shakes my hand, bursting into laughter. "I like ya, bucko. Hugh is still pissing blood after ya clocked him good."

I shrug, unmoved.

"I've been meaning to call ya. 'Ave a pint with me."

Erin slams our drinks onto the bar, making it clear she doesn't approve. Liam ignores her however and gestures I'm to follow him. I leave Cian and Rory to milk any information out of Erin and casually walk to where Liam and Aidan are sitting.

As Aidan raises his glass in salute and his tattoo shines under the light, I decide then and there that I'm going to kill him. Liam and Hugh share the same ink as him, but they're too young to be the man who attacked my ma.

This has me guessing that this tattoo is a rite of passage as such; I just need to find out what that rite of passage is.

"Sup, boys," I say, taking a seat at the table.

"Y've got some bollocks on ya, lad," Aidan says, slapping me on the back as though we're friends.

"What can I say, I missed y'all," I reply with a grin.

Liam clicks his glass against mine. "Cheers, mate."

I drink my stout, waiting for Liam to make the first move. Me being here is enough of a hint that I want in on whatever he's offering. And he takes the bait.

"Glad that yer here. I have a proposition for ya."

Nodding, I gesture that he's to go on.

"Someone didn't pay my family for a service we provided," he explains, deliberately leaving out what that service is. "I'd take care of it myself, but—"

"Say no more," I interrupt, wanting him to know no further explanation is needed. A good dog doesn't ask questions.

Aidan is pleased with my loyalty. "Are ye busy now?"

Throwing back my drink, I wipe my mouth with the back of my hand. "Nope."

"Grand. Ye animal, let us go then."

Aidan and Liam exchange a look between them. I don't know what it means, but I'll take my chances.

"Thanks, Mike. I won't forget it. Aidan will make sure ya get paid for yer troubles. I'll call ya tomorrow." And I know that he will.

He'll want to know if I had the balls to do whatever it is they want me to do. But little does he know, I'm about to go rogue.

We shake hands, and I follow Aidan through the crowd.

Cian and Rory are sitting by the window, and when they see me, I nod subtly. They know to give it a couple of minutes before they follow.

Aidan exits the pub, and the lights on a red Audi parked out front flash, hinting this is our ride. We get in, not saying a word. He starts the engine and takes off into the night. The GPS on my phone is synced with Cian and Rory's phones, so they can track where we're going.

"How ya liking Ireland?" he asks, making small talk.

"Love it," I reply, mentally taking note of landmarks in case I need to retrace my steps. "The boys and I were thinking of going to Belfast next week."

Aidan laughs, but it's not in happiness. "That place is a dead loss. Y'd be better off going to Scotland," he sarcastically says as both options in his opinion are as bad as the other.

"Oh, you've been?" I ask, playing dumb.

"Ack, not for a very long time."

"Why not?" Mike from America asks, while Punky from Northern Ireland sits back and waits for this fucker to sign his own execution order.

"'Cause I wouldn't take a slash on thon place if it were on fire. It's filled with nothing but maggots. Good fer nothin' *Protestants.*"

Sitting on my fists to stop myself from connecting his forehead with the steering wheel, I coax him to elaborate. "Oh, so this is a religious thing? You're Catholic?"

"Aye, that I am. But naw, religion is just an ounce of why I hate that place. There is a certain family there that think they're the quality. But they're nothin' but ignorant culchies. Not a word of a lie. It's easy thinkin' yer a dab hand at selling the gear in a city the size of Belfast.

"There's no competition, well, so they think not."

I mentally count to three before I reply. "Competition? Is that where we're going tonight?"

Aidan turns to look at me briefly, smirking. "Ye cute hoor. That's the element. Too bad yer leaving so soon. We could really use someone like yerself.

"My family value honesty and loyalty, somethin' the Kellys know nothing about."

He mistakes my silence as me lost in translation, but in reality, I can't speak in fear I'm going to kill this fucker with my bare hands. *My* family, meaning the Doyles. So which Doyle is he?

"The Kellys are our rival family. The Protestant fuckers who think they're better than us. But they have no idea shit's about to hit the fan."

Adrenaline courses through me because it seems I've hit the jackpot. Pushing my murderous urges aside, I need to focus because this is the start of something good.

"Good luck to them then," I reply, and the ballbag falls for it as he grins smugly.

We drive for about thirty minutes, and there is definitely a change in scenery. The city life is long gone. Everyone is locked away safely in their houses, and the only ones remaining out here in the darkness are monsters like us.

"All y'll see are bogtrotters out here," Aidan says as we pass a sign saying Ratoath. I catalogue it, along with everything else I've learned tonight.

"Where do you live?" I ask casually.

"Dalkey. All mi family's there. My brother, Brody, owns a property on one and a half acres. I live not too far away," he brags, but all I hear is the word *brother*.

So, Aidan is Liam's uncle, Brody's brother. The tattoo hidden below my shirt sleeve itches—a psychological response to what tonight holds. I never anticipated this. This really is too good to be true.

Aidan turns down a dark street, and instantly, the quaint village vibe is replaced with desolation, and when I see an abandoned house up ahead, I know the tour is over. Shite is about to get real.

He parks the car and turns to me. "This wee fucker deserves no mercy. Let us see what yer made of then."

He'll be experiencing that firsthand soon enough, but I nod coolly. I know better than to ask questions and reach for the backpack I packed "just in case."

We exit the car, the closing doors echoing out here in the silence. There are no houses nearby, but still, this is hardly ideal.

Sloppy work on the Doyles' behalf, but then I have a thought; maybe they don't care who sees or hears them, and that's because they own this fucking town.

That makes what I plan on doing wild craic.

I follow Aidan who unlocks the front door. When he turns on a light, I'm surprised there's electricity, but focus on my surroundings because if this is a kill house, then I need to memorize every nook and cranny.

I'm not an eejit. I know this is a test to see if they can trust me. I'm here to do their dirty work, and if I prove valuable, they just may not kill me. But I'm disposable, so I need to make my mark.

Aidan turns over his shoulder, eyes animated when we walk down the hallway and hear the unmistakable sound of someone's gagged cries for help. I have no idea what I'm walking into. Aidan opens the door, and the person I see bound to a chair in the middle of the bedroom—which resembles a squatter's den—clarifies what shite hitting the fan really means.

A black T-shirt serves as a blindfold, and a dirty rag is shoved into his mouth, gagging him, but without a doubt in that chair is Ronan Murray—one of my men. A fucking traitor.

Connor thought Nolen Ryan was the only traitor among us; he thought wrong.

This isn't good. This is a reflection on our leadership. If two men had no issues consorting with the enemy, then this means they don't respect us. They don't fear the consequences of what happens when doing business with a Doyle.

Something needs to change because I fear Nolen and Ronan are just the start of many.

But now, I need to deal with this shitshow because Mike from America isn't supposed to know who this man is.

"Hello, Ronan," Aidan happily says, announcing our arrival.

Ronan's cries are muffled around the gag, so Aidan reaches out and roughly removes it. Ronan moves his jaw from side to side, while I'm seconds away from tearing out his traitorous tongue.

"I don't know anything!" Ronan pleads, which sickens me more than I already am.

"Ach, don't lie to me. We're past this. Yer job was easy—deliver us the Kelly gear."

So Ronan was the man Connor wanted me to "talk" to. I didn't get a chance to ask who because I had other pressing matters to deal with, like finding out that I may not be a Kelly. But regardless of who I am, Ronan betrayed me.

He betrayed Cian, Rory, and I, and that cannot go unpunished.

"I tried mi best, but Connor knew I was a couple of kilos short. I can't keep comin' up short."

"Not my problem," Aidan replies, unmoved. "Ya said ya could do this."

He did? Why did he seek the Doyles out in the first place? More money? I don't understand any of this.

"Ya don't know Connor. Ya don't know his son, Pu—"

Before he has a chance to say another word, I leap forward and connect with his jaw. His head jars back with the force.

Aidan's eyes are wide, surprised by my sudden need for violence, but Ronan cannot say my name. I have no doubt the Doyles know who I am, but the less they know, the better.

Aidan's shock soon turns to delight as he claps happily. "Ronan, meet Mike."

Ronan frantically shifts his head from left to right, attempting to gauge where Mike is. I make that clear when I punch him again—in the nose this time.

"Janey Mack!" Aidan shouts, elated, stepping out of the way as he doesn't want to get blood on his white shirt.

I need to know what Ronan has told the Doyles.

"Think you can run with the big boys?" I say, knowing he won't recognize my voice, thanks to my flawless American accent. "I don't know who these Kelly people are, but—"

"That's right," Ronan interrupts, taking the bait like I knew he would. "They're the biggest drug dealers, among other things, in all of Northern Ireland."

"Then why are you double-crossing them?"

Aidan allows the interrogation, appearing just as interested in his response as I am.

"'Cause things are about to change. The *Doyles* are going to change that."

Holy fuck.

"Aye," Aidan agrees, nodding happily. "Ya chose the right side, Ronan. Even though yer a Protestant. But that doesn't seem to matter much."

Of course, it fucking matters. What the fuck is going on here?

"I'm sorry, Aidan. Let me make it up to ya. Connor's twins...I'll bring them to ya. He loves them wains."

The walls close in on me, and my darkness snaps its jaws, demanding bloodshed.

"All right then," Aidan says with a grin. "Seems fair. Brody can decide what to do with them. Use them as collateral. Raise them as Doyles. Or sell them. The possibilities are endless."

These people he speaks so flippantly about are my siblings—whether they're flesh and blood or not, it doesn't matter. They are innocent in all of this, just as I once was.

But innocence escaped me long ago.

Aidan appears happy with their compromise and removes Ronan's blindfold. He blinks rapidly, attempting to adjust to the lighting and when he does, a gasp leaves him because all he sees is me—the *Kelly* he fucking betrayed.

"Naw, it can't be," he wheezes, and when Aidan turns slowly, not understanding why it appears Ronan knows me, I know it's time.

It doesn't matter if I'm a Kelly or a Doyle. In the end, I'm one fucking pissed off human being who is about to deliver revenge to all who betrayed me.

Aidan quickly reaches into his pocket, but it's too late and I kick him in the throat. He staggers back, clutching at his neck because the blow has compromised his windpipe. Ronan frantically tugs at the ropes around his wrists, fruitlessly attempting to break free.

"I'm sorry!" he pleads, knowing what his fate is. "It was a trap."

"Shut up," I demand, curling my lip, disgusted with his lies. "Yer *trap* involved negotiating with my siblings? Are ye jokin'? I'm not fucking thick."

Aidan's wheezes stop when he hears what I just revealed. "Yer Irish?"

"Naw, I'm Northern Irish," I declare, standing tall. "And I'm a fucking Kelly. My name's Puck Kelly. What's the craic?"

Aidan, who is still struggling to breathe, knows it's now or never and makes a wild dash for the door, but no one is leaving this room. Blocking the exit, I raise my elbow and strike him in the nose, breaking it. He tumbles back, blood gushing through his fingers as he cups his nose and attempts to gulp in mouthfuls of air.

Opening my backpack, I reach for my knife, shove Aidan against the wall, and twist his arm high above his head. He launches forward, but he's not going anywhere, and I make that clear when I drive my knife into his palm, crucifying him to the wall.

His howls are music to my soul.

One arm is still free, so he swings out, trying to grab me, but I step back, laughing. "Take the knife out," I dare him. "That's the only way yer comin' off that wall."

When he attempts to do so, I seize his free hand and bend it backward until bone snaps. It flops lifelessly as his wrist is broken.

"Shh, shh," I hush him, slamming my palm over his mouth as I level him with an amused stare. "I just wanna talk with ya."

His cries are muffled beneath my hand.

Yanking back the cuff of his sleeve, I glare at his tattoo. "What does this mean?"

His eyes dart to his tattoo, and I suddenly realize the symbolism behind this is even bigger than I thought.

Removing my hand carefully, warning him not to scream, I wait for him to answer my question. Instead, he spits in my face. "Fuck ya, Kelly."

Tonguing my cheek, I lift my face to the ceiling and exhale. "Is that right?" I ask, unsure why he believes that question was optional.

Maybe he needs further encouragement.

Opening my bag, I reach for my face paints and brass knuckles. I don't need a mirror because each stroke, I know by heart, thanks to him and the two other cunts who robbed me of my life. Placing the brass knuckles into my pocket, I unscrew the lid on the white paint and circle my fingers in the container.

Once they're coated, I slather my face with no real method

to my madness and paint my face white. Aidan stares, horrified, as I open the black paint container and draw a sinister grin from cheek to cheek. I use my middle finger to slash downward across my mouth, before blowing him a kiss with it.

My blue eyes are shadowed in black as I angrily rub circles around them. I repeat the same action down my nose.

My face is now painted to how it was when I saw him as a wee chile.

"Yer not the full shilling. Yer a molly, is it? No wonder, yer a Kelly, after all."

I don't bother addressing his slander, nor do I correct him that I actually don't know who I am.

"Yer tattoo, I want to know what it means."

"Why? Ye want one of yer own?"

With a smirk, I tug back my sleeve. "I already have one."

Aidan's confusion is clear when he sees our matching tattoos. "How'd ya know?"

It's time to reclaim what he stole from me.

"When I was five years old, I saw ya. I saw whatcha did to my ma—Cara Kelly. Remember her?"

"Naw, I don't. No Kelly is worth remembering."

Regardless of his denial, I continue with my story because even if he wasn't there, he has answers I want.

Shaking my head, I begin to whistle the song that was playing on the radio when he raped my mum. When I take a breath, I see it—recognition. He remembers. He *was* the fucker who was there that night.

Reaching for the black paint, I dip my finger into the container and draw a single line down my forehead. I've waited for this moment for what feels like an eternity.

As I stand in front of Aidan, he doesn't cower when I tilt my head, examining him closely. This is my bogeyman, the fella who took something which can never be replaced—my soul.

He tries to fight me as I dig into his pockets until I find what I'm looking for—his wallet and phone.

The leather is soft as I open the wallet, immediately finding what I'm looking for. "These yer kids?" I ask, running a black painted finger over their photograph.

Two boys and one girl. The wee dote is wearing a T-shirt with the words Four Leaf on the front of it.

My attention focuses on his license. Now that I have his address, he realizes he's royally fucked. "All right. Thon tattoo, ya stupid gobshite, is what every Doyle gets when they kill one of ye! A fuckin' Protestant. Almost all Doyles 'ave one 'cause ye Kellys are weak as piss."

Tsking him, I keep my cool—only just. "Who were the other two fuckers with ya that night?"

Aidan laughs angrily. "Dunno what yer talkin' 'bout."

"Ach, maybe ya need remindin' then?"

Taking out my phone, I do a quick search, and it doesn't take me long to find out that Four Leaf is a preschool. "Yer wain looks to be the star pupil," I say, turning my screen around so he can see what I've found.

His daughter is on the website, her fingers dipped in paints.

"I'll fucking kill ya!" he threatens, lunging for me.

"Go on then," I challenge, folding my arms across my chest. "All ye gotta do is pull that knife out."

He roars in frustration because with one hand broken, that only leaves the hand pinned to the wall as functional. "Everything we do, we're taking the piss outta ya. Just like stealin' one of yer men. Ye have no idea who yer up against."

Clapping slowly, I catch Aidan unaware as his wee tale was supposed to upset me. All it did was piss me off even more. He clearly doesn't think I'm serious, so I decide to call in reinforcements. Sending a text, I wait for the boys to arrive—who I know are outside, waiting for my instructions—and when they do, both Aidan and Ronan gasp.

"Whataboutye?" I cheerfully ask Cian and Rory as they enter the bedroom.

"Well then, I wouldn't mind a wee cup a tae, but this'll do," Cian sarcastically says, whistling when he takes in the carnage.

Rory curses when he sees Ronan tied to the chair. "Ya wee fucker. Ya workin' for the Doyles then?"

His bloody nose is enough of an answer.

"Lads, Aidan Doyle needs some encouragement. Here"—I offer them his license over my shoulder—"can ya pay his family a wee visit?"

Rory snatches the license from my fingers. "Beezer! Love

to."

I can see it. I can see Aidan grappling with his loyalties. Loyalty to his family. And loyalty to being a Doyle. And just like me, just for the reason of all this, his family wins out.

"All right, I was there! That geebag got what she deserved."

Inhaling, I take a moment to process his confession because it almost doesn't feel real. "Mind yer mouth," I warn, awful serious. "Who were the other two fellas with ya?"

I realize that he could be lying because if what he says is true and every Doyle gets a tattoo for every Protestant they kill, then any Doyle with a tattoo could be responsible for my ma's death. But the reason I believe it's him is because of how personal this kill was.

My ma was sleeping with Brody, and if what Uncle Sean says is true, then they wanted her dead because she was a liability and a nuisance. If they had wanted to start a war with Connor, then they would have made that clear. Her death would have been their calling card.

But the reason she was murdered had nothing to do with being a Kelly, but everything to do with wanting to be a Doyle.

"I think the fucker who slit her throat, that was yer brother, Brody."

Aidan pales but doesn't confirm or deny it.

I want to ask him about my ma, and if he knew about her affair, but I can't voice those words aloud.

"Think whatcha want," Aidan snarls. "But yer ma was

nothin' but a whore. She spread her legs for whoever looked her way. She was weak, just like you. Yer not gonna hurt my—"

Aidan never gets to finish his sentence because without a second thought, I loop my fingers through my brass knuckles and silence him for good.

I connect with his jaw so hard, a tooth dislodges and somersault's to the floor. But it's not enough. I hit his cheeks, his temple, until his face is slathered in blood. Hitting under his jaw, his head cracks into the wall with a ferocious thud.

Panting, I flex my fingers, appreciating the flesh and blood coating my knuckles. Aidan's chin flops to his chest with a wet squelch, a trickle of bloody spittle trickling from his mouth as he attempts to breathe. There is one last thing he needs to do before he stops—breathing, that is.

Unlocking his phone, I scroll through his contacts until I reach Liam's number. Gripping Aidan's hair, I yank his head back and sneer, "Yer gonna tell yer nephew that everythin' is beezer. That I can be trusted."

"Why would I do that?" he pants, peering at me through one swollen eye. The other has been perforated.

"To save yer wains," I reply, promising him that no harm will come of them. And I mean it. "I only want my revenge on those who deserve it. When they're grown, if they want the same thing, A'll give them the chance.

"It's only fair—an eye for an eye." No pun intended.

"Yer word means nothin' to me," he wheezes, his chest

rattling with every uneven breath he takes.

"Then, the alternative is I'll take you to yer house and ya can watch me kill yer family…just how you made me watch mine."

Aidan doesn't have a choice. He is to sacrifice himself to save his family. It'll be the only honorable thing he'll ever do in his lifetime.

Dialing Liam, I put the phone out in front of Aidan, and when Liam answers, I wait for Aidan to make his choice.

"The cute hoor did it," he says, surprising me with his acting skills. "It's taken care of. We can trust him."

"Grand. Why're ye so breathless?" he asks, and I arch a brow at Aidan, hinting he's to try harder.

"I got a diddy in ma gob."

I scrunch up my nose because now he's just being disgusting.

Liam laughs loudly. "I am in me wick! What'll Aunt Fia say?"

"Act the jig if she asks, lad," Aidan replies. "I'm gonna take a couple of days off. I'm jacked."

"Aye, good idea. Call me when yer done with yer floozy." Liam seems to think his uncle's adultery is something to laugh about.

"Good on ya," Aidan says, flinching as he shifts.

He suddenly quietens because he realizes that this is the last conversation he's to ever have with his nephew. If I cared, I'd let him live, but I don't.

"Talk to ya later then, Uncle."

"All right, bye."

Liam hangs up, none the wiser, while Aidan sniffs, accepting this for what it is.

I want to watch him suffer, but the truth is, he is only a small fish in a big pond, and honestly, looking at his face only a mother could love, I want this done. I know he isn't the one who slit my ma's throat or unlocked the wardrobe.

That fucker was tall. I remember that much.

But that doesn't mean Aidan's reckoning has been deferred. He's just a taste of what's to come.

"My brother's gonna kill ya. Yer nothin'," he spits, not begging for his life, which I have respect for. "Yer nothin' but a Kelly."

Whistling, I mock, "Are ye lonely? Is this how ya make friends?"

It doesn't matter that he hasn't revealed who the other two men were. I'll find out, just as I found him. There are no coincidences in our world. My ma was slain because she was lost to a life that showed no mercy.

Connor Kelly may as well have wielded that knife because Ma's fate was decided the moment they met.

Gripping Aidan's chin, I tilt his head back and examine him closely. "I don't know who I am," I confess. "But what I do know is that I'm gonna enjoy killin' ya."

His Adam's apple bobs as he swallows, the first sign that

he's scared.

I want to humiliate him, just how he did to my ma, and someone like Aidan—someone who called me a molly 'cause I wear this warpaint with pride—would be utterly disgraced if I used him as a canvas before I slit his throat.

Turning around, I see Cian and Rory standing by Ronan. He is having a complete cack attack at what's headed his way. I'll deal with him later. Grabbing my paints from the ground, I smile when Aidan groans.

"This face," I share, rubbing my fingers into the white paint and mixing it with the red blood on my hands. "This is the face *you* created when I was locked in the wardrobe watchin' ya rape and humiliate my mum.

"I know it wasn't you who slit her throat," I state with poise as I slather his face in white paint. When he tries to move, I grip his chin. "I also know y'll not tell me who did. But that's all right...I already know."

"Ya know nothin'," he sneers, baring his teeth when I ensure I've covered every part of his face.

"Ach, I'm pretty sure yer brother was the one. The third fucker, though. Tell me who he is, and I'll kill ya quick."

"I don't rat, so go ahead and kill me," he spits, and fair balls to him for not being a grass. "Ya have no idea who yer fightin'. This is bigger than ya can ever guess. Yer life is over. Done. My family will hunt ya. Ya have no idea what's coming for ya!" He looks ridiculous, threatening me when he looks like Casper the

Friendly Ghost.

Stepping back, I smirk at my handiwork. His face is a blank backdrop for me to create carnage. Tossing the white container over my shoulder, I rub circles in the black face paint with my fingers and fill in the blanks.

"Imagine that?" I mock, drawing a black line from his cheek to his mouth. "Me afraid of a Doyle? Too bad I'm not."

Once he wears a big, painted grin, I tap my chin, unhappy with what I'm seeing. The artist in me strives for perfection, and that'll only be achieved with a few minor adjustments. Yanking the knife out from Aidan's palm, I elbow him in the face to stop any last-ditch efforts to escape. As he gasps for air, I grab his lips and slice them off.

They drop to the floor with a plop.

I coat my finger in the blood pouring from his wound, and strike down his forehead once—one down, two to go.

"Do ya not think that's better, lads?" I ask Cian and Rory, admiring a lipless Aidan as he incoherently muffles for help.

"Fucking class," Cian exclaims, clapping in approval.

"A masterpiece," Rory agrees, and places a blade in my hand. "But I think one more thing is needed."

Turning over my shoulder, I look at my friend and nod in both agreement and thanks. This isn't his fight. This vendetta has nothing to do with him or Cian, but here they are, and I know they'll never leave my side.

It doesn't matter what surname I bear; these two lads will

always be the family I belong to.

Opening the butterfly knife, I slip my fingers through the knuckle guard and the five-inch blade becomes an extension of my hand. Aidan has dropped to his knees as the fight in him has conceded defeat. He commences the Lord's Prayer—as best he can without any lips.

"Our Father who art in heaven, hallowed be thy name. Thy kingdom come…"

"Thy will be done on earth, as it is in heaven," I conclude, walking behind his praying stance. I grip his hair, yank back his head, press the blade against his throat, and sweep across it brutally.

The sticky warmth coating my hand thaws the chill from my bones, and for the first time in a long time, there is silence. Aidan gurgling on his blood is the only sound filling the still room as I absorb what I just did.

I killed.

Releasing Aidan, he flops onto his stomach, blood pooling around him as he wheezes in his last breaths of life. I stand over him, knife in hand, watching and waiting until eventually, he simply stops being. Filling my lungs with air, I exhale slowly, savoring this moment as it has set a benchmark for things to come.

I use my foot to turn him onto his back and peer down at the painted, bloody mess. I feel absolutely nothing.

Cian and Rory stand on either side of me, also examining

the carnage before them. This is the beginning of the end.

"What do we do with him?" Rory asks.

I lift my shoulders, untroubled. "We leave him someplace where his family will eventually find him."

"D'ya not think we should hide the body?"

"What for? I want them to find him," I declare. "I want them to see he entered the afterlife baring the scars on his face which are carved onto my soul."

I want the Doyles to know someone is after them. I want them to know that they're next. I didn't just kill Aidan—I tortured and humiliated him, just like he did to my ma. This is personal, and I want every Doyle to know that.

"What of Ronan?" Cian questions. "What are the Doyles wantin' our gear for? They've got their own. I don't understand it."

Looking at Ronan, I know he won't tell us anything because he doesn't know anything. He's merely a pawn; all of us are.

"I don't know. But I'll find out."

"Do we tell the aul' lads about him?" Rory asks.

Ronan whimpers, begging for mercy when he deserves none for what he's done. But he's more valuable to me alive than dead.

Shaking my head calmly, I reply, "Naw. We do not. 'Cause of them, Ronan and Nolen thought they could get away with this. We don't tell them anythin'. What we do is *their* job…it's time we claimed back our kingdom, boys."

TEN

PUNKY

Someone is in my room.

Without thought, I spring up and reach for the gun in the top drawer of my bedside table. But when I hear who it is, I halt.

"Ack, ya won't be needin' that, cub."

Uncle Sean sits in the chair by my bedside, reading the morning paper. He is untroubled by the fact that I was seconds away from shooting first and asking questions second.

Running a hand through my snarled hair, I sit up against the bedhead, indicating if he wants to speak, then better he does so now. I'm still gutted he lied to me for all these years. I know he thought he was protecting me, but I'd have preferred the truth.

"Are ya still angry with me?" he asks, lowering the paper and looking at me over the rims of his glasses.

"No." My short response is hardly convincing.

"When yer older, y'll—"

But I don't want to hear his excuses.

"Spare me the fucking lecture." Kicking off the blankets, I stand, hinting I'm not interested in continuing this conversation. But Uncle Sean won't let this go.

"Please, Punky, I'm sorry. It's done, so it is. No matter what, y'll always be my blood."

And we'll find that out for certain once I get a paternity test sorted.

A blood test is out of the question, but that doesn't deter me. It means I just need to be creative as there are other ways to get someone's blood, like breaking their nose. I need anything that has Connor's DNA on it, so I plan on getting a sample of his saliva and hair as well.

"Oh, happy fucking days." I sarcastically smirk.

Uncle Sean sighs, and even though it upsets me to see him this way, I've got other things to deal with.

We flipped a coin—heads, we do Ronan in. Tails, he lives.

It was tails.

But he left Dublin barely alive as it was a warning of things to come if we ever saw him again. He said he acted alone, but we don't believe him, which is why we're suspicious of everyone. Until we can confirm everyone is with us, they're all the enemy.

Uncle Sean cannot know that we plan on giving our operation an overhaul because he'll stop me. Just as he didn't tell me the truth about my ma, he will want to protect me for the rest of my life. But I'm grown, and I don't need him protecting me.

I can do that myself.

"If yer done havin' a face like a Lurgan spade, don't forget the party. It's in a few hours."

Oh, fuck.

I completely forgot about Connor's fifteenth wedding anniversary.

It's going to be a proper affair because Chief Constable Moore—among other people of "importance"—will be attending. This is Connor's way of appearing like every normal Joe Soap, while working over the people he wants in his corner.

Connor doesn't do anything just cause. There is always an ulterior motive.

"Quit yer yackin', I'll be there," I reply with half a smile.

Uncle Sean smirks, but it's strained. He knows we've got a long way to go before we're sound again. "Have ya not heard about Ronan?"

"I can't say that I have," I reply calmly.

"We think he's been stealin'," he explains, taking off his glasses and rubbing the bridge of his nose. He's knackered. "But no bother."

"Ack, it sickens ye. He's probably long gone by now, though."

I need to send him off course. No one can know that he's gone for good.

Uncle Sean nods. "Aye, yer right. Yer some pup. Smarter than me when I was yer age."

Laughing, I open my wardrobe and see my suit hanging up, freshly pressed. I'll thank Amber when I see her later. "That was some time ago, aul' lad."

"All right, ya smart-arse. I'll see ya later." He playfully slaps the back of my head, before leaving to no doubt help with the *fur coat, no knickers* festivities inside.

Once he's gone, I exhale, that was close. No one can know about Ronan. Rory, Cian, and I will deal with this our own way because our fathers have dropped the ball. For the men to think they can go behind our back is a sure sign they're not afraid of the repercussions.

I want to rule with respect, not cruelty, but it seems we might not have a choice. I can't shake this feeling that we have a mole in our midst. What Aidan said has been playing on my mind since he said it.

"Ya have no idea who yer fightin'. This is bigger than ya can ever guess."

What does that mean? My guess is that it's the *Doyles* were fighting, seeing as they're the enemy. So why would he phrase it like that? Like I'm supposed to guess who's behind the secret door. I need to speak to the boys about it because it doesn't make sense.

I shower and get ready for tonight's façade. I wonder what Connor has up his sleeve to impress the chief constable? I'm already done.

Looking at my phone, I'm tempted to send Babydoll a message. I don't know what I'd say. Sorry for being such a bastard would be a good place to start. But I can't do that. My life is a fucking mess right now.

It's best I leave her be because I have absolutely nothing to offer her. But that doesn't mean I won't do everything in my power to find out who hurt her. They're going to pay. Her wounds, they were inflicted by someone whipping her.

Such a barbaric act. I don't understand why or who would do such a thing. But I don't know anything about Babydoll, and that is troubling, especially now. I need to treat everyone like the enemy.

Looking at my reflection in the bathroom mirror, it's amazing what a mask can hide. I look like everyone else, but I'm not. I smile, laugh when prompted, but it's all just an illusion to make people feel safe because when they do, they lower their guards and then I can see *their* true faces.

I must be ruthless because that's the only way I will succeed.

Once I'm dressed, I decide to head to the main house and see the twins. I doubt they'll be allowed out of their rooms as Connor will see them as just getting in the way. I can hear distant voices up ahead as the house will be a panic of people, not wishing to upset the hosts.

Amber and the twins are in the backyard, flying a kite. She places her hand over her eyes to shield the sun and when she sees me, she waves.

My mum's gardens once thrived here. Her roses grew tall, but they're no more. Fiona made sure of it when she dug up the gardens and left nothing in their place. She just wanted to destroy something that was my ma's.

I walk over, smiling when I see the twins fighting over whose turn it is.

"Y've already had yer turn," whines Hannah, as Ethan tongues the corner of his mouth in concentration. "I'll tell Da!"

"Ya will not," I say with a smile when I'm within earshot. "What did I tell ya about dobbin' on yer brother?"

When Hannah sees me, she smirks and throws herself in my arms. "He's being a dick," she states, while I try not to laugh.

"And what did I tell ya about usin' bad language?"

She wraps her arms around my neck, hugging me tightly. "I've heard ya say worse."

I look at Amber who shrugs with a grin as we both know she's right.

Pulling Hannah out at arm's length, I see her pink dress has grass stains all over it. "I like yer dress," I say, kissing her forehead.

"I hate it," she argues, pursing her lips together. "I want to wear trousers, but Amber said Ma wanted me to wear this."

Of course, Fiona did. They have to look like the perfect

family. I'm surprised she allowed me to attend, seeing as I ruin her charade. But Dad wants me there to be a lickarse with the chief constable. He's away in the head if he thinks that's happening.

"Best listen to Amber then. She helped dress me too."

Amber smiles, brushing a piece of hair behind her ear.

"Yer turn!" Ethan yells to Hannah, but she shakes her head.

"I wanna stay with Punky."

"Naw, I wanna," Ethan wails, losing interest in the kite as it sails to the grass.

Amber swoops forward and saves it from becoming a tangled mess as Ethan drops the spool and comes running over to me. I bend and pick him up as well.

The twins are small, so I'm able to hold them both at the same time. It won't be much longer however until that changes. I wonder who they'll grow into. I can only hope someone not like me.

"Is yer face all right?" Ethan asks, examining the fading bruises. I heal quickly, but it's been a tough week.

"I'm all right. Don'tcha trouble yerself."

"We heard Mum tellin' Da yer a dirty wee hallion," says Hannah, awful upset as she narrows her eyes. "That one day, yer gonna end up dead like yer ma. She said she wouldn't cry. We don't wantcha to die, Punky. We'll protect ya. A'll never let anyone hurt ya."

Amber averts her gaze, hinting she heard this too.

The twins are too small to realize what that means, and I want to keep it that way. The longer they hold onto their innocence, the better for them. I wish I'd had that luxury.

"I'm not going anywhere, rascals," I promise, kissing their cheeks. "And it's my job to protect youse. Okay?"

They both nod, but I can see the fear in their eyes. Fiona has always been jealous of my relationship with the twins. I have no doubt I'm in her prayers; prayers that I leave and never return.

"She said yer a Catholic lover. What's that mean?" Hannah asks, always curious.

When I see Fiona headed our way, I narrow my eyes but try to act calm. "Don't ya be troublin' yerself with that."

"Hannah!" she cries out. "You're jokin' me? Look at yer dress! It's ruined."

Hannah clings to me tighter.

When I make no attempts at putting them down, Fiona arches an unimpressed brow. "Something troublin' ya?"

"Aye, ya could say that. Cover yer ears and sing yer favorite nursery rhyme," I instruct the twins, who immediately do as they're told.

I would say Fiona looks scared, but thanks to all the Botox she's had, I can't distinguish what her facial features are anymore.

"Don'tcha *ever* talk about me in front of the twins again," I calmly order, holding onto them tightly. "What I do is my business. Stay outta it 'cause y've no idea whatcher talkin' about."

She pulls back her shoulders. "I was only consolin' yer father. He was troubled about the rosary—"

"Imagine that, a world where I give a fuck what you and Connor were doin'," I interrupt, not interested in hearing her gurn. "And don'tcha ever mention my mum again."

Fiona's lips pull into a thin line. "Yer father will be hearin' about this."

Laughing, I state coolly, "There ya go again, thinkin' I give a fuck."

"Ack, y've got no respect."

"For ye? No, I do not."

Fiona's nostrils flare as she's realized this is a losing battle. We've never gotten along, and that'll never change.

"Come," she orders the wains, gesturing they're to get down. "I want ya to say hello to Pastor Diffin."

They look at me, their singing growing quiet as I lower them to the ground. "Go with yer ma."

Both of them screw up their faces but do what they're told.

Fiona roughly snatches their hands. "We're payin' ya to work, not talk," she snaps at Amber, who pulls in her lips, embarrassed.

Fiona storms off, kids in hand, leaving Amber and me alone.

When she's gone, Amber exhales loudly. "She's insufferable."

"I'd have said she's a fucking bitch, but that'll do."

Amber turns to me, a smile breaking out across her cheeks.

"The twins shouldn't have told you that. I'm sorry."

"What are ya apologizin' for? You didn't say what was overheard."

"I know, but I don't like seeing you upset," she says softly.

"It's gonna take a lot more than that to upset me, doll. But thanks."

She wrings her hands in front of herself, appearing to want to say something. I don't know what's going on. "Punky, I wanted to ask you…um, this is really awkward."

"What is it?" I ask, suddenly worried. "Has the aul' lad done somethin' to ya?"

"What?" she questions, before shaking her head quickly when she realizes what I mean. "No, nothing like that. I just…I was wondering if you'd like to get a drink sometime?"

My worry soon turns to surprise. This is the first time Amber has openly asked me to do something with her. And I know she doesn't mean as friends.

I like Amber, I would be an eejit not to. But we just don't… click that way.

"I'm flattered, I really am, but I can't," I say, not wanting to lead her on. "I've got a lot on, and it's not fair—"

But she doesn't buy it.

"Is it because of that girl? Poppy?"

I want to deny it, but I don't want to lie to Amber. She's wild craic, and I don't want to insult her that way. But she catches me off guard.

"You don't think her accent is…off?"

"Off?" I question, unsure what she means by that.

She nods, chewing her bottom lip. "She doesn't sound like she's from London. I was in London for six months before I came here, and trust me, I know what a Londoner sounds like."

I haven't noticed anything strange, but I suppose that could be because I've been trying to work out what her motives are.

"Where d'ya think she's from then?"

Amber weighs over my question. "I don't know, but what Londoner says y'all?"

And the mystery just continues to grow…

"I better go inside. I'm sure Fiona has met her quota for doting mother of the year already." She leans forward and kisses my cheek. "Be careful, Punky. I don't want to see you get hurt."

She leaves me standing in the middle of the yard, pondering over what she just said.

I don't want to believe Amber, but she wouldn't lie to me just to spite Babydoll. If she believes something is weird, then it's worth investigating. But how do I do that? I know nothing about Babydoll. It's like she just appeared from nowhere.

"What's the craic?"

Turning, I see Rory and Cian walking toward me. They're also in suits and looking as uncomfortable as me.

"Was that Amber?" Cian asks, looking in the direction of where she's walking.

"Aye, it was."

"Somethin' troublin' ya?" Rory questions, sensing my mood.

"Still no luck findin' anythin' out about Babydoll?"

"Naw," he replies, shaking his head. "It's weird. I can't find much under that name."

"Maybe that's not her name then," Cian says with no real thought as he's still looking at Amber. But Rory and I turn to one another, thinking the same thing.

I never thought this was a possibility because the Clerys confirmed she worked for them. And what little information was online all pointed that she was who she said she is. But with what Amber just shared, I'm beginning to think Babydoll is hiding a lot more than I originally thought.

"I tell a lie, yer not a complete eejit," Rory teases, while Cian gives him the middle finger.

We decide to get this over with as we have some investigating to do. Some of our "colleagues" are coming, and there is nothing like a wee bit of alcohol to loosen the lips. We have to be on our A game, so no going on the piss for us, which is a shame because dealing with this sober is going to be brutal.

The house is chaos, with countless people rushing around, ensuring everything is in place. They know what happens when Connor Kelly is unhappy. The castle sparkles, and I wonder how many hours Fiona's slaves were forced to scrub every corner of this place.

"With all this, y'd think our aul' lads knew what they were

doin," Rory whispers, whistling when he looks at the hanging crystal chandelier.

And he's right.

This wealth was built on blood money, and our fathers believed they were untouchable. But the last few days have proven otherwise.

"I've been thinkin'," Rory says, keeping his voice low as we casually walk down the hallway. "About what Aidan said. I think we have a double agent working for us."

"Aye, I was thinkin' the same thing," I reply with a nod. "Nolen and Ronan were workin' for the Doyles, but who put them in contact? They don't have the brains or the bollocks to do that themselves. They're small fry. We need the whole fuckin' ocean."

Rory hums in agreement. "And why? What are the Doyles offerin' them? To consort with Catholics, it's sacrilegious. Not just for us Protestants, but if other Catholics found out that the Doyles were dealin' with us…they'd be shunned. This is bigger than we thought."

"Can ya ask yer uncle Sean?"

"What should I ask him, Cian? How's it hangin', Uncle? Who'd ya think would betray us? Oh, and I've gone into Dublin in hopes of tryin' to infiltrate the Doyles."

"Aye right," he says, while Rory laughs. "It was just an idea. Yer uncle wouldn't lie to ya."

But as soon as the words leave him, he realizes the mistake

he made. Uncle Sean *has* lied to me and will do so again if he thinks I'm getting too close. This is why we need to do this on our own.

When we come to the family portrait bar me, both Rory and Cian stop, needing a closer look. "That fuckin' bitch," Rory says, shaking his head.

"Aye, she has a face like a baten bear." Cian gags, shuddering.

A waiter walks by with a bottle of champagne. Cian stops him. "I'll be havin' that. Cheers."

Cian doesn't give him a chance to argue and snatches the bottle from his hands. He legs it away from us, scared.

A photographer takes our picture. It's a little over the top, but it seems Fiona has gone all out.

"I think we deserve a wee drink." Before I can protest— considering we agreed not to drink—Cian shakes the bottle rigorously, aims it at the painting, and pops it open, showering the canvas with expensive champagne. "Much better."

Rory chuckles while I tilt my head to the side, admiring the adjustment. It looks class.

"Away ta fuck," Rory mumbles under his breath. I have no idea why, until I peer in the direction he's looking and almost rub my eyes in case I'm seeing things.

"Who's thon?" Cian asks, the remnants of the bottle trickling all over the floor.

"Babydoll," I say, not answering his question, but rather, speaking my disbelief aloud.

Standing down the hallway is Babydoll, a silver tray in hand. A man speaks to her and she nods, like she's taking note of his instructions. Is she working this event?

"*That's* her?" Cian whistles as we all stare.

Rory has seen her picture on social media, so he recognized her, but no picture can capture how beautiful she really is. She is innocent, but fierce all in the same breath. It doesn't make sense, nor does her being here.

Amber's warning plays over in my mind, and I push aside the happiness I feel at seeing her because I must stick to my guns—everyone is the enemy until I can prove otherwise.

Inhaling deeply, I dig my hands into my pockets and walk to where she stands. When she realizes she's not alone, she lifts her eyes, and as they lock with mine, her mouth parts. I try not to think about how those lips felt when I claimed them as mine—wild craic, that's how.

"How's it goin', wee doll?"

She rolls her eyes. "It was great until about five seconds ago."

She attempts to push past me, but I sidestep, blocking her exit. It seems to be our go-to move. "Ach, that's not nice."

"I wasn't trying to be nice," she snaps, just turning me on further.

She has every right to be ragin'. The last time we were together, I was a fucking bastard to her, but if only she knew why. The reasons seem to evade me, however, because seeing her now, all I want to do is beat my own arse for being such a prick.

"Hi, I'm Cian." He offers his hand, which Babydoll shakes.

"Rory." He waves from a distance.

I don't know what to say or do as I've never been in this position before. I've never been interested in anyone as I am with Babydoll.

She clears her throat, clearly uncomfortable. "Your father isn't paying me to chat, so I better go."

I hate that she's waiting on these fuckers, so I ask, "How much is he payin' ya?"

"That's none of your business."

Cian snorts, awful amused with Babydoll's smart mouth.

Digging into my pocket, I retrieve my wallet and pull out six hundred pounds. "This enough?"

When I offer it to her, Cian groans, shaking his head.

She steps back, her mouth ajar. "Are you fucking serious? I don't need or want your charity. I work for my money. I don't have the luxury of everything being served to me on a silver platter—literally. Now, if you'll excuse me…kindly fuck off."

She bumps her shoulder into mine as she pushes past me, offended. When she's gone, I look at Rory and Cian, confused.

"Ach, that went downhill awful quick," Cian says, doing a poor job of concealing his grin.

"Really, Punky?" Rory asks, eyebrow cocked. "Ya may as well have called her a millbeg."

"What?" I put the money into my pocket, suddenly feeling scundered.

"It's true," Cian butts in. "Really sorry, but the fuck? Why would ya think that was a good idea?"

"'Cause I don't want her servin' these arseholes. She's better than that," I argue, still not seeing what the big deal is. "I was trying to be…nice."

Cian slaps my back playfully. "Maybe try being a little less patronizin' next time," he suggests, smirking. "She doesn't strike me as the type of girl who appreciates charity."

"Charity?" I scoff. "I did no such thing. I offered her money—" But I stop midsentence as I realize what I just did. "Fuck."

I meant well, but the boys are right. I may as well have flashed my wealth in her face because six hundred pounds is nothing to me, but to others, it's a lot. I insulted her by trying to be considerate.

"This is why I don't do nice," I say, running a hand down my face.

"If that was yer attempt at being nice—"

"I'll knock yer melt in if ya want to see nice," I interrupt Cian, who bursts into laughter.

All laughter is long forgotten however when Connor walks down the hallway. "There y'are," he says, adjusting his black bow tie. "The chief constable has arrived."

"And?" I challenge, not jumping to command.

Connor pauses from rearranging his too tight tie and looks at Cian and Rory. "Yer fathers are lookin' for ya."

This is a not so subtle hint that they're to leave.

Nodding discreetly, I give them the okay that I'll be fine. They both leave, knowing better than to argue with Connor.

Once they're away, Connor steps close so no one can earwig. "Tonight is very important. Don't fuck it up."

"Aye," I smartly reply, folding my arms. "It's the day ya married the love of yer life, so ya did."

"Quit yer gurnin'. I won't have ye runnin' yer smart mouth, ruinin' this," he warns, not appreciating my sarcasm. "I don't need to remind ya what happens if we make an enemy of the chief constable."

The chief constable should be the least of his worries. He needs to sort out his men first because it doesn't matter who's on our side if we don't have a side. But that's how arrogant he is. He thinks everyone is blinded by his bullshit.

"I'll not tell ya again."

He leads the way, expecting me to follow, and I do 'cause the quicker I get this done, the sooner I can find Babydoll and apologize. Guests greet us as we walk through the castle, talking utter bollocks, but I nod and smile, pretending to give a fuck.

Connor's ability to shit talk still amazes me because you'd think he cared if you didn't know any better. When the chief constable, and who I'm presuming is his wife, appear up ahead, Connor quickly excuses himself and casually makes a beeline for them.

He gestures that a waiter is to follow him, which is my opportunity.

"Chief Constable Moore," he says, snaring two glasses of champagne from the server's tray, offering them to the chief constable and his wife. "And you must be Mrs. Moore."

Both accept the glasses, but I can immediately see the chief constable doesn't appreciate lickarses.

"Mrs. Moore is Donovan's mother. I'm Lana," his wife says, extending her hand, which Connor kisses the back of.

Reaching for my own glass, I throw it back in one gulp, needing to wash the disgust from my bake. I notice Donovan watching me closely. This is the first time he's seen me, but no doubt, he's heard a lot about me.

I'm known for being a bad wee rip, and that's why the peelers have left me be, but I think that's about to change. Donovan Moore is no friend. He is foe.

"This is my son, Puck Kelly."

Smiling without enthusiasm, I grab another glass of champagne, not interested in making small talk. It seems Donovan feels the same way.

"I know who he is," he says, sipping his drink.

"Ach, I'm flattered," I reply smartly, while Connor glares at me.

"I'd love to speak with ya later on," Connor says, wishing to change the subject.

"Grand," Donovan replies, not fooled by Connor's charms. "How's business then?"

Connor smiles, but it's strained. "Always busy in the manufacturin' business."

That's his cover story. That the Kellys earn what we do because Connor is the CEO of a company that manufactures aluminum casting products for the automotive industry. This is how we're able to import and export our product—which has nothing to do with cars—without detection.

Everyone knows it's bullshit, because although this business does exist, it makes little to no money operating legally. It's just a front, and it's worked until now.

Connor reaches for a glass of champagne, clearly sensing this for the dog's dinner that it is. When he takes a mouthful, I zero in on the glass because I want it.

Thankfully, Cian's da appears, who Donovan seems to take a liking to more than Connor. When Connor places the empty glass on a passing waiter's tray, I don't bother excusing myself and follow the waiter through the room.

When he turns the corner, headed for the kitchen, I stop him. "I'll be havin' this."

I don't give him a chance to ask why I need an empty glass as I walk away with Connor's glass in hand. I head toward the bathroom and lock the door when I'm inside.

Opening the vanity drawer, I reach for the swab and rub over the rim to collect as much of Connor's saliva as I can. Once done, I drop the swab into the specimen jar and screw the lid on tight. One down, two to go.

Leaving the glass on the vanity, I open the door and what I see has me wishing I didn't leave it behind as I'd have used it to gouge out the eyeball of the fucker who has his hands all over Babydoll.

"What's goin' on here?" I coolly ask, walking toward the ballbag who is definitely a peeler.

"Mind yer business," he snaps, looking over Babydoll's head to address me.

"This *is* my business," I contest. "And soon it'll be yer hand I'll be breakin' if ya don't let her go."

Babydoll turns over her shoulder to look at me as the fucker has a hold of her wrist. She looks worried, but not scared as she yanks herself free.

"Do ya know who I am, ya dirty wee hallion?" he threatens, puffing out his chest.

"I don't give a fuck who ya are. Touch her again and y'll know who I am."

"I know who ye are, ya wee blurt."

"Dead-on," I mock. "Then we don't need any introductions."

Babydoll looks between us, chewing her lip.

I stand my ground, daring this bastard to fight me, but he realizes the consequences are not worth it. "Ack, have yer slut. Yer welcome to her."

He shoves her into the wall, and just as she's about to

advance and give him an earful, I beat her to the punch—literally. I elbow him in the nose before making good on my promise of breaking his hand.

He howls, his bravado quick to break, like his nose and hand.

Taking a hold of Babydoll's hand, I quickly lead us down the hallway and through the kitchen so we can exit out the back door. Once outside, I let her go.

"What happened?"

"Nothing," she replies, catching her breath. "Just a sleazy old man who wouldn't take no for an answer. I can take care of myself."

"Ach, it sure looked that way," I sarcastically state, shaking my head.

"I don't understand you," she reveals sincerely.

"I don't understand myself either."

She mulls over my comment, her anger toward me simmering when she reads the truth behind my admission.

"I'm sorry for insultin' ya."

"Which time?" she quips, folding her arms.

She isn't making this easy for me, and she shouldn't. I did a shitty thing. Well, many shitty things.

"I don't know what it is about ye, I just…ya make me… feel."

"Feel what?" she questions, but she's misunderstood.

"Make me feel…full stop," I clarify. "I can't get my head

around it. I was taught feelin's make ya weak. And they do. I was full of feelin' when—"

"When what?" she coaxes as I pause, realizing what I almost shared.

But what would happen if I did share my darkest secret with her? Would it change anything? The answer is no.

"When I watched my ma being killed. I was so full of feelin' that I didn't do anythin' when I should have done more."

Babydoll covers her mouth with a trembling hand. "Oh God, that's h-horrible. That's why the brooch means so much to you? Because it's the last thing you have of hers?"

She should not know me this well, but there are a lot of should nots where Babydoll is involved.

"Aye, ya could say that."

"How old were you?"

"I was five."

Babydoll shakes her head, processing what I just shared. Something which has burdened me for so long suddenly feels a little lighter because it's not a secret any longer.

"Is that what your face paint means?"

She isn't thick; she understands the significance of it.

"Three men raped and killed my ma and because of them, that mask allows me to accept what I must do."

"And what's that?" she asks, stepping closer to me.

"It's what I did to some fucker last night."

She gasps, eyes wide as she doesn't need me to draw a

diagram. She understands I took a man's life and feel nothing for doing so.

"You know who they are?"

Nodding slowly, I reply, "I do. Brody Doyle is goin' to pay for everythin' he took away from me."

I realize she has no idea who that is, but I suddenly want her to know.

"This man, he's the one who killed your mum?"

"Aye. I killed his brother last night, and it's only a matter of time before I come for him."

Silence.

Babydoll pales, her eyes focused in the distance. I cannot read her expression.

"Poppy?" I ask, using her name for the first time.

But she leaves me speechless when she leans forward, stands on her toes, and whispers into my ear, "The police are going to raid your home. They're looking for drugs, guns, anything that can bring you down. You have to get rid of it. All of it. Now.

"And call me Babydoll."

Pulling away slowly, I attempt to deal with her brutal confession. Is she telling the truth? But the better question here is, how does she know?

Angrily shoving her against the wall, a panicked gasp escapes her as I lower my face to hers. Her chest rises and falls frantically. Her fear is a drug to me. "If yer lyin', so help me God…"

"I'm not," she firmly replies, not intimidated by my anger.

And I believe her.

I slam my fist against the bricks, and she flinches but doesn't cower. She understands what she's just done by sharing this with me.

Gripping her chin between my thumb and finger, I arch back her neck and snarl, "Then God help ya."

Before she has a chance to speak, I slam my mouth against hers, stealing her breath just as she does with mine. She fists my shirt, pulling me toward her as we kiss without apology, not caring who sees. Her smell and taste are like a punch of adrenaline, and I growl possessively because she is mine.

Without a doubt, Babydoll has an ulterior motive. I doubt our meeting was coincidental either. Babydoll is a liar...but I don't fucking care.

I kiss her hard, not caring that she can scarcely breathe. All I care about is marking her like a caveman because this wee liar, this wee thief is mine...mine...mine.

She loops her arms around my neck, moaning into my mouth as we tease one another, fighting for dominance. She suckles my lip ring, tugging hard with her teeth, before sweeping her tongue along my bottom lip.

Her aggression is what I need, what I want, and I lift her, coaxing her to wrap her legs around my waist. She does, and when her pussy presses against me, memories of when it was last in my mouth, on my tongue assault me, and I almost lose it right where I stand.

But I can't. This is just a taste of what's to come.

Severing our kiss roughly, I'm pleased to see her breathless and writhing in need. Even though she is a liar, and I can't trust a word that comes out of her mouth, I can trust her body's response to me. And I plan on exploiting that to get the truth.

"A'll be seein' ye awful soon, wee doll."

"What are you going to do?"

"The only thing I can do. I need to find my uncle Sean."

"And you trust him?"

With bitter conviction, I confess, "He's the only person I trust."

Her eyes narrow, and her worry is replaced with anger, for she knows what I do; her confession has done nothing to pardon her betrayal. Leaving her against the wall, I run inside, on the hunt for the only person who can help me.

Uncle Sean.

To my knowledge, we don't leave any gear at home, in case something like this happens. But because this has never happened before, I'm worried it's made Connor complacent. He's already a cocky bastard, and the two are not a winning combination.

I see Uncle Sean talking to a pretty woman, but it'll have to wait. The moment he sees me, I gesture with my head that we're to talk in private. He senses the urgency and is over within seconds.

"Don't ask me how I know, but we're about to be raided."

"Are ye havin' a laugh?" he asks, but when he sees I'm far from laughing, he curses and runs a hand through his hair. "Fuck."

He storms away, but I quickly follow because from his response, it's clear if we get raided, we're all going down. He takes the stairs two at a time, profanity spilling from him, and when he kicks open Connor's door, I understand why.

"How could he do this?" he mutters under his breath, fuming at Connor.

Uncle Sean pushes aside the wooden blanket box, and when I see a hole cut into the carpet to make room for a safe, I know things are about to turn to shite. He drops to his knees, punches in a code into an electric panel, and when the door pops open, Uncle Sean shakes his head.

He frantically pulls out brick after brick of white gear. "Flush it!" he orders me while I stand still, unbelieving what I'm seeing. "Punky!"

His scream wakes me the fuck up.

I grab as many bricks as I can and leg it to the en suite, hunting through the drawers for scissors. What I find is Connor's comb, which I slip into my pocket. When I see Fiona's silver nail file, I snare it off the vanity. Flipping open the toilet lid, I stab the nail file into a brick and drag it downward, splitting open the plastic.

Tearing apart the seams, I desperately empty the packet

into the toilet. Once it's gone, I do the same to another brick and then another until I'm done. As I enter the bedroom and see another fifteen bricks, I shake my head.

"Why does the aul' lad have this?" I shout, ragin' that he could be so stupid.

Uncle Sean doesn't answer me. Instead, he gathers as many bricks as he can, and I do the same. As we're in the bathroom, frenziedly flushing the gear, we hear shrieks erupt from downstairs.

She was right. The peelers are here.

"Cub, burn the packets," he orders, gesturing to the bathtub.

I collect all the empty packets which still have traces of drugs inside. Although the gear is gone, this is still evidence. We need all of it gone.

Throwing everything into the tub, I reach for the pack of matches and light one, tossing it onto the plastic. It sets alight instantly, a wee boney. Uncle Sean continues passing me things to burn. I cannot believe Connor could be this stupid.

"How'd ya know?" Uncle Sean asks between flushes. "Who the fuck tipped the peelers off?"

"I can't tell ye." Before he can argue, I add, "Because I don't even understand it myself. But once I do, I swear it, I'll tell ya."

He doesn't press as we have other issues to deal with—like getting rid of the remaining bricks before the peelers bust down the door. I turn on the taps to douse the flames once there is nothing left but black ash, which I push down the drain.

We both sprint into the bedroom to gather the remaining bricks and push the trunk over the safe. Everything looks the way it should.

As Uncle Sean is cutting into the last one, we hear loud voices just outside the door.

"I won't let them take ya. Ya play stupid, ya hear?"

"They already know I'm guilty," I say, appreciating him taking the fall for me. But I won't allow it.

The last of the gear is down the toilet when the door bursts open. Uncle Sean frantically flushes it while I open the window and toss the last packet out. It sails to the ground and gets caught in Fiona's flowering bushes.

Even if the peelers find it, they can't prove it's ours. And even if they do, it's an empty brick. Hardly enough to have us lifted.

Connor storms in with Donovan and two peelers following close behind. When he sees us, standing casually, he arches a brow. Uncle Sean pats himself down, and when he finds his fegs, he offers me one. I take one with a smile.

"We have a warrant to search the property," Donovan says, producing a piece of paper.

Uncle Sean shrugs offhandedly, lighting his feg with a match. "And this couldn't wait until tomorrow?"

"I've called our lawyer," Connor states angrily, no longer interested in being Donovan's friend.

"Why bother? We've got nothin' to hide." Uncle Sean blows

a smoke ring.

"Why does it smell like smoke in here?" asks a peeler, sniffing the air.

Raising my feg, I give him a reason. But Donovan isn't convinced. He peers into the bathtub and although he can see small specks of black ash, that doesn't prove a thing.

"Have ya not heard? One of my men had his hand broken. Ya don't happen to know anythin' about that, I suppose?"

Pretending to think over his question, I eventually shake my head. "I can't say I do."

He knows I'm lying, but with no evidence, he's got nothing.

The peeler won't say what happened because he has two witnesses. If it were only me, he'd have no problem ratting me out, but my response to Babydoll has him guessing she'll tell Donovan the truth.

"Don'tcha be going anywhere," Donovan warns, gesturing to his men that it's time to tear the place apart.

They start in the bedroom, and it's wild craic knowing they're tearing up Fiona's love nest.

"Yer joking me? Ya think this is funny?" Connor says in a low voice when he notices me smiling.

Taking a drag of my feg, before calmly blowing it out, I reply, "Slap it up ye."

Connor advances forward, shoving Uncle Sean aside as he tries to stop him, and slaps my cheek. He doesn't want any blood spilled when the peelers are here, that's why he didn't punch me. But I don't care who's here.

Without hesitation, I punch him square in the jaw.

His head snaps back with a crack, and when I see I've busted open his lip, I inhale, overjoyed.

Two birds, one stone.

"I'm going to check on the twins," I say, butting out the feg in one of Fiona's expensive bars of soap.

He doesn't argue. I've won this war—for now.

With blood coating my knuckles, I walk past the peelers, daring them to stop me. They don't.

The moment I'm out in the hallway, I unfasten my tie and wipe it over my knuckles, soaking up all the blood. Once I've got it all, I place it into my pocket, alongside the comb.

I have everything I need. Saliva. Hair. Blood.

Looks like tonight wasn't a waste, after all.

ELEVEN

Babydoll

He's here.

Before I have a chance to flee, he's on top of me, arm over my throat, pressing us nose to nose. The slither of moonlight peeking in from the curtains illuminates his eyes. They glow, like a hungry predator's and I'm his prey.

"Get off me!" I cry, slapping at his arm. His hold isn't tight, but it's rigid enough that I can't escape.

"I think not." His voice is smooth, dangerous, and in the darkness, it's amplified tenfold. "Awful soon is now, wee doll."

I don't know how Punky found me, but he can't be here. It's not safe…for either of us.

"I think we need to have a talk."

"About what? I told you everything I k-know."

"Bullshit!" he sneers, pushing harder against my neck. "Yer gonna tell me how ye knew about tonight."

"I can't," I pant, squirming beneath him.

"Can't? Or won't?"

"Can't. How'd you know where I live?"

Punky loosens the pressure but doesn't let me go. "Y've got a brass neck on ye like a jockey's bollocks, Baby! I've met no one like ya. Most would be pleadin' for their life, but not you. Yer asking *me* questions instead."

"I told you, I'm not afraid of you," I state with conviction because Punky is the good guy—even if he doesn't believe it.

I'm not making excuses for his behavior because he's done some really shitty things, but so have I. We've both got an agenda, but it seems we'll happily sacrifice that to protect the other. It doesn't make sense. I don't understand why we connect this way, but I feel like I've known Punky my entire life.

I was sent here with an ulterior motive, one I will *never* divulge, but pretending to like him has never been the problem because I like him *too* much. *That's* the problem.

I knew the consequences of telling him that he was going to be raided. But I had to tell him because I was the one who planted those drugs. But I had no other choice. This was just another way to get what they want. That's why I was working at the party.

But when Punky confessed his past, about what *they* did to him, to his mother, I just couldn't do that to him as I knew he would go down too. And now, that choice has fucked everything up beyond repair. But I wouldn't take it back.

I need to find another way to get what I want. And using Punky isn't one of them.

"Connor doesn't let just anyone into the house. The work form ya filled in had all the information I needed."

Shit.

Frantically scanning over everything I wrote on there, I realize my address is the only thing Punky knows.

"I answered yer question, it's time ya answered mine."

"I overheard one of the waiters—"

"Quit yer lyin'!" he exclaims, not buying into my bullshit. "I'll not tell ya again."

"It's the truth!" I cry, twisting madly, desperate to break free.

"What, *who're* ye protectin'?" he asks, putting two and two together.

I stop fighting and turn my cheek, ashamed of the looming tears. I have no right to cry. "I can't tell you, Punky, because if I do...he'll kill me."

Silence.

The room is eclipsed in total darkness, and it's just Punky and me versus the world.

He realizes I'm not being melodramatic. "Who will? For fuck's sake!"

"Do your best," I challenge, my breaths growing panicked.

"You don't understand what's at stake."

"I'm askin' ya to tell me."

"And I'm telling you that I can't."

And this is something I won't budge on. The lives of the people I love most in this world rely on me. Failing isn't an option. I don't trust *him*…but better the devil you know.

"Amber thinks yer accent is off. That ya don't sound like a Londoner."

And that's because I'm not.

I knew she'd be onto me. This is spiraling out of control. "I thought Amber was a nanny, not the FBI."

"Get up."

Before I can ask what's going on, he launches off the bed and pulls back the curtain on the window to let in the moonlight. My eyes adjust to the change in lighting, and I see that he's still in his suit but missing his tie and jacket.

I wonder what happened tonight. The fact he's here means the police didn't find anything. Everyone was escorted from the residence, much to the horror of all the gossipers. The Kellys reputation is notorious for another reason now.

They're no longer untouchable as the chief constable isn't playing by their rules. He's in cahoots with another family.

I won't cower. I didn't get this far being a coward, so I toss aside the blanket and stand angrily, daring Punky to do his best. But his best tests my bravado.

"Those welts on ye, I reckon they were punishment for not

givin' the right answer. They show how hard it is to break ye. I respect that."

I stand perfectly still, watching Punky closely.

"But, wee doll, I'm just as stubborn as you," he warns, interlocking his hands behind his back. "I have an advantage over whoever that fucker was, and that's 'cause I think ye'd like me to punish ye."

A gasp leaves me because…he's right.

Losing control with Punky is a taste of freedom which I've become addicted to. Being shackled against my will with invisible manacles has crushed my very soul. But being with Punky is the only time I feel free.

He is dangerous, vicious, and ruthless, but that just makes me want him all the more. I know he'd never really hurt me. He could, but he won't, and that's because he knows I can hurt him too.

We share an equal playing field, although I have an advantage—I know who's hunting him. They're hunting me, too.

"Cocky much?" I quip, pretending I'm not quivering at the thought.

His grin catches the moonlight, and I remember how utterly sinful he looked with his face slathered in war paint. He scares me…and I like it.

"Only one way to find out. Ya can take that off, or I will."

He's referring to my nightgown.

This is a test. He doesn't know how to break me, so he's trying to scare me instead. But I'm not easily scared.

Without hesitation, I slip the nightgown over my head, and it pools by my feet as I drop it, unapologetically. The darkness helps with my confidence, and I wonder if this is the reason he didn't turn on the light.

We both thrive in the darkness because it's here, where our demons can play.

His unhurried examination of me both excites and terrifies me in the same breath. Every part of me craves his touch. I know what his hands, his mouth, his tongue feel like, and my body wants more.

"Who're ye?" he asks, his confusion, his frustration clear.

"I'm Babydoll," I whisper, happy to be anyone other than me.

"I could force ya to tell me."

"You can try," I challenge, my naked skin prickling with goose bumps.

"Aye, I could," he hums, running his thumb along my bottom lip.

I'm embarrassed at how breathless I am, while Punky's breaths are even and in control.

I know Punky won't hurt me like *they* have. His touch is welcomed, and no matter what he says, I know there's a line he won't cross. But that doesn't mean he won't coerce me to straddle that line until we're both breathless in need.

"Go on then, Puck Kelly. Or are you all talk?"

A low growl echoes deep, and I grin, pleased with the response I elicited from him.

He grips me by the throat and arches my neck back. We're pressed nose to nose when he whispers, "Get on yer knees."

If I had any objection to his demands, I wouldn't have a choice anyway as the hold he has on me is tight. But he doesn't need to force me. I go willingly.

His hand is still around my throat, and he squeezes gently. I swallow deeply, eagerly awaiting what's to come. I'm wet between my thighs. I can't help it. This rough play with Punky turns me on. I know these hands have hurt, they've killed, but when they've touched me, it's been with nothing but affection.

I confuse Punky, and that's because he doesn't know the truth. It's getting harder and harder not to reveal why I'm here.

"What now?" I question, peering up at him from under my lashes.

He lets me go and calmly walks behind me. The darkness conceals the wounds on my back, but I'm certain Punky can still make them out. On a relaxed exhale, he kneels. I want to turn to see what he's doing, but I don't.

"Ye frustrate me, Baby," he states into my ear, his warm breath gliding down my neck. "So it's time I frustrate you."

I gulp, fearful of what's to come.

It merely takes one finger, one simple touch for me to whimper in need when he traces along the column of my neck sluggishly. He can no doubt feel the thrashing of my pulse, echoing the wanton disturbance within my chest.

He trails down my shoulder, then my arm. When he gets to the crease in my elbow, he changes direction and focuses on my stomach. With torturous circles, he caresses my navel, his large hand almost covering my belly whole.

He touches me with purpose, and that's to drive me insane. I discreetly open my legs a little wider in a silent invitation, but Punky merely chuckles in response. My nipples are begging for some attention, as all it would take is for him to shift a little higher. But this isn't about gratification—this is about teaching me a lesson.

"Y'know I will find out who ye are." It's not a question, but rather, a statement.

"I know." My voice quivers, betraying my nerves.

"Tell me and make it easier on yerself." He strokes inches above my pussy, always teasing, always in control.

"Nothing in my life has been easy thus far. And I don't want it to be. I fight for what I want."

"And what's that?" he asks, leaving heated lashes in his wake as he continues stroking me leisurely.

"I just want to protect the people I love," I reveal, surrendering because I want to. I'm sick of fighting him because this is a war I don't want to win.

He hums deeply, before giving me what I want. He rubs two fingers along the seam of my pussy, before sliding them deep inside. Gasping, I sag forward, as the intrusion is a wicked kiss down low. Wrapping an arm around my waist, he anchors me, waiting for me to adjust. He then begins to move.

He fingers me slowly, almost too slow as he's skating close to the edge, denying me the friction my body so desperately wants. When I try to place my hand over his, begging he go faster, he shrugs it away, his husky chuckles warming my ear.

I'm pinned as he's holding me prisoner with both hands.

"Punky," I moan, writhing because he's driving me crazy.

"Aye, wee doll?" He wants me to beg. "Frustratin', is it?"

Biting the inside of my cheek, I don't reply and only hope he'll give in to what we both want as I can feel his hard-on pressed into my back. It pleases me that I can stir this response in him because Punky has mastered the perfect poker face. This, however, proves he's just as turned on as I am.

"I want that too," he shares, sinking his fingers in and out, in and out. "Even though my ma is dead, I'll protect her memory by killin' those who killed her."

He just revealed that he has no qualms killing. His admission should scare me, but it doesn't. It only has me falling harder for him.

The way he touches me, it's like we've met before, like our bodies, our souls have known one another for an eternity. I've been with guys before, but with Punky, it's different. I come alive, and after being numb for so long, I've become addicted to the taste.

He lays a single kiss just behind my ear and the simple action coupled with what he's doing to my body has the scorching knot within my core beginning to unravel.

"I should leave ye be. Yer trouble, I know that. But why can I not?"

He feels it too.

This undeniable pull will surely get us into irreparable trouble, but neither of us seem to care. This feeling liberates us both. I never want it to end.

"We're bad for one another, Punky. One of us will get hurt," I state, moaning when he rubs over my clit. "And that person will be…you."

He scoffs, amused by my claims. "Yer so confident, are ya? I don't get hurt, Baby. I'm the one who causes pain."

To emphasize his point, he begins to finger me relentlessly. I desperately want to come, but he won't permit it. I like and hate his dominance all in the same breath.

"And when I find out who y'are…y'll regret not tellin' me when ya had the chance."

My body is a live wire, demanding a release, and when Punky plays with my clit, I think he's going to give in. But nothing is ever that simple with him.

Rocking my hips, I encourage him to go faster, harder, but just as I gasp, on the cusp of letting go, Punky removes his fingers.

"No!" I cry, slumping forward in desperate anger.

"Imagine that, ye thought we were done," he mocks, his deep voice filled with humor.

"Fuck you," I snap, frustrated in every sense of the word, which causes my accent to slip and reveal what I really am… American.

He said he was going to return the favor and frustrate me—mission accomplished. He broke me, just how he knew he could.

"Ach, Amber was right then." I'm expecting him to push me away and call me out for being the liar that I am, but he doesn't do that.

He grips my chin, roughly tilts my neck back, and kisses the living fuck out of me. The angle is painful, but I don't care. All that matters is this.

Our lips can't keep up with our frantic kisses, and my body is about to explode. I need him to punish me because being an American is just the start of who I am.

"Don't talk about her when you're with me this way," I caution from around his mouth. The relief at being able to expose this small part of myself to him is incredible.

I knew my accent wasn't perfect, but I thought my performing arts degree, which I was halfway through at a community college in Illinois, would have fooled the locals. But because Amber is American, she saw through the bullshit easily.

"Thon shade of green suits ye."

He won. I'm officially frustrated and will do anything to appease this hunger within.

Spinning around so we're pressed chest to chest, I frantically unfasten his buttons. But it's taking too long. My fingers are trembling with impatience. So, without thought, I fist his shirt and split it down the middle. Buttons scatter all along the floor, and I don't regret a thing.

He tosses his now ruined shirt to the side, latching onto my nipple as I moan, fumbling with getting his belt buckle undone. Once it's unfastened, I unbutton his pants and yank down his zipper. The moment I slip my hand down his pants and feel him flesh to flesh, we both moan as the hunger between us just grows.

Punky isn't wearing any underwear, and that just makes him all the more hotter. I grip his shaft and am overwhelmed by his size. I've been with two guys before, but they're a distant memory because I've never felt this desire as I do with Punky.

I commence stroking him, whimpering because it's sensory overload. I'm getting off by the way Punky suckles my breasts, cupping them so he's able to indulge himself full, but the guttural growls erupting from his chest as I jerk him off is the biggest turn-on of all.

Knowing I'm the one provoking that response pleases me immensely. My "mission" was to seduce Punky so I'd be able to infiltrate the Kellys' empire and bring them down—Trojan Horse style. But I don't need to pretend that I want him; to stop wanting him is the problem.

"Don't mistake this for weakness," he growls from around my lips. "If yer a threat...I'll kill you."

"I know you will," I pant, pumping his cock quickly. "But you'll have to catch me first."

A sated moan escapes him as he pumps his hips, desperate for more.

"So yer my enemy then?" he questions, still searching for answers to who I am.

"No, Punky." I moan when he slaps my hand away and yanks me up from the floor.

Without apology, he tosses me onto the bed, where he comes after me. His weight pressed against me is the antidote I need. He doesn't check if I'm ready as he aligns us in a way we both crave. He knows that I am.

And when he slips into me painfully slow, I pant. "You're mine."

He sinks into me, taking my breath away because my confession has done nothing to stop something which was bound to end this way. We're on a collision course, and the explosion will leave no survivors.

When he's sheathed all the way, he halts, allowing me to feel every hardened inch of him. I lock my arms around his nape and arch my back. This shouldn't make sense, but Punky's world has taught me that things don't operate how they would in the "normal" world. One day feels like one hundred because you don't know if it'll be your last, and if that is true, if this betrayal will get me killed, then I intend to march into the afterlife with no regrets.

"Y'll be the death of me, Babydoll. And I do not care."

He begins to move, gripping my chin and slamming his mouth over mine. I can barely breathe, but that's okay. I would happily perish locked this way with a man who robbed me of air the moment we met.

He's not gentle. He sinks into me deeply, his movements quick, and it's everything I want. When I try to caress down his back, he seizes my arms and pins them above my head. With my wrists secured in one hand, he dominates every inch of me, and I surrender because I want to be lost and never found.

His cock fills me full, before he pulls out, only to rock back into me. His brutal strokes shift me up the bed, but I only want more. Wrapping a leg around his waist, I open myself up to him and deepen the angle—I feel him everywhere.

"Oh fuck!" I curse, throwing my head back and squeezing my eyes shut.

Punky tightens the hold around my wrists. "Yer American," he says in disbelief. "What else are ye hidin' from me?"

I moan in response as his strokes grow more frantic, reflecting his anger. He knew I wasn't telling him the entire truth, but to lie about where I'm from, he can guess this will only lead to a bigger deception.

"For a liar, ya feel fucking amazin.'"

I can't speak. Punky owns me—mind, body, and soul.

The animalistic sounds spilling from him just fuel this fire inside me, and when he switches position, I'm seconds away from coming. He comes up on his knees while moving my legs so they rest on his broad shoulders. He does all this while still being rooted deep within me.

He places his arms on either side of me and drives into me intensely. I grasp the sheets, almost tearing them to shreds because this position allows him to dominate while I'm submissive. I know he's done this with intent. As his movements quicken, I grip his muscled arms and pull myself toward him, meeting him thrust for thrust.

He leans over to dominate me further and change the angle to hit me even deeper. I scream in response. The moonlight allows me to see his victorious grin.

This position is brutal as he isn't holding back. I want to come so badly, so I reach down and begin to play with my clit. The pressure combined with what he's doing sends me over the edge. I come hard, crying out as my body thrashes uncontrollably.

The release is so euphoric, it brings tears to my eyes. But as Punky continues driving into me, I know things have just begun.

"That was the first and only time I show ya mercy," he warns with dangerous intent. "Now y'll see who I really am."

My orgasm is slowing, but Punky doesn't let me bask in the

afterglow. He pulls out and flips me over, coaxing me to rest on all fours. Winding my long hair around his fist, he holds on tight as he slams back into me.

My neck is arched back, and I desperately want him to move, but he doesn't. He simply allows me to feel every pulsating inch of him.

"Punky," I beg, wiggling my ass, hinting I want more.

And more I get when he slaps my ass cheek—hard.

I jolt forward with the force, but Punky doesn't let me fall as he grips my waist. I'm held prisoner as he begins to move. He holds me in place, fucking me senseless, and I love every depraved second of it.

His movements are filled with control and punishment because even though I've defied him, he still wants me. He could punish me harshly, forcing me to talk, but he won't, he can't, and that's because he cares about me when we both know that he shouldn't.

I'm not noble. I've lied, cheated, and stolen. And I'll do so again if it means getting what I want.

Letting go of my hair, he grips my throat and squeezes softly. "Yer heart is beatin' so fast, and that's 'cause ye know I could kill ye right now."

"Do it," I challenge, swallowing deeply.

A growl gets caught in his throat as he brutalizes me in the most delicious of ways. "Naw, that'll be too easy. And where's the fun in that?"

His threat isn't empty. Now that I've unintentionally let a small part of me slip, he won't stop until he gathers all the pieces of the puzzle. But I'm hoping what I overheard will help cushion the blow.

After the Kellys' party, I went to see *them* and told them the Kellys had been tipped off. They were fuming, but they had a plan—a plan which I eavesdropped on.

They said someone named Mike was going to be their fall guy. I don't know what he's going to take the fall for, but it seemed to take the heat off Punky. Mike is the key to their devious plans, which means Punky is safe—for now.

Whoever Mike is, I feel sorry for him because they made clear he won't be getting out of this alive. I wonder what he did to be involved with them. But if his sacrifice saves Punky, then it's each man for himself.

He tightens his hold around my neck as he fucks me unapologetically. "I will not stop until I find out who ye are."

As I gasp for air, the knot of pleasure begins to build once again.

This isn't lovemaking; this is raw, carnal, depraved sex, and I've never felt safer or more desired in my entire life.

Punky knows I can ruin him, but he continues to devour my body because we can't stop this. We're powerless. We are each other's enemy, and in no way do we trust one another, but that doesn't seem to matter because good sense is thrown to the wind and given way to…this.

As I'm on the cusp of blacking out, Punky releases his grip and holds my waist with both hands, sinking into me raucously. I can't take in air fast enough, and the urgency has me whimpering because I think I'm going to come—again.

Punky reaches around my hip and commences playing with my clit. I shudder, as it's all too much. My breasts are swinging, my nipples grazing the sheets with Punky's brutal strokes. He's everywhere, and I know I'll never get enough.

I can't handle his carnality any longer, so I collapse, but Punky won't allow the reprieve. He props himself up on one knee while placing his other foot on the floor. He then grips my arm and secures it behind me as he fucks me hard.

I'm half slouched onto the bed, turned onto my side as Punky anchors onto my wrist and hip, controlling and dominating me so I have no other choice but to bend to his demands. I'm floppy, my body Jell-O, but Punky won't stop.

"Had enough?"

"No," I stubbornly cry with my cheek pressed into the mattress.

"I fuck ye like I should hate ye," he breathlessly states, moaning when I rock back on his shaft.

"You should hate me because this means nothing to me," I arrogantly lie. "You're a good lay. That's all."

"Is that right?" He chuckles, not believing my dishonesty. "This has come as a huge relief, ya can imagine, 'cause I wouldn't want ya gettin' attached."

"That won't happen."

"Glad we're on the same page," he says, the slapping of our flesh so erotic, I bite my cheek to stop my pleasured moans. "But I know that yer lyin'. Ye may want to hate me, but yer body is tellin' me otherwise. This warm, wild body which fits around my cock perfectly."

I can't handle it.

Punky's actions and words send me over the edge, and I chase my release, unable to hold back my screams because I'm so fucking close. He's won. He knows he can hurt me, which means I'm in so much trouble. We both are.

"Yer a parful wee liar, Babydoll. I own ye. Whether ye want me to or not. Say it," he orders, then suddenly stops as I desperately rock back, begging he put me out of my misery.

"That'll never happen," I pant, reaching around, pleading he continues to move. But he does the complete opposite. He pulls out.

I sag forward, crying out in frustration. "No!"

"Say it," he commands calmly while my winded breaths betray me.

Stubbornly, I begin rubbing over myself because if he won't bring me to climax, I'll do it by my own hand. But he slaps my hand away and flips me onto my back. I fruitlessly fight him, but he pins me with his weight as he draws my arms above my head.

"I'll not ask ya again," he cautions hoarsely.

His erection presses between us. I whimper when he rubs it against my needy center. I don't want to give him the satisfaction of giving in, but eventually, I concede because there is no point in fighting the inevitable.

"I'm a parful wee liar," I angrily cry.

"And?"

"And you fucking own me!"

"Aye, Baby, that I do."

He hums in satisfaction, knowing that he's won, knowing that this changes everything. He can hurt me. And I can hurt him. We're at a crossroads where no one wins, but losing has never felt more like winning than it does right now.

On a sated exhale, he sinks into me, both of us moaning because this depravity hurts so good. He bends down, kissing me languidly. Changing the pace of our coupling, he confuses me with his kindness. His lip ring brushes against me, and I reach up, running my finger over the barbell in his nipple.

I can't stop wanting him.

He increases the tempo, stroking me in just the right way where I don't stand a chance and come loudly, finally letting go. My moans are unrestrained, but I don't care. I cling onto him, his skin slick and warm. It's nothing short of perfect.

The moment the last cries leave me, he pulls out and spills his seed over my stomach with a guttural growl. The moonlight allows me to see his silhouette, neck arched, back bowed—he is a vision. And I know I own him as much as he owns me.

His breathless pants echo in the room as he gets off the bed, and before I can ask what he's doing, he uses his shirt to wipe me clean. The gesture just confirms what I knew the moment we met—we're so fucking screwed.

TWELVE

PUNKY

L iam is late, and I know that's no coincidence. I also know they've found Aidan's body.

I was expecting this call, seeing as I was technically the last person to see him alive. They've called bullshit on his story, which means they're looking for answers. And they're thinking those answers sit with me.

He's testing me, as this pub is full of Doyle spies. If I look nervous, then he'll assume I know more than I'm letting on, which is why I calmly sip my pint, pretending to be engrossed by a game on my mobile phone.

How my life has changed. I'm living a double life, but then again, it seems everyone is—Connor, Uncle Sean, and Babydoll.

I can still taste her, and it's been three days. But I'll never be able to rid myself of the taste.

She scares me more than the Doyles, and that's 'cause she can hurt me. Even though I know she's a liar and a thief, I can't stay away. Her being an American is merely the tip of the iceberg, and when I uncover who she really is and why she's here, I know I'll have to deal with it.

But hurting her, I don't think I can.

What we shared wasn't just sex; it was something else entirely. I'm in way over my head, and I'm fearful for what's to come. This is why I haven't thought about it. My life is complicated enough.

When Liam finally makes an appearance, I quit thinking on this nonsense and become the character he thinks I am.

"Bout ye?" he asks, taking a seat at the table. It's hard to believe this bastard could be my half-brother.

His tone is far from friendly, but I look up from my phone and smile. "Hey. What's up?"

"We've got a fierce situation, Mike. My uncle Aidan is dead."

No foreplay, it seems.

I knew this was coming, so I slip on my surprised face. "What? You're fucking with me?"

"No, I wish that I was. But we found his mutilated corpse not too far from his house. Whoever did this wanted us to find his body."

"Fucking hell, man. I'm sorry."

Liam nods, watching for any signs of deceit. He won't see

any. "I need ya to tell me everythin' that happened that night."

Peering around, pretending to scope out our surroundings, I lean in close and say, "I took care of your *problem* until he was barely breathing, and then left. Aidan said he'd handle the rest."

"He did not say what he was doin' with our *problem*?"

We're speaking so flippantly about a human life because that *problem* is Ronan. It sickens me. But I shake my head.

"No. He said once he was done, he was seeing a lady friend. That's all."

Liam mulls over my admission. "Ye see, the funny thing is we've found Uncle Aidan's body, but not that of Ronan."

"You don't think…"

I leave the question open, but what I'm hinting at is that Ronan was the one responsible for Aidan's death. Ronan is long gone by now, so the Doyles won't find him. He's the scapegoat. That's what he gets for being a fucking traitor.

"I don't know," he confesses, leaning back in his seat with a sigh. "The usual place Uncle Aidan would dispose of our problems is undisturbed. That leaves you and that pile o' shite the last people to see my uncle alive.

"He called me afterward and said I could trust ya. Says him to me that he was with some floozy. But when I called his mots, they said they haven't seen him."

Nodding, I remain calm because Liam has nothing on me. He's searching for any signs of betrayal in my mannerisms.

"I don't know what to tell you. Anything you need help

with, I've got your back."

Liam isn't convinced, but he doubts I have the bollocks to go up against his uncle and win, which gives me the advantage. He's underestimated me, and that's what'll allow me to take the Doyles down.

His phone rings, and when he sees who it is, something comes over him. I listen to the conversation discreetly, and when I find out who he's speaking to, I understand his strange response. "It's under control, Dad."

But it seems Brody Doyle doesn't trust his son.

Liam offers me his phone. "My da wants to talk with ya."

And just like that, my chance to speak to the devil has come.

I remain calm because Mike has no idea he's about to talk to the kingpin of Dublin. But Punky does, and he doesn't know how he's going to refrain from telling him his days are numbered.

I don't know what to expect. Aye, I've googled him, but the Doyles, just like the Kellys, are very private people, so I couldn't find anything of use. We're put in the public eye when we want to be, which means it benefits us somehow.

Anything else is just ammo for the enemy. And we can't be having that. We rarely have our pictures taken as this allows our foes to know what we look like.

I knew killing Aidan and leaving his body where we did was bait the Doyles couldn't ignore. It worked a charm. This is it, the moment I've been waiting for.

"Hey, what's up?" I coolly greet him.

"I thought ya could tell me that." Brody's voice is deep and firm. No one would doubt the power he holds. "Liam's told ye what's happened?"

"Yes, Liam told me. I'm really sorry about Aidan. I told Liam when I left him, he was alive and well. He said he was going to take care of everything."

Brody processes what I've just shared. "Aye, lad, I believe ya. Mi daughter, Erin, seems to think yer trustworthy. So did mi brother," he says, which pleases me. Having Erin in my corner has worked in my favor. "That arsehole is to blame. Or at least, the family he works for."

He means us. He's assuming Connor had a hand in his brother's death.

"That's what I get for trustin' a Protestant. My brother will be avenged. And we need yer help."

And that's the real reason Brody wanted to speak to me.

"I don't expect ye to understand this, but my family is at war with another. They're from Northern Ireland. I want what is theirs and I'm close to gettin' that. Ronan worked for them, but he came to us when he realized the Kellys' days are numbered."

In and out, I remind myself to breathe.

"There is a shipment of yokes and sneachta that I want. The lorry is due for arrival in Belfast next Tuesday. We plan to be there when it does."

I know exactly what he's talking about as this is Uncle Sean's deal. He has organized a shipment of cocaine to come in from Central America. The street value of this haul is £200,000. The yokes are ecstasy tablets coming in from the Netherlands.

This is a huge deal for us, and if it doesn't go to plan, it'll be a brutal loss.

"You're going to intercept the lorry?" I ask casually.

Brody laughs. "No, we're goin' into Belfast. It's time we make ourselves known. As I see it, Connor Kelly took my brother, so I'll take his."

The blood drains from my face, but I keep it together.

"Which is where ya come in. We need a face they won't recognize. Ye see, our fellow Catholics won't take too kindly to us dealin' with them Protestants. We need to be discreet, but there is no way Connor is getting away with this.

"My brother was painted up like some muppet. Ach, this was personal."

Yes, it was, and I wanted the Doyles to know I was coming for them, but not like this. Uncle Sean's life is now at risk.

"I took his wife. Nothing more personal than that," he boasts like I'm supposed to be impressed.

Clenching my fists under the table, Brody has just confirmed what I already knew. He and Aidan took my ma's life. If what he says is truth, does that mean he's my da? Did he kill my ma, knowing I was his son?

My hatred for this cunt continues to grow. Dad or not, I'm going to do unto him what I did to his brother. What he did to my ma.

This is a test. The Doyles know if I say no, then my story is rubbish. But if I do this, then their trust in me will strengthen. I'll be able to infiltrate their operations even more than I already have. I'll be able to save Uncle Sean.

"What's in it for me?" I question because that's the only reason any stranger would agree to this.

"How about twenty-five thousand American dollars?"

For that amount of money, this isn't as simple as Brody makes it out to be. There's a reason they want me there. And I plan on finding out what that reason is.

With a smirk, I say, "You've got yourself a deal."

"Good, lad," Brody replies, his excitement suffocating me. "Liam will letcha know the details closer to the day."

Of course, he will. They wouldn't want me to get cold feet and chicken out. Or worse yet, dob them into the peelers.

"No problem."

Our conversation is done. "I'll be seein' ya soon."

And he hangs up.

"If y'll excuse me." Liam doesn't give me a chance to reply as he gets up, leaving me alone.

I don't care why he's pissed off. I got what I wanted—to gain access to the Doyles and make them pay accordingly. But for that to happen, I need to do one thing…and that's come clean to Uncle Sean. I need to tell him everything, and I need to do that now.

There is no easy way to do this because I know Uncle Sean is going to be ragin' either way. Aye, I'm coming to him with information which will give us the upper hand, but how I got that information is going to leave Uncle Sean wired to the moon.

He's in his office, which is in the opposite wing to Connor's, so I know he'll be alone. Knocking on his door, I prepare for anything because for the first time in my life, I don't know if Uncle Sean will side with me on this.

He opens the door, and when he sees me, he arches a brow. "Whatta ye knockin' for? Yer always welcome."

"I'm not too sure y'll think that once I tell ye what I did."

He doesn't say a word. Instead, he opens the door wider, permitting me entry as he walks to the table in the corner of the room that has his bottle of scotch. He pours two glasses as I close the door.

"What did ya do now?" he asks, offering me a glass.

Accepting, I throw it back before revealing it all. "I was in Dublin tonight. Meetin' up with Liam Doyle."

Uncle Sean pauses mid sip of his scotch.

"I've been undercover, I guess ya could call it. They think I'm Mike from America. They trust me. I killed Aidan Doyle."

Uncle Sean doesn't speak. He slumps into his leather chair, gutted.

"I found an address in Connor's drawer when I broke into his office. The address was for a pub in Dublin. The Doyles' pub."

The less he speaks, the more I do.

"I earned their trust by winnin' a fight against Hugh. They think I'm just some stupid foreigner which is why they're havin' me do their dirty work. But tonight, they told me they're comin' to Belfast. They plan to rob us."

Uncle Sean places the empty glass onto his desk, his eyes void of emotion. I've never seen him like this. "Uncle Sean?"

"Aye, cub?" he says, and I wonder if he's gone into shock.

"Are ye all right?"

He rocks in his chair, considering my question, and what he asks next confirms he's shook. "Why d'ya call him Connor? He's yer da."

After everything I've just revealed, *this* is what concerns him the most?

"I don't know that. He's never been a father to me."

"Is that why ye did this? To get back at him?"

"Course not," I argue, shaking my head. "I did this 'cause no one in this fuckin' family has told me the truth! I was sick of being lied to. Can't ye even try to understand that?"

"Yer a buck eejit, so ya are," he says, finally addressing the issue at hand. "Do ye have any idea what y've done? Is this why ya knew the peelers were raidin' us?"

"No, that was someone else." And that someone, I will never rat on.

"Oh, for fuck's sake, Puck!" he exclaims. "What a dog's dinner this is. Ya should have come to me. Y've got blood on yer hands now, Doyle blood, and they will not stop until he is avenged."

"Aye, sure, this is it."

"I'm just needin' a minute." He shakes his head at my dismissive response.

I give him some time because I know this is a lot to take in, but he needs to know it all.

"Ronan was workin' for the Doyles. He double crossed us."

Uncle Sean's eyes narrow. "And how would ya know that?"

"'Cause I was sent by the Doyles to take care of him. He was stealin' from us. Giving our gear to the Doyles. I think they want Northern Ireland as their own. They're recruitin' our men who are disloyal because we've allowed it.

"For them to do this, they don't fear or respect us, and it'll only be a matter of time before the Doyles get their wish. I think they have someone here in Belfast workin' for them. They're sellin' our stolen gear, testing the waters to see how easy it'll be."

I didn't understand why they wanted our drugs when they had their own, but this must be why.

To have control of all ports—here and in Dublin—gives them total power. They can import gear into Belfast and sell here without risking driving across the border and being caught by the peelers. The less movement, the better.

We all know that. Every time a lorry goes out, we're at risk of being caught. Or one of the drivers betraying us. But if the Doyles had connections inside Northern Ireland, this would eliminate the risk.

"Why do ya think that?" Uncle Sean asks, and I'm thankful he's listening and not giving me a lecture.

"Why else are they interested in our gear? They've got their own contacts, their own drugs in Dublin. But takin' our men, our drugs, that gives them knowledge into how we run our business. They want to set up base here. And they need an inside man to do that."

I cannot believe I didn't see this sooner.

"What of Ronan?"

"I let him go as I needed a scapegoat for Aidan's murder." I decide to leave out Cian's and Rory's involvement in this.

"Yer some pup, Punky," Uncle Sean says in a tone which sounds like praise. "What ya did was stupid and very dangerous, but ye did good."

The relief I feel is overwhelming. I should have known that no matter what, Uncle Sean would stick by me.

"So what's the plan then?"

Uncle Sean appears deep in thought, staring straight through me. "We do what those fuckers want. We go, and then we ambush them. They think yer someone else. We have the advantage here."

"Brody, he says to me that he…that he took ma."

Uncle Sean squeezes his eyes shut. I know this is a lot to take in.

"Aidan was the other man who was there. That's why I killed him. He deserved to die, and I'd do it again given half the chance."

"Ya told me there were three men. Who else was there?" he asks, reopening his eyes. He looks knackered.

"I don't know. But I'll find that out. This tattoo"—I hold up my wrist—"Aidan told me every Doyle gets one when they kill a Protestant. Have ya heard that?"

"I have not," he replies angrily. "I cannot believe this. This is my fault. And yer fa—"

He stops himself before correcting, "Connor's. It never should have gotten this far. Those fuckers have been under our noses this entire time, and we didn't even know. It sickens ya."

"Aye, but we know now."

Uncle Sean nods, looking at me with nothing but pride. "If Brody is yer father, yer okay with killin' him then?"

Without missing a beat, I reply, "I'm not just goin' to kill him, Uncle Sean, I'm goin' to torture him until he begs me to put him out of his misery. And even then, I will not. He is going to suffer in ways unimaginable, and I won't feel a fucking thing about that."

Uncle Sean is stoic. He's never heard me speak this way. I

realize it's a lot to take in. He still sees me as the innocent wain he helped rear, but it's time that stopped.

"I have to tell Connor," he finally says.

"He's the reason for this," I state. "If he had control over his men, instead of being such an arrogant bastard, none of this would be happenin."

"I'm at fault as well."

This is so like Uncle Sean to blame himself. But we both know this is Connor's show. Nothing goes unless he gives it the green light. He was supposed to be our leader, but he's just a fucking joke.

"Stop that," I argue, refusing to stand here and allow him to take the blame. "This is Connor's doin'. Everythin' is his fault. He's about to ruin this family, and even if I'm not a Kelly—"

But Uncle Sean stands abruptly. "Don'tcha finish that sentence, ya hear me? Yer a Kelly. Yer my blood"—he thumps his hand over his chest—"I care not what anyone says. Ye fight like a Kelly. Ye die like a Kelly."

Nodding, I don't let my sentiment show as I appreciate this more than he'll ever know.

Connor hasn't even bothered to address this issue. He dropped the bombshell, and that was it. But in a few days, I'll know the truth because once that paternity test comes back, it'll tell me if I'm a Kelly or not.

"Thanks. No matter what, y'll always be my uncle."

He averts his gaze, touched by my words. But he soon clears

his throat. "All right then, I'll make some calls. Ya did the right thing tellin' me this. We'll deal with these Doyles once and for all. Belfast is ours, and any fuckin' Catholic who thinks they can come here and steal it from us will suffer desperately."

"Nice one," I hum in agreement, unable to wait for more bloodshed. But now, I need to phone the boys and fill them in.

I'm about to turn and leave, but Uncle Sean steps forward and hugs me. It's a tight embrace. It's one filled with affection. "Be careful, cub."

I'm not exactly sure what I need to be careful of as everything has gone to shit, but I hug him back. If anything were to happen to him, I don't think I'd survive this. I pull away, not wanting to make a fuss.

He smiles, and I'm relieved I told him. He is the only person I trust. He and the lads, that is. Speaking of, I can't avoid them for much longer. Since the party, I've been dodging their calls as I don't want to tell them about Babydoll.

The reason for that is I know they'll tell me what a fucking eejit I am for not being more cautious about her. She's a liar, a liar who refuses to tell me the truth. If this were anyone else, they wouldn't be left standing.

But when I left Babydoll's house, I knew I was in deep. There is no way I can hurt her. Liar or not, that doesn't change my feelings for her. I don't know what those feelings are, or how to deal with them, but what I do know is that I'll protect her because she is mine.

"I'll talk to ye later."

Uncle Sean nods and takes a seat at his desk. I guess he's got a few phone calls to make.

Closing the door behind me, I reach for my mobile and see three missed calls from Rory. I can't avoid him any longer.

"All right, then?" I casually say when he answers.

"Have you spoken to Cian?"

The panic in his voice troubles me. "No, I have not. Why?"

"'Cause that arsehole usually phones me about ten times a day, and I haven't heard from him in a few hours."

I can't help but laugh. "I'm sure he's fine. He's probably out on the pull."

"Ach, yer right," he agrees. "Where ye been then?"

Keeping my voice low, I reply, "I've a lot to tell ya. Call on me tomorrow?"

"Oh, happy fucking days," he sarcastically mumbles. "Is she who she says she is?"

He doesn't need to clarify who.

"Don't ye be concernin' yerself with that." My response is as good as a no.

"Ye buck eejit. Ridin' the enemy is not smart."

"She's not the enemy. Well, I don't think she is."

"Is that you and yer cock talkin'?"

With a smirk, I reply, "Me and my cock will see ye tomorrow then."

I hang up, not interested in any lectures.

As I make my way outside, I decide to call Babydoll as I haven't spoken to her since I left her home in the middle of the night. I don't know what the protocol is for after sex talk as I've never been interested in revisiting a one-night stand.

But this isn't that with Babydoll.

Even though there wasn't any cuddling after we had sex, me leaving was a mutual thing. I could sense she wanted me to leave, and I think it's 'cause she was worried about getting caught. But caught by whom? She's an adult and can ride whoever she wants.

But the urgency was her fearing for my safety. I haven't wanted to think about this because I have so many issues going on in my life right now, but this is one which cannot be solved with violence. And a wee part of me doesn't want to know the truth.

But I can't dodge the truth forever. I need to know.

I dial her but am surprised when a voice tells me the number is no longer in service.

Sighing, I place my phone back into my pocket and add this to the ever-growing pile of shite I need to deal with.

THIRTEEN

PUNKY

"It's my turn."

"Y'already had a turn," Hannah says, using her elbow as a barricade as Ethan tries to steal the remote control from her.

The twins got a motorized toy sailboat from Connor and wanted to sail it on the lake behind the castle. These gifts come from him every so often to make up for being a shitty dad. The problem is, he always seems to forget there are two of them. He's so self-absorbed, he thinks he's doing them a kindness, but all it does is leave them bickering.

"Hey, no one will have a turn if you can't play nice," Amber warns sternly.

She's kept her distance since the party, which is why I didn't want anything to happen between us. I enjoy her company, but now, things are just fucking weird.

My phone rings, and when I see a number I don't recognize, I excuse myself so I can answer it in private.

"Hello?"

"Is this Puck Kelly?" asks a male voice I don't recognize.

"Aye, it is. Who's this?"

"Oh, Mr. Kelly, this is Dr. Dunne from Oak Park Clinic. Yer results are here. I understand the urgency, so I wanted to phone and tell ye—"

"What are they?" I ask, cutting him off.

Finding someone who wouldn't tell Connor what I'm up to was near impossible, but Dr. Dunne is new to Belfast and not yet aware of the Kelly reputation. I could have used those home paternity tests, but going to a clinic would give me the most accurate results.

"If ye wanted to come in—"

"I don't mean to be rude, Doctor, but please tell me the fuckin' results."

He clears his throat. "The samples of hair, blood and saliva you provided, well, they conclude that the subject is excluded as the biological father."

Excluded...

"Mr. Kelly? Did ye hear me? The data gathered from the test do not support a relationship of paternity. I'm awful sorry. However, if—"

I don't bother listening to anything further because what would be the point? The results all confirm that Connor Kelly is not my father. That I'm not a Kelly.

"Thank you, Doctor." I hang up, 'bout to lose my shite. All I can hear on repeat are the words *excluded as the biological father.*

I don't know how to feel. Relieved in some ways not to be related to that pile o' shit, but the alternative is just as bad.

When my phone vibrates, I'm about to hurl it into the lake. But it's Cian's number that flashes on my screen. I've been trying to get a hold of this fucker all day.

"The fuck ye—"

But the panic in his voice has me forgetting everything. Something is terribly wrong.

"Punky, they think I'm you," Cian pants. "And I've let them think it."

At first, I think he's hammered, but then I realize he's breathless because he's hurt.

"Cian? Where are ya?"

"I don't know," he confesses, wheezing in pain. "But ye can't come here. They'll kill ya."

"And if I don't, they'll kill you instead. Who's got ye? Cian?" I press when he doesn't reply.

"The Doyles. But—"

There are no buts in this situation.

"I'm coming for ye, brother. I promise ya. Please hold on."

"I'm sorry, Punky. I—"

But the line goes dead.

I frantically try to call him back, but his phone is switched off.

"Fuck!" I scream, blinded by nothing but mad rage. I regret my outburst as I know the twins are scared, but if anything happens to Cian…

"Punky?" Amber asks, but I don't have time to explain. If the Doyles have Cian, all gloves are off, and no one is safe.

"Amber, go inside and lock all the doors, ya hear me? Don'tcha let anyone in."

"What's going on?" I know she's afraid, but I can't console her. I don't have time.

"Please, just listen to me. Keep the twins safe, all right? I'll explain everythin' later."

She nods quickly, sensing the urgency to my demands. "Kids, let's go inside and put on that movie you wanted to watch."

Hannah and Ethan look at me for guidance, and at this moment, I realize it doesn't matter that we're not blood. They will always be my kin.

"Go with Amber," I say with a strained smile.

They may only be small, but they understand when something is wrong. They're Kellys, after all, and nothing is ever right in our fucked-up world.

Both of them come running over to me, their fighting over

the boat long forgotten. They cling to me tight as I crouch down to hug them.

"Yer coming back?" Hannah asks, choking on her tears.

"Of course, I am."

Ethan doesn't say a word.

"Yer the man of the house, all right?" I say, pushing him out at arm's length. "I need ye to be brave for me. Can ya do that?"

His head bobs, but he's afraid. "I love you, Punky."

"Me too. I love ya both. Go now. A'll see ya soon."

I gently coax them to leave with Amber who nods, promising me she'll look after them.

Once they're gone, I run to my gaff and dial Rory. I don't give him a chance to talk.

"Can ye trace Cian's phone?"

"I've tried doing that all day, but it's turned off. What's going on then?"

"He just phoned me about two minutes ago. He's in trouble, Rory." I kick open my door and storm over to the painting hanging above the fireplace. Ripping it off the wall, I punch in the code to my safe.

I can hear the frantic clicking on a keyboard as I gather guns, knives, and money and stuff them into a bag. I don't know why the Doyles have Cian, but I'm going in prepared for every possible scenario.

"Holy fuck," he says, and I know this isn't good. "The call

came from the bungalow where yer grandparents are. He's there."

"Fuck," I curse, not understanding any of this. "We've got to go. The Doyles have him. They think he's me."

"If the Doyles are there, and we go, they'll know yer not Mike. They have Cian because they don't know who y'are. All of yer hard work would have been for nothin', and the upper hand ya have will be lost."

My body is vibrating in anger. I can barely stand it. Rory is right. If I go there now, the plan to ambush the Doyles with Uncle Sean will be ruined. They'll know that I'm not Mike and that I've played them, and then we'll never get to the bottom of who's behind all this.

This proves there is a mole amongst us, but why do they think Cian is me?

Desperately searching the room for an answer, I see it scattered on the coffee table—my face paints. It's not foolproof, but when they see the face I paint, the same one which I etched onto Aidan's, they'll only see that—the face that killed a Doyle.

Whoever has him can't be Liam or Hugh because they met him at the pub. It's someone else. I can only think of one other Doyle—Brody.

Snatching the paints from the table, I throw them into my bag. "I have an idea. Be here in ten."

My hand is surprisingly steady as I apply the final downward stroke on my sinister grin. Looking into the sun visor mirror, I realize how comfortable I am wearing this face.

I make no apologies for what I've done and what I plan to do.

I feel nothing.

Rory now knows everything and agrees that someone is using our gear as a test run. We won't stop until we find out who that is. He also knows that Babydoll isn't from London. He reacted how I thought he would—he called me a fucking eejit.

When he asked if I thought Babydoll had anything to do with this, I answered honestly; I really don't know.

When he asked how I felt about not being Connor's son, I replied with the same response.

I don't know anything anymore, but what I do know is that I'm going to kill every fucker who laid a finger on Cian. As for my grandparents…I really am walking into the unknown. The only advantage we have is that we've been here before.

We park down the road, taking in our surroundings as it's dusk. We don't have the moonlight to hide behind. We decide to jump the fence on the side of the property as the thick shrubs and hedges lining it will provide the coverage we need.

The absolute silence scares me. I don't know what we'll find inside this house of horrors.

We quietly jump the fence, hiding behind the hedges. The curtains are drawn across the window, so we can't see anything. I gesture with my head that we're to move.

"Ya need to be quiet. Quieter than a mouse."

All I can hear is my ma's voice. The words she spoke to me before our lives changed forever.

This house is riddled with nothing but bad memories, and the fact my "family" has no issues being here, shows they don't care about what happened to my ma. Being here makes me want to vomit. But they stay here of their own accord. It's beyond fucked up.

I may not be a Kelly, but I'm not a Foster either. I don't know who I am. And I'm okay with that.

When Rory and I peek into the window at the back of the gaff, I hold my breath because this room is where my ma was slaughtered. And it's the room where my best friend was beaten to a bloody mess.

The curtains are parted a fraction, so we can see in, and what I see has me clenching my fist, promising to kill every last fucker who laid a hand on Cian.

"He's breathin'," Rory whispers. "Only just."

"I need ya to stay out here," I order, placing my bag onto the ground and quietly unzipping it. "Don't let anyone in. Or out."

When I give him a gun and a knife, he understands what

we need to do when the enemy approaches.

"Y'll be all right on yer own?"

Nodding, I arm myself and slip on my hood. "Aye. It's this gaff which taught me what bloodshed was."

"See ye soon." He extends his hand, which I slap and shake.

I don't know what's going to happen, but Cian won't die in my place. I'll do everything I can to save him.

Without hesitation, I walk toward the back door and peer around the doorjamb. It's unmanned, so I open it quietly. The moment I step foot inside, I'm hit with Ma's perfume, her warming smile. This place is entrenched with her memories.

My boots don't make a sound as I tiptoe through the gaff, refusing to give way to the memories which plague me with each step I take. The fact there is no one in here troubles me as to what I'm about to find. As I peer around the corner, I see a man standing in front of the bedroom door.

He's holding a machine gun.

There is no way I can sneak up on him, so I look for a distraction. I see one in the shape of a small rock near my foot. Picking it up, I throw it against the back window. It makes just enough of a sound to alert the arsehole.

His slow footsteps echo in the silence. I hold my breath and arrange my hood low over my brow. The barrel of his machine gun is the first thing I see as he cautiously walks through the hallway. Focusing his attention on the window is his error because before he knows what's happening, I strike out and elbow him in the face, blinding him.

Before he can fire his weapon, I snatch the machine gun from his limp grip and knock him out cold. I catch him before he hits the floor and quietly rest his unconscious form against the wall. He stays upright for now.

With machine gun in hand, I commence my walk down the hallway, the carpet muting my footsteps. With a deep breath, I prepare myself for anything as I kick open the bedroom door, gun raised, ready for battle. But I only see Cian and my grandparents.

Where is everyone?

I can ponder on that later.

"Cian?" I whisper, gently slapping his bloody cheek.

He moans in response as bloodied spittle dribbles from the corner of his mouth. They beat him good.

"Punky?" Keegan wheezes as he shifts in the chair he's tied to.

"Shh." I place my finger over my lips. "Where are they?"

"Havin' a feg," he replies. "There're two of them."

I quickly cut through the rope binding his feet and wrists. "Can ye walk?"

He's beaten just as badly as Cian, but I need him to help me get Imogen out of here. She's unconscious and doesn't look to be in a good way.

The stubborn aul' lad nods and ignores his shaking legs as he stands. I reach out to help steady him. "They think he's ye," he whispers, gesturing to Cian. "They kept sayin' she told them so."

She?

Who the fuck is she?

Quickly cutting the rope binding Imogen, Keegan lifts her limp body into his arms. "My friend is out back. He'll help ye."

Keegan doesn't need to be told twice. "For what it's worth, thank ye, lad. I know we letcha down. But ye still came for us."

"I didn't come for you," I blankly reply, not interested in playing happy families. That time has come and gone.

He nods, accepting this for what it is, and staggers out the door.

Cian moans, and when he shifts, I see blood spurting from his side. He's been stabbed.

"Always gettin' yerself in trouble, aren't ya?" I say, attempting to deflect the severity of his injuries as I carefully cut him free.

He coughs, a winded breath leaving him as he tries to speak. "She. Who's she?"

"Shh, mate. Save yer energy, all right?"

He flops forward when I cut the rope at his wrists, unable to hold up his weight.

Reaching out, I slip my arm around his waist and help him stand. He leans against me, panting. He's hurt really bad. I doubt he'll be able to walk down the hallway, so I look at the window. It's not a great option, but it's the only one I have.

However, when I hear the front door open, followed by

jovial voices, I realize there is another option; one which saved my life.

"Cian," I whisper, dragging him toward the wardrobe. "Y've got to hide."

"Naw, lemme fight," he argues, attempting to dig in his heels.

This conversation hits too close to home.

Opening the wardrobe, I gently place him inside and give him the machine gun as he sags into a half-sitting position.

"Ya can fight from in here."

He arms himself as best he can. "I'm sorry, Punky. I was careless."

"Don't be worryin' about that," I cut him off, shaking my head. "Just stay quiet."

He nods, his face a brutal mess.

Closing the wardrobe door, I press my back against the wall, preparing for battle. I only need one of them alive. Two of them come bursting through the door, looking at the empty chairs, confused, which is when I strike.

I stab one in the thigh while I kick the other in the stomach, winding him. He staggers back, tumbling over one of the chairs. He doesn't have a chance to get up because I drop to one knee and slam my fist into his face, once, twice, before he's out cold.

The man howling in pain as he tries to pull out the knife just feeds this guttural anger, and I slowly turn toward him and laugh. I know this arsehole.

"Ya take that out, y'll bleed to death in seconds," I warn calmly as I've stabbed him in the femoral artery.

His bloody hands pause from removing my blade.

I come to stand, watching the way his face twists in recognition.

"You," he snarls, while I wave my fingers.

"How're ya doin', Hugh?"

Hugh Doyle and I meet again, but this time, he will not leave with his life intact.

He shuffles backward to lean against the wall. "*Yer* Puck Kelly then?"

I shrug with a smirk. "Maybe."

"Maybe? What the fuck d'ye mean maybe?"

Grabbing a chair, I spin it around and straddle it as we have a lot to discuss. "Who told ye?"

Hugh chuckles, clutching at his thigh. "That stupid aul' fella," he mutters under his breath. "He trusted her when I told him not to."

"Who?" I press, trying to piece this together.

"He thinks he's got it sorted, that he's got the advantage, but none of them can be trusted. For fuck's sake! When I saw yer friend, I didn't know what to think. I didn't want to believe ye t'ree could fool us."

"Listen to me. Yer goin' to answer me, or I'll make sure ya die awful slow."

Hugh spits in response. "Yer gonna kill me, anyway."

"Aye, that it is."

Realizing he won't rat on his family, I get up and walk over to him. He looks up at me with nothing but hatred. Gripping the collar of his shirt, I drag him along the floor and toss his arse into the chair. When he tries to fight me, I punch him in the jaw.

He's still struggling as I use the discarded rope to tie his hands behind his back, but I eventually get him bound. The other guy who I don't know is still out cold, so I pick him up and tie him to another chair.

"Ye killed mi uncle?" Hugh asks, looking at my face paint.

"Yes, I killed him, just how he killed my ma. In this house, actually."

Rolling back the sleeve of my hoodie, I reveal my own tattoo, the one I bit off Hugh's wrist. His eyes widen. "I saw it. I saw what they did to her, and I promised myself that I would kill every last Doyle to avenge her death."

"Yer ma was stupid. That much is clear. She married a Kelly, for fuck's sake."

"Aye, but she was fucking a Doyle," I quickly counter. "Yer dad, to be clear."

"Yer nothin' but a liar!" Hugh roars, cheeks blistering red.

"Afraid not. We may be brothers. Imagine that," I mock, laughing.

"I don't believe ya."

"I care not what ye believe. But maybe y'll see the

resemblance. Hang on."

Hunting through my bag, I retrieve my face paints, and before he can object, I slather his cheeks with white. He struggles frantically, but he's not going anywhere. Once his face is painted a stark white, I dip my fingers into the black paint and roughly circle around his eyes.

When I get to his mouth, I draw a messy line from cheek to cheek, but I'm not satisfied. Yanking the knife out of his leg, I press the bloody tip into the apple of his cheek. He doesn't squirm. He doesn't scream. He dares me to do it.

And I do.

My blade slices through his flesh with ease.

"Aye, now I can see it," I say with a smile, admiring my handiwork.

His right cheek is sliced to the corner of his mouth, emphasizing his sinister grin as bloody spittle seeps from the wound. Digging into his pocket, I take his phone and snap a picture, so he can see the work of art his face now is.

"Yer my double," I sarcastically say, showing him the picture.

His chin sags to his chest. It's only minutes before he will bleed out.

"Don'tcha worry, the rest of yer family will be joinin' ya soon."

I search through his contacts and send the photo to Brody and Liam, and then to every other Doyle listed in Hugh's phone.

The man next to Hugh comes to with a groggy groan. When he opens his eyes and realizes he's the one now tied to a chair, he shrieks, trying to break free.

He sees me standing before him, a painted nightmare from hell.

"Tell me who organized this, and I'll let ye go," I say to him.

"Shut yer bake," Hugh warns, his caution a whistle as he tries to speak with a hole hacked into his cheek.

When the man sees his state, he shakes his head, not wishing to end up like his mucker. "Doyle's dau—"

"Shut the fuck up, will ya?" Hugh shouts, blood jetting from his wounds.

"I'll not end up like you," the man says, scared. "Doyle's daughter did."

"Erin?" I ask, confused. Why would she say Cian was me? She knows us as Mike and Kanga. I don't understand any of this.

"Y've no idea what's comin' for ye. None of ye Kellys do." Hugh's grin is menacing, and even though he's moments away from dying, he has the upper hand because he'll take his secret to the grave.

Rory comes charging through the door, peering at the carnage before him. "We need to go. Now. There's a van coming up the road. Where's Cian?"

"Fuck!" I curse. It's not enough time, but if we don't go now, all of this would have been for nothing. "He's in the wardrobe."

Rory runs over to the door, yanking it open while I exit the room, fire burning through my veins, which gives me an idea.

Fuck the Doyles.

And fuck this house.

Raiding the cupboards, I snare a bottle of scotch and a box of matches off the kitchen bench. I bump into Rory as he holds an unconscious Cian.

"Way with ye. I won't be far behind."

Rory doesn't argue as he knows we're running out of time and pushes past me.

As I re-enter the bedroom, the man begs for mercy, but where was Cian's mercy when he almost killed him? Dousing both him and Hugh with the scotch, I light a match and flick it without feeling. They instantly set alight, their screams doing nothing to appease the demons within.

They need more.

Looking around the bedroom, I realize this house is where it all started. I fixate on the carpet, the spot which was once stained with my ma's blood, where I laid beside her stiff corpse. The carpet may be new, but the memories associated with this house are not. They deserve to be burned along with these two fuckers.

"Goodbye, Ma," I say, using the rest of the scotch to douse the carpet, the curtains, and lastly, the wardrobe.

Taking one last look at the place which has been my prison for years, I smile as I light a match and toss it onto the alcohol.

It ignites instantly. The room cackles a red hue, complementing the screams of the two men who are burning to death.

I wish I could watch them take their last breath, stand around the human boney, but this will have to do.

As I'm running down the hallway, a picture on the wall catches my eye. I missed it before. It's of my ma. This is the only thing worth saving.

Yanking it off the hook, I stuff it into my backpack and gather all the bottles of liquor I can find. Tossing them down the corridor, I light the box of matches and throw it onto the trail of alcohol. It instantly goes up in a fireball, engulfing the gaff.

Running out the back door, I jump the fence and sprint to where Rory has parked the car. When he sees me, he speeds down the road and opens the passenger door. I dive in, and he rakes away from the mess I've made.

Keegan looks over his shoulder at the gaff going up in flames. He doesn't say anything however as he knew it would always end this way.

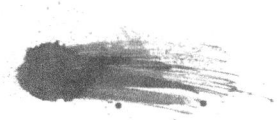

It's after two a.m. when I get home.

Cian insisted he was fine and didn't need to go to the hospital. I sent Amber a text, asking if she could check on him however. She's got her first-aid credentials and is pretty good with this stuff as the twins are always getting into trouble.

Rory is staying over to watch him, so I think he'll be fine. But what he said in the car, I don't know what to think. Aye, he's delirious after taking a beating, but he seemed quare lucid when he said that someone had told the Doyles about me.

They knew I had a nose ring—as does Cian—which is why they mistook him for me. He also said they knew a lot about me. But they never told him how they knew. The man I burned alive had said it was Erin, but how would she know this?

Someone must be relaying information back to her. But who?

The moment I unlock my door, I know someone is inside. Flicking on the light, I see Babydoll curled up on the couch, asleep. I don't know why she's here, especially since she's been ignoring me for days.

I'm about to shower and wash the paint from my face, but she stirs. "Punky?"

"Aye."

She sits up and rubs the sleep from her eyes. "Your face."

I'm still coming to terms with her American accent. Not because I don't like it, but rather, that I still don't know who she is.

She jumps up and makes her way over to me. I stand tall, allowing her to gently turn my cheeks so she can take a closer look at my face.

"What happened?"

"What happened was my best friend was beaten within an inch of his life. If he hadn't called me, I don't know what would have happened."

I don't know why I'm telling her this. But she has this effect on me. I just can't say no to her.

"Why is your face painted like this?"

She understands the significance of it. She knows something serious went down.

"Because someone thought he was me."

She casts her eyes downward, obviously disgusted with what that means.

"These hands," I say, turning them over. "They've killed, and they won't stop killin'. Y've got to leave me be, Babydoll. I can offer ye nothin'."

Her silence is deafening.

I don't know where she's been, but honestly, I don't care because I'm so happy she's here now.

"I know what I'm getting myself into," she finally speaks, caressing my cheek. "And besides, it's not like I don't have baggage of my own."

"Who are ye?" I ask again, hoping this time she'll finally tell me the truth.

She bites her bottom lip. "I can't tell you."

Frustrated, I remove her hand and take a step away from her. "Ye need to leave. I don't trust ya."

Tears swell in her green eyes. "I understand that. I haven't given you reason to. But have I ever hurt you? Haven't I always had your back? Can't you just trust me?"

She's right, although she's lied to me, she's always had my back. But I don't trust her. "I can't trust ya," I confess. "I don't know who y'are."

"Trust your…feelings for me," she says softly. "They're real. I know they are…just how mine are for you."

Her face is heavy with emotion, begging I confirm what she just said.

"Where've y'been?" I ask in vain as I know she won't answer me.

When she doesn't reply, I shake my head. "This is exactly the reason I can't trust ya, regardless of my feelin's. Ya need to go."

I turn my back, but she reaches out and snares my forearm.

Peering down at her fingers, I give her a silent warning. If she has a point, best she makes it now. "So you admit you do have feelings for me?"

"What difference does it make? Those feelin's mean fuck all without trust. I know yer not tellin' me somethin' because yer afraid. But I'd never hurt ye. I'd never judge ye. But ya still won't tell me, and those feelin's of betrayal are more important than any others.

"I've been lied to my entire life. I'm done with it."

She nods, holding back her tears. "I promise, all of this will make sense soon. Can you just trust me until then?"

"I don't know that I can," I reply honestly.

Her grip around me trembles, but I stand firm.

"For what it's worth, I've never felt this way about anyone," she confesses, permitting her tears to fall. "I know you probably don't believe me, but I've risked so much…for you. I knew the consequences, but I didn't care. If only you knew what that meant, you'd understand why I'm doing what I am.

"I fall to pieces when I'm with you, and I don't even care because I know you'll be there to help me heal. You've always been there.

"We don't make sense, but you can't deny this attraction. It was there from the first moment we met. Not just physically, but in here as well." She places her hand on my chest over my hammering heart. "This is as honest as I can be for now. Please let it be enough."

Every part of me is demanding I throw her out. It's what I should have done ages ago, but instead, I place my hand over hers. "Sure, this is it."

She smiles, cementing how fucked I really am. I know this is wrong and probably one of the biggest mistakes of my life, but I'm knackered fighting a war I don't want to win.

She loops her fingers through mine and leads me toward the bathroom. I go willingly. I allow her to unzip my hoodie and watch as she drops it to the floor. Without a word, she takes off my T-shirt, coaxing me to lift my arms so she can slip it over my head.

Once I'm topless, she turns on the tap and wets a facecloth with hot water. Wringing it out, she commences to wipe my face clean. The act is filled with kindness and care. I've never been tended to this way before.

A knot forms in my stomach because I'm falling for Babydoll, and I know I've passed the point of no return.

Once my face is clean, she chews her bottom lip and slips out of her blue dress. She stands before me in a black bra and matching underwear. She then reaches around her back and unhooks her bra. The moment she allows it to fall and I see her beautiful tits, I sigh, feeling at home being with her this way.

She clutches onto my belt buckle and draws me toward her, where she unfastens my belt and then my jeans. I'm not wearing any boxers, so a small gasp leaves her when she sees me semi-erect. I step out of my jeans and await further command.

Her cheeks turn scarlet, but she loops her fingers in the waistband of her underwear and takes them off.

I love her body—supple but strong. I know she's embarrassed with me looking at her this way, but I can't stop.

She reaches into the shower and turns on the water, using her hand to test the temperature. When it's right, she steps inside and offers a hand, welcoming me inside. I accept, and the moment I step under the spray, a sated groan leaves me as the scalding water feels perfect against my skin.

Babydoll lathers the sponge with the soap and proceeds to

wash my body, standing on her toes to reach my upper shoulders and back. I allow her to tend to me because I like it. I like her looking after me because her strength, her stubbornness, shows me that she cares.

Babydoll is my equal in every sense of the word. She said she's risked so much for me, and I believe her. For her to tell me about the raid, to give back my brooch, to be here now, tending to me when I've been nothing but an arsehole to her, confirms that she has fought for me, for us, regardless of the consequences.

And that's the reason I can't push her away.

I'm sick of losing the people I lo—

I soon stop myself from thinking such thoughts because love is something I know nothing about. But what I feel now for Babydoll, it comes fucking close.

The water falls around us, and I resist the urge to lick the trickles off Babydoll's perfect tits. She washes over my chest and stomach, caressing over the barbell in my nipple, driving me fucking insane. When she dips low, brushing over my erection, we both hiss at the connection.

But she doesn't let that distract her from getting me clean.

She washes my thighs and just as she is about to drop to her knees to wash my calves and feet, I stop her. "Never drop to yer knees for a man."

Aye, she's been on her knees before, but this is different. Being on her knees is for me to bring her pleasure, not to serve me.

"I don't mind doing it for you. I want to take care of you," she whispers, waterdrops sticking to her lashes. "I like it…I like you."

I can't stand it any longer.

Bending low, I slam my mouth against hers, kissing her with an urgency that leaves me breathless. She loops her arms around my neck and stands on her toes to reduce the height difference, but I pick her up, coaxing her to wrap her legs around my waist.

I slam her back against the shower wall, needing to be inside of her right fucking now.

Lifting her, I position her over my cock, and without delay, I lower her onto my aching shaft. She shudders. I fucking growl.

She bounces, working my cock as I slam into her over and over again. Our bodies are slick with water and our desire, and each time I pull out and sink back into her pussy, I curse because she feels so good.

Breaking our kiss, I bend and take her nipple into my mouth. I suckle it, enjoying the gasping moans slipping past Babydoll's parted lips. She clutches my hair, tugging firmly and holding on as I ride her hard.

I lift her arse, encouraging her to bounce on my cock, and when she clenches her muscles around me, I almost come. "Fucking hell," I curse, increasing the tempo.

She slides up and down, her pussy hugging me tight, and

when she shudders, I know she's going to come. Just as the last shudder leaves her, I pull out, spin her around, and press her body to the tiled wall. I slip back into her pussy, bending my knees to deepen the angle.

I ride her hard, unable to stop this hunger I feel for her. I spread her arse cheeks so I can see the way her cunt hugs my cock—it's fucking amazing. We fit perfectly.

She splays her hands against the wall, arching her back to take me in deep. She is fearless in everything that she does. I want to fuck her for hours, but being lost in Babydoll is a drug like no other, and when she reaches down to play with herself, I'm hooked to the taste.

After two violent strokes that shift her up the wall, I pull out and come on her lower back with a sated groan. My heart is beating so fast, I'm certain I'm about to have a heart attack.

Babydoll is still playing with herself as I'm coming, but my girl won't leave here deprived.

I spin her around and drop to my knees before her, as it should be—a man bowing before his queen. She peers down with nothing but love reflected in her eyes as I lower my mouth to her pussy and eat her out.

Her tiny whimpers as she tugs at my hair get me hard once more, but this is about Babydoll and showing her how much she means to me. I may not be able to say it, but I hope she understands this is so much more to me than a casual ride.

She spasms around my tongue, coming once again. I lick

every honeyed drop. The moment she sags, I catch her, and we sluggishly kiss as I allow her to taste herself on my lips.

I need her again.

Turning off the water, I dry us off quickly before leading her into the bedroom, where I toss her onto the bed. She crawls up the mattress, watching me with wide eyes.

"These feelings don't make sense," she confesses, reflecting my thoughts perfectly.

"Aye, they do not." I chase after her, pressing my body against hers.

She opens her legs, welcoming me home because that's how I feel when I'm with Babydoll—she's my human.

"But I do not care because this is what I want. *You* are what I want."

She blinks back what looks like tears. "No one has ever said that to me before."

"That's 'cause y've been speakin' to the wrong people."

"Sometimes, you can be quite charming." She gasps when I show her how charming I can be when I sink into her pussy.

"Don'tcha tell anyone," I whisper into her ear, biting the shell as I commence riding her.

"Cross my heart."

"Hope to die," I conclude, not realizing how significant that phrase is.

FOURTEEN

Babydoll

I can't take my eyes off him.

Watching Punky draw gives me a sense of peace. It's here, in the silence where we can both be ourselves. The way he composes himself is a work of art within itself.

We've spent the past few days together, which means something has happened to *him*. No one has come looking for me, but I don't mistake that as freedom. I know they're just biding their time. Something big lingers on the horizon, which is why I'm going to tell Punky the truth.

I can't lie to him any longer.

I know what that means for everyone involved, but we'll figure it out because I trust him. And to gain his trust, I need to tell him who I am and what I was sent to do.

Nervously wiping my sweaty hands on my jeans, I decide I'm just going to blurt it all out and hope for the best.

"C'mere," he says, his smooth accent eliciting a sprinkle of goose bumps from head to toe.

Rising from the sofa, I walk to where he sits in front of his easel. I look at his sketch in black charcoal. The image is slightly abstract, but there appears to be a person with their arms stretched behind them. They look like they're about to take flight. It's beautiful.

"D'ya like it?"

Placing my hands on his bare shoulders, I lay a single kiss on his stubbled cheek. "I love it."

"Each person I meet, they know somethin' I don't. I take that piece of information and learn from it. No matter how small that teachin' may be," he shares, his philosophical view on life just adding more depth to the amazing man he is.

"I woke up next to ye this mornin' and this is what I saw inside my head."

"It's hauntingly beautiful," I say, admiring his strokes and how, if you stare long enough, you can begin to make out her eyes, her lips, her hands. Others may see a man, but I see a woman, and that's the beauty of art—it's subjective. Nothing in life is ever black and white.

"I don't know whether she's comin' or goin', but she doesn't either, and that's okay 'cause I know she'll always come back to me."

Tears begin to well because I understand why Punky has drawn this. He still doesn't know who I am, and it plagues him. If I were anyone else, they'd never have gotten away with what I have. But here he is, drawing a picture of how he feels, how he sees me.

I don't deserve him.

He's gone against everything he knows is right and given in to me because we're both impervious to these feelings between us. I've never been in love, but with Punky, this feels something like love.

"Y'll always come back to me, will ye not?" he gently asks.

Unable to take the gravity to his tone, I lift his chin and kiss him over his shoulder. He kisses me back softly, a promise that no matter what, he'll always be my true north.

"Yes, Puck, I'll always come back to you. I promise."

I don't know what's caused the need to pledge this between us. Maybe he too senses a change is coming. But whatever the reason, I want him to know I'm his.

I break our kiss to drop to my knees in front of him. He said never to drop to my knees for any man, but he isn't merely any man—he's my man. And I want him to know this isn't a casual fling for me.

I know what's at risk. I know what happens if I don't succeed. But I can't stop the inevitable. I don't want to.

Peering up at him as I unfasten the zipper on his jeans, I relish in the way his blue eyes darken and turn predatory because I'll happily be his prey. When his cock springs free, my core clenches because I want him.

He threads his fingers through my hair, gently playing with the strands. These hands have killed, but when they touch me, I don't feel anything but love.

He's already hard, so I take him into my mouth and take my time pleasuring him. Punky is a generous lover, always ensuring my needs are met before his. Yes, he's rough and likes to tease, but I want it. I wouldn't have it any other way.

I grip his thighs and take him deep, tears leaking from the corner of my eyes as I gag on his length. He tries to pull out, but I suck him harder and bob my head, savoring the way his body shudders under my touch.

With a long sweep, I lick the underside of his shaft, loving how he tastes and feels.

"Ach, fuckin' hell," he curses, gripping the seat beneath him.

Increasing the tempo, I use my hand to grip his base and work in unison with my mouth. Tonguing over the slit in his cock, I hollow my cheeks and suck him hard. The pleasure I get from going down on him and being in control has me rubbing my legs together, desperate to soothe the ache down low.

He sweeps my hair to one side, and I can feel those astute eyes watching me as I take him in deep. "Yer fuckin' beautiful," he pants, thrusting his hips and hitting the back of my throat. "Yer the only thing that makes sense to me."

I understand what he means. It's the reason I was so

drawn to him in the first place—we're two broken people who somehow became a little less broken the day we met. Hardly eloquent, but to me, it makes perfect sense because I doubt either of us will be whole ever again.

But together, we complete the other. Punky lends me his strength to mend my wounds, and I offer the same to him.

"Fuck." He tries to push me away, but I'm not going anywhere…in every sense of the word.

He's helpless to my demands, and with three quick thrusts, he spills his hot seed down my throat. I swallow every last drop, humming at the fact that a part of him is inside me.

The moment he's done, he lifts me and slams me onto his lap, where he kisses the ever-living fuck out of me. Just as he's undoing my jeans, there is a sharp knock on his door.

"I'm sorry, lad, but we need to head soon."

Punky groans against my lips. "For fuck's sake. It's my uncle Sean."

With one last kiss, he slaps my ass and takes me with him as he stands. I understand whatever his uncle needs him for is important.

"I—"

But Sean's knocking on the door interrupts me. "Punky? Y've got ten minutes."

"Can we finish this later?" Punky asks as he does up his jeans. "I'm sorry."

I nod, as what I have to tell him will need more than ten

minutes to spare.

"Quit yer yackin'. I'm comin'."

Punky kisses me quickly. "I'll call on ye tonight. I have somethin' to take care of first."

I raise an eyebrow because this doesn't sound good. I could press and ask what that entails, but I'm in no position to question him when he doesn't even know my real name.

"All right. Be careful."

"I always am." He smirks, stealing my breath away. But who needs air when I've got this?

He heads into the bathroom, where I hear the shower turn on.

Gathering my things, I take one last look at the drawing, realizing I owe Punky so much. I see his uncle through the window. He's on his cell, talking animatedly to someone. A sudden sense of foreboding overcomes me.

Deciding to start small, I reach for a pencil and write a note in Punky's sketch pad. Tearing off the page, I fold it and slip it into the pocket of his hoodie where it's draped over the back of his chair. I don't know why I feel the need to do this. Something inside me tells me it's the right thing to do.

Once I have everything, I open the front door and get onto my bike to ride home. Sean has gone, but that's okay. I've already told him what I need to…unbeknownst to Punky.

Yet another truth I keep from him.

As I ride home, I think about the mess I find myself in. The night I came to see Punky, I was going to tell him everything. But I bumped into his uncle first. Punky told me he trusted his uncle with his life, which is why I decided to tell him what I knew.

I wanted to tell Punky the truth, but his uncle assured me that he'd deal with it accordingly. With Punky's temper, he was bound to act first and ask questions later, which would result in all of this being for nothing. I trust Sean because of Punky, so I hope I did the right thing.

Sean was very understanding, and when I started, it was like I couldn't stop. He knows my entire life story. He knows who I am. He had every right to throw me out and tell me to leave his nephew alone. But he didn't.

He promised me it would be all right, and that Punky would be safe. I just hope Punky understands.

Even though Sean has asked I don't tell Punky the truth until he says it's okay, I don't feel right lying to him any longer. I told Sean in the belief that this would be over. But all it's done is make me feel guilty for confiding in Sean and not Punky.

I find myself caught in a deeper web of lies, and I want out. I knew this wasn't going to be easy, but two wrongs don't make a right. She'll forgive me. I know she will. But I won't forgive myself, because I failed her…which is why I need to tell Punky the truth.

Maybe, just maybe, he can help me. I don't know what else to do.

I chain my bike in front of my flat and make my way inside. There is nothing special about this place, but he rented it for me with a purpose. I needed to be close to the Kellys.

As I unlock my door, I see *him* sitting in my armchair, casually smoking a cigar. "Ack, finally, lass. Where ye been?"

Tossing my keys into the bowl near the door, I shrug out of my coat, playing cool. "Where do you think? Doing your bidding, that's where. Where have *you* been these past few days?"

He ignores my jab. "Hugh's dead," he reveals, winding me. "Burned alive. But not before his face was painted like Aidan's. When we got there, it was too late to save him. But we saw what was done to him."

Face painted?

I remain calm, measuring my breaths because I think I know who's responsible. I don't think he is, however, because if he was, Punky wouldn't be alive.

"He was a knacker, but he was a good boyo."

I refuse to agree because Hugh Doyle was a sick motherfucker.

"Ach, what's done is done. I'm here to tell ya, yer gettin' yer wish."

"What wish?" I ask, walking into the living room slowly.

"To go home. Now, in fact."

I've clearly not heard him right. "W-what? Now? Like, right now?"

He digs into his inner jacket pocket and produces a plane ticket. "Aye. Yer job 'ere is done. I'll make sure yer ma gets what she needs."

The world begins to spin, but I quash down the urge to vomit. "But, what about—"

"Enough now," he warns, his cool demeanor swiftly replaced with the monster who was merely sleeping. "I'll not tell ye again. Pack yer things."

This is happening too fast. I need more time.

"From the looks of ya, ya'd think ya didn't want to leave."

Is this a test?

Hugh's death was just the beginning, but the beginning of what?

I need to warn Punky. If he said my *job* is done, then that means Punky's life is in danger. They have everything they need to carry out whatever fate they think is owed to him. I don't know what that is because they never told me.

But I can guess that it ends with his death.

All of this…because of a fucking name.

"Awesome," I say, slipping into the character I've been forced to become. I need to get out of here before it's too late for Punky. "I'll just go pack. Make sure my mom gets what was promised to her."

She's the reason for this. She and my little sister are innocent victims in all of this.

"Y've my word."

Turning on my heel, I don't run as I don't want to make a scene, but my heart is bursting from my chest as I enter my bedroom and reach for my suitcase. My hands tremble as I gather my minimal possessions. All I can think about is warning Punky.

As I turn, I jump, startled to see him standing in the doorway. "You can go," I say aloofly, gathering my cosmetics from the vanity. "I'll catch a cab."

I tell myself to keep calm because he's watching for any signs of deceit. One wrong move, and everyone will pay.

"Naw," he says with a sharp smile. "I'll run ye over."

"That won't be necessary," I counter, folding my T-shirts quickly. "I'm more than happy to—"

But he makes clear this isn't optional, and that's because he knows me better than I think. Punky's life isn't the only one in danger—mine is too.

"I won't hear of it. Nothin' but the best for my…daughter."

Oh, fuck me.

FIFTEEN

PUNKY

"If yer uncle finds out, he'll kill us," Cian says, limping as we head toward the warehouse.

He's still wounded, but insisted to come with Rory and me. I agreed because he deserves to be here after the lamping he took. Besides, tonight is the time for change in more ways than one.

Liam Doyle sent me a text early this morning with where I was to meet them tonight. They plan on intercepting the lorry on a backroad, a road which would only be known by someone who works for us. That's why Uncle Sean was in such a hurry to haul arse. We need everything in place to ensure our ambush doesn't fail.

But I need to do something before I go, and Uncle Sean

cannot know what that is.

The warehouse is packed with our men, and their "leader," Connor, is giving his usual bullshit speech about loyalty. He believes this is the way to keep them in line. That this is enough to keep them loyal. But he's about to see what a true leader is.

We enter the abandoned warehouse, which, thanks to Patrick Duffy, is now Connor's new secret lair. Lorries come and go from the premises, picking up gear which comes off the boats. It's risky because sooner or later, the peelers will be onto us.

But Connor believes changing location is the smart way to operate, and in most cases, it may be, but not with the organization we run. We need to have no ties, no links to our name. We can't gather in the masses any longer because this gives Chief Constable Moore a paper trail.

We need to operate incognito.

Our online dealings have had no issues, and this is the way to go from here going forward. It's time for change.

Connor doesn't know that, however. But he will.

"How 'bout ye give me some warnin' next time," Connor says to Danny, who is Ronan's mate.

He's just the man I want to talk to.

"Bout ye, Puck?" he says when we come up behind Connor. He's hoping to take the heat off himself. But he's got a lot to learn.

Connor turns, surprised to see me and the boys, as we don't

usually attend his "sermons."

He's been keeping scarce since the party, probably consoling Fiona, who's awful scundered that her perfect party was ruined by the peelers. She can pretend the money she spends isn't dirty money, but others aren't as easily fooled.

The Kellys' front—us being a family who struck it rich legally—is all bullshit. Everyone knows it, but no one has the bollocks to say it. Not until Connor made an enemy out of Chief Constable Moore.

"What're ye doin' here?" he says under his breath, but I have no interest in playing happy families.

I push past Connor and punch Danny square in the face. The men gasp, confused with what's going on. Danny cups his jaw, knowing better than to fight back.

"Now that I have yer attention," I say, standing in front of the men. "We need to 'ave a wee yarn."

Connor grabs my arm, attempting to pull me in line, but I'm done being his little bitch.

"Ye made a right bags of this, Connor." I coolly remove my arm from his grip, leaving him scundered in front of the men he's supposed to rule.

"Don't give me any of yer guff," he warns, but I laugh in response.

"Or what?"

Connor is not used to me talking back, and he definitely isn't used to me disobeying him.

"Yousens may have noticed that we're a couple of lads short?" The men look around at one another, unsure what's going on. "Bout ye, Danny? Missin' yer man, Ronan?"

Danny soon realizes what this is about. "Catch yerself on. I know nothin'."

Clucking my tongue, I calmly fold my arms across my chest. "Now, I know that yer lyin'. I think yousens are, and the reason for that is 'cause I know Ronan and Nolen were double-crossin' arseholes."

"Shut yer gub or ah'll shut it fer ye," Connor furiously whispers. But he doesn't seem to understand this isn't his gig anymore.

"Give it a lash. I dare ye," I reply, and for the first time in my life, I see that Connor is afeared of me.

"Yer a rocket," Danny exclaims, looking at Connor for backup. But Connor stays quiet.

"Aye, that I am," I confirm with a sinister grin. "That's why I had no issues barrin' Ronan from Northern Ireland. If I see him again, I'll do to him what was done to Nolen."

Silence.

"This is yer first and only warnin'. If I catch ye, and I will catch ye, goin' behind my back, I'll do ya. That's it. No second chances. Y'hear me? And anyone who thinks they can outsmart me…more power to ye."

Danny doesn't seem convinced. "Thon boy sits down to pee," he says, looking at his friends with a condescending grin.

"That's a cracker yarn, but how 'bout ye—"

Before he has a chance to continue, I punch him in the nose, breaking it. He howls, putting an end to defying me.

"Ronan was in business with the Doyles," I reveal, silencing Danny's cries. "And this was allowed because yousens don't respect or fear Connor Kelly. But ya *will* respect me, or I'll be breakin' more than just yer noses.

"I know who yer family are. I know where ye live. Trust me when I say, ye don't want to fuck with me, lads. I don't care about ye or yer families. Yer nothin' but a worker who is easily replaced, and when I say replaced, I mean no one will ever find yer corpse."

And just like that, the atmosphere in the room changes. I can smell their fear.

"Away now. We're done. These wee meetin's are no more. Ye do what I tell ya, or yer gone. Any questions?"

Silence once more.

"Didn't think so. Fuck off now."

With blood pouring through Danny's hands, he shouts, "Connor, yer gonna let this dirty blurt talk to us this way? Clean his clock!"

Before Connor has a chance to reply, I reach for the gun in the small of my back and shoot Danny in the kneecap. He collapses to the ground, shrieking and writhing in pain.

I look at Connor. "Is this the son ye'd be proud of? The son ye'd be proud to call yer own?"

He is expressionless. "Y'heard the lad, fuck off then."

The men don't know how to react, but soon realize this is a new empire in which there are new rules—my rules. They soon clear out, leaving me alone with Connor, the lads, and a gurning Danny.

"What's this about the Doyles?"

Looking at Cian and Rory, I gesture that they're to take Danny and dump him on his doorstep. Let his wife deal with him. They know what the plans are after that, so they nod.

Gripping him by the collar, Cian drags Danny through the warehouse, whistling a jolly tune. Once they're gone, Connor makes it clear that it's time I explained.

"The shipment of yokes and sneachta, the Doyles are comin' into Belfast for it," I bluntly reveal.

"Yer jokin' me?" Connor says, shaking his head.

"Does it look like I'm jokin'?"

Uncle Sean didn't want Connor to know any of this. He knew what that would mean for me, but I'm not afraid of Connor anymore. This arsehole deserves to know that his empire is crumbling before his eyes.

"How would ye know that?"

It's now or never…

"'Cause I broke into yer office and found the address of the Doyles pub in Dublin hidden in yer drawer. I went there and became friends with the Doyles. They trusted me, and in return, I killed Aidan and Hugh Doyle for their mistake.

"Liam and Brody think I'm an American, but someone has been tippin' them off. That's how they knew about our lorry. That's how Ronan and Nolen thought it was okay to go behind our backs.

"Someone almost killed Cian, thinking he was me. I don't know who told them that. Erin Doyle is apparently involved, but I don't buy it. So tonight, I'm going to get to the bottom of this. And I'm goin' to avenge my ma."

Connor is shook. His anger has taken a back seat as he processes everything I just said.

"Brody knows a Kelly took his brother, so he's gonna take your brother."

"Sean knows about this?"

I nod. "Aye. He knows it all."

"And ya didn't think to tell me this?" he exclaims, fists bunched by his sides.

"I'm tellin' ya now," I reply, unmoved by his theatrics.

Connor advances with his fist raised, but I reach out and seize it in my palm. "Y'll never raise a hand to me again. Or the twins. I'll kill ye if ye do. Come with me. I've a lot to tell ya."

He fumbles over his feet as I push him away. "Ya speak to yer da this way?"

I toss my head back, laughing. "Yer not my da. Ye never were. I've the test to prove it. I may not be a Kelly, but I'm the one who's about to save this family. So quit yer yackin', we're away to the lorry."

I don't wait for him as I turn on my heel and head for the car. His frantic footsteps reveal he's following. I order Connor's driver to go home as we won't be needing him.

As I get into my car, the passenger door is almost ripped from its hinges as Connor opens it. He gets in, ragin'.

"Don't forget yer seat belt," I quip, unable to wipe the smile from my bake.

He fights with it, but eventually gets it done up.

Once we're buckled up, I start our journey to where Uncle Sean and his reinforcements lay waiting in hiding. Liam is expecting me, so my face is one they're expecting to see. The others, however, not so much.

"Why'd ya have their address and not do anythin' 'bout it?" I ask, deciding to fill the uncomfortable silence with even more awkwardness.

"What did ya want me to do?"

"Um, how 'bout the right thing: killin' every last fucker who murdered yer wife?" I offer like it's a no-brainer.

"That's not how this works, Puck."

"It worked a beezer for me," I challenge, gripping the steering wheel. "But I suppose ye stopped carin'. Ya moved on with yer new life and that."

"I never forgot yer ma, contrary to what ye think. I loved her."

This would be the moment in a film or a book where the son forgives his father, and they work together and make amends for the past. But this is neither. This is my life, and no matter what Connor says, I'll never forgive him for what he did.

"So ya got the tests done?"

"Aye, you are not the father," I say, mimicking Maury Povich—Amber's favorite daytime TV host. "That's come as a huge relief, I can imagine."

"Naw, I can't say that it has."

His comment unsettles me.

"Why did ye have all that gear in yer bedroom? Y'know better than that. I can't get my head around it."

Connor turns to me. "Aye, I do, which is why I didn't put it there."

"I just cannot believe it. If ye didn't put it there, then who did?"

He shrugs, turning to look back out the windscreen, leaving me with this mankin' feeling in my guts. I don't want to believe him because if he didn't do it, the only other person who knew about the gear was Babydoll.

"Ya feelin' all right?" Connor asks with a hint of sarcasm. "Minus craic altogether knowin' y've been made a fool of."

Touché, fucker.

Refusing to give him the pleasure of seeing me ragin', I focus on the road and park the car where Uncle Sean directed me to. He has set up surveillance around the area, so the ambush will go off without a hitch. Looking at my watch, I see that it's time to go.

"Uncle Sean is comin' in north from Old Brewery Lane. Meet him there."

I open the door, but Connor reaches out and grips my arm. "Yer goin' alone?"

"Aye," I confirm. "I'm undercover, remember? I can't exactly have ye taggin' along."

"I don't like this plan."

"Well, stay in the car then." I yank my arm out from his grip. I don't have time for this. I arm myself and open the door.

"Puck!"

He leaps from the car and runs to where I stand. "I'll come with ye."

"That's not happenin', aul' lad. I didn't come this far for you to mess it up." I slip on my hoodie, positioning it low. "If ye want to help, go find Uncle Sean, will ya."

"This feels wrong. Ye tell me y've killed Hugh and Aidan. No way Brody is coming to Belfast, alone."

"Uncle Sean has it sorted. It's an ambush."

"And yer the bait? Is that it?"

"Sure, this is it," I reply angrily. "I brought ya here 'cause I wanted ye to see the mess y've made. If y'd sorted this years ago, then we wouldn't be here. But I refuse to let those cunts walk into my country, thinkin' they can steal from me!

"I may not 'ave yer blood in my veins, but themens killed my mum, and they're to pay for what they've done."

Connor doesn't say a word. Maybe he knows this isn't

negotiable.

With a sigh, he nods. "Ye may not be my chile, but y'll always be a Kelly, Punky."

This is the first time he's called me Punky. I don't know what it means, but I can't let sentiment get in the way.

"I'll go to yer uncle. Be careful."

He turns in the direction of where Uncle Sean will be waiting, but I stop him.

"Here. Take it." I offer him my gun, but he places a hand over mine.

"Naw, I'll be fine."

I don't insist and watch as he treks through the long grass, knowing this landscape like the back of his hand as this route is his.

Once he disappears, I inhale deeply, needing a second to compose myself. This is it. The moment I've been waiting for since I was locked in thon wardrobe and forced to watch my innocence be destroyed.

I walk in the opposite direction of Connor, ready to meet Liam and whoever else he has with him. I want to think it'll be Brody, but I'm not sure. Either way, a message will be sent to every Doyle left standing—don't fuck with Puck Kelly. Belfast is mine.

It's a ten-minute walk which gives me more than enough time to think about what Connor said. If he didn't put the drugs in the safe, who did?

I refuse to believe it was Babydoll, but when it comes to her, I've a bad dose of denial. I know that. But I can't believe she would plant drugs, only to tell me they're there. It doesn't make sense. None of this does.

Connor's got to be lying. But I don't think he is. However, when I see a black van ahead, I push away those thoughts and focus.

Liam said he'd be waiting at this precise spot, exactly five minutes before the lorry was headed this way. His knowledge of the driver's schedule has me guessing Ferris is also in cahoots with the Doyles. Or at the very least, in contact with whoever the rat is.

"This is for you, Ma," I whisper aloud, adrenaline coursing through me.

When Liam sees me, he waves. I instantly notice the gun concealed in the small of his back. He's come prepared for bloodshed too it seems.

"Hey," I say as I step over the banjaxed fence. "You could have told me I had to hike through the wilderness. This place is off the map."

Uncle Sean purposely had me take this precise route as I was to be on lookout for any Doyles, keeping dick on us. The coast was clear.

He laughs, appearing amused. "Sorry 'bout that. But we had to keep it low key."

"No worries. So what's the plan?" I ask, keeping my cool.

"The lorry should be here in"—he peers down at his gold watch—"four and a half minutes."

"And then what? You were a little vague on the details."

"Ach, bucko, why're ye askin' so many questions? Anyone would think ya were nervous."

Something is different about Liam. His usual cockiness is replaced with urgency. Something is wrong.

"Nope, what would I have to be nervous about?" I ask, watching Liam closely.

He reaches into his pocket, while I'm ready to reach for my gun. But when he lights a cigarette, I tell myself to calm the fuck down.

Taking his time, he shrugs. "Don't know…maybe 'cause yer not who ye say y'are."

Fuck…

The van door opens and out steps a man who is about to change the course of everything.

Here stands Brody Doyle—the fucker who was involved with Ma and could be my father. When I see him, I'm instantly hit with the air of authority all men in power hold. Connor's is almost suffocating, but Brody's is different.

Unlike Connor, Brody is a chameleon. He draws people in with a fake smile, a pleasant demeanor, but I know these are just tricks he's mastered to lure in his prey. He's tall, in good shape, I can see why Mum may have fallen for his charms. I look for any similarities between us, but I refuse to believe that

I'm his son.

"Hello, son."

Does he mean that term literally?

These are just tricks men like him play. I know better. I need to get it together.

"What's up?" I casually say with a wave. The lorry will be here soon. I just need to stall them until then.

"Nice to finally meet ya." His accent is smooth, refined.

He offers his hand, and the moment we shake, rage overtakes me.

"You too. You're Liam's father? I recognize your voice," I say, playing coy. But we both know he didn't come up the Lagan in a bubble.

"I admire yer tenacity, lad, but let's stop the bullshit."

"I'm sorry?"

Four minutes...

Brody smiles, but there is nothing pleasant about the gesture. "I know you, do I not?"

"Nope. Don't think so," I reply, not disguising my annoyance.

Brody examines me. I wonder what he sees. "We've got a lot to talk about. But I cannot do that with ye lying to me. I can hardly call ye Mike when that's not your name."

"Who do you think I am then?" I pose, as I want to uncover how much he actually knows.

Liam's footsteps announce he is getting closer and closer to me.

"I don't think, lad, I know yer a Kelly. Puck Kelly. I know yer the one who killed my brother and my son. I know ye were the one who painted their faces like ya paint yers. They were at fault for trustin' ya. They knew better. So does Liam."

Three minutes and thirty seconds…

"You're mistaken," I press, continuing to stall. "I don't know who told you all this, but they're wrong."

Brody nods, but he doesn't buy it. "Ach, I'm sorry then. We must have got our wires crossed," he says, gesturing with his chin toward the van.

The door opens, and the person who is shoved out of the van has me questioning everything. But I don't allow my emotions to betray me. I can't.

Babydoll is escorted over to Brody by some arsehole. Her chin is downcast. She can't even look at me. Is she his prisoner? Has he captured her as he did with Cian? I don't understand.

"Don't be afraid," Brody soothes Babydoll who is trying her hardest to suppress her sniffles. "If what ye say is true and ya don't know him, then that's my mistake. But if yer lyin'—"

He grabs a hold of Babydoll's ponytail and tugs her head back.

I instantly advance. "Let her go."

Brody smirks, knowing he's won. "Ye don't know him, do ye?"

Babydoll holds her ground. "No, I do not." She doesn't disguise her accent, so Brody knows she's American.

"All right, my mistake then," he says, but he doesn't believe her. "If ya don't know him, then it wouldn't bother ye if I killed him in front of ye. Or maybe I should make him watch me kill you. Get on yer knees."

He lets Babydoll go, and she stumbles, attempting to find her footing. The fucker behind her forces her to her knees as she fights him savagely. Brody reaches into his holster and produces a gun.

"I'm sorry," she mouths to me, tears running down her cheeks as Brody presses the gun to the back of her head.

But it doesn't end this way for us.

Reaching for my gun with speed, I point it at Brody, who laughs animatedly. The time has come for this to end once and for all.

"Let her go, ya fucker," I say, Mike from America long gone. "Aye, I'm Puck Kelly, and I killed yer brother and son. I would do it again given half the chance."

Babydoll shakes her head, squeezing her eyes shut.

"Y'll need to give me a minute because I've been dreamin' of this day," Brody says, unable to contain his excitement. "Y've caused so much trouble, lad."

"Cheers, thank you," I sarcastically reply. "Get up, Babydoll."

Babydoll's lower lip trembles as she comes to a cautious stand. I expect her to come over to me, but she doesn't. She stands by Brody.

"Babydoll?" he questions, laughing.

I never take my gun off Brody, but that doesn't bother him.

"I never thought this would work."

"What would?" I question.

"This," Brody replies, gesturing with his gun between Babydoll and me.

"Spare me the fuckin' theatrics," I snap, not interested in playing his games.

"Punky, don't—" Babydoll warns, fresh tears rolling down her cheeks.

"It's too late for that. He deserves to know. Should I tell him? Or do you want to?"

I beg of her to explain what he's talking about, but all she does is look at me with nothing but desperation. "I'm sorry. Please forgive...me."

I lower my gun, suddenly realizing it'll do no good because I'm in this alone. No one here is a friend; they're all my foes.

"Did ye really kill my ma?" I ask Brody, peeling back the layers and starting at where it all began.

"Aye, I did," he affirms with a slow nod as he puts away his gun. "Ye know why?"

I ignore his question because there is something else I need to expose first. "Who else? There were three men. I know one of them was yer brother. Who was the other man?"

Brody smiles, as if reliving the memory of raping and killing my mum is one to be happy about. "Someone very close to home, Puck. He's the reason she died."

"Who?" I ask between clenched teeth.

"I don't want to cause any trouble."

Advancing, I press the gun to the middle of Brody's forehead. "Too late for that. Tell me."

He knows I won't shoot, not until I get the answers I seek. The messed-up thing is that he's the one person who can tell me the truth and I'd believe him because he has no reason to lie.

"It was Connor, lad. He was the one who killed yer ma."

"Ya lie," I gasp, my grip on the gun tightening. Not yet, I tell myself. His time is coming.

"Ach, naw, I tell ye the truth. Connor was the one who unlocked the wardrobe for ye, Puck. He knew ya were there. He wanted Cara to suffer, and the only way to do that was through ye."

I don't believe him. It can't be true. But he knows about someone unlocking the wardrobe, how that act seemed so personal.

"Cara was a beautiful woman. But she knew too much. She was nosy and smart, just like you. I knew sooner or later ye'd find out what we did, which is why I needed to get to yer first."

"What d'ye mean?" I'm hardly holding it together.

"The Kellys and the Doyles, we're private people. I hadn't seen ya since ye were a wain. I didn't know whatcha looked like and I needed to."

"Why?"

"'Cause I knew it'd eventually come to this. Yer collateral, and I needed a backup plan, just in case. It doesn't make sense. But it will."

Thoughts of the lorry arriving are long gone because all that matters is this. I don't want to believe Brody, but I do.

"So, when my Camilla came to me, ye can imagine my excitement. It was the perfect plan."

"Who the fuck is Camilla?" I exclaim, confused.

But when Babydoll finally meets my eyes, I understand what she's sorry for. "Me. But call me Cami."

Brody places his arm around her, like he didn't just hold a gun to her some minutes ago. "Aye, y'are. When Camilla phoned me, telling me her ma was sick with cancer and she needed help, it was like the Lord himself delivered her to me.

"I needed someone ya didn't know to befriend ye. But she did more than that, didn't she?"

I beseech she tell me he's lying, but Brody Doyle has spoken no lies. Ironically, he's the only person who's told me the truth.

"It was a fair trade—find out everything she could about the Kellys, about ye, and tell me everythin' she found out. In return, I would ensure her ma was taken care of financially as cancer treatment is quare expensive in the USA.

"She wormed her way into yer world, workin' for the Duffys so she could give me all the information to properties I could buy anonymously in Northern Ireland. And to also tell me which yer da was workin' out of. He's very secretive, he is."

"I'm sorry," Babydoll—Cami—cries, her lower lip

trembling.

"Why didn't ye tell me?" I ask, numb.

"I wanted to. So many times. But my mom, my sister, if I didn't do this, they'd suffer. My mom will die, and I have no money, no family to look after my little sister. I had no choice," she explains, but all I hear are excuses.

"I've worked my ass off since I was twelve years old, but since Mom got sick, I've cared for her, and it just…it became too much. I needed help. I didn't know what else to do. When he told me what I had to do, I didn't know who you were. I didn't know I'd fall in lo—"

"Enough!" I warn, not wanting to hear those words leave her deceitful lips.

"Please, Punky, understand it from my point of view. This"—she gestures around us—"is all because you wanted to protect your mom when you couldn't, but I have that chance. Please don't hate me for it. I swear to you, I tried to stop this when I had the chance. I tried to protect you, even when I knew I was putting my mom and my sister at risk.

"I told you about the police coming to your house because… because I was the one who planted the drugs. Brody threatened my mom if I didn't do it! But I felt guilty. I couldn't do that to you. So I told you the truth."

I shake my head, disgusted with myself

"I gave you back your brooch even though I got whipped for it."

Why did they want my ma's brooch? And now I know why she got those welts—because of me.

"How can I trust a word that comes outta yer mouth?" I question, angry with myself for not seeing her for what she is.

"Check your pocket."

I do what she says and when my fingers pass over a folded piece of paper, I pull it out. Unfolding it, my heart squeezes inside my chest as I read over Babydoll's handwriting. It's come too little, too late. And it changes everything beyond repair.

I was sent to spy on you. To make you trust me. I was sent to make you fall in love with me. But I didn't have to pretend because I do...I love you. My name is Camilla Doyle. Brody Doyle is my father. Please forgive me.

"Yer a...Doyle?" I ask, my voice dangerously low.

She nods, a tear trickling down her cheek.

"I didn't tell you because I knew you'd hate me...well, hate me more than you already do. I didn't even know who I was until a few months ago. I didn't understand this war between the Doyles and Kellys. Catholics versus Protestants."

Brody grins victoriously, and why shouldn't he—he's outsmarted us all. "Camilla's ma used to work for me. What can I say? I have a thing for blondes," he says flippantly.

Babydoll curls her lip, disgusted as I am. "My mom left Ireland and came back to America, pregnant with me. She never told me who my father was, but when she got sick, I went through her things and found out who he was. I was desperate. She needed me, and after being there for me my entire life, I needed to be the strong one.

"I just didn't know what I was getting myself into. I didn't know that my father was a selfish son of a bitch."

Brody grins, unbothered. "My sons and brother didn't know about my plan, which is why ye were able to infiltrate our operation, 'Mike.'"

"*You're* Mike?" Babydoll asks, eyes wide. "Oh my God. I thought you were safe because they were going to use Mike. But they were going to use you. You lied to me, *Father*."

Brody shrugs, untroubled, as he continues his story. "We needed a scapegoat, someone to take the fall for what we have planned. They wanted ye to trust them so when the time came, ye'd serve yer purpose.

"They must have trusted ye 'cause they knew."

"Knew what?" I ask, my anger close to boiling point.

"That yer family."

Babydoll looks between us, confused. She doesn't know what this means. But I do.

Brody reaches into his pocket and produces a piece of paper. He offers it to me. "Here are the answers ya want. I always had my suspicions. Dr. Dunne is a good friend of mine and called me with the news."

Snatching it from him, I read over the information, still not believing it even though it's printed in black and white. How would Dr. Dunne have Brody's results on file?

But the letter is from the same paternity clinic I used to find out Connor wasn't my dad, and it's the same clinic to tell me who is—I'm a Doyle. I'm Brody Doyle's son. It's a perfect match.

Liam snares the paper from my hands, obviously kept in the dark about this wee fact, that I'm his half-brother, which means Babydoll is my…half-sister.

Vomit rises, but I hold it down because I deserve this. This is what I get for trusting someone I shouldn't have. Although we didn't know, it doesn't make a difference. It can never erase what we did, over and over again.

"What is it?" she asks, afraid.

I can't speak. I can barely think.

"Camilla, Puck is yer half-brother." Brody looks at us proudly.

"*What?*" she gasps, placing her trembling hand over her mouth. "That's n-not possible."

"It's very possible," Liam says with disgust, tossing the piece of paper at her.

She catches it and reads over the evidence, shame and disgust coloring her scarlet. "Did you know he was my br— what he was?"

Brody shakes his head. "I knew it was a possibility, but it wasn't confirmed until recently. What a plot twist. No wonder ye were drawn to one another. Yer blood."

"Just stop," she cries, shaking her head. "Why didn't you tell me Connor wasn't your father? And that Brody could be…"

I want to console her, but how can I? Not only is she a liar, she's my fucking sister and touching her the way I want is a thing of the past. A past I want to forget.

"He killed Uncle Aidan and Hugh. Brother or not, he's going to pay!" Liam declares, untouched by this impromptu family reunion.

"This is yer fault, boyo. If ye didn't go behind my back and act like a big man, then none of this would have happened. Ye didn't think I had a plan this whole time?"

And now, the truth to why we're here emerges.

The lorry comes down the road, just on time.

"Ye didn't think I could do this alone, is it? I always had someone on the inside, workin' together and bidin' our time. That time is now."

"Who?" I ask, broken in ways I never thought possible.

"He's been under yer nose this entire time. Ye brought him here. This was all possible because of you two."

I did?

Babydoll cups her face, sobbing. All she wanted was to help her ma. Just like I did. But this sacrifice has cost us so much, and we'll never get it back.

There are so many holes in this story, and I know I won't get the full story until I uncover who Brody's partner is. None of this makes any sense. All I know is that Babydoll isn't the enemy. She wasn't the one who organized all of this. Someone else did.

But who?

"Camilla played a part, of course. If it wasn't for her, we wouldn't know what we do. She told me everything."

I suddenly realize why they thought Cian was me. "Yer the one who told them Cian was me?"

She nods. "I didn't know what to do. I didn't think they were going to hurt him. When Brody asked me who you were, I pointed at your friend. The photo was taken the night of the party."

I remember the photographer taking a picture of us. We should have known better than to be so careless. This is why we're careful. I was able to remain undetected with Liam and Aidan because they didn't know who I was.

But Brody knew, and Babydoll failed his test. She played right into his hands. This was his way of finding out just what she was prepared to do to save me. We were all his pawns. But I still don't know why. I don't know how he found out I wasn't Mike.

This isn't just about drugs. This is personal. But then again, it always has been.

There is so much to process, but now isn't the time because when the lorry comes to a stop, it's time to uncover the rest of this fucked-up tale.

"Ye feeling all right, son?" Brody sarcastically asks, touching my shoulder.

"Don'tcha call me that ever again," I warn, recoiling forcibly.

"Ach, ye may change yer mind when ye find out who's behind all this. But don'tcha bother yerself with that. I'll take care of them. They can't be trusted, and just like you, Camilla, my sons, yousens played a role, but playtime is over now.

"There's room for only one leader. They think I'm playin' by their rules, but I'm not."

I turn over my shoulder to look at him. I don't know when or how, but one way or another, I'm going to kill this cunt and everyone who played a part in this show.

Ferris kills the engine and exits the lorry. I'm expecting to see Uncle Sean with him, as that was the plan. But he's not here.

"Ferris, how's the wains?" Brody asks like they're old friends catching up—they probably are.

Liam looks as surprised as I am, which confirms he played no part in this new plan. Robbing us was always part of the plan, but Liam was kept in the dark with the details. His anger is reflective of mine.

"Ack, they're always wantin'," Ferris replies. When he sees me, his eyes widen as he obviously wasn't expecting me here.

"Puck?"

"Bout ye?" I stare him straight in the eye.

"What's he doing 'ere?" He nervously looks at Brody.

"Surprise, shitehawk."

"Everythin' inside?" Brody asks, wanting to get down to

business.

Ferris nods, his apprehension evident.

"Thanks, mate. Really appreciate it."

Before anyone has a chance to figure out what's going on, Brody takes out his gun and shoots Ferris between the eyes. He's dead before he hits the ground.

I stand emotionless because Ferris chose his fate. Just as we all have.

Brody steps over Ferris, gesturing Liam is to follow him. I could end this right here, right now and kill Brody where he stands. But I cannot. I do that, and I'll never find out the truth.

Babydoll keeps her distance. No matter that I know her real name, she'll always be Babydoll to me.

Just as Liam is about to open the back of the lorry, Brody turns to me. "C'mere. You can do the honors."

I'm not thick. I know Brody is concerned that whoever his partner in crime is will double-cross him. Is that why he needed me as collateral? It's the only thing that makes sense. I'm valuable to this person. Or so Brody thinks I am.

With nothing to lose, I walk forward, but that's as far as I get because rustling from the dense bushland alerts us that someone is coming, and that someone is Connor.

"Don'tcha move, Puck," he orders, stepping onto the gravel road. I look behind him but don't see Uncle Sean. Where is he?

"Connor Kelly," Brody says with a wide grin. "Y'always knew how to make an entrance."

"Fuck ye," Connor spits, looking at where Ferris' corpse is strewn on the ground. "This wasn't supposed to happen."

Brody shrugs while I look at Connor. What's that mean?

"We had a deal. Why would ya break it? Why now?"

"Deal? What fuckin' deal?" I question. This is the first time I've ever heard this. As far as I knew, Connor hadn't seen Brody for years.

A sinking feeling hits me low and I begin to fear for my uncle.

I brought Connor here, thinking I was teaching him a lesson, but what if Uncle Sean didn't want him here for a reason. What if what Brody said was right, and it *was* Connor who killed Ma. What if Connor is the inside man?

It makes sense. For someone to be able to penetrate without detection would mean they know the workings of our business like the back of their hand. I suddenly regret my actions. Did I welcome the enemy into this with open arms?

"That deal was made long ago," Brody replies calmly. "Things change. People change."

"Ye made a deal with a *fucking* Kelly?" Liam spits, just as in the dark as I am.

"Ach son, don'tcha be speaking about things ya have no idea about. I did what I had to for this family. I never wanted a part of Belfast."

"And I with Dublin," Connor counters, but something's changed.

What? What's changed for them to be here now?

"Puck is my son," Brody states, smiling when Connor's surprise is clear. "I've the test to prove it."

Connor turns to me, guilt and sorrow reflecting in his eyes. "Y'll always be a Kelly," he says, and I believe him. "No matter what the tests say, y'll always be my wain. Mine and yer ma's."

"Do ye know who killed my ma?" I ask, begging he tell me the truth once and for all.

He sighs, complete exhaustion overtaking him. "Aye, I do. And I'm sorry for everything. But I'm about to make it right."

I stand utterly still when he reaches for me and cups the back of my neck, drawing me close.

"Look after the twins for me," he whispers into my ear.

When I desperately try to break away, he holds me tight. He's not done.

"Yer all they have now. I was hard on ya because I knew one day…y'd rule this country. And that day is now. No matter what name ye bear, y'll always be my wain. Y'll always be Puck Connor Kelly, and don'tcha be forgettin' it.

"Yer a leader. Lead with the compassion yer ma gave ya. And rule with the cruelty I taught ya because it's the only way to survive in our world. I'm sorry I never told ya this…but I love ya, and I'm proud of the man y've become."

Before I have a chance to ask what he means, the doors on the back of the truck are kicked open and gunfire erupts around us. Connor shoves me out of the way while I attempt to process what the fuck is going on.

I take cover behind the wheel of the lorry, focusing on the bedlam that is happening feet away. Masked men appear out of nowhere, shooting one another. I don't know who is on our side, but when I see Uncle Sean jump out of the back of the truck and take aim at Brody, I realize he was just biding his time to ambush this fucker. He and Connor were.

Connor has taken cover behind the door of the lorry, ducking his head out to shoot anyone game enough to try to take him down. Instantly, my survival instinct kicks in, and I reach for my gun, focusing on where Babydoll is.

She's hiding behind the back of the van, but it won't be long until she's picked off by these men. She's unarmed and afraid. I can't leave her alone.

Keeping low, I scope out my surroundings and see about thirty men shooting at one another. Some are Kellys. Some are Doyles. Neither family came into this unprepared. Uncle Sean knew Brody wouldn't come unmanned, which is why he's rounded up our troops.

I can't see their faces as they're wearing balaclavas, but if Uncle Sean trusts them, then I do too, which is why I take a deep breath and make a run for the van.

Gunshots tear around me, but I shoot first, taking down two men who advance toward me, guns raised. I don't know where anyone else is because all I see is a masked man running toward the back of the van, ready to shoot.

"Baby!" I scream to be heard over the gunfire.

She pokes her head around the van, and I gesture for her to run. But it's too late, and a shot is fired.

With adrenaline coursing through me, I charge through the chaos, shooting anyone who stands in my way. My boots kick at the gravel as I scramble to get to Babydoll, and when I do, I almost cry in relief.

Sliding along the ground, I cover her with my body, and she hugs me tight. "Your uncle shot h-him," she states, her voice trembling.

The man lies in a crumpled mess, feet away. I rip off his balaclava, and when I see it's Danny, I want to kill him again. Even with a busted kneecap, his loyalty knows no bounds. Every one of our men are traitorous fuckers, and it's time they all paid.

"Rule with the cruelty I taught ya because it's the only way to survive in our world."

Connor's words echo inside my head, and although I'll never forgive him, I understand why he did what he did. He raised a ruthless, heartless monster because he knew it would always come to this. Opening his heart is what got him in trouble, and he never wanted that for me.

In his own fucked-up way, he was trying to teach me not to be like him. Love and emotion are what got him here. A leader cannot love because love leads to destruction…

Prying the gun from Danny's lifeless hand, I give it to Babydoll. Looking into the back window, I see the keys are in the ignition.

"Get inside the van and drive away from here."

"Punky—" she argues.

"I'll not tell ya again! The next town is only over the way. Go."

"I won't leave you," she cries, brushing the hair from my face.

Turning my cheek, I hate that I still crave her touch after everything I know. "Ya must."

She realizes why I turned away from her and gasps, removing her hands with shame. "We didn't do anything wrong. We didn't know," she says, tears streaming into her lips, lips I want to kiss over and over again.

"But now we do. And we have to stop. I can't be around ye, Babydoll, 'cause I want ya how a brother should not want a sister. Please go. I need ya to be safe."

She looks at me, pleading I tell her it'll be all right. But it won't be. Nothing will be ever again.

She slams her mouth to mine, kissing me with finality because we both know this is goodbye. We cannot deny these feelings for one another, and until we learn how to deal with them, then we need to be apart.

"I…love you," she whispers against my lips, cupping my cheeks and drawing us brow to brow. "And I'm so sorry for betraying you."

I taste her salty kisses and surrender—one last time. "I love ye, too. I always will. But I can't be anywhere near ya. I promised ya if ye were a threat…I'd kill ye. But I can't hurt ya. Nor can I trust ya. So, goodbye, Baby."

She nods jerkily, still clutching onto me, never wanting to let go. "Ex favilla nos resurgemus," she says, reciting the tattoo across my collarbone. "From the ashes we will rise…I'll never give up."

Planting a soft kiss to her forehead, I let go of my humanity because I'll never love anyone as much as I do her and that makes me weak. Something I refuse to be ever again.

"I'll cover ya," I say, gesturing she's to make a run for the driver's side.

She hugs her gun, taking three deep breaths.

A thought suddenly occurs to me. "How'd ya know he was my uncle?"

Babydoll said Uncle Sean shot Danny. How did she know who he was? I never introduced them.

Before I can ask her, however, I hear footsteps advancing toward us.

"Go!" I scream, coming to a stand and guarding Babydoll with my body as I lead her toward the driver's side.

My focus is straight ahead, which is an error I'll regret for the rest of my life, as I don't see a masked man emerge from the dense bushlands to my right. He aims his gun and fires a bullet which lodges into my chest.

But I persevere. It's merely a scratch.

Only a couple more feet and Babydoll will be safe.

Just as I'm about to open the door and shove her inside, someone screams my name, and that person is Connor, who dives in front of me, before collapsing into a twisted heap on the ground. Everything comes to a screeching halt.

"Connor?" I ask, suddenly feeling faint, and when I press a hand over my chest, I realize that *scratch* is actually a lot worse than I thought.

I drop to my knees beside Connor, gasping for air.

"Punky!" Babydoll cries, catching me from falling. "Oh my God. You're hurt b-bad."

I lean into her, my lungs wheezing as I attempt to breathe. But it doesn't end this way.

"Connor?" I shove at his shoulder, flinching when my hand is saturated in his blood.

He groans, his eyes flickering open. "Do-don't…" He attempts to speak, but blood trickles from his mouth.

"Save yer strength," I say, pressing my hands over the wound to his stomach. "Help is comin."

"Babydoll, call the peelers!" I don't care that they'll find a lorry full of drugs. I'll take the blame as long as it'll save Connor because he just saved me. He took a bullet for me.

"They're comin," Connor pants, peering up at me, gulping in mouthfuls of air. "I called them."

"*What?*"

"I told them what I did. We were all going to pay for our

crimes. But yer…" He splutters up blood but won't go down without a fight. "I didn't kill yer ma. I lo-loved her. So much. The deal I made was to save ye."

Babydoll cries beside me, holding me up as I fight to stay awake. "Who killed her?"

Connor reaches up and with trembling fingers, he wipes away the tears I didn't even know I was shedding. "Don't trust him," he pants, struggling to breathe.

"Who?" I scream, placing my hand over his. He's freezin'.

"Yer uncle," he pants, flinching in pain. "Don't trust…Sean."

His hand grows limp, but I press it to my face, refusing to accept this. No, this is not the end. He can't leave the earth like this.

"Connor?" I wheeze, squeezing his hand, begging he take my strength and make it his own.

"Punky, he's g-gone."

But I refuse to listen to Babydoll's pleas. There is no way he's gone. This man is the strongest arsehole I know.

"Aul' lad?" I press, shoving at his chest, the chest which no longer fills with air. "…Dad?"

Grief tackles me, and I'm transported back to that bedroom floor when I pleaded for my ma to wake up. But just like her, Connor won't. He's dead. I've watched both my parents perish, and I still don't know why.

With his blood mingled with mine, I swipe three fingers down the middle of my forehead, promising that his death won't be in vain.

Coming to a wobbly stand, I look for Uncle Sean and see him fighting with a masked man. I clutch Babydoll by the arm and shove her into the van. She tries to fight me, but I lean inside and buckle her in.

"Drive."

With bittersweet tears, she makes the promise I asked of her. "I'll come ba-back to you."

And I hope one day she will.

Slamming the door shut, I ignore the tingling in my limbs as blood gushes from me and shoot any man who stands in Babydoll's way.

Uncle Sean turns, and when he sees me shoot, his eyes widen.

Don't trust…Sean.

Before I leave this earth, I need to know why.

So, with my gun raised, I hobble over, demanding he give me the answers I seek. I don't even know where Brody is, and honestly, I don't care. All I care about is finding out why I shouldn't trust the one man who I do trust with my entire being.

"What did ye do?" I scream, training the gun on Uncle Sean.

He shoots two men who come running for him. "Punky, yer jokin' me? Yer gonna shoot me, are ye?"

"Why did Connor tell me not to trust ya? Those were the

last words to leave him!"

"Connor is dead?"

"Answer the fucking question!" I hear the van's motor start. It's almost over. She's safe.

"I don't know, lad!" Sean cries, lowering his gun, but I don't lower mine.

"How did Babydoll know who ye were?"

"Because she told me. When she came to the house lookin' for ya, she told me everythin'. I promised not to tell ya because I had a plan."

"*This* was yer fucking plan?" I exclaim, arms out wide.

"Naw. Connor was never meant to be here. Why did ya bring him? He's called the chief constable. They'll be here in minutes. We've got to go."

When he tries to reach for me, I recoil. His hurt is palpable, but I don't know who to believe.

"I'll explain everythin', but now, we've got to go. If we don't, we'll go to prison for a very long time. That lorry is full of drugs!"

"I don't care anymore," I confess, everything becoming murky.

"Stop that!" Uncle Sean scolds. "We go now, and we let the Doyles take the blame. They're here when they're not supposed to be. It's the perfect plan. It's what I wanted to happen."

"Is it now?"

Uncle Sean looks over my shoulder as the barrel of a gun

presses to the back of my head. Turning around slowly, what I see changes the course of everything once more.

Brody and Liam have three people who trusted me at gunpoint, revealing no one will get out of this alive. I thought she had fled in the van. But that would have been too easy, and nothing in life ever is.

Cian, Rory, and Babydoll are their prisoners, and the only exchange acceptable is my life for theirs. They put up a fight, as they're bloody and bruised, but it wasn't enough.

Cian and Rory got ambushed while keeping dick—I have no doubt about that. They were only here because I asked them to, because I believed our plan would work.

"Let them go," Uncle Sean warns, coming to stand next to me, gun pointed at Brody.

Brody grins. "Really sorry, but I can't do that. Ya see, someone has got to take the blame for this."

Sirens wail in the distance. Connor *did* call the police, knowing he would be held accountable for this entire thing.

"And that won't be me."

I look at Cian, who nods discreetly. He and Rory can take Liam and Brody. But what Brody says next, seals the deal.

"If I go down, then all of ye will too; that includes yer ma, Camilla. That's why I brought ye here. Ya were always collateral. Ye were always my get out of jail free card because I knew Puck would do anythin' to save ya."

Babydoll shakes her head, blood trickling from the corner

of her mouth.

"I go to prison, yer ma gets nothin'. I will make sure she suffers, and yer little sister, well, ya saw firsthand how cruel the Doyle men can be. We like to keep it in the family. I'm sure ya came to learn that from Hugh. He punished ya, did he not?"

What does that mean?

When she lowers her eyes, ashamed, I understand that Hugh was the one who whipped her and did so much more than I expected.

"Ya bleedin' fucker," Uncle Sean spits, his arm never wavering from Brody.

Five men appear from the bushes, surrounding us, guns raised.

Uncle Sean closes his eyes, defeated.

This was never an ambush; this was a suicide mission. We thought we had the upper hand, but the Doyles were always ten steps ahead. This was supposed to work, and it would have if they weren't tipped off. I still don't know by whom.

"Okay then, let it be me." Uncle Sean lowers his gun and raises his hands in the air.

Brody laughs, and I have no idea why.

"Naw, I think not, Sean. Somethin' else is headed yer way."

It happens in the blink of an eye.

Brody fires, and Uncle Sean drops to his knees before collapsing onto his front with a thud.

I stare at my uncle and my dad who lay feet apart,

slaughtered by the Doyles, but the ironic thing is, they aren't to blame—I am.

If only I'd let matters be and not pursued who killed my ma, then things would have been different. If I never went to Dublin, then none of this would have happened. But the bloodshed around us, it's my doing.

All of it is.

So many have suffered because of me…this is my fault.

Cian elbows Liam in the stomach, but the masked men ascend on him, beating him and Rory while Brody stands back with a smile.

He wants me to see what I caused. The mayhem I brought onto the people I love.

When one of the men pulls Babydoll's hair and yanks her head back, licking along her neck, I know what I have to do. I hurt the ones I love and it's time I stopped it. Stopped it all.

"Ya won, Brody. Let them go," I coolly say, standing tall, regardless of my wounds. "Promise me they'll be all right."

Brody orders the man who has Babydoll to let her go.

"Ye 'ave my word."

"She gets everythin' ya promised her?"

"I swear it."

Babydoll tries to fight, but the man grips her waist, holding her back. "No! Let me go. Don't do this, Punky! You'll go to jail for a very long time."

I ignore her and focus on Cian and Rory. "I'm sorry I got

ya involved."

"Y've got nothin' to be sorry for," Cian says, tears in his eyes. He knows we can't win this, not with Uncle Sean and Connor dead.

Uncle Sean thought he had men on his side, but if only I'd told him sooner about Ronan and my theory about the traitors among us, he would have known the men fighting with him weren't with us—they were against us.

"My da—" Rory starts, but is soon cut off.

"Yer da will suffer the same way as Connor Kelly if ye retaliate. We know who they are. We were willin' to let matters be, but then ye had to stick yer nose in business that didn't concern ya," Brody states confidently.

This is our punishment for thinking we could outsmart a world we know nothing about.

"There is so much ye don't know, Puck. Maybe one day I'll tell ya."

"Should we head?" Liam asks as the sirens get closer and closer.

"That's up to yer brother."

Cian and Rory look between us slowly, confused. But I don't have the time to explain.

"Aye, head on. I'll deal with the peelers."

"NO!" Babydoll cries, running over to me. "Punky, no! Fight. Tell the police the truth."

"Who are they going to believe, I do wonder?" I say, looking at Brody. "And I don't do this, yer ma, she dies. I won't allow that. Y've a chance to help her, and I've a chance to make this right."

"I'll n-never stop fighting for y-you," she cries, throwing her arms around me.

I hug her back, allowing myself this comfort because I won't feel it ever again. "I'm doin' this so we're even. But I don't want to see ye again. No matter what ye did, ya lied to me, and now I have the deaths of my family on my hands. I cannot forgive ya. And ye shouldn't forgive me."

I gently push her away, gesturing to Brody to take her away.

"Punky?" she questions, violently ripping free when one of the men try to drag her toward the van. "This isn't your fault!"

But I don't want to hear it.

"Ya save her fuckin' ma," I order Brody. "Whatever money she needs, ya give it to her. If she dies, I'll tell the peelers everythin'."

Brody nods. "And Belfast? Who rules now?"

Cian and Rory avert their gazes because even though they and their dads are involved, this business only succeeded because of the Kellys. Now that the Kellys are no more, they know it won't be the same. Look what Brody was able to achieve with Connor and Uncle Sean alive.

With them dead, the strongest links in our chain, we don't stand a chance.

"It's yours."

Brody tips his face toward the heavens, inhaling in victory because this is what he has always wanted—Belfast.

I'll never find out who his partner was, but it doesn't matter. The people I love are dead. This is the only thing I can do to ensure that the ones left standing don't suffer because of me.

"Punky, we'll find a way," Cian says, rushing forward and hugging me. "I love ye, brother."

I hug him back numbly. "Look after the twins for me."

Look after the twins for me…

I now understand why Connor asked this of me—he called the peelers because he was going to take the fall. He knew he couldn't win against Brody. He knew that his empire had crumbled because he let it. But his faith in me allows me to see that he believed I could repair the damage he had done.

And I would have.

He allowed the traitor to bring our kingdom down, brick by brick, and him going to prison was the punishment he would accept for his crimes. But he never anticipated that something he thought he wasn't capable of would bring him down—his love for me.

His death, Uncle Sean's death; they're on me.

"My dad will get his lawyer—"

"No," I argue, consciousness slipping away. "Ye leave it be. Too much blood has been shed and for what? You live yer life, the life ye deserve, away from this, away from me. Mind this for me."

Digging into my pocket, I give him my ma's brooch. I don't need it anymore.

"I won't let ye rot in prison!" Cian shakes his head stubbornly, as does Rory, but after today, I won't see them ever again. They'll fight me, but after a while, they'll forget.

And I want them to.

Rory puts his arm around Babydoll, who sobs violently, offering the comfort I cannot.

"I'll be seein' ye then," Brody says, snapping his fingers.

Everyone hustles to command.

Cian and Rory don't fight as they know the war is over. The corpses around us confirm this. "Ye make sure they get a grand burial."

Cian nods, a tear trickling down his cheek when he looks at my da and Uncle Sean.

The remaining men disappear into the bushlands while Liam forces Cian, Rory, and Babydoll into the van. If this were some romance film, she'd turn over her shoulder to look at me. But this isn't, so she doesn't.

This is real life. My life which I fucked up by my own hand.

Brody is the last to leave. "I promise ye, when the time is right, I'll tell ya everythin'."

"Fuck you," I reply, not interested in anything he has to say. "Keep those I love safe. That's all I want from ya."

Brody smirks as he lights a cigar. "Ye really are a Doyle."

"Naw." I shake my head with a grin as I steal his cigar. "I'm not. Ye may be my dad, but I'll always be a Kelly. Don'tcha ever mistake me for anythin' but that."

Brody's confidence simmers, as he reads the warning for what it is. *If he crosses me, I will tell the peelers everything. Blood or not, I'm hunting him.*

"Aye. I understand. Yer to make sure yer dead to the life ya once knew. No visitors, no contact with anyone. This is the only way it'll work. For me to start afresh, y've got to be gone."

What he means is for our colleagues to want to deal with him, they have to know I'm not coming back and that he's the only one in charge.

"How can I trust y'll keep to yer word?"

"I'm sure y'll hear otherwise if not."

He's right. I'm sure the officers would love to tell me how my loved ones died by the hands of a Doyle if that ever happened.

"Fair play."

"If I hear y've gone back on yer word, they'll all pay. That includes those wains Connor loved. The deal will be off."

"I heard ya the first time," I reply firmly, but he has nothing to worry about. *I'm doing them a favor by removing myself from their lives. I wish I could see the twins grow, but I cannot.*

He nods, understanding this as goodbye. I don't know what he has planned, but that's not my business anymore. He walks away, taking my kingdom with him. When the van drives away, I stare into the distance, bidding goodbye to my family, bidding goodbye to me.

When I can no longer see it, I hobble toward the lorry and boost myself into the back and take a seat. The vegetables behind me are hiding £200,000 of drugs. The sirens grow closer before eventually, I see a convoy of cars coming over the hill.

I calmly smoke my cigar, awaiting my doom.

"Hands where I can see them!"

"Fucking hell, it's a massacre."

"We're gonna need backup."

That's all I hear as I sit, laughing maniacally at the carnage I caused.

"Get on yer knees!" Chief Constable Moore orders as he yanks me from the lorry.

The arsehole who was manhandling Babydoll at the party is on my other side. "Now ya know who I am, ya dirty wee hallion," he says, spitting on me. "Check the lorry, boys. See what's onboard."

"I'll tell ya what's onboard," I say as I'm forced to my knees. "Drugs, and a quare amount."

"Are ye thick, lad? Why would ya tell me this?" asks the chief constable.

When the peelers look at Connor and Uncle Sean, I accept my fate. "'Cause I'm the one responsible for all of this. I killed my uncle and dad because they got in the way. This is all on me."

"That's not what we heard."

"Well, ya heard wrong. D'ye see anyone else here? D'ye see anyone left standin'?" I pose with a grin.

Chief Constable Moore knows I'm lying, but a haul such as this will make his name notorious. And with no one else to blame, this closed case means an easy win for him and the police. He put an end to the infamous Kellys and their illegal dealings.

There is no justice in this world, just survival of the fittest.

"Puck Connor Kelly, yer under arrest…" The chief constable handcuffs me, reading me my rights while I tip my face to the heavens, finally free, finally saving the people I love.

SIXTEEN

PUNKY

One Year Later

"O i, y've a visitor."

The light burns me because the darkness is where I've slept for the last…I don't know how many days? Months? I've lost count.

I've no windows, just a door and concrete walls. Where I was sent is not a normal prison. I'm locked away with a cesspool of degenerates, ensuring I pay for my crimes in the most heinous of ways. This tiny cell has become my home, where a monster has found solace in silence. Claustrophobia doesn't bother me anymore.

The day I surrendered was the day I let go of my humanity

and succumbed to the demons. They were always going to win. This was always my fate.

I didn't want a trial. I admitted to everything, confessed to the crimes I did commit. Chief Constable Moore warned me of the repercussions, but I didn't need a lecture—I knew I was going away for a very long time.

Not only did I have the drug distribution charge, but the trail of dead bodies had the judge punishing me in ways I wanted. I will never see the light of day again.

But I don't think about the past. I don't want to. I don't want to reminisce on the good ole days because there are none. The people I left behind are better off without me because people have a tendency to die when they're around me.

And besides, the person I once was is no more. The person they remember died the day I surrendered. I wish for them to remember me that way because this person I've grown into is not someone I want anyone to meet.

"Tell 'em to fuck off."

The door slams shut.

Four Years Later

"Are ya goin' to tell me who did this to ye?"

Turning my cheek, I shift on the soft bed as I'm not used to luxuries such as this anymore. But I suppose I'm not used to a lot of things like walking without chains binding my feet and wrists. And using a real fork.

Those are a thing of the past, a past I've forgotten because that world is dead to me, and in its place is this—hell.

The system didn't know what to do with a young offender like me as my crimes were unlike anything they'd seen before. They wanted to put me into a YOC, but at the insistence of the chief constable, I was thrown into Riverbend House—a prison reserved for the depraved.

On the outside, things may seem "normal," but on the inside, it's anything but. I've been beaten, starved, and tortured, and no one does anything about it because no one cares. We're merely playthings to the officers and other prisoners.

It's kill or be killed, which is why I'm sporting a five-inch gash across my guts. I'm no one's little bitch, and when a new inmate tried to make me his, I slit his fucking throat.

I've got nothing to lose out there, but everything to gain in here by reinforcing that no one fucks with Puck Kelly. I suppose my reputation is notorious because what I did five years ago shook Northern Ireland. Tales have been spun, but at the root of it was the truth—that I killed my father and uncle in cold blood.

Even though I didn't pull the trigger, I was still responsible. I've heard some ridiculous retellings from new prisoners trying to be my friend, but they were just bedtime stories mothers told their wains to frighten them. I was a basis of comparison.

Ye don't wanna end up like Punky Kelly, do ye now?

Why let the truth get in the way of a good story?

"Who's Cara?" the nurse, Aoife, asks.

I haven't heard that name in so long, I've almost forgotten it. But the memories those four simple letters awaken have me remembering like it was only just yesterday.

"My ma."

Aoife smiles—she's too sweet to be working here. "Ya can't be that bad if y've got yer ma's name tattooed on yer knuckles."

I deadpan her. "Naw, I'm worse."

She pauses from stitching me up, her lower lip quivering. "I don't believe it. There's somethin' different about ya."

"What don'tcha believe?"

Her fingers tremble against my stomach.

I know she likes me. I've been in this sickbay too many times to count, and each time, I see the way she looks at me. "The stories about ye. That ye killed thirty men with yer bare hands."

Laughing, I take great pleasure in seeing her turn a lovely scarlet. It's been so long since I've been with a woman. The last woman was…

Refusing to give way to those memories, I decide to make room for new ones, so they're the only ones I remember from this moment going forward.

"Ye shouldn't believe everythin' ya hear. It was twenty-five, but who's countin'?" I reply, eyeing her up and down.

She brushes a strand of brown hair behind her ear before slowly getting up and drawing the blind on the door. She then locks it.

With her back pressed to the door, she plays coy, but I sit back, already topless, waiting for her to make the next move.

"Don'tcha tell anyone," she says, slowly undoing the zipper on her white uniform. She's wearing a black bra and matching underwear.

"It'll be our secret," I assure, beckoning her over with my finger.

She walks over to the bed, and if this were any other prison, there'd be a prison officer inside the room. But this is Riverbend House and anything goes. She peers down at me, licking her lips. With nothing but time on my hands, I work out a lot. I was muscular before, but now, I've grown into that body.

She is beautiful, but she isn't who I want. But who I want, I can never have.

"C'mere," I softly order, and Aoife obeys my command.

She straddles me, and the feel of her on me is almost suffocating, but I wrap my arms around her waist, almost forgetting how soft a woman feels. When she tries to kiss me, I turn my cheek because I don't want that sort of intimacy.

Instead, I reach around and unhook her bra.

Her tits bounce free, and I bend low, taking one in my mouth. She moans, rubbing herself against my cock. She quickly lowers my trousers and takes me into her mouth.

I see stars because this feels fucking grand, but as I brush her hair aside so I can see her pretty pink lips take my cock in and out of her mouth, all I think about is how it isn't her I want. She doesn't rouse the hunger in my loins. She doesn't get me rock-hard.

There is only one doll who does, and the sick fucker that I am wishes Aoife was her. I wish my half-sister was sucking my cock, the pleasured sounds spilling from *her* sinful mouth.

I'm disgusting, I know it, but I can't help the way I feel, which is why I angrily lift Aoife and take her with me as I stand and slam her front to the wall. She doesn't have a chance to object when I rip off her underwear and sink into her warm pussy from behind.

When I hit her hard, she whimpers and arches her back. She wants more.

I ride her long and hard, wishing I could fuck away the desire I feel for Babydoll, but it'll never go away. I could have all the pussy in the world, and there'd only ever be one I want.

"Harder," Aoife demands, bouncing on my cock as I fuck her without remorse. I come only after she does, hoping that I'll forget the face and body I really want. But I don't.

It only makes me want her all the more.

Once I'm done, I clean away the mess I've made on Aoife's

back and get dressed.

She shyly slips on her uniform, and I wonder if I'm the first person she's broken the rules with. But I'm not naïve, I'm no one special.

Aoife sews me back up, since my stitches split open while I was riding her hard, and slips me some prescription drugs when she's done.

"Naw, thanks." I refuse the offering because they are the reason my life turned to shite.

"Maybe I can see ye next week?"

She surprises me, but I nod. "If I'm still alive, then aye."

I'm not being melodramatic. I live each day, not knowing if I'll wake come morning. That's my life now.

An officer comes to get me, cuffing my ankles and wrists before we commence a walk to my cell. "Y've got more letters," he says stiffly. "That's twenty this week. Who's writin' ye?"

With a shrug, I reply, "I can't say I know who."

And I mean it because since being here, I've not read one letter. Nor have I seen one visitor. There've been many of each, but I'm not interested in either. Nothing they say, nothing I read will make a difference.

"What d'ya want me to do with them?"

With nothing but firm resolve, I state, "Burn them. Burn them all."

Five Years Later

Days and nights, nights and days, I don't know what's real anymore.

I've been locked in solitary confinement now for a hundred, or maybe it's two hundred days? I really don't know. I don't mind the quiet. It's here where I can lose myself to fiction, a life where I live happily ever after.

I barely remember their faces anymore, the faces which shaped my past. I cling onto small memories, my fragile mind filling in the blanks because I haven't seen another human being in months. The door whines open, blinding me as the light fractures the darkness.

"Get up and shower," an officer demands. "Someone is here to see ye."

I try to speak, but no words come out. Maybe I've lost my voice. The scratching on the walls I made with my fingernails is the only way I communicate; it was the only way I could speak all those years ago. Chief Constable…I've forgotten his name, forbade me to have any paints. He said a murderer doesn't deserve any luxuries, and he's right.

When I think I can speak, I hoarsely utter, "Just leave me be."

Letting prisoners "out" for an hour a day for exercise, access to showers and phones, and receiving visitors is seen as the officers respecting us as human beings, but when they remember, we're made aware that they're doing us a favor—a favor they'll call in on in one form or another.

But this officer is different.

I've forgotten his name, but he's different because he cares.

"Come now, ye surely don't want to see yer sister lookin' and smellin' the way ye do."

Sister?

"Will ya do me a kindness and tell her to fuck off?"

He laughs, standing in the doorway as I curl myself into a ball on the hard floor. "We'll get ya sorted. Come on."

This arsehole won't take no for an answer, but I don't want to see Babydoll. She is the last person I want to see.

"Tell Camilla—"

"Camilla?" he says, interrupting me. "She says to me her name is Hannah."

Hannah? This is the first time an officer has told me who's come to see me.

But Hannah is a chile. Why would Fiona allow her to come here?

Confusion pounds at my temples, but I push past it because Hannah can't be anywhere near these animals. I know what men in here would do to a wee girl like her.

Coming to a shaky stand, I use the walls as support as I stumble out. The officer helps me stay upright as he leads me down the long corridor. I suddenly miss the confines of my cell. It's too open…too real. I don't want real.

The officer tosses my arse into the shower where I clean myself, scrubbing the filth from my skin. Once I'm dressed, I look at my reflection in the mirror, looking over my shoulder because the reflection I see isn't mine.

This aul' lad…is this me?

My hair is long, as is my beard. There are creases around my eyes, probably from constantly squinting in the dark. I don't recognize this man, this man who looks so much like the man I killed.

"Ya feelin' all right?" the officer asks.

"Happy days," I reply, prodding my cheeks.

"We're away to the visits room," he explains like I'm supposed to know what that means.

Once he cuffs me, he leads me through the prison while I keep my head down. I'm not interested in knowing where I am. I just want this done and over with. Once we get to a room surrounded by bars, he stops and goes to uncuff me.

"Naw, leave them on," I say. I don't trust my hands. I don't trust they won't reach out and throttle Fiona for bringing Hannah here.

He nods and unlocks the door.

There are a few families speaking with their loved ones. Tears are being shed as they catch up on what's happening outside these walls. I search the room, but I don't see Fiona. The officer leads me to a table where a young woman is sitting, obviously uncomfortable being here.

When he stops by the table, indicating she is here to see *me*, I arch a brow, confused. "We should head. I don't know her."

But when she turns over her shoulder, when I lock eyes with her, I realize that I do know her. I just don't know this version of her.

"Bout ye, Punky?"

I stare at her, words escaping me because there is no way this is Hannah. She's a wee chile. But this girl sitting before me is no chile.

"Will ye sit?"

All I can do is slump into the hard seat, placing my cuffed hands on the table as I try to get comfortable. The cuffs make her uncomfortable.

The officer nods with a smile and leaves us alone, but he stands close by.

"Hannah?" I ask, utterly shook.

She nods slowly. "Aye, it's me."

"But yer so grown."

"That's what happens when ye get older. Ye grow," she sarcastically says, rolling her eyes. "Maybe if ya bothered to see me, or answer my letters, y'd know it was me."

"How old are ye?"

Her lips part, and pity overcomes her. "I'm sixteen. Almost seventeen. Y've been in here for ten years."

Shaking my head, I refuse to accept this future. The Hannah I know was scraping her knees and fighting with Ethan...

"Ethan?"

When tears fill her eyes, the truth slaps me the fuck awake, and after ten fucking years, I see clearly. I see the life I've missed.

"What's happened to him?"

She wipes her nose and sighs. "Why wouldn't ya see anyone? Why did ye push us away? Ya promised me ye'd come back, but ya never did."

"Yer coming back?"

"Of course, I am."

Those words were spoken a lifetime ago.

"We wrote. We visited. Ya didn't even want to come to Dad's funeral. How could ya turn yer back on us, Punky? Ye were all we had."

Connor's funeral. I'd forgotten about that. I hope he and Uncle Sean had the sendoff they deserved.

"And that's the reason so. I'm nothin'. I offer ye nothin' but trouble. Yer better off without me."

She narrows her eyes, and at this moment, I see her—the stubborn six-year-old I left behind without an explanation as to why. I broke her heart.

"Ach, that's fucking bullshit!" she spits, her anger also

growing with age, it seems. "No one told us what happened. Ya just disappeared. D'ya know how that feels? The day Dad died, ya died with him. We lost everythin'."

I do understand how that feels because that's what happened to me when my ma died. And I did the same thing to the twins. I'm ashamed.

But her comment has me arching a brow.

"What d'ye mean?" That wasn't supposed to happen.

"Ma couldn't afford the lifestyle she wanted to live, and after sellin' all our things, we left our home so that Ma could move onto a new man. She tried to sell the castle, but she couldn't."

"And why not?" I ask, none of this making any sense.

"Because it wasn't hers to sell. It's yours, Puck. Da left everythin' to you."

The room spins, and I grip onto the table, scared I'm going to faint like a wee pussy.

"Here." She offers a plastic cup of water, which I throw back as best I can while still cuffed.

"Cian came to see ye with a lawyer. But ya kept refusin' to see anyone. The castle now sits abandoned, a place where kids go, expectin' to see the Kelly ghosts."

I can't tell her why. I can't tell her that was the deal I made to keep them all safe.

"I'm sorry, but there are things ya don't understand."

"Explain them then," she poses, refusing to back down.

When I don't elaborate, she shakes her head, annoyed.

"Ya think we could all just move on without ya? Like ye never existed? Well, we couldn't. We didn't want to. I know Connor wasn't yer da."

I shift uncomfortably. I don't want to talk about this. But Hannah doesn't give me a choice.

"But neither is Brody Doyle."

"Don't talk about things ya don't understand," I gently warn as she's bringing up memories I wish to forget.

Her tenacity makes me bleedin' proud, even though I want to wring her neck.

"Officer, take me back to my ce—"

"No, not this time," Hannah interrupts, sliding a piece of paper across the table to me. "Aye, these results are of that of yer da, but it's not Brody's DNA."

Looking over the paper, I see the test results I last saw ten years ago. I don't know what's changed. "Whose is it then? If it's not Connor or Brody, then who is my dad?"

Hannah works her bottom lip. "Ma didn't get rid of everything. Cian, Rory, and…Cami, they made sure of it."

Why did she pause? Does she know what I did?

"It's taken me ten years to find this, but I knew he was still alive. At first, I thought it was a ghost. Or that I was seein' things. But when Ethan disappeared without tellin' me where he was, I knew there was only place he'd be."

"Hannah, what's happened to Ethan?" I reach across the table, and with my heart in my throat, I touch her hand.

We flinch as the touch is foreign to us both.

Tears trickle down her cheeks as she passes me a leather-bound journal. There is a ribbon bookmarking the page she wants me to read.

"Read that and tell me what ya think."

I have no idea what I'm about to read. I have no idea how this will change my life forevermore.

He will find out what I did. Sooner or later, he'll know that I killed her. He'll know that Cara died because she found out I was dealing to the Catholics. To the Doyles. She betrayed me after she told me she loved me. After she promised she'd never leave me. That I was the one she wanted, not him.

She was going to leave him, she told me so. But she lied. She was going to leave us both. All she wanted was to save her wain. That's all she cared for. I couldn't let her go. She had to die. She'd have told Connor the truth.

So I killed her, asking the Doyles to help me. Brody knew what that would do to Connor, so he agreed. But he also knew this secret would destroy us both. If Cara told Connor the truth, he would put an end to the Doyles and to me.

I told Connor she was having an affair with Brody, however, and that's the reason he never avenged her death. But she never touched Brody. She never would. He believed me because their marriage was already broken long before—that's how I managed to seduce her.

Her secret would destroy me, and I couldn't allow that. I couldn't allow her to ruin everything I worked so hard for. But there is no such thing as no strings attached with the Doyles and Brody has become greedy, seeing there is profit in Northern Ireland.

He's threatened to tell Punky what I did, so I have to take care of it...again.

That wee hallion is in too deep. I know it was him who killed Aidan and Hugh, he painted their faces just like his.

He trusts me. He shouldn't.

I watch him when he sleeps, he looks so much like Cara. So much like me...

I will ask Brody to lie, ask him to tell Punky that he is his father as I need Punky to hate Connor more than he already does. I'll make sure Punky thinks Connor was the one who killed his ma. I need him to denounce his Kelly ties so that when I kill Connor, I'll be in line to inherit everything...not him. No matter that Connor knows Punky isn't his, he'll still leave everything to him because he loves the boy.

Brody will agree because he thinks he'll benefit from this too.

I've been in business with him for years. He trusts me. This won't fail. He believes if he does what I say, he and I will share Belfast together. But there is room for only one leader.

I was the one sending our men to Brody. They trusted me as Connor was a laughing stock when I told them I fucked his parful wife. Brody had Camilla plant the drugs the night of the party in hopes the chief constable would bring me and Connor down. But then that little whore told Punky. She then told me who she was in a moment of guilt.

She confided in me, thinking she was doing the right thing. But all she did was let me in on Brody's plan—he wants me dead. He doesn't trust me as I thought he did, and so he shouldn't. He, Punky, he was always Brody's backup plan.

Brody has what I want—Dublin. And I have what he wants—Belfast.

But now that I know, I have the upper hand over everyone.

I will rule both Belfast and Dublin, and no one will stand in my way. There was never going to be a partnership.

Punky's loyalty will either get him killed or sent to prison. I'm fine with either outcome. The ambush will play out how I plan it. I will "die," allowing everyone to believe the Kelly name is dead. But a smart predator awaits their prey.

I'm pretty certain Punky will bring Connor as he thinks it's a lesson he needs to learn, and it's the perfect place for me to shoot my brother dead with no questions asked. Before this happens, I will convince Connor to change his will. Nothing can be left to Punky—nothing. I don't want to rule with anyone. This is all mine.

Punky is headstrong and smart—I need someone I can control.

Brody will believe he's won, but I have a plan...just how I did with Connor's men, I plan on doing the same with Brody's. I'm going to persuade them all, making them see I'm the better leader.

And when I do, it's then when I'll strike.

It doesn't matter if it takes five, ten years. I'm going to build my own empire, and when it's impenetrable, I will be king. No more coming second best.

Connor had it all. It's now my turn, and I don't care who I have to sacrifice to get what I want.

Forgive me, Cara, I needed a fall guy, and that guy is Punky... our son.

Although I've seen the words with my own two eyes, I cannot believe it. I just can't.

"Punky?" Hannah apprehensively asks. "Please speak to me. I need ya. Ethan needs ya."

This journal belongs to Uncle Sean, and his sins are written on pages upon pages. My mind is racing, but one thing is clear—Sean is the puppet master. He was playing us all. He is responsible for everything.

He made out like my mum was some whore, but in reality, she made one mistake which cost her her life. I know how charming Sean can be. Look at where I am, where I've been for the past ten years because of him.

There was never an affair, well, with Brody. But there was one, with Sean...my father.

Every conversation which never made sense smashes into me, and I can't believe I didn't see it sooner.

"Ya have no idea who yer fightin'. This is bigger than ya can ever guess."

Aidan's words echo loudly because I finally know what they mean. He never told me what he knew, thinking Sean was their friend, but they were all using one another.

Brody merely went along for the ride as he wanted me out of the picture for his own selfish reasons. I needed to believe I wasn't a Kelly so that he could take what is rightfully mine when he killed Sean. I may not be Connor's son, but I am Sean's.

I *am* a Kelly.

For ten long years, I carried this guilt with me. I thought Connor's death was on me, and it was, but I played right into Sean's hands.

These ramblings are from a madman, but from what I can decipher, Sean was always going to backstab Brody, as was Brody to Sean. Babydoll was Brody's pawn, his way to get information on me.

"'Cause I knew it'd eventually come to this. Yer collateral, and I needed a backup plan, just in case. It doesn't make sense. But it will."

Now it does make sense—Brody knew Sean would double-cross him, which is why he wanted to get there first. He used Babydoll to learn everything there is about me, about the Kellys, so he would know what Sean's next steps would be.

Connor said he made a deal with Brody—what was it? I

need to find out what it was.

Brody and Sean were merely using one another because both needed the other to get what they wanted. And it was a race to the finish line, where the winner would take it all.

They never trusted one another. They played nice because they had to. There are so many things I don't know because this story has only just begun. But there are two things I do know.

Sean is a psychopath.

He is responsible for everything. He killed my mum because she uncovered his dirty secret. He slandered her name to Connor, who believed him—we all did. I wonder if he ever loved her, or just wanted something which belonged to his brother—the man he hated.

He hated me because he was jealous that my ma loved me more than him, and as punishment, he made me—his own flesh and blood—watch him kill her. Then, to punish me further, he tricked me into thinking he cared about me.

It must have given him great satisfaction seeing Connor beat me time and time again as I hated the wrong man and only he was privy to that secret.

He sent our men to the enemy, knowing full well that he'd need them on his side when he took over Brody's domain. He was sick of coming in second best. He was sick of living in Connor's shadow. This was all about greed, pride, and his wee ego being bruised.

Babydoll only did what she had to do to save her ma. I can't be ragin' over that because look at what I did to avenge mine. We were both puppets to Sean and Brody who used us to wage their war over one another.

And I also know that…

"Brody isn't my father," I say aloud, needing Hannah to confirm what I just read.

"No, he isn't."

A thought suddenly hits me, and I sit back, winded. "And that means…"

"She isn't yer sister."

So she does know.

This entire time, I was so disgusted with myself, thanks to Sean and Brody punishing me and Babydoll for something we never wanted a part in.

"Have ye shared this with anyone?"

She shakes her head. "I found that in a box in storage. They all tried to help, but there was just so much. Ma wouldn't let anyone near those boxes, but I broke in and searched every night until I found that."

"I saw him get shot," I say, shaking my head, incredulous.

"I don't know who we buried, but it's not him. No doubt Uncle Sean fooled someone else to do his dirty work."

"How do ye know he isn't dead?"

Hannah looks away, ashamed. "At night, I would sneak out

and go back to the castle. It reminded me of happier times. It reminded me of you."

I reach for her hand, and this time, the touch is easier.

"I was certain I saw him there, but didn't want to believe it, not after I'd lost so much. But I followed Ethan to the castle one night. He was talkin' to a man, and that man was Uncle Sean.

"Uncle Sean is trying to mold Ethan into ye. He wants a righthand man he can trust and with Da dying and ye being gone, Ethan trusts him. And what scares me the most is that Ethan is lyin' to me. When I ask him where he's been, he tells me he's been out with friends.

"He's never lied to me before. He's my twin, but I feel like I don't even know him anymore."

She bursts into tears, but quickly sniffs them back as my brave Hannah won't let anyone see her cry.

"Punky, what does this mean?" She brushes over the cross tattoo on my wrist.

I'd forgotten this marks my skin because I had forgotten who I was. "Why, wee one?"

"Because Ethan has one. Right where you do."

The blood drains from my face because this mark—it's the mark of death, and sooner or later, Ethan will be me.

Sean's plan is to take over Dublin and Belfast, knowing his past efforts have failed because he was too exposed and he relied on others. But this plan will work because he's had years to perfect it. Rome wasn't built in a day…

I know what this means, and my stomach turns at the thought. There is only one person who can help me, the last person I ever want to ask for help. But I need an inside man, and that man is Brody Doyle. He is clueless to Sean's plan. He has no idea he's still alive.

He'll work with me because we both need the other to get what we want. And when I do…I will finally finish what I started ten years ago.

But first things first, I need to get the fuck out of here.

"Thank you for never givin' up on me."

"We never did," she says, not wanting credit.

Clearing my throat, I need to ask the inevitable. "How's Cian? Rory? Babydoll?"

When Hannah tongues her cheek, I know she's hiding something. She was never a good liar. "They're grand. Ya can find out for yerself when ye get out."

"How do ya propose I do that? In case y've forgotten where I am." I gesture around the room.

"Darcy wants to help."

"Duffy?" I ask, pulling a face.

"Aye. She's a lawyer now. A fancy one too."

"Who would have thought it."

How things have changed. The world continued to turn with or without me. I was the one switched off to change.

"She's gone over yer case. She thinks she can get ye out. Something to do with Chief Constable Moore being a dirty pig."

My mouth drops open. "Yer jokin' me?"

"Maybe if ye read my letters, ye'd know this already."

"Aye, yer right."

"I'll organize for Darcy to come see ya then."

I can't believe my wee sister has done this for me. "I don't deserve this, Hannah. I'm sorry I left ya. There was a reason, I promise ya."

She nods, but her hurt is still clear.

"I cannot believe how grown y'are."

"I cannot believe how *old* y'are," she teases, laughing when I'm left with a mouth full of nothing.

But she's right. I've wasted so much time.

The officer alerts me I have five minutes left.

Hannah gathers her things, ensuring to pack the journal away safely. She stands, looking awful awkward, and I realize why. I turn to the officer, who nods. I offer him my hands and when he unlocks my cuffs, the invisible manacles holding me back break free as well.

"I haven't done this in a very long time," I confess, while Hannah gulps, unsure of what I mean.

When I open my arms, I give her the choice—but there never was a choice to be made.

She steps into my embrace and hugs me tight, transporting

me back to better times. "I've missed ye. So much," she whispers into my ear, her tears wetting my cheeks.

"I'll make it right. I promise ya."

As I hold onto her, my world finally comes back into focus, and I realize who I am. I don't know what I'm walking into, whether Brody has taken over Belfast or if someone else has taken his place. I don't know if Cian and Rory will ever forgive me. And I don't know what this means for Babydoll and me.

But whatever faces me, no more hiding in the darkness, for I'm a Kelly. They all thought I was dead…but the real story has only just begun.

BOOK TWO COMING SOON

Subscribe to my Newsletter:

https://landing.mailerlite.com/webforms/landing/b4j1v6

Thy Kingdom Come Playlist:

https://open.spotify.com/playlist/3lQ2n3FSOfoTnrZntlap79

ACKNOWLEDGEMENTS

My author family: Elle Kennedy and Vi Keeland—I love you both very much.

My husband, Daniel. Love you. Always. Forever. Thanks for putting up with my craziness.

My ever-supporting parents. You guys are the best. I am who I am because of you. I love you. RIP Papa. Gone but never forgotten. You're in my heart. Always.

My agent, Kimberly Brower from Brower Literary & Management. Thank you for your patience and thank you for being an amazing human being.

My editor, Jenny Sims. What can I say other than I LOVE YOU! Thank you for everything. You go above and beyond for me.

My Irish Queens—Shauna McDonnell and Aimee Walker, your advice was priceless. Thank you so much for allowing me to pick your brains.

My proofreaders—Aimee Walker and Rumi Khan, you are amazing!

My Beta Reader—Rumi Khan. Thank you for loving Punky as much as me.

Michelle Lancaster—you took this story and created an image which is utter perfection. Your vision and talent are absolutely mind-blowing, and I feel so blessed to have worked with you. Your photos SLAY! Actually, YOU slay!! That makeup was FANTASTIC!! I love your face! #mytribe

Lochie Carey—dude, like wtf?! You are incredible! You are my Punky. Thank you for bringing him to life.

Giana Darling—thanks for your rubber stamp. I adore you.

Lauren Rosa—this cover was born because of your suggestion. I thank you so much for always being there for me.

Conor King—Thank you so much for everything. Your narration was perfect! PS. I owe you a pint. Or two. And I'm excited to see Milk play a gig soon!

Sommer Stein, you NAILED this cover! Thank you for being so patient and making the process so fun. I'm sorry for annoying you constantly.

My publicist—Danielle Sanchez from Wildfire Marketing Solutions. Thank you for all your help.

A special shout-out to: Bombay Sapphire Gin, Ashlee O'Brien, LA Casey, Christina Lauren, Natasha Madison, Tillie Cole, Lisa Edward, David King, Cheri Grand Anderman, Louise, Kimberly Whalen, Ben Ellis—Tall Story Designs, Nasha Lama, Heyne, Random House, Kinneret Zmora, Hugo & Cie, Planeta, MxM Bookmark, Art Eternal, Carbaccio, Fischer, Sieben Verlag, Bookouture, Egmont Bulgaria, Brilliance Publishing, Audible, Hope Editions, BookBub, Paris, New York, Sarah Sentz, Gel Ytayz, Jessica—PeaceLoveBooks.

To the endless blogs that have supported me since day

one—You guys rock my world.

My bookstagrammers—Your creativity astounds me. The effort you go to is just amazing. Thank you for the posts, the teasers, the support, the messages, the love, the EVERYTHING! I see what you do, and I am so, so thankful.

My ARC TEAM—You guys are THE BEST! Thanks for all the support.

My reader group—sending you all a big kiss.

My beautiful family—Mum, Papa, Fran, Matt, Samantha, Amelia, Gayle, Peter, Luke, Leah, Jimmy, Jack, Shirley, Michael, Rob, Elisa, Evan, Alex, Francesca, and my aunties, uncles, and cousins—I am the luckiest person alive to know each and every one of you. You brighten up my world in ways I honestly cannot express.

Samantha and Amelia— I love you both so very much.

To my family in Holland and Italy, and abroad. Sending you guys much love and kisses.

Papa, Zio Nello, Zio Frank, Zia Rosetta, and Zia Giuseppina—you are in our hearts. Always.

My fur babies— mamma loves you so much! Dacca, I know you're hanging with Jaggy, Dina, Ninja, and Papa.

To anyone I have missed, I'm sorry. It wasn't intentional!

Last but certainly not least, I want to thank YOU! Thank you for welcoming me into your hearts and homes. My readers are the BEST readers in this entire universe! Love you all!

ABOUT THE AUTHOR

Monica James spent her youth devouring the works of Anne Rice, William Shakespeare, and Emily Dickinson.

When she is not writing, Monica is busy running her own business, but she always finds a balance between the two. She enjoys writing honest, heartfelt, and turbulent stories, hoping to leave an imprint on her readers. She draws her inspiration from life.

She is a bestselling author in the U.S.A., Australia, Canada, France, Germany, Israel, and The U.K.

Monica James resides in Melbourne, Australia, with her wonderful family, and menagerie of animals. She is slightly obsessed with cats, chucks, and lip gloss, and secretly wishes she was a ninja on the weekends.

CONNECT WITH
MONICA JAMES

Facebook: facebook.com/authormonicajames

Twitter: twitter.com/monicajames81

Goodreads: goodreads.com/MonicaJames

Instagram: instagram.com/authormonicajames

Website: authormonicajames.com

Pinterest: pinterest.com/monicajames81

BookBub: bookbub.com/authors/monica-james

Amazon: https://amzn.to/2EWZSyS

Join my Reader Group: http://bit.ly/2nUaRyi